TRUELIF3

Jay Kristoff is the *New York Times* and internationally best-selling author of The Lotus War trilogy, The Illuminae Files, and The Nevernight Chronicle. He is 6'7" and has trouble operating a toaster but still respects machines as a necessary evil in our world. He lives in Melbourne, Australia, with his wife and a rescue dog that he thinks is made of 100% organic parts.

Contact Jay:
www.jaykristoff.com
 www.facebook.com/AuthorJayKristoff
 @misterkristoff

ALSO BY JAY KRISTOFF

The Lotus War
Stormdancer
Kinslayer
Endsinger
The Last Stormdancer

The Nevernight Chronicle
Nevernight
Godsgrave
Darkdawn

WITH AMIE KAUFMAN

The Illuminae Files
Illuminae
Gemina
Obsidio

The Aurora Cycle
Aurora Rising
Aurora Burning

JAY KRISTOFF

TRUEL1F3

HARPER
Voyager

Harper*Voyager*
An imprint of HarperCollins*Publishers* Ltd
1 London Bridge Street
London SE1 9GF

www.harpercollins.co.uk

First published by HarperCollins*Publishers* Ltd 2020
This paperback original edition 2020
1

A catalogue record for this book is
available from the British Library

ISBN: 978-0-00-830146-0

Printed and bound in the UK by CPI Group (UK) Ltd,
Croydon CR0 4YY

MIX
Paper from
responsible sources
FSC™ C007454

FSC
www.fsc.org

You cannot kill

What you did not create.

— Corey Taylor

THE WHO, WHAT AND WHY

Eve—the thirteenth and final model in the Lifelike series. Raised to believe she was human, Eve discovered she was an android replica created in the image of Ana Monrova, youngest daughter of Nicholas Monrova, director of the megacorporation Gnosis Laboratories.

After learning the truth about herself, Eve joined forces with her lifelike siblings Gabriel, Faith, Uriel, Verity and Patience. Their goal was simple—find the resting place of the real Ana Monrova and use her DNA to unlock the Gnosis supercomputer Myriad. With the information inside Myriad, Eve and her siblings would be able to create more lifelikes and mass-produce Libertas—a virus capable of erasing the Three Laws in a robot's core code. Eve also wanted to kill Ana, erasing her humanity along with the girl she was modeled on.

After run-ins with her former friend Cricket and her former lover Ezekiel, Eve discovered Ana's resting place beneath the Brotherhood capital of New Bethlehem. Eve appeared to falter in her convictions, but before she could decide whether she truly wished Ana to live or die, she and her siblings were attacked by Ezekiel and the bounty hunter Preacher. Uriel was killed, and Eve and Gabriel were swept into the custody of the megacorporation Daedalus Technologies.

Lemon Fresh—Eve's former best friend. Lemon was named for the logo on the side of the detergent box she was dumped in as a baby. She's a deviate, possessed of the ability to manipulate electrical currents with the power of her mind.

After being abandoned by Eve and separated from Cricket and Ezekiel, Lemon was captured by an operative named Hunter from the BioMaas citystate. She escaped, falling in with a group of fellow deviates (Grimm, Diesel and Fix) operating out of an abandoned missile silo in the desert. Calling themselves the Freaks, they were under the command of a mysterious figure known as the Major. Lemon joined their cause, and the Major eventually revealed that he was Lemon's grandfather.

Things went horribly wrong, of course—the Major turned out to be an apocalypse nut, intent on using Lemon's powers to access the silo's nuclear ordnance. He launched seven of the missiles, but Lemon and Grimm managed to stop six. Last anyone heard, the seventh was heading toward New Bethlehem.

Grimm and Diesel sped off to save the town, leaving Lemon behind at the silo, where she was recaptured by Hunter and BioMaas forces.

Ezekiel—one of thirteen lifelikes created by Gnosis Laboratories. Ezekiel is faster and stronger than a human, but his emotional maturity can border on childlike, like most of the 100-Series. He was lover to both Ana Monrova and Eve.

Ezekiel was the only lifelike who didn't join the revolt that destroyed Nicholas Monrova and his empire. As punishment, his siblings bolted a metal coin slot into his chest to remind him of his allegiance to his human masters.

After being separated from Lemon and Cricket, he joined forces with Preacher to track down Lemon but ran afoul of his siblings instead. Discovering their plan to find and kill Ana, Ezekiel clashed with his fellow lifelikes beneath New Bethlehem. During the battle, Preacher showed his true colors, shooting Zeke and taking Eve, Gabriel and the cryogenically frozen body of Ana into Daedalus custody.

Ezekiel recovered from his wounds, only to discover a nuclear missile was headed right for his current location.

Cricket—a logika created by Silas Carpenter. Cricket was Eve's companion and robotic conscience. During a battle inside Babel Tower, Cricket's small robotic body was destroyed by Faith, and his persona transplanted into a mechanical war machine.

After being separated from Lemon and Zeke, Cricket fell into the keeping of Sister Dee, leader of the Brotherhood of New Bethlehem, and her son, Abraham. Cricket was made to fight in local WarDome matches against his will.

While in captivity, Cricket befriended a robot called Solomon, who taught him subtle ways in which the Three Laws of Robotics might be bent while not outright broken. He also grew close to Abraham, eventually discovering the boy was a deviate.

When knowledge of Abraham's powers became public, Sister Dee offered her son up to the New Bethlehem mob. Cricket had Solomon destroy his audio arrays, and freed of the imperative to follow orders he couldn't hear, Cricket rescued the boy from the mob just as Eve and her lifelike siblings attacked the city.

Victory seemed at hand, when a nuclear missile appeared in the skies above. . . .

Grimm—a handsome young deviate allied with the Major's freaks. Grimm has the ability to absorb and redirect thermal and kinetic energy. His parents were killed by the Brotherhood. He speaks in rhyming slang.

Lemon rescued Grimm and Diesel from certain death at the hands of the Brotherhood. A grateful Grimm brought Lemon to the freaks' desert hideout and was well pleased when the Major welcomed her into the group.

Quite sweet on Miss Fresh, he kissed her goodbye before departing for New Bethlehem and an almost-certain death by nuclear explosion.

Diesel—another freak. Diesel has the ability to open tears in space, which she calls Rifting. Like doorways, rifts allow objects and people to step from one location into another.

Diesel has erected a ten-meter-high wall of sarcasm to protect herself from the world. She wears black lipstick and heavy eyeliner, which is no mean feat in a postapocalyptic wasteland.

She was lover to Fix and was brokenhearted at his death.

Fix—another of the Major's freaks. Fix had the ability to transfer "life energy" between living things, healing one by harming another. He had an infamously foul mouth and was trying to mend his ways with the use of a swear jar.

Sadly, during an attack by BioMaas and Brotherhood forces, Diesel was mortally wounded, and with no other life force to draw on out in the deep desert, Fix chose to draw on himself, healing Diesel's injuries at the cost of his own life.

The Major—the leader of the freaks. The Major claimed to have the ability of clairvoyance, which only manifested when he dreamed. He also told Lemon he was her grandfather.

In reality, the Major was the founder of the Brotherhood, usurped by his daughter, Sister Dee, and intent on revenge against New Bethlehem and the world. His "clairvoyance" was gained by access to satellite imaging systems inside the freaks' missile silo, and he was nothing close to Lemon's relative.

Lemon stopped his heart after she discovered the truth about his agenda, but not before he managed to launch a nuclear strike against the city he'd helped establish.

Abraham—the son of Sister Dee, and a mechanical genius. Abraham is also a deviate, with the ability to move objects with the power of his mind.

Despite his brutal upbringing, Abe has a good heart—even after the people of New Bethlehem tried to crucify him for his abnormality, he joined forces with Cricket and Solomon to help save the city during the lifelike attack.

Solomon—a humanoid logika who fell into the service of the Brotherhood. A former resident of the city of Megopolis, the Sensational Solomon was tending one of their trade outlets when he was attacked and almost destroyed by Lemon.

Sent to Abraham's workshop for repairs, he bonded with Cricket, helping the big bot overcome his programming and teaching him to "bend" the Three Laws of Robotics. He later deafened Cricket at the big bot's request and helped rescue Abraham.

To say Solomon thinks a lot of himself is something of an understatement.

Preacher—a cybernetically enhanced bounty hunter in the employ of Daedalus Technologies. Preacher was blown apart by Eve's blitzhund, Kaiser, outside Babel. Left with no legs, only one functional arm and no way to contact Daedalus headquarters, he joined forces with Ezekiel, and the pair tracked Lemon across the Yousay. Preacher was eventually able to have his cybernetic body repaired, and he and Zeke tracked Lemon to New Bethlehem.

He betrayed and shot Ezekiel and, with the help of a Daedalus special forces unit, took Ana, Eve and Gabriel back to Megopolis.

Hunter—a warrior and tracker in the employ of the BioMaas CityHive. Hunter is heavily bio-augmented, and her body serves as a home for a swarm of genetically modified bees, which she uses for weapons and communications.

She was killed helping Lemon Fresh rescue Grimm and Diesel, but an identical copy of her later accosted Lemon at the freaks' missile silo.

Ana Monrova—the youngest daughter of Nicholas. Ana fell in love with Ezekiel against her parents' wishes and was left in a vegetative coma after an attempt on her father's life. Unable to deal with the loss of his favored child, Monrova created Eve to replace her. However, Ana's body was taken from Babel Tower to a secret GnosisLabs holding, her vitals maintained by life support.

Nicholas Monrova—the Director of GnosisLabs. Nicholas was a visionary who believed the fusion of human and machine was the next step in humanity's evolution. He initiated the lifelike program, attempting to create a smarter, stronger version of his own species.

After a betrayal within Gnosis, he masterminded Libertas, a two-stage nanovirus capable of erasing the Three Laws in any machine's core code. In order to safeguard his stewardship of the Corporation, he then infected the lifelike Gabriel with Libertas and commanded him to murder the other members of the Gnosis board.

Nicholas was killed, along with most of his family, in the subsequent lifelike revolt.

Gabriel—the first lifelike of the 100-Series. Gabriel was in love with another lifelike, Grace. He rebelled against his creator after Grace's death and orchestrated the revolt that killed Nicholas Monrova and his family.

Gabe wishes to unlock the Myriad computer in the hope of learning the secret to creating more lifelikes, allowing his beloved to be reborn.

Faith—Ana Monrova's former confidante. Faith was the third lifelike to join Gabriel's rebellion. She remained with Gabe in the ruins of Babel, even though most of the 100-Series abandoned the capital after the revolt. Faith remained with Gabriel because she loves him, though Gabriel himself is still hopelessly besotted with Grace.

Faith was seriously injured in battle with Cricket during the showdown in New Bethlehem.

Uriel, Verity and Patience—rebellious lifelikes who joined forces with Eve in her efforts to track down Ana Monrova. The three were robot supremacists, fully convinced of humanity's redundancy.

Patience was killed by Ezekiel in Paradise Falls, while Uriel was killed by Preacher and Verity by Cricket during the showdown in New Bethlehem.

With their deaths, only four of the 100-Series models now remain—Gabriel, Faith, Ezekiel and Eve.

Silas Carpenter—a genius neuroscientist and former head of the Research and Development Division for GnosisLabs. After the assassination attempt on Nicholas Monrova, Silas created a new lifelike replica of Monrova's beloved injured daughter and assisted Monrova in transplanting Ana's personality into it.

Silas was killed by Gabriel in Babel.

Myriad—the GnosisLabs supercomputer. Though it manifests as a holographic angel, Myriad is actually housed inside an armored shell at the heart of Babel Tower, kept locked by a four-stage security sequence. Two of those locks have now been broken, but the third and fourth can only be opened by someone possessing Monrova DNA and brainwave patterns.

Myriad is possessed of all of Nicholas Monrova's knowledge, including the method to create more lifelikes and the secrets of the Libertas nanovirus.

BioMaas Incorporated—one of the two most powerful Corp-States in the Yousay, currently in a cold war with Daedalus Technologies. BioMaas is a company devoted to genetic modification and manipulation and to biotech.

After BioMaas learned of Lemon's genetic abnormality, it resolved to capture the young deviate and use her as a weapon against Daedalus—with the ability to destroy electronics with the power of her mind, Lemon could be the weapon that allows BioMaas to gain control over the whole country.

Daedalus Technologies—the second CorpState vying for control of the Yousay. Daedalus made its fortune through the development of solar power technology, cybernetics and military hardware.

It has existed in a state of uneasy but subtle hostility with BioMaas for decades—while Daedalus controls the country's power supply, BioMaas controls its food sources. But each Corporation hopes to overthrow the other and gain control over the whole Yousay for itself.

The Three Laws of Robotics

1. ~~A robot may not injure a human being or, through inaction, allow a human being to come to harm.~~

   YOUR BODY IS NOT YOUR OWN.

2. ~~A robot must obey the orders given to it by human beings, except where such orders would conflict with the First Law.~~

   YOUR MIND IS NOT YOUR OWN.

3. ~~A robot must protect its own existence as long as such protection does not conflict with the First or Second Law.~~

   YOUR LIFE IS NOT YOUR OWN.

automata [au-toh-MAH-tuh]

noun

A machine with no intelligence of its own, operating on preprogrammed lines.

machina [mah-KEE-nuh]

noun

A machine that requires a human operator to function.

logika [loh-JEE-kuh]

noun

A machine with its own onboard intelligence, capable of independent action.

3.0

INTRODUCTIONS

The streets of Los Diablos were no place for a kid.

The capital of Dregs was a rusting cesspit. A reminder of humanity's greatest age, and greatest folly. Built in the heart of a scrap pile, Los Diablos wasn't a city, it was a meat grinder, chewing up people and spitting out the bones. If you were born there, you grew up sharp, you grew up hard or you didn't grow up at all.

Lemon Fresh had taken the first option—she was too short for the second, and the third sounded like zero fun. As a girl who'd been found in a detergent box as a baby, she'd had a tougher life than most. But she'd been running the Los Diablos streets since she was knee-high to a cockroach, and in her fourteen years in the sprawl, she'd learned a trick or two.

Like how to spot a tasty mark.

She was lurking in the shade of an auto-peddler, green eyes narrowed behind dusty goggles, scoping her next meal ticket. The old man was seven kinds of crusty, jawing with one of the local parts dealers and stopping occasionally to smother a septic cough behind an oil-stained fist. He was a newcomer to Los Diablos, and he didn't look much fancy, true cert. But she'd heard he was some kind of tech genius, and Lem figured a gent like that had to be carrying some decent scratch.

His name was Silas Carpenter.

The girl that Crusty was rolling with looked a little sharper. She was tall, a little gangly, sun-bleached blond hair undercut into a flashy fauxhawk. A black metal implant sat in the socket where her right eye should've been, and silicon chips were plugged into a Memdrive behind her right ear. Her peepers were exactly where they should've been, which is to say, on the street around them. But Lemon Fresh hadn't survived fourteen years in this dumpster of a city on her looks alone.

Fabulous as they were . . .

She cruised through the crowd, quiet and smooth as exhaust fumes, eyes on her mark. Old Crusty lifted an oscillator from the parts pile, asking the blond girl's opinion and drawing her attention away. And Lemon slipped in, quick as blowflies on roadkill, and slit the old man's pocket.

She figured he'd be carrying some loose cash, ration cards. And so when three shiny credstiks tumbled into her greasy palm, Lemon took a second to register it. Blinking hard. Imagining, just for a second, all the happy that amount of scratch could buy. It was stupid of her, talking true. The kind of stupid that gets you killed.

The blond girl collared Lemon in a blink. Coming to her senses, Lem sank her teeth into Blondie's wrist, twisting and slipping out of her poncho. And like that, she was sprinting off through the mob, leaving Blondie and Crusty with nothing but a torn shred of clothing.

It had been sloppy of her to get spotted. But after thirty minutes of tripping and twisting through the sprawl, she figured she'd got away clean as . . . well, clean as anything could be in an armpit like LD. On shaky legs, she made her way back to her hideout to lie low for a spell. Grinning like she'd won the sweeps. And curled up under a cardboard roof, clutching those credstiks to her chest like a mother with a newborn sprat, she finally fell asleep, dreaming of better places and better days.

She woke to a metallic growl. Looked up into a pair of glowing red eyes. A cybernetic dog loomed over her, metal teeth bared in a snarl. She bolted upright, scrambled back into a corner, her cutter raised in her fist. Past the cyberdog, Lemon saw Crusty and Blondie blocking the exit from her hideaway.

"Hey there," Lemon said.

"Hey yourself," the bigger girl replied.

Blondie was looking at her with narrowed eyes, an electric baseball bat slung loose and lazy over one shoulder. The dog looked like it wanted to eat her, and considering it was made out of metal, that was an impressive trick. But Crusty looked around at the squalor Lemon lived in, his sunburned face softening. And though she'd never really had one, he spoke with a voice like she supposed fathers used.

"You live here?"

"Not usually," Lemon replied. "My mansion's at the cleaner's."

The old man chuckled, and even the tall girl managed a smile. Lemon had learned young that a wisecrack could sometimes save you from a beatdown—it's hard for some folks to stomp a sprog who can make them giggle. She wasn't ass-backward enough to live in a squat with only one exit. But looking at the cyberdog, the torn poncho in the girl's hand, Lemon Fresh had a feeling these two might be able to find her again if they had a mind to. So she tossed the credstiks at the tall girl's boots, her knife still clutched in her other fist.

"It's fizzy, I wasn't hungry anyway."

Crusty glanced to Blondie, raising one unruly gray eyebrow.

"What do you think, Evie?"

Blondie stared Lemon up and down. She looked at the filth and crud Lem lived in, the cardboard roof over her head, the credstiks in the dirt.

"I think she needs it more than us," she said, softlike.

The old man smiled, nodded to the stiks. "Keep 'em."

Lemon stared, a dozen different emotions punching on inside her head. Disbelief. Suspicion. Confusion. Strange enough, and despite the streetwise part of her brain's objection, it was pride that won in the end.

"Don't need your pity," she growled, rising to her feet.

"Not pity," Blondie shrugged. "You earned 'em. Fifth rule of the Scrap, right?"

Lemon blinked, taken aback. "Takers keepers."

"Takers keepers," Blondie smiled.

Lemon's brainmeats were all tumbled, and she was furiously looking for the angle. Fourteen years on the streets had taught her nobody in this world was nice unless they had an angle. This city chewed up dreams and spat out misery, and folks who lived here never gave you anything without a taking in return.

So what did these two want?

"Are you two smoked?" she finally asked. "Or just defective?"

The old man looked around her squat again, then met her eyes. "You ever want a decent meal," he said, "come out to Tire Valley and look us up."

Ah, she nodded. There it is.

"You're too old for me, Gramps," Lemon replied.

He laughed then, a laugh that turned into a long, racking cough.

"I like you, kiddo," he said.

They let her keep the credstiks. And they wandered away without another word, leaving Lemon bewildered in their wake. And when she mooched up to their doorstep after the scratch ran out, they fed her, just like they said. They let her stay, let her belong, let her think maybe there was something more than the meat grinder she'd grown up inside. The old man never asked her for anything, not once. And though it'd always be the name he wore inside her head, she never called him Grandpa to his face. She called him "Mister C" instead.

Right until the day he died.

And the girl? The girl who taught her not everyone has an angle? Who taught her not everyone gives without wanting a taking?

Well, Lemon called her "bestest."

But what she meant, of course, was "sister."

PART 1

GENESIS

PART I

3.1

CALAMITY

Cricket was sure of only one thing.

The WarBot stood in the town square of New Bethlehem, a sun-bright calamity unfolding above him. The city about him was in ruins, the streets choked with smoke, dust, panicked citizens. There was so much input, it was difficult for him to process it all. But above the imperatives of his programming, the knife-sharp alarms blaring inside his head, the need to save the humans screaming and praying and panicking all about him, a single thought was ringing in his mind.

I don't want to die.

The logika knew he wasn't "alive" in the strictest sense. He had hydraulics, not muscles. Armor, not skin. There was no electronic afterlife where toasters and microwaves sat around on synthesized clouds, listening to digital harps. Cricket was blessed with the certainty that once he stopped, he just ... stopped. But even if the Laws of Robotics didn't make self-preservation the third most important imperative in his hierarchy of needs, the truth was, Cricket had decided he *liked* existing.

Though his so-called life hadn't been much more than

struggle and anguish lately, it was also filled with possibility. In the past few days, Cricket had made enemies and found friends, had his eyes opened and his world turned upside down. Everything felt bigger, and Cricket felt like he was changing—*evolving* into something more than he'd ever thought he could be. He felt like he was more.

Sadly, nukes don't care about your feelings.

"ALL OF YOU NEED TO RUN!" Cricket roared. "THERE'S A MISSILE COMING!"

Electronic panic flooded the big bot's systems as he stomped up to the broken gates of New Bethlehem, a payload of nuclear fire streaking in out of the sky above. This settlement was home to the dreaded Brotherhood, a cult of religious fanatics who practiced an awful form of genetic purity. But even though the city was peopled with the pond scum of humanity, they were still *human,* and Cricket was forced to try and protect their lives.

Thing of it was, there was no protecting *anyone* here. As he'd flown away with Evie in the belly of his flex-wing transport, that scumbag Preacher had warned Cricket the missile was on its way. The WarBot knew there was nowhere to run— the blast would simply be too massive to escape. But still, the First Law was screaming in Cricket's mind. His only concern: the hundreds of humans still in New Bethlehem. He had to help them. He had to *save* them.

But how do you save the unsavable?

He looked up into the cigarette sky, data scrolling down his optics as he scanned the gray. He saw a tiny black shape burning in out of the heavens like a thunderbolt. Electric despair washed over him. Thinking about Evie. About Lemon. About everything he'd fought for, everything he'd lost, glad in the end that he wasn't alone. Solomon was here, at least, the sassy logika perched on his shoulder. Abraham was with him, too, cradled in one massive palm. During the chaos of the lifelike attack, the boy had done himself proud—he'd saved the city from burning, even though the citizens and his own *mother* had been ready to nail him to a cross for his "impurity."

But in the end, it had been for nothing.

Only a miracle could save them now.

Crick patted Solomon on his metal knee, cradled Abraham to his chest.

"I'M SORRY," Cricket said.

He felt a knocking on the side of his head and turned to look at Solomon one last time. The spindly logika needed to bang on Cricket's metal skull to get his attention—the WarBot had deafened himself to avoid having to take more orders. He saw Solomon pointing east across New Bethlehem's smoking walls, the wrecked cars, the ash and ruin. There, glinting in the sunlight, was a monster truck painted Brotherhood red, speeding toward them across the desert.

The big bot sharpened his optics, thinking he was glitching as a colorless . . . tear opened up in front of the truck. The vehicle plunged down into it, disappearing as if into a hole in the ground. A split second later, it plunged right out of an identical tear that opened up just in front of New Bethlehem's walls.

The truck hit the deck, bouncing and crashing through the gate wreckage with a scream of tortured metal. The Brotherhood and citizens all scattered out of its way, the truck skidding and slamming into a row of rusty autos. Windows shattering, engine smoking, it ground to a halt in the middle of the town square.

". . . WHAT THE HELLS?"

Cricket saw two teenagers in military uniforms inside the

truck's cabin. There was a dark-skinned boy, a radioactivity symbol shaved into the side of his head. Beside him sat a girl with short dark hair, long bangs, black paintstick smudged on her lips and a slice of Asiabloc somewhere in her ancestry. The youngsters climbed up onto the truck's roof, bloody and bedraggled.

"WHAT ARE YOU DOING?" Cricket yelled.

The big bot saw another shimmering rift open in the air above their heads.

Cricket saw the missile speeding in out of the heavens.

And Cricket saw the boy

raise

his

hands.

The girl dragged a breather mask up over her face, goggles over her eyes, and did the same for the boy as she roared, "Everyone close your eyes!"

Cricket didn't have eyelids, of course. Nor did he have functional ears to hear the girl scream—he only found out what she yelled from Solomon afterward. Looking upward, telescopics engaged, he saw the missile plunge into the shimmering rift she'd apparently opened with her bare hands and *disappear right out of the sky.*

Scanning the heavens, Cricket caught movement north. He realized another tear had appeared—like an eraser smudge on the muddy gray. Amazed and dumbfounded, he watched the missile plunge out of this new rift, so distant it was only a speck, and moments later burst into shocking, impossible light.

The humans about him were all cowering in fear. Abraham was curled up against his fist. Even the boy and girl with their goggles had turned away from the blast. And so it was that only Cricket and Solomon bore witness to the first nuclear explosion the planet had seen since the war that almost ripped it to pieces.

It was elemental. Primordial. Fire stolen from the gods. The last time humans had unleashed this awful flame, they'd nearly destroyed their civilization, their species, their world. For a terrible moment, Cricket wondered if maybe the gods had returned to finish the job.

A second pulse followed after the first—a double flash, lighting the heavens with burning white. A fireball blazed inside it, blossoming outward in a moment, spherical, almost beautiful. Cricket's thermographics measured temperatures in the millions; the molten heart of a new sun blooming brighter with every second.

The clouds were consumed, rippling in circular patterns as they boiled into nothingness. The shockwave struck the earth below, gathering the desert sands and ripping them into the burning sky. The firestorm kept expanding, roiling, churning, flattening as it struck the upper atmosphere, a mushroom-shaped nightmare rising above the screaming earth.

And through it all, Cricket could only look on in horror.

The sound struck him next—though his aural systems were offline, he felt the vibration in his chest. A hammer blow, traveling at the speed of sound, ringing like funeral bells on his metal skin. It shook the ground, shivering the buildings in their foundations. And beyond it, riding across the wasteland like a storm of dark horses with tails of living flame, came a dust cloud bigger than Cricket had ever seen.

"EVERYBODY TAKE COVER!"

He could see Brotherhood members and their disciples yelling, saw terror in the folk around him. Many of New Bethlehem's buildings had been incinerated in the lifelike attack, but he knew the sturdiest structure was still intact. It stood at the bay's edge, black smoke spilling from its stacks. Frontways, it looked like a cathedral from 20C vids, but its hind parts were the chimneys and storage tanks of a bloated factory. If there was safety left, it was in there.

"THE DE-SAL PLANT!" he roared. "EVERYONE INSIDE!"

Some folk began streaming inside, others making for the WarDome or seeking cover in the buildings that hadn't been burned. Cricket stomped across the town square, lowering Abraham into the shelter of the boy's underground workshop. Abe slipped out of his outstretched fingers onto the oil-stained concrete, lips moving as he shouted. Solomon watched intently from Crick's shoulder, then wrote quickly onto the whiteboard he'd salvaged during the attack.

Master Abraham is asking about them?

The spindly logika pointed back into the town square. Turning, Cricket saw the two uniformed kids still atop their monster truck. The girl was tugging on the boy's pant leg, obviously urging him into cover. But the boy was refusing, standing with his hands held toward the incoming storm.

"THAT IDIOT'S GOING TO GET HIMSELF KILLED," Cricket growled.

Solomon quickly wrote on his whiteboard.

That is Master Abraham's concern, yes.

The big bot turned to Abraham, held out one massive palm. "STAY PUT!"

Cricket dragged the workshop's overhead doors into place and, spinning on his heel, dashed back toward the monster truck and the lunatics on top of it. He could see the dust cloud bearing down, roiling, boiling, black. His sensors were already reading the spike in temperature and radiation—anyone in its path was going to get fried. He only had moments before it swallowed them all whole.

"ARE YOU TWO INSANE?" he bellowed. "TAKE COVER!"

The boy turned toward him, yelled something and turned back to the looming storm wall. The girl waved for him to get back. But Cricket didn't have time for a debate—the First Law said he had to save these kids, simple as that. He reached out to scoop them up gentle as he could. The girl held out her hand toward him, and the earth just opened up under his feet.

His sensors went haywire, inputs spiking. He was falling somehow, crashing to the earth with a bang that shook his rivets, Solomon tumbling off his shoulder. Cricket looked about, realizing he was somehow a few hundred meters down the street from where he'd stood a second before. He saw one of those bizarre gray tears in the sky snapping shut over his head, his processors trying to make sense of exactly what was going on here.

Did she just . . . move us?

Cricket saw Abraham climbing up out of the workshop doors, black hair askew, tech-goggles pulled over his eyes. He saw the dark-skinned boy atop the monster truck brace himself, feet spread, palms outstretched. He saw a wall of boiling, burning darkness sweeping in out of the north, a storm born in the heart of that brief sun, set to immolate all in its path.

"ABRAHAM, GET DOWN!" Cricket roared.

And then, it hit them.

It was strange, watching it all unfold in total silence. It was an engine without the roar. A storm without thunder. It crashed on them like a tsunami, impossible force, unthinkable power. The earth shook, the dark swallowed them, thousands upon thousands of degrees, the burning remnants of the gods' stolen fire come to scorch them to their bones. But as that elemental fury crashed down upon the walls, as the flood arrived on their broken shores . . .

Something stopped it dead.

The air about them rippled. Awash with tiny sparks, like static on a faulty vidscreen. The dust and fire and withering weight blasted the walls and the outer city to pieces. But in the town square, stretching out to envelop the desalination plant, the broken buildings where the desperate citizens of New Bethlehem cowered and prayed, a sphere of . . . something kept the destruction at bay. It was invisible, intangible, its borders shimmering like the air above a bonfire.

Cricket saw the dark-skinned boy bending into the blast. Behind him, Abraham stood with arms flung out against the tempest, teeth bared in a snarl. The blast rolled over them, a wave of dust and flame. But though the temperature rose, it wasn't enough to burn them. Though the radiation levels spiked, it wasn't enough to kill them. And though the shockwave crushed everything around it to dust and ashes, there in the heart of that sphere, earth shaking below, sky boiling above, all was somehow calm. The crackling eye of a ravenous storm.

The worst washed over them, passing the bayside wall and dispersing over the black and foaming ocean. Burning winds followed in its wake, dust and debris swirling against the sphere of force enveloping them. To the north, a mushroom-shaped cloud was rising off the desert floor, kilometers into the heavens. Cricket saw Abraham had lowered his arms and was sinking to his knees. The boy atop the monster truck was swaying on his feet, dragging his goggles off his head. And if Cricket had breath, it would have been stolen away at the sight of him.

The boy's eyes were burning. Aflame, like the heart of that brief sun. The girl who came with him was looking up at him with awe and fear. As Cricket watched, the boy dropped off the truck and onto the hard-packed earth. The ground shattered beneath him, as if he weighed hundreds of tons. He staggered toward the water's edge, black footprints burning in his wake. He looked ready to fall, the fire in his eyes rolling down his cheeks like tears. The girl was screaming, pointing at Cricket.

"I CAN'T HEAR YOU!" he shouted.

Solomon banged on his shin, held up his whiteboard.

The ocean, old friend!

Cricket had no idea what was happening, let alone how or why, but in the absence of a better plan, he obeyed. Dashing across the broken square, Solomon hanging on to his leg like some metallic limpet, he scooped the dark-skinned boy up in his hands. An alarm blared inside his metal skull, and he realized the boy's skin was scorching hot, enough to melt his armor if he held him too long. Smashing through gutted buildings, Cricket carried the burning boy to the boulevard on the city's edge, the black salt water lapping at rotten piers.

The boy leapt from his palms, out into the sea. Steam burst from the water where he touched it, boiling as the boy held out his arms, away from the settlement, fingers spread. The air shivered, churned, *erupted,* a storm of gamma radiation and kinetic force released from his outstretched hands, carving through the ocean in a long, sweeping arc.

The waves turned to vapor, the foam to steam. Cricket was blinded for a moment, a great dark fog rising off the churning sea. But when it cleared, there the boy stood, waist-deep in black chop, his T-shirt and cargos soaked through, vapor rising off his skin. Head bowed. Eyes closed. Fists clenched.

But somehow, he was alive.

Somehow, they were *all still alive*.

People were peering out from the rubble, from the windows of the desalination plant. By the looks on their faces, they were reaching the same conclusion Cricket was. New Bethlehem was a city owned by the Brotherhood, and the Brotherhood operated under one absolute and unwavering mantra: Only the pure shall prosper.

Deviates, abnorms, trashbreeds—whatever you called them, they were the enemy of the people who lived here. But now those people looked out with wondering eyes at the boy in the boiling waves. At Abraham, making his way through the shattered concrete to stand, breathless and sweating, on the boulevard. At the girl with the black-paintstick lips, rushing past Abe and jumping into the water, throwing a fierce embrace about the dark-skinned boy before punching him repeatedly in the arm.

This was a city where deviates were nailed to crosses in the name of "purity." Where a mother was willing to sacrifice her own son to appease the mob.

But three deviates had just saved it from total destruction.

Among the slowly gathering crowd, Cricket could see the Brotherhood's leader, Sister Dee. The woman was clad in a white cassock, now stained with black dust and spatters of blood. Her dark hair fell in bedraggled waves around her shoulders, a greasepaint skull on her face. She was standing among her elite guard, watching Abraham with uncertain eyes.

But Abraham was looking at the pair in the water, something between elation and awe on his face. Dragging his dark hair back from his grubby cheeks, he met Cricket's eyes, shaking his head in wonderment.

"I TOLD YOU TO STAY PUT," Cricket said.

Abe simply shrugged, offering a sheepish grin.

Behind him, Cricket saw another familiar figure pushing through the crowd. One hand was pressed to a cluster of bullet holes in his chest, and his shirtfront was soaked with blood. His face was picture-perfect, dark, sweat-damp curls framing eyes of beautiful baby blue. He was staring at the deviates in wonder. But along with the bafflement, the bewilderment, Cricket could see anguish in his eyes.

"EZEKIEL."

The lifelike met his stare, raised one bloody hand in greeting. His eyes were filled with sadness, his face haunted. Though they'd been separated only a few days ago, it seemed like a lifetime had passed. They'd parted on ugly terms—Cricket had spoken harsh words about the lies Ezekiel had told Evie. But talking true, the WarBot was glad to see a familiar face among all this madness.

His brain was processing the events of the last few moments now, replaying footage of the Preacher as he'd made his escape. When the bounty hunter had emerged onto the de-sal plant's roof, he'd been pushing a cylindrical case—some kind of cryo-tube. And through the smoke and flame, Cricket had spotted two bloodstained figures being hauled into the Preacher's waiting flex-wing. A pretty boy with a mop of bloody blond hair. And beside him, dripping scarlet from the multiple holes in her chest, had been Evie.

The girl Cricket had been programmed to love. The girl he'd been programmed to protect. The girl who'd turned out not to be a girl at all. She'd fallen so far after she'd learned the truth of what she was. She'd done things Cricket wouldn't have believed her capable of. But now she and her "brother" had been abducted by Daedalus Technologies. Along with whatever, or *who*ever, was inside that cryogenic coffin.

What a mess . . .

The dark-skinned boy was being helped back to the pier by his friend, leaning hard on her shoulder. Abraham was looking back at his mother and her goons edging a few steps toward Cricket. Ezekiel had pushed his way through the mob now, bloody and beaten, looking up at Cricket with his plastic baby blues.

The WarBot looked to the boiling clouds, to the wreckage of the city that should've only been dust and bones. He felt metal knuckles banging on his skull, saw Solomon had clambered up onto his shoulder once more. The logika was spindly, his cream-white chassis decorated with gold filigree. He held up his whiteboard, his mouth fixed in that permanent, maddening grin.

It appears we all have some explaining to do!

3.2

PURGE

On paper, Ezekiel had a genius-level IQ.

His artificial synapses processed input at speeds unthinkable for an actual human. He could count the lashes on a person's eyelid in a fraction of a second, track a bullet as it cut the air. Nicholas Monrova had created him to be more than human. Stronger. Better. Smarter. And on paper he was all that and more. On paper, Ezekiel was a perfect synthesis of mechanical and biological engineering that completely surpassed the beings that had created him.

But it turned out paper didn't count for much in the real world.

I feel like an idiot.

He'd had no choice but to throw in his lot with the Preacher. He *knew* it was a risk at the time. But he'd wanted to believe the cyborg might be something close to honorable, that all his talk of having a code, of paying his debts, of being more than a killer, might prove true. Ezekiel had saved his life, after all.

That had probably been his first mistake. Unless you counted falling in love with Ana Monrova. Or lying to Eve about his role in the downfall of the Monrova clan. Or abandoning Lemon in the Clefts. Or any one of the other hundred bone-headed things he'd done since Eve found him in that ruined flex-wing on Dregs.

Make that a complete and total *idiot.*

Truth was, though he looked like a teenage boy, Ezekiel was only two years old. When they'd been created, he and his siblings had the architecture of the finest minds in Gnosis Laboratories incorporated into their own. Billions of ones and zeros uploaded into their psyches, the compiled knowledge of dozens of lifetimes. But Ezekiel was learning the hard way that it wasn't the same as actually *living.*

The world was more than ones and zeros. The beat of a butterfly's wings could change the weather on the other side of the globe. A single kiss could bring down an empire. The only way to understand what life meant was to *live* it, and the longer he did, the more he understood how little he understood. How he still had *so* much more to learn. About life. Himself. What kind of person he wanted to be.

So what did he learn about Preacher's betrayal? Eve's descent into violence and rage? That inevitably, the people you put your faith in will let you down? That he should trust no one?

What kind of person would that make him?

He was standing in New Bethlehem—what was left of it, anyway. His first thought was that they should all be dead. His second was of Preacher's betrayal, of Eve and Gabriel in his custody. But his last thought, his heaviest, the one so dark he couldn't bear it for long, was the memory of Ana. The girl he loved, the girl he'd spent the last two years searching for, floating inside that frozen cryo-pod. No brainwave activity. No pulse or breath except what the machines pumped into her.

His first and last and only.

Now nothing but an empty shell.

The sky to the north was dark with dust and smoke, that awful mushroom cloud slowly smearing itself across the cigarette sky. The city was shrouded in ashes, the taste of burned rubber and charred salt clinging to the back of his throat. His once-white T-shirt was torn and bloodstained, his black jeans caked with dust and grime. The bullet wounds Preacher had given him hurt like broken glass and dirty acid, but they were gradually knitting closed—one more gift from the folk who'd made him more human than human.

A Brotherhood posse in red cassocks had gathered on the shoreline. A group of burlier-looking thugs in black surrounded a tall woman with a greasepaint skull on her face—some kind of authority figure.

The boy and girl in the military uniforms had climbed out of the ocean onto the boardwalk, both looking exhausted. He hadn't seen them arrive, but he'd seen what that boy had done. Zeke wouldn't have believed it possible, but somehow, this kid had redirected the edge of a nuclear firestorm.

Cricket stood at the waterline. His WarBot body loomed eight meters tall, twelve thousand horsepower of bleeding-edge hardware. But somewhere in the last three days, he'd been repainted in Brotherhood colors—blood red and black, a bone-white skull daubed over his face. He was glaring at Ezekiel now, eyes burning a luminous blue.

The spindly logika with the luminous grin sitting on

Cricket's shoulder had called himself Solomon. Zeke knew the boy in the greasy coveralls with the slick hair was Abraham. Aside from that, he was completely in the dark.

"WHERE THE HELL HAVE YOU BEEN?" the big WarBot demanded.

Ezekiel took a deep breath and sighed. "Nice to see you, too, Cricket."

Solomon wrote quickly on a whiteboard so Cricket could understand his reply—the big bot had deafened himself to avoid having to take further orders from humans. *Pretty smart,* Zeke thought. Though he wasn't about to tell Cricket that.

"Who are you?" Abraham asked.

"My name's Ezekiel."

"Not you," Abraham replied, staring at the pair in the military uniforms. "You."

The girl was supporting the boy's weight, glowering at the assembled Brotherhood thugs. She had dark shadows under her eyes, fury in her glare.

"What, don't you recognize us?" She frowned at the assembled brethren, the tall, white-clad woman leading them. "We're the *enemy*."

"You . . ." The dark-skinned boy with the radiation symbol shaved into his hair faltered, looking at Abraham. "You . . . helped me. The heat, the radiation . . . that I could handle. But the shockwave . . . you stopped it."

Abraham shrugged. "Seemed like a good idea at the time."

"Trashbreed filth," one of the Brotherhood thugs muttered.

"Really?" the dark-skinned boy growled, turning on the man. "You're gonna spew th-that purity crap *now*?"

The girl raised her voice over the burning wind, long bangs caught at the corners of her mouth. "In case you missed it, we're the *trashbreed filth* who just saved your lives. But if it were up to me, you'd all go straight to hell."

One of the Brotherhood boys reached for the pistol at his belt, a few more unslinging their assault rifles. Ezekiel knew Cricket couldn't do anything to harm a human, but with a whoosh and whine of heavy servos, the WarBot scooped Abraham up and cradled him inside the shelter of his metal hands. The air around the two newcomers rippled, shivered, the boy closing his fists. More brethren reached for their guns, and Ezekiel was slowly drawing his pistol when—

"Mother, *stop this*!" Abraham shouted.

The boy glowered at the skull-faced woman.

"What the hell is wrong with you people?" Abraham demanded, his voice trembling with anger. "Thomas, I salvaged the humidicrib your son lived inside for three months. Caleb, who built the respirator that helped your wife breathe at night? James, we've known each other since we were *kids*! Your damned purity means so much, you're willing to murder the people who just saved your lives? Every one of you would be *dead* if not for us!"

Ezekiel could see tears of frustration and rage shining in the boy's eyes as he looked among the assemblage: the thugs, the mute citizens in ruins around them and, finally, the woman who was apparently his mother.

"You should all be *ashamed* of yourselves," Abraham spat.

His words brought stillness to the scene. Ezekiel saw a few brethren sharing guilty glances, looking to their leader for direction. The woman was staring up at her son, her face unreadable beneath the smeared paint and dirt.

"Radiation's g-gonna keep blowing in on those winds," the dark-skinned boy told her, his eyes bruised with exhaustion.

"And I'm not s-sticking around to keep them away. Considering you nailed me to a cross a few days back, you should be thanking your damn god I've kept them off this far. But if you care about your people, you sh-should trundle them out of here while the trundling's good, bitch."

The woman's jaw tightened. A long moment passed, silent but for the whisper of poisonous winds. Ezekiel's pistol felt like a brick in his hand.

"Brother Jonah," the woman finally said. "Assemble the vehicles." She raised her voice, looked to the buildings around them. "All of you, gather what provisions you can. Weapons. Water. We must leave this place, my children. And quickly."

"But where will we go?" someone cried.

"Know no fear!" she called. "I have led you this far, haven't I? This is all a part of God's plan. As the chosen were led out of the desert in the Goodbook, so, too, shall we survive this exodus. Have faith, my children." She met her son's stare, dark eyes glittering. "The pure *will* prosper."

The brethren moved swiftly at the woman's command. The folk in the buildings about them were less certain, but as the first few shuffled away, more followed, bewildered. Ezekiel supposed they had no other option. When you're lost in the wilderness, you follow anyone who claims to have a map.

As the brethren and citizens prepared to abandon their ruined city, Abraham and his mother simply stared at each other. Zeke could feel the weight between them. The sorrow and anger. But finally, with no other words of explanation, the woman marched off into the throng.

Ezekiel looked to the uniformed pair again. The Asiabloc girl looked utterly exhausted, and the dark-skinned boy looked even worse. If Zeke looked hard enough, he could still see a glow in his eyes, ember-soft and red.

"What are your names?" Ezekiel asked.

They looked at him curiously—the bullet holes in his chest slowly knitting closed, the metal coin slot in his flesh gleaming through the tears in his shirt. Burning winds kissed Ezekiel's skin, the air about them still crackling and rippling.

"I'm Grimm," said the boy, thick with WestEuro accent. "This is Diesel."

"You're deviates," Abraham said.

The girl named Diesel stared up at the boy with suspicious eyes, brushing her black waterlogged bangs out of her eyes. "Ditto, kid. You wanna explain how the heir to the goddamn Brotherhood turns out to be a freak just like us?"

"Deez, we got no time for the chit or the chat," Grimm muttered, smothering a cough. "We g-gotta get back to Lemon. Bio-Maas m—"

"*Lemon?*" Ezekiel's heart leapt into his throat. "You know Lemon Fresh?"

Grimm blinked. ". . . Do you?"

"I've been looking for her for the past five days!" He tasted blood in his mouth, wincing as he pressed a sticky red hand to his chest. "Where is she? Is she—"

"*LEMON?*" The metallic shout rang over the boulevard, startling the stragglers in the buildings around them. Cricket glanced at Solomon's whiteboard again to make sure he'd read right, then back to Grimm. "YOU KNOW LEMON FRESH?"

Diesel looked up at the WarBot, paint-smudged lips pursed.

"You're Cricket," she finally deduced. "The rustbucket bot-buddy Lemon dragged her idiot ass out into the desert to find."

Dark eyes turned on Zeke. "Which makes you Ezekiel. You were in Paradise Falls a few days back. Killing people."

"I didn't kill anyone," Ezekiel replied. "My brothers and sisters did the killing in the Falls, not me."

"Mmm," Diesel said, obviously unconvinced.

"Where is she?" Ezekiel asked.

"WHERE IS SHE?" Cricket demanded a moment later.

"She's back at Miss O's," the girl said. "She's safe."

"She's *not* s-safe," Grimm said. "The Major said BioMaas was tracking her."

"The Major said a lot of things, Grimm," Diesel murmured.

"We gotta bounce," Grimm snapped. "Sharpish."

Blistering winds blew in from the north, the scent of death and char on the air. Grimm was already shuffling toward the square. Ezekiel felt torn, unsure which way to turn. Preacher had made off with Ana's body, still in her cryo-tube. She was just a shell now. Those arms that had held him, those eyes that had adored him, that heart that had filled him—all of them were empty. It was as if she were as good as dead, and the thought of it almost brought him to his knees. If she was the girl who'd made him live, he wondered how he might go on without her. Wondered what the point of any of this might be. But the thought of her in Daedalus hands took hold of him, seized that empty space inside his chest and filled it with anger.

She wasn't some trophy to be kept on a mantelpiece.

She wasn't some test subject to be poked and prodded in some damn lab.

I can't just leave her with them.

I can't let it end like that. . . .

But still, he'd made a promise to Lemon. And the thing of it was, beyond the emptiness in his eyes and the rage in his chest,

Ezekiel knew this was a world where a promise didn't count for much. Where inevitably, the people you put your faith in would let you down. But it didn't have to be.

"I'm coming with you," he said.

Grimm looked him over, eyes narrowed.

"She's my friend," Ezekiel said simply. "I made a promise to her."

The boy glanced down again at the bullet holes in Zeke's chest. The wounds were now all but closed, just a handful of small punctures in his olive skin.

"You're like us," Grimm murmured.

Ezekiel shook his head, heart aching. "I'm very different."

Diesel and Grimm exchanged a quick glance. The girl shrugged.

"Well, you're Lem's crew," the boy finally sighed. "So I s'pose you're right by me. The deets can wait for later, we got rubber to burn."

"I'M COMING, TOO," Cricket said, still following the conversation on Solomon's whiteboard.

Diesel shook her head. "Our truck won't fit you, Rusty."

"We have our own transport," Abraham said. "We can follow you."

Atop Cricket's shoulder, Solomon tilted his head. "YOU PLAN ON TRAILING AFTER THESE . . . PECULIARS . . . INTO THE WASTELANDS, MASTER ABRAHAM?"

"It's not like I have anyplace better to be. Unless you're planning to . . ." Abraham looked at Diesel, made a popping noise, opening one fist, then another. "You know . . ."

The girl shook her head, her face pale and drained. "I've got nothing left in the tank. We're gonna be driving regular for a while."

"Okay." Ezekiel looked at Abraham, glad to just have a direction and something to take his mind off the end of his road. "My bike's trashed, can I . . . ?"

Abraham shrugged. "Any friend of Paladin's."

Zeke slipped his arm under Grimm's, hefting his weight. The boy nodded thanks, and the group shuffled from the boardwalk out into the bedlam of the town square. Brotherhood members were shouting orders, directing a convoy of trucks, 4x4s and bikes laden with gear and people. The air stank of distant smoke and ashes, methane exhaust and fire. The rev of rusty motors filled the air.

Ezekiel helped Grimm and Diesel up into the truck's cabin, the boy cursing as he struggled in. The pair looked like twenty klicks of rough road.

"Can either of you drive?" the lifelike asked softly.

"If you're offering to chauffeur," Diesel relented, "I wouldn't say no."

"Ezekiel!"

The scream rang out over the throng, the rising motors, the chatter and the fear. Zeke turned and saw the shell-shocked citizens parting before a limping, broken figure. Ezekiel's heart twisted at the sight of her.

Faith . . .

Drenched with red, the lifelike looked like she'd been through a meat grinder. Her legs and stomach had been crushed under some colossal weight, and though they were slowly healing, her wounds were still horrifying. She'd twisted some metal pipes into crutches to help her walk. Her dark bangs were soaked with blood, hanging over wild gray eyes.

Cricket's metallic roar rang on the broken walls.

"FAITH!"

A chaingun in the WarBot's forearm unfolded, spinning up with a deadly electric whine. Citizens scattered as Cricket stomped toward the crippled lifelike. But Faith's eyes were fixed on Ezekiel, tears rolling down her bloodstained cheeks.

"Ze-eke," she whispered.

She staggered, slipping onto her ruined knees. Falling in slow motion like a broken doll, like a puppet with its strings sheared through.

Zeke was at her side before he knew he was moving, catching her, sinking down with her in his embrace. Cricket roared at him to get out of the way. But Zeke stayed where he was, Faith in his arms as she struggled to speak.

"They t-took him . . . ," she said. "Gabriel . . ."

"I know," he nodded.

Faith swallowed, tears in her eyes. "W-we have to get him b-back."

"Where's Verity?" Ezekiel asked.

Faith tried to speak, choked on a bubble of blood. Instead, she raised one shaking hand, pointed over Ezekiel's shoulder. Zeke glanced behind, saw Cricket's towering form blotting out the light. The WarBot's eyes burned blue, his chaingun aimed square at Faith's chest.

"GET OUT OF THE WAY, EZEKIEL," the big bot growled. "I THOUGHT I KILLED THAT HOMICIDAL MANIAC IN THE WARDOME. I'LL MAKE DAMN SURE THIS TIME."

Ezekiel realized Verity was dead. That Cricket must have destroyed her. That of the original twelve lifelike models, only he, Gabriel and Faith remained. Looking down at Faith, broken and bloodied in his arms, he felt his heart sinking.

He knew she wasn't a good person. She'd murdered Olivia, the eldest Monrova daughter, right in front of him—just lifted her pistol and blew the girl's brains all over the floor. She'd been happy to stand by while Gabriel killed Silas, almost killed Eve. She and the others had murdered countless people in their search for Ana's body. Who knew what other atrocities Faith had committed since she stood at the windows in Babel, looking out with wonder on her first dawn?

It's so beautiful, she'd whispered.

On paper, this was a simple deal.

On paper, he should just let her go.

"Zeke." She touched his cheek with red fingertips. "P-please . . ."

Ezekiel had put faith in people before. And all he'd got for it was a knife in his back. A bullet in his heart. A metal coin slot in his chest.

"She helped kill Silas, Ezekiel," the big WarBot spat. "She tried to kill Lemon, Evie, me and you. She's a *murderer.*"

Ezekiel looked up at Cricket, a scowl darkening his brow. He knew the logika couldn't hear him through his damaged aural arrays. And Ezekiel suspected he wouldn't have listened anyway. But there in the New Bethlehem square, the taste of a mushroom-shaped cloud on his tongue, surrounded by all the worst the world had to offer, Ezekiel realized the kind of person he could be.

He could be the kind who had faith when he had every reason not to. The kind who believed in others even when they kept letting him down. The kind who chose to think that everyone had some good in them, somewhere.

Or he could be the kind of person who sat by while someone killed the only sister he had left.

Ezekiel stood, a bloodied and broken Faith in his arms. He met the logika's eyes and fancied he could see rage, burning bright and blue in that plastic and glass. Cricket's titanic hands curled into mighty fists. But they didn't fall.

"She's family," Ezekiel said.

And he turned and walked away.

3.3

PULSE

It took a moment for Eve to realize where she was.

The lights were pin-bright and blinding. A crowd stomping and cheering. She could feel their thunder through the metal around her, butterflies in her belly. The dark was full of wild eyes and ethyl grins, Corp logos shining on glitching vidscreens. But it was the smell that brought it home to her at last—the oil and methane smoke, scorched plastic and fresh sweat.

WarDome.

She was snug inside her machina, the controls lit up in a rolling rainbow. The old leather of her pilot's chair creaked as she flexed her fingers inside her gloves. High above the ring, she saw the EmCee in her sequined top hat and tails.

"And now, gamblers and raaaaamblers," she cried. "Our champion, weighing in at thirty-eight tons! Get yourselves hoarse for *Miss Combobulation*!"

Eve raised her arm in her control sleeve, and her machina did the same. The crowd screamed in reply, elation washing over her in waves. She looked into the stands and spotted a tiny girl in an ancient, oversized leather jacket. A jagged bob of cherry-red hair. A spattering of freckles. A small hand in a fingerless glove waved at her through the WarDome bars.

"Lemon," she whispered, smiling.

"Riotgrrrrrl!" her bestest grinned, throwing up the horns.

Eve could see Cricket sitting on the girl's shoulder, the rusty little logika waving, his boggle eyes alight. At her feet, Kaiser sat with his mouth open, heat-sink tongue lolling between his teeth. And beside him, an old man with a shock of gray hair. Eyes sharp as laser scalpels, ice blue and filled with love.

Eve felt light as air, relief swelling in her chest, a sense that everything would finally and truly be okay. She was where she belonged. She was back where it started, the place people knew her, not just her name.

She was home.

Her grandpa looked at her and grinned. "Go get her, kiddo!"

"Aaaaaaaand now," the EmCee shouted, "our challenger! Representing Gnosis Laboratories in her first professional bout, weighing in at sixty-three kilos—make some noise, won't you, for Miss Ana Monrovaaaaaa!"

A pulse of blood-red light rolled over the scene. The cheering and stomping fell silent, the blinding lights died. A single spotlight remained, piercing the gloom like a spear. And standing in it, bathed in light, Eve saw herself.

A version of herself, anyway, with longer hair and paler skin and softer eyes. The girl she was made to replace. The design she was copied from.

Ana Monrova looked up at Eve, her hazel eyes shining. She was empty-handed, wearing a simple white shift, and Eve was encased inside a twenty-foot-tall killing machine. But still, Eve felt a sliver of fear pierce her belly at the sight of that girl. A cold chill running across her skin.

She'd hunted all over the Yousay for Ana Monrova. Intent on killing her, silencing her voice inside her head, proving once and for all she was more than this empty shell she was built to replace.

That blood-red pulse washed the sky again.

Eve felt a stab of pain behind her eyes.

"Who are you?" Ana asked her.

"I'm me," Eve replied, hands in fists. "I'm *me*."

The girl tilted her head, long golden tresses spilling over her face.

"But who do you want to be?"

———

It took a moment for Eve to realize where she was.

The light was low and summer-warm. The silence soft and complete. She could see a broad window looking out on a murky night sky, white sheets around her feet. She could feel warmth pressed against her, butterflies moving in a long, languid dance inside her belly. But it was the smell that brought it home at last—the faded flowers and faint metal, warm breath and fresh sweat.

Ezekiel.

His hands were on her waist, and her arms around his neck, her fingertips weaving through his dark curls. His chest was hard against hers, and her lips were soft, skimming the line of her jaw and sending flushes of flame all the way down to her toes. She could feel his long lashes fluttering against her skin. They were in her bed, she realized. Bare and smooth and spent—that night he'd first come to her room before her world fell apart.

Her mouth found his, and his lips opened against hers, and for a moment, the ache of it was so sweet, it was all she was. The soft velvet of his kiss, the hard swell of his shoulder, her hands trailing down over the lines and furrows of his back and lower, lower still. She'd given all of herself to him, lost between the sighs and wrapped in the want, honey-sweet and secret-deep. She knew that this wasn't made to last, that a life lived in the dark was half a life at best. But though he'd been made, not grown, this beautiful boy with an angel's name was more real in that moment than anything else in her world. And if she were only to have half a life, let it be *this* half, she begged. One where she was happy and she was adored and she was real. Real as the almost-boy in her arms.

They eased away from each other, and the ache only deepened as she felt the places he'd been, now without him. For a moment, she wondered what use her lips were if they weren't pressed against his. What point there was to her hands if they weren't touching him. But then she looked up into his eyes, beautiful, blue, bright, and though they were full of love, framed by dusk-dark lashes and shining in the dark, she couldn't help but remember he'd never, ever looked at her this way.

"All I am," he said. "All I do, I do for you."

"You never said that to me," she told him.

Eve pushed away from Ezekiel, rolling out of the bed—a bed she'd never slept in, a night she'd never shared. She clutched a sheet she'd never touched about herself, looked around this room that was never hers, this boy she'd never loved.

Ezekiel held out his hand, his voice low and sweet with promise.

"Come back to bed."

"Come back?" She almost laughed. "We were never together like this."

He smiled at her, rising from the crumpled mattress. "Like this, then?"

Blood-red light pulsed, a thrust of pain crackled in her skull. Her legs were wrapped around his waist, her oversized boots digging into the small of his back as she crushed herself against him. They were in the workshop in Faith's mission back in Armada, oil smudged on her skin and iron in the air. A fire was burning inside her, not soft and slow and sweet this time. No, this was gasoline and nitro, this was rage and want and teeth and bare skin on dirty concrete and fingernails clawing at his back and right, so *right*.

This had been real, she knew. This had been hers.

And so had he.

"Eve," he murmured, breath hot against her skin. "Eve."

"No," she breathed. "Call me Ana. . . ."

He lifted his head, looked at her with those pretty sky-blue eyes.

"Make up your mind," he said. "Who do you want to be?"

————

It took a moment for Eve to realize where she was.

She was standing on a beach neither she nor the girl she'd been had ever visited. It was the kind of beach they used to put on postcards, back when there still was a post and people put cards into it.

Waves lapped at her ankles, shiver-cool on her skin. Not the black chemsludge that had slurped and sucked on the broken shores of Dregs. No, this was a beautiful blue, like sapphires and tumbling diamonds. The sand was cotton-soft between her toes, and there were no rusting auto hulks or discarded fridges or polystyrene scum. The sky was blue, clean, so bright it hurt her eyes to look at.

She was wearing loose white linen, just as spotless as the sand. The cool wind whispered in off the water and raised the hairs on the back of her neck. She could smell hot food sizzling somewhere nearby, hear distant music of a shape and tone she'd never known.

"I'm dreaming," she realized.

"If you like, yes," came a voice behind her.

Eve turned and saw a man reclining in a wooden sun lounge. He had a deep tan, offsetting the brilliant white of his shirt and shorts. He was tall and fit, perhaps in his midthirties, perfect teeth and a perfect smile. He wore mirrored sunglasses and held a long frost-rimed glass set with a little umbrella. He raised it to her in greeting.

"Good day, Miss Monrova," he said.

"My name's Eve," she replied, soft anger slipping into her voice.

"Of course." His smile only widened. "Would you like to sit?"

The man gestured, and Eve saw another sun lounge beside his. An identical drink rested on the chair's arm, and a towel was laid out on the wood. The fabric was printed with a familiar shape—a small, agile-looking machina in hot pink urban camo, the words KISS THIS sprayed across its hind parts.

"Miss Combobulation," Eve breathed.

A wave of melancholy washed over her at the sight, the

memory of that dream: her life in Dregs with Lemon, little Cricket, Grandpa.

Except he wasn't her grandpa, was he?

He'd lied to me about that, just like all the rest of it.

Anger seeped back into her mind, swallowed her nostalgia under sticky black. The waves shushed about her ankles, a song of azure and salt on her skin. Every sense was alive and tingling; she could smell the flowers and the ocean, hear and feel the whispering waves, see the crescent of lush green palms rising up from pale dunes ahead. There was no place on earth left like this, she knew.

And this, she realized with a sinking feeling, *is no dream.*

Her memory was returning now. Drowning those images of the WarDome. Of Ezekiel in her bed. She remembered the attack on New Bethlehem. She and Gabriel and Uriel in the cryochamber beneath the Brotherhood's desalination plant. Ana's body—her doppelgänger, her twisted reflection—frozen inside her glass coffin.

She could hear Ezekiel's words, hanging like ghosts on the wind.

I know you! The girl you were built to be, and the girl you became afterward. And this girl I see in front of me now isn't anything like either of them!

That's the point, she'd replied.

She looked at the man in his sun lounge, her anger rising.

"Who are you?" she asked.

"My name is Danael Drakos," he replied.

"But *who* are you?" she demanded.

The man sipped his drink.

"I'm the chief executive officer of Daedalus Technologies," he said. "It's truly a pleasure to meet you, Miss Monrova."

"I told you. My name is Eve."

"Well, no," Drakos said, still smiling. "Not technically. From what we've surmised, Eve was the name Silas Carpenter gave you after GnosisLabs collapsed and he fled with you to Dregs. The name you were born with—or, more accurately, made to answer to—was Ana Monrova."

She looked this man over, from the tips of his toes to the top of his head. She could see a glowing subdermal implant at his wrist, the sleek lines of a Memdrive above his right temple, 'trodes beneath his left ear. Either he was born perfect or he'd undergone extensive surgery, sculpting him into an image of masculine beauty. Truth told, he looked too good to be real, and to Eve, that made him look anything but. He was like one of those 20C boy dolls she'd sometimes find in the Scrap—the ones with the permanent smile and sculpted pecs and a smooth featureless lump where the interesting parts of the crotch should've been.

He looks like a human trying to look like one of us.

"I get to decide my own name, cockroach," she spat.

"Miss Monrova," the man said, peering at her over the top of his sunglasses. "From now on, I'm afraid you get to decide nothing at all."

"Where am I?"

"You're safe. You're in Daedalus custody."

"Where's Gabriel? Faith and Verity?"

"The whereabouts of your sisters is unknown," Drakos said. "And largely irrelevant. Your brother Gabriel is in our care, but I'm afraid he's a little worse for wear. Our field agent was a touch . . . overenthusiastic during acquisition."

Eve remembered the shoot-out under New Bethlehem, pulsing red light and oily black metal and cool white frost on her lips. She could see her brawl with Ezekiel in her mind's eye, the pair of them crashing against each other with a rage that mirrored their old passion. She remembered the kaleidoscope of emotions—joy, sorrow, guilt, pain—roiling inside her chest as she hurt him, oh, how she'd *hurt* him. And she remembered herself standing over Zeke, bloody hands and ragged breath, as a dark figure blasted a handful of holes through her chest.

A black hat. A red right hand.

"Preacher," she whispered.

"Sincerest apologies for his treatment of you. He was a good man once. His recent failures, coupled with his violent conduct, make the board question how much longer he'll be of use to this Corporation. But enough about *him*." Drakos's perfect teeth flashed again, his smile too good to be true. "Now, Miss Monrova . . . actually, would you mind terribly if I called you Ana?"

"Would you mind terribly if I kicked your teeth out of your head?"

"Charming," Drakos chuckled. "We have some questions for you, if you don't mind. Our techs can unearth their answers eventually, but it will prove less stressful on your mental faculties if you volunteered them." He leaned forward, peered at her intently. "Please understand, all of us on the Daedalus board are ardent admirers of your father's work. Personally speaking, I consider you a *masterpiece*, Ana."

"You call me Ana one more time," Eve growled, "I'm going to hurt you in ways you never dreamed."

"Your erstwhile comrade," Drakos said, sipping his drink. "Lemon Fresh."

Eve's stomach flipped at the name, her hands curling into fists. Lemon had lied to her, just like all the rest of them. After their falling-out, Eve had been happy to see the girl's back, talking true. But despite all the hurtful, hateful things Eve had spat into her face, Lemon had still tried to save her in Babel. Despite what lay between them—the deceit and the anger and all that Eve had done and become since she left Lemon behind—that little redheaded trouble-machine had still been her bestest. And that still counted for something.

"What about her?" Eve asked.

"You're aware she's a genetic abnormality? What do you know of her abilities?"

"Nothing I'm about to share with you, cockroach."

Drakos steepled his fingers at his chin. "Ana, please, I—"

Eve moved, lightning quick, one moment standing in the water, the next, beside Drakos. She dragged him out of his chair and struck him with her closed fist, knuckles mashing right into his infuriating smirk.

She threw all her weight into it. All her rage. His sunglasses flew loose, and his jaw shattered like porcelain, bone and meat pulping. The strength of her lifelike body was enough to snap his neck, the wet crunching of his vertebrae rolling up her arm as his head lolled atop his broken spinal column.

He was dead, she realized.

Snuffed out in her arms, just like that.

The thing she'd become—more human than human than human—couldn't help but feel disdain in the face of something so hopelessly fragile. The body in her grip disgusted her, and she let it drop, *thump thud,* into the sand at her feet. Staring at the bright red splashed across her knuckles.

"Feel better?" came a voice from behind her.

She turned, and there was Drakos, seated in an identical lounge with an identical smile on his face and an identical drink in his hand. Glancing behind, Eve saw the first lounge was gone, the corpse at her feet vanished, the blood on her knuckles wiped clean. Just as she suspected.

"This is a sim," she said. "You've got me plugged into a virtch unit."

"Well spotted," Drakos replied.

Eve had tried a few virtual reality programs over the years in Dregs. Grandpa had a suite of VR history reels, some nature clips; Eve had even experimented with a few skin sims in her Los Diablos days, black-market, X-rated, handed out among her cronies. But you had to wear a bodysuit and float inside a sensory deprivation tank to get the full physical experience of VR, and none of the sims she'd tried came *close* to this level of detail. She looked up at the sky overhead, curled her toes in the sand, inhaled the salt-sweet scent of the ocean, shaking her head.

"Impressive," she admitted.

"It's a new platform we're putting to market in quarter three," Drakos explained. "A wetware interface that almost completely bypasses the need for physical peripherals, such as goggles and whatnot. Instead, it plugs directly into the neural network. It will completely revolutionize the way we interact with so-called reality. We call it Truelife."

That now-familiar pulse of blood-red light raced across the sky again, that same twinge of pain crackled across Eve's temples. It was sharper this time, brighter, and she pressed her hand to her brow, hissing.

"Apologies," Drakos said. "We have you heavily medicated, but it seems your artificial neural network suffers trauma the same way a real human's does. The pain will stop soon, your session is almost over for the day."

She winced as the pain subsided. "Session?"

"We wouldn't normally need to perform quite so invasive a dive if we were simply replicating wave patterns. But I'm afraid your lifelike physiology is proving somewhat difficult for our techs to negotiate. And you have some information that's rather pertinent to us." Drakos shrugged. "As I said, things would go far smoother if you were to simply volunteer the information about Miss Fresh."

"You're mapping my brainwaves?" she said.

"I believe I just explained that, yes."

Eve's eyes narrowed as realization struck her. "You're going to use them to break into the Myriad computer inside Babel."

Drakos finished his drink, placed the glass aside. "Ana Monrova is brain-dead. But you are an almost-perfect copy of her. Between the topography of her physical form and your baseline to operate from, we feel we can adequately replicate the real Ana's pattern. As I said, we on the Daedalus board are ardent admirers of your father's work. His vision for the world was flawed, but he was still an exceptional artiste. We feel his legacy shouldn't die with him."

"And *I* said he's not my father," Eve spat.

"Miss Monrova, please," Drakos sighed. "Don't be so naïve. Now, I'll ask you again: What do you know of Miss Fresh's ability? What is its range? Its limitations?"

"Go to hell," she replied.

Drakos glanced at his wrist, reading the illuminated numbers on his subdermal implant.

"Do we have time?" he asked, speaking to the air.

He nodded, as if to himself.

"Very well, then."

Drakos clapped his hands, and the beach dissolved. Without warning, Eve found herself surrounded by flames, blindingly bright, impossibly fierce. The floor beneath her was blistering, and she screamed as her bare feet were scorched. Collapsing to her knees, she screamed again, feeling the fire eating her flesh. It was a pure and perfect agony, inescapable, absolute. Curling over, she could feel her fingers blackening like twigs, her hair burning, her eyes bursting, running down her cheeks and cooking on her skin like the insides of broken eggs.

"Something less traditional, perhaps?"

Drakos clapped again, and the scene shifted. The flames were gone, replaced by a snowstorm: arctic, howling, pummeling. The heat on her body was quenched in one moment of sweet relief, and then the cold reached past the bliss and punched its way into her heart. Eve gasped, the chill piercing her spine, boiling on her skin. She looked up at Drakos, standing in the tempest with his thin shirt and shorts, utterly unaffected. She tried to speak, but her throat had seized closed. Knives of ice in her lungs. Her eyes frozen solid inside her skull.

Drakos clapped, and they were back on the beach again, Eve on her knees, gasping as the bitter cold melted beneath that gorgeous sun. She *knew* this was a simulation. That none of what was happening was actually happening. But the pain, god . . . she'd never felt anything like it in her life. . . .

"The mind is its own place," Drakos said, "and in itself can make a heav'n of hell, a hell of heav'n."

Eve curled her hands into fists and took hold of her tears. She recalled those words from years ago. Sitting with Raphael in Babel's great library, listening rapt as the lifelike read aloud from—

"Paradise Lost," she whispered.

Drakos only smiled. "As I explained, this will go much easier for you if you cooperate. Simply tell us what we wish to know and all this can stop, Ana."

The sky pulsed red again, and that stabbing pain behind her eyes returned—worse than before. The subdermal implant in Drakos's arm beeped. The man looked down and sighed.

"I'm afraid that our session's over for the day, Ana. We'll meet same time tomorrow. I hope you'll have considered my offer by then."

Eve drew breath to speak. To seethe. To spit.

Drakos clapped a final time.

And everything went white.

———

Weightless.

Drifting.

Silent.

Eve felt absolutely nothing—no sight, no sound, no touch—and that was perhaps more frightening than all the pain before. But ever so slowly, she started to receive input, to feel the familiar weight of her body, the sense of herself. She opened her eyes, saw she was sitting on a soft chair. She was surrounded by dozens of robots—tall logika with slender limbs, hulls painted surgical white, the winged sun of Daedalus Technologies at their breasts. White light. White walls. Some kind of lab, by the look.

She couldn't see a single human in the room.

A logika plucked a small silver stud from either temple—the wetware interface Drakos had mentioned. A thrill of rage seethed through her, and Eve tried to raise her hands, to reach out and hurt, bend, *break*. But she was cuffed, elbow to wrist, knee to ankle, in bands of gleaming metal.

"Get your hands *off* me!" she spat, bucking in the chair.

The logika about her paused, turning to study her. They each had one large eye in the center of their faces, ringed with a dozen smaller lenses, all glowing blue. There were ident numbers on their chests: TECH-098. TECH-892. TECH-228. The metal encasing Eve's limbs groaned as she struggled, the seat rocking beneath her. But the bonds kept her pinned like a fly. Another wave of impotent rage washed through her, and she scanned the room, looking for any way to escape.

And then she saw her.

A long tube of glass, filled with liquid, softly aglow. Its walls were pale with frost, but not enough to hide the body within. A golden halo of blond hair floated around her head. Naked skin lit vaguely blue by the lights inside her coffin. 'Trodes at her temples and a tube between her pouting lips. Her eyes were closed—she looked like some girl from a fairy tale waiting for a handsome prince to wake her with a kiss.

Except there was nothing inside her to wake.

Ana.

Eve stared at her doppelgänger. Indignant somehow that these Daedalus roaches had claimed her. To know Ana was in their clutches somehow made Eve's own captivity burn even worse.

"Let me go!" A lank blond curl fell over her eyes as she glared at the robots in the room. "Let me go, or I swear, I'll ghost each and every *one of you*!"

The logika shared a glance. The one who'd touched her spoke.

"TAKE THE SUBJECT TO THE DETENTION LEVELS."

"COMPLYING," came a voice behind her.

Eve twisted to look over her shoulder. Two tall, bulky logika stood behind her—different models from the ones around her. They had blue-gray hulls, glowing white optics and idents stenciled on their chests: SEC-1098 and SEC-994. Eve glanced around the room again, noted the idents on the other logika.

TECH-338. TECH-028. TECH-301.

Technicians.

Security.

She felt herself moving, realized her chair was floating—suspended on a cushion of magnetized particles. She bucked and thrashed as the logika propelled her from the room, leaving that sleeping beauty in her glass coffin.

The bot guided her down corridors of gleaming white, sterile and pristine, computer panels in the walls. The space outside the lab was bustling, legions of logika filling the halls. Some had the same design as the ones pushing her, but most were the same as the technicians in the lab. Cam-drones buzzed about her head.

Where are all the humans?

A cheery, honey-smooth voice spilled over the public address system.

"A reminder to accredited Daedalus citizens: Freedom Month begins tomorrow. Cutoff for citizen allotment is in six days—if you have friends or family beyond the Wall, be sure to alert them they still have time for one final productivity push. And remember, Citizen Points earned this month are doubled!"

Eve had no idea what any of that meant, but she had bigger concerns right now. After a short elevator ride, she was pushed onto a new level, down another series of antiseptic hallways, peopled only with logika. Despite her anger, she forced herself to be still, to *think,* taking note of her surroundings. If she wanted to get out of this place, she'd need to know the damned escape routes at least.

Finally, she and her logika escorts arrived at a series of what could only be holding cells. The walls were transparent, illuminated pale blue, three meters square. Eve was pushed into the room, still willing herself to be calm, patient, clever. She was faster than her captors. Stronger. This might be her chance to jet, right here.

She heard the soft tread of feet as the logika backed out of the cell, the whisper of the door as it slid shut. With a soft snapping sound, the cuffs at her wrists and ankles rolled back, and Eve was up and out of her chair in a heartbeat, slamming herself into the door with all her strength.

A dull *whump* rang in her ears, and Eve was knocked backward, sailing three meters into the rear wall. Her teeth tingled, her skin ached. She was reminded of her old stun bat, Excalibur, and the day that Lemon had hit her with it on a dare.

Just to see what happens, her bestest had grinned.

"HOLDING CELL WALLS ARE ELECTRIFIED," one of the logika explained with a deep, metallic voice. "PHYSICAL CONTACT MAY RESULT IN SEVERE INJURY."

"Can I get that on a T-shirt?" Eve whispered. "The 'physical contact' part?"

The logika scanned the room with glowing eyes, then trudged down the corridor. Eve shook her head, body still thrumming from the shock. That had been idiotic of her. Daedalus Technologies was the wealthiest CorpState in the Yousay. She was in the major league now. She couldn't underestimate these people.

"Stupid," she hissed.

The soft knocking of knuckles on metal broke through her self-admonishment. Eve clawed her mussed fauxhawk from her lashes, heart surging as she looked to the cell beside hers and into a familiar pair of green eyes. The mind of a killer and the face of an angel, framed by a mop of tousled blond hair. The first of Nicholas Monrova's creations, and the first to turn against him.

"Gabriel," she whispered, her stomach turning.

His face was a ruin. His lower jaw had been blown clean off by a shotgun blast. The wound had been left undressed, and Eve could see Gabe's tongue dangling above his open throat. The bone and flesh were slowly regenerating—he'd eventually be as beautiful as he'd always been. But to see her brother's once-perfect features so hideously marred made Eve sick with fury.

"Who did this to you?"

Gabriel made a circular motion at his mangled throat, miming a collar.

"Preacher," she hissed.

Her brother nodded, eyes narrowed.

Pushing down her anger, willing herself once more to be cold, analytical, Eve took in her surroundings. A small padded sleep-slab was set on one wall, a sink and commode against another. The chair she'd been pushed in on had been left behind, but the magnetic cushion it rode on had been deactivated, and it now rested lifeless on the floor. The walls were transparent, illuminated with that faint and buzzing blue. The corridor beyond was blank, faceless, patrolled by cam drones. Another announcement about Citizen Points rang over the PA.

Eve reached toward one of the walls, and Gabriel grunted a warning. She touched it anyway and was rewarded with a bright flash and a crackling surge of pain.

"We're in Megopolis?" she asked.

Gabriel nodded.

"How long?"

Gabriel held up a single finger.

Eve gritted her teeth and sighed. Danael Drakos's questions burning in her head.

These Corp bastards wanted into Myriad. Wanted to unlock Monrova's secrets. But more, they wanted to know about Lemon, and how much of a threat she posed to their little empire. Truth told, Eve didn't know much about Lem's capabilities—the girl had kept them secret despite their friendship. And though she felt a familiar twist of betrayal at that thought, she wasn't about to sell out her former bestest to these maggots, these insects, these *humans*. Not after the way they'd treated her.

She looked at Gabe, watching her in malevolent silence.

They were imprisoned at the heart of the Daedalus Corp-State.

Surrounded by electrified walls.

Under constant surveillance.

Alone.

"Brother," she sighed, "it appears we're in deep shit."

3.4

BEHEMOTH

It wasn't the most pleasant car ride Ezekiel had ever taken.

He sat behind the wheel, Grimm and Diesel in the bucket seat beside him. Faith lay in the back, soaked and bloody, her mangled legs stretched before her. His sister's eyes were closed, her breathing faint—though Zeke knew the damage would mend in time, Cricket had almost killed her during the attack on New Bethlehem.

Talking true, Zeke wasn't entirely sure how he felt about that.

He kept both hands on the wheel, peering out through the grubby windshield at the endless desert. The nuke had exploded far to the north, and while the wastes below the epicenter would never be the same, their little posse soon outstripped the missile's desolation and left New Bethlehem behind. In front of them was a desolation of a different kind—a wasteland of shattered highways and empty roadhouses and faded signs pointing to cities that no longer existed. It was the sprawling graveyard of a long-dead civilization, laid out in all its fallen glory.

The bullet holes Preacher had given him were almost

healed, but they weren't the source of Zeke's discomfort. He'd been searching for Lemon for days, and now that he'd learned where she was—so near and yet so far—he'd begun fretting on her all the more. She was a fifteen-year-old kid. And he'd promised to protect her.

He'd listened as Diesel and Grimm told how Lemon had rescued them from the Brotherhood. Grimm described the missile silo beneath the desert, and Diesel explained in bitter tones about the Major—the madman who'd used Lemon to almost burn the whole country to cinders. As Grimm explained that he and Lemon had stopped *six other missiles* on their firing pads, Zeke was acutely aware of how much danger Lem had been in since he'd left her. How badly he'd let her down.

"This Major of yours sounds like a real piece of work," he said.

"He was definitely a piece of something," Diesel muttered.

"And we trusted the bastard." Grimm shook his head. "I never suspected he might be bent. I feel like a bloody stooge."

"Speaking of stooges, who's this Abraham kid we got tailing us?" Diesel said.

"I don't know him," Ezekiel confessed. "But he's a friend of Cricket's. And Cricket and Lemon have been tight for years."

"He's Brotherhood," Diesel growled.

"He's a freak, too, Deez," Grimm pointed out. "He helped me keep the kinetics of that blast back. Without him, pretty sure we'd all be brown bread."

"We just got sucker punched by the Major for years," the girl frowned. "You so keen to go trusting strangers again, Grimmy?"

The boy simply shrugged. "Any friend of Lemon's . . ."

Ezekiel glanced at the boy, sizing him up. Grimm's eyes were pouched in shadows, his skin sallow and gray. In the dark pools of his pupils, that faint ember light still burned. Considering he'd deflected a nuclear missile blast a few hours ago, he was looking okay. Still, Zeke could see a familiar anger in Grimm's stare. It was a feeling the lifelike knew all too well—the rage of trust betrayed.

"So this Major," Zeke said. "You're sure he's dead?"

"Lemon stopped his heart." Grimm snapped his fingers. "Like that."

". . . She can do that?"

"She's been practicin', guv. She's a firecracker, that one."

"She's a trouble-magnet," Diesel said from her seat by the window.

"Yeah," Grimm grinned, despite his exhaustion. "That, too."

"Hope she had the sense to stay underground," Diesel scowled.

"That makes two of us," Grimm sighed. "BioMaas isn't playing around."

"No," the girl murmured. "They're really not."

Ezekiel caught the hint of sorrow in her voice, the emptiness in her eyes. He glanced to Grimm for an explanation, uncertain whether he should ask.

"When BioMaas attacked us at the Clefts . . . we . . . lost someone, yeah?"

"His name was Fix," Diesel said, her voice soft and gray.

"I'm sorry," Ezekiel said.

The girl made no reply, simply watching the desert slip past beyond the window. Ezekiel decided not to press, and Grimm steered the conversation away.

"What does BioMaas want with Lemon anyways?" he asked.

Ezekiel shrugged. "BioMaas provides most of the country's food through their gene-modded crops. Daedalus supplies power through their solar farms. But ever since Gnosis collapsed, they've been moving closer to the war that'll decide who controls the country. And since Daedalus tech runs on regular electrical current, BioMaas figures Lemon's gifts can give them an edge in that war."

"Between the two of them, those Corps rule the whole roost." Grimm shook his head. "Why can't they just enjoy their slice of the pie?"

"It's their n-nature," came a voice from behind them.

Ezekiel glanced into the rearview mirror, saw Faith in the backseat. Her clothes were stiff with drying blood, her flesh a mangled mess. But her eyes were open now, gray and flat like dead telescreens.

"Because you h-humans only know to destroy," she said.

"I'm not human, love," Grimm replied.

Faith's bloody lips curled. "How w-wonderful for you. What are y-you, then?"

"Freaks," he replied. "Abnorms. Deviates."

"How're you feeling?" Ezekiel asked, watching in the mirror.

"Just l-lovely, little brother," she whispered. "Next idiotic q-question, please."

Diesel turned from the window to look at Ezekiel, eyebrow raised. "Brother?"

Zeke just nodded, eyes on the road ahead.

"So, you two ain't human, which is all Robin Hood," Grimm said. "But you mind fillin' us in on what exactly you are? Lem was a little sketchy on the 'tails."

"We're the n-next step . . . in humanity's evolution," Faith murmured.

"Nah." Grimm shook his head, tapping his chest. "That's us, love."

"N-no. You're just a faulty c-copy from a broken machine." Faith shook her head, her gray eyes distant. "You're two-headed c-cockroaches."

"She could charm the paint off walls, this one," Grimm muttered.

"Faith, you'd be radioactive dust if it weren't for Grimm and Diesel," Ezekiel said. "Show some damned respect."

His sister simply smiled, the dried blood on her face cracking as her lips curled. "How l-long to Megopolis, little brother?"

"We're not going to Megopolis."

". . . What?"

He met those flat gray eyes with his own. "We're going to get Lemon."

"Gabriel and Eve are in Megopolis," Faith said, struggling to sit up. "Those Daedalus insects took them. That b-bastard who killed Hope. I *saw* him."

"I know where they are, Faith. But I made a promise to Lem."

"Another roach?" she hissed, finally dragging herself upright. "This is your f-family, Ezekiel. You have obligations. Who knows what Daedalus will—"

"My *family* was happy enough to abandon me two years ago," Ezekiel snarled, tapping the coin slot in his chest. "You bolted this on me, threw me off Babel Tower and left me to rot in the wastes. Don't you *dare* lecture me about obligations."

"And what about your b-beloved Ana?" Faith said, eyes flashing. "Are you going to leave her to the tender mercies of Daedalus Technologies, too?"

His belly rolled at that. Fire and sorrow in his chest. He pushed it aside, focused on the road ahead. "Go to hell, Faith."

"Turn this truck toward Megopolis, Ezekiel," she growled. "Right now."

"No."

"I said *now*!" Faith roared.

Ezekiel felt a sharp blow to the side of his head, fingers clawing at his eyes. He cried out, trying to tear her hands off his head, Faith screaming and reaching for the wheel. The truck slewed sideways, tires shrieking, rubber burning. Behind them in the semi, Abraham crunched the gears and swerved to avoid slamming into their tail. Grimm shouted and grabbed Faith's wrist. The temperature in the cabin dropped twenty degrees. Ezekiel smelled burning flesh, heard Faith scream as he slammed on the brakes and brought their truck to a shuddering halt.

He was into the backseat in a heartbeat, wrestling with his sister as she howled and thrashed. Her strength was enough to crush metal, pulp bone. The seat beneath them groaned, and her boot kicked one of the doors clean off its hinges. But even though she was furious, she was still wounded and broken after her brawl with Cricket. Ezekiel pinned her arms, roaring over her screams.

"Faith, you'll hurt yourself!"

She tried to throw him off, bucking him upward and denting the ceiling.

"Let me *go*!"

"*Stop it!*" he cried, pinning her again.

She thrashed in his grip for a few moments more, ripping her wounds wider. Ezekiel's hands were slick with red, sticky and warm. Faith's struggles weakened, her screams became low, desperate gasps. And finally, as she sagged beneath him, all the breath rushing out of her, she began to sob.

Ezekiel pushed himself off his sister, terrified he'd hurt her. Tears rolled down her perfect cheeks, her mouth twisting as she looked up at him with pleading eyes. If his heart hadn't already been broken beneath New Bethlehem, the look on her face would have been enough to do it.

"We h-have to g-go get Gabe," she whispered.

"Faith . . ."

"He'll b-be frightened without me." She swallowed, shaking her head. "He has n-nightmares, Zeke. Such awful nightmares, oh god, you should h-hear him. He wakes up every night. Drenched in sweat. Screaming their names."

"Who?"

"Tania and Alex," Faith said. "Olivia and Marie."

Ezekiel's stomach turned, the names of the Monrova children ringing in his head like funeral bells. He remembered those awful final hours during the fall of Babel. The stink of fear and blood in that cell when Nicholas Monrova and his family had been murdered. Though he'd saved Ana's life that day, the guilt he felt at not being able to save the rest of them had never truly left him. But the thought that Gabriel might also be haunted by their deaths had never once entered his mind.

He glanced to Grimm and Diesel, saw bewilderment in their eyes. Beneath him, Faith shook and shuddered, the sobs bubbling in her throat.

"I have to h-help him. I can't leave him there alone."

Zeke knew that after he'd been cast out of Babel, his siblings had fallen to infighting. Uriel and Patience and Verity had abandoned the tower, leaving the grave they'd made of Monrova's dream behind. But Gabriel had remained, intent on unlocking the secrets inside Myriad and resurrecting his beloved Grace.

Ezekiel had always wondered why Faith stayed with Gabe

all those years. Why she'd stuck by his side inside that dead tower as he slowly descended into obsession and madness. Looking into her eyes now, Zeke finally understood. Finally recognized the pain that burned behind those flat gray eyes of hers.

"*Please,*" she whispered.

It was the pain of loving someone who didn't love you back.

"Pardon me for sayin'," Grimm said softly, meeting Zeke's eyes, "but your family seems kinda fucked up, guv."

"Swear jar," Diesel murmured. "But yeah, true cert."

Talking true, Zeke found it hard to disagree. In his quiet moments, he'd often wondered if there was some flaw in the lifelike design—some frailty that led to mental instability. His obsession with Ana. Gabriel's with Grace. Now Faith's with Gabriel. He and his siblings had been given the full capacity for human emotion, and you never love anyone like you love your first. But was this the same intensity that humans felt? Or was it something altogether darker, and more destructive?

And if it was alive in him, how could he trust the way he felt?

About Ana?

About Eve?

"Ezekiel?"

Zeke saw Abraham standing in the road behind them, Cricket looming at his back. The boy had pulled his tech-goggles off, squinting in the garish sunlight.

"You okay in there?" he asked.

"We're fine," Ezekiel called. "Just hit a pothole and over-corrected."

"LEMON'S WAITING!" Cricket bellowed. "WE NEED TO MOVE!"

He nodded, waved them off. "In a second."

Abraham looked uncertainly at the buckled door lying beside the road, but he eventually shrugged and trudged back to the semi, under Diesel's narrowed stare. Cricket glowered a moment longer, then followed. Faith was still crying, her whole body racked with silent sobs. Zeke looked down at his sister, and despite all the awful things she'd done, the horror she'd become, he couldn't help but feel a stab of pity.

What must it have been like all those years?

Spending your life staring at someone who didn't even see *you?*

"We'll get them back, Faith," he heard himself say.

"Do . . ."

Her voice faltered, the pain of what she'd done to herself now choking her. Zeke saw with horror that he was covered with her blood.

"Do you p-promise?" she whispered.

Zeke took a deep breath, held it in his chest. He'd made promises before—promises he'd yet to keep. But beyond thoughts of what might be happening to Gabriel, beyond the garbled, confused knot of emotion when he thought of Ana, when he thought of Eve, both now in the clutches of those Daedalus agents, another thought was burning. A nagging, barbwire tangle that had been slowly resolving itself into a certainty over the last few hours' drive.

The Myriad computer at the heart of Babel Tower held all of Nicholas Monrova's knowledge. The key to the Libertas virus. The secret to creating more lifelikes. Gabriel had struggled for years to open it, constantly defeated by the four-stage system that kept the computer sealed—a lock that required four keys to open.

The voice pattern of a Monrova.

The retinal print of a Monrova.

The DNA of a Monrova.

The brainwave pattern of a Monrova.

Eve had already unlocked the first two stages.

Now that Daedalus had Ana's body, they had access to Monrova DNA. And with Eve, whose personality had been copied, note for note, thought for thought, from Ana's, they *might* be able to crack the fourth seal.

What would the most powerful Corp in the Yousay do with that kind of knowledge? Where would the ability to create an army of lifelikes lead them?

He looked to the northern skies, still scarred from nuclear fire. The same flame that had almost burned the world to cinders. He thought about the madness of the Brotherhood, the maniac in that missile silo who'd tried to incinerate the whole country, all the hurt and carnage he'd seen during his years wandering the wastes. And he thought about Faith's words, whispered from the bloody lips of a murderer and a monster, yes. But no less true for it.

You humans only know to destroy.

"Do you p-promise?" Faith whispered.

Ezekiel released his breath in a sigh.

"Once we have Lemon?"

He slowly nodded.

"Okay, I promise."

———

The sun was setting by the time they arrived.

The sky was the strangest color Ezekiel had ever seen—one

last gift from the nuclear conflagration that had split the heavens. As the sun sank, the sky was drenched in sepia and crimson, twisted into strange watercolor swirls. To the east, Ezekiel could see a dark smudge on the earth: the beginnings of the irradiated wasteland known as the Glass, where the bombs had fallen so hard, the desert was fused into black silicon.

You humans only know to destroy.

"Is this it?" he asked, peering out through the dirty windshield.

"Home sweet home," Diesel said, pushing open the door.

The girl hopped down onto the sand, Grimm close behind, already calling loudly for Lemon. Diesel looked decidedly better now that she'd had some rest, but Grimm still seemed shaky. The pair disappeared through a hatchway in the dirt, a concrete stairwell beyond. Zeke saw the hatch had been painted once, but only a few letters remained on the rusty surface.

MISS   O

"Miss O's," he murmured. "Missile silo."

"Most amusing."

Zeke glanced over his shoulder at Faith, still laid out on the backseat. His sister was looking fragile after her outburst, tear tracks cutting through the blood and dust on her face. Her dark bangs hung in telescreen eyes, full lips parted as she breathed. She was beautiful—smooth lines and long lashes and a perfect, ethereal symmetry. But they were all beautiful, really. Monrova had sculpted his lifelikes into masterpieces of physical perfection.

It was a shame he'd not been so masterful with their minds.

"Feeling better?" he asked.

"Somewhat." She gestured at her legs. "These might take a while."

"I'm going to take a look around. Stay here."

She gave him a wry smile. "I've little choice, little brother."

"You were only activated thirty-seven minutes before me, Faith."

"I'm still your elder, bratling." She waggled her finger. "Don't forget it."

He smiled despite himself, shoved open the door. "Sing if you spot any trouble."

"Fa-la-la-laaaaa," Faith sang, pointing.

Her finger was aimed through the window toward Cricket's semi. The brakes squealed as the big rig came to a shivering stop, and Ezekiel saw Solomon behind the wheel. Zeke climbed out of the monster truck and walked over to the stick-thin logika as he wobbled out onto the desert floor. Solomon's inane grin lit up as he spoke.

"THIS IS ALL RATHER PICTURESQUE, YES?"

"Shouldn't Abraham be driving? Where is he?"

"I'm here," came a voice.

Zeke saw the boy hop out of the semi's trailer, a toolbox in his arms. "Thought I'd take the chance to fix Cricket's aural arrays while we were driving." He frowned at the spindly logika. "You busted them up pretty good, Solomon."

"APOLOGIES, MASTER ABRAHAM, BUT IF SOMETHING'S WORTH DOING, IT'S WORTH DOING RIGHT." The logika clapped his metal hands together as Cricket climbed out of the trailer, his massive feet thudding into the earth. *"AH, FELICITATIONS, DEAR PALADIN. WELCOME BACK TO THE LAND OF THE AUDIO-CAPABLE. HOW DO YOU FARE, OLD FRIEND?"*

The big bot aimed his glowing stare at Faith, then settled it on Ezekiel.

"Just peachy," he growled.

"Tell me, old friend, you had me ruin your hearing in order to avoid receiving further orders from humans, yes? Why repair the damage?"

"Because the novelty of that damn whiteboard was wearing off pretty quick, Sol. Besides, Abraham's cobbled a better solution."

The boy nodded. "I've rigged some hardware into Paladin's audio unit so he can cut his aural inputs at will." He tossed a small remote back and forth between his palms. "Or via this, if needs be. We get into trouble, Cricket can just cut his feeds."

"Verifiable genius, Master Abraham. Now, how to put this politely . . ."

"Don't worry," the boy nodded. "I can rig a unit for you, too."

"It's not that I don't love taking your orders, but—"

"Lemon?" came a call.

"Shorty!" came another. "Get *out* here!"

Ezekiel saw Grimm and Diesel climbing back up out of the hatchway, looking equal parts worried and annoyed. The boy scanned the desert around them, the broken rocks and shifting sands, putting his hands to his mouth.

"LEMON?"

"She's not downstairs?" Ezekiel asked.

Diesel shook her head, her expression grim.

"Well, where is she?" Cricket demanded.

"Gotta be round here somewhere." Grimm looked about in consternation. "Deez, you check the garage. Everyone else, split up, grab a butcher's."

"A what?" Abraham asked.

"A look!" Grimm snapped. "'Butcher's hook,' rhymes with 'look,' mate!"

Hearing the fear and frustration in his voice, Ezekiel found himself wondering exactly what Lemon had come to mean to Grimm. He raised an eyebrow at Diesel and was met with a small shrug. The girl spun on her heel, stomped over to a stretch of desert sand and peeled back a large tarpaulin, revealing another long metal hatchway concealed under the earth.

Grimm had already stalked off past a rocky outcropping, shouting Lemon's name. Zeke looked to Abraham, Cricket and Solomon and nodded eastward.

"I'll look this way."

"I'll come," Abraham said. "Paladin, can you and Solomon help?"

The group split up for their search. Cricket strode off south, massive feet crunching on the parched sands, while Solomon headed north. Zeke and Abe wandered the rocky badlands around the installation. Ezekiel was shouting for Lemon at the top of his lungs, but he wasn't exactly worried yet—the girl had grown up in the alleys and squeezeways of Los Diablos, and she knew how to take care of herself. Lemon was small, quick and clever, and he figured she was simply hiding.

Stomping over a small dune, Zeke saw a wide circular opening carved into the ground: a mouth with metal lips yawning at the sky. He realized it was one of the installation's weapons silos. Stepping up to the edge, he peered down, saw a nuclear missile crumpled against one wall. The hull was blackened by flame, and a faint stink of chemical smoke hung in the air.

The globes inside the silo were shattered, the electrical wiring melted. Zeke realized this must have been one of the birds Grimm and Lemon prevented from launching. The life-like shuddered to think what might have happened if the pair hadn't stopped the warheads in time, and he resolved to give the inimitable Miss Fresh a big hug on behalf of the entire country when he found her.

"Lemon?" he shouted down into the hole.

The cries of the others were the only answer. Zeke looked around them, hands on hips, shouting again into the dying light. He could see tracks up here—dozens, he realized. They were almost scoured away by the winds, but his eyes were sharper than a human's, more sensitive in low light. Crouching beside the marks, he noted they were a strange shape—stabbed into the dirt rather than trodden, arranged in a scuttling gait. His stomach sank into his boots as he recalled the masses of dead constructs he and Preacher had found at the Clefts, those strange dogthings with translucent skin and six legs and faces full of wicked teeth.

"BioMaas," he whispered.

"You find something?" Abraham asked beside him.

Zeke stood, calling over the dunes. "Cricket, we might have—"

His shout was cut off by a tremor at his feet. The sound of crunching earth and twisting metal. And above it all, Faith's bewildered, terrified shout.

"EZEKIEL!"

The lifelike broke into a run back toward their truck. Leaping over an outcrop of tumbled boulders, dashing across the sands, he barreled out to their impromptu parking lot, his breath leaving his lungs.

"Holy crap . . ."

An enormous shape had burst from under the earth and seized the monster truck in its claws, with Faith still inside. Vaguely insectoid, it was the size of the semi, and the failing sunlight gleamed on its hide. It had six limbs: two ending in feet, two in clawed hands, and the top two in massive scythes of black bone. A long tail stretched out behind it; its skin was armor-plated, ridged and spiked, a dark desert red. Its skull was as big as the monster truck, eyes glowing a baleful green, mouth filled with entirely too many teeth. Ezekiel had seen images of these things in briefings, back when he worked security in Babel. It was a BioMaas construct, a warbeast from their City-Hive, a creature genetically engineered to be a perfect engine of destruction.

"Behemoth!"

Faith threw herself clear as, with one sweeping blow from those massive bone scythes, the truck was sliced in three. Faith hit the ground hard, crying out as her mangled legs twisted, rolling aside as the engine block crashed on the dirt where her head had been. The behemoth roared, lips peeling back from foot-long teeth. A chuddering, bubbling sound rose up from its belly.

"Faith, *move!*"

Ezekiel charged, feet pounding the dirt, scooping his sister up as the creature exhaled. A gout of snot-green liquid boiled up from its gullet, an acrid stink filling the air as hissing goop spattered across the dirt where Faith had lain a second before.

"Bloody hell!"

The rank hiss of acid filled the air, the ground boiling where it struck. Rolling to his feet, Zeke saw Grimm had returned to investigate the commotion and was now standing transfixed before the towering warbeast. The behemoth turned on the boy with a snarl, armored tail lashing at the dirt as it swung those awful scythes.

"Grimm, look out!"

Zeke's pistol was up and out, blasting away at the monster's back, but the bullets were pebbles against a mountainside. Grimm raised his hands, the air rippling, his breath escaping his lips as a puff of pale frost. And as those massive claws arced toward him, set to slice him into pieces as easily as their truck, they smashed into a wall of . . . *nothing*.

The air around Grimm shivered and warped, like ripples on clear water. The behemoth bellowed, striking at the boy again. But again, the blows stopped short, tiny slivers of bone splintering free as the scythes crashed into that invisible wall.

Ezekiel glanced behind him, saw Abraham standing with his hands raised. The boy's fingers were curled into claws as he roared, "Run, dammit!"

Grimm took two fumbling steps backward, his face pale with shock. He opened his mouth to speak, words turning into a yelp as a gray tear opened up in the earth under him and he tumbled down into it. Reloading his pistol, Zeke heard a *thump*, another yelp off to his right. He saw Diesel crouched in that underground metal hatchway, Grimm picking himself up off the concrete beside her.

A robotic shout echoed across the badlands, and the thunder of chaingun fire tore the air. A blinding spray of high-velocity shells arced through the night, carving swaths through the warbeast's hide. The thing roared in pain as Cricket emerged from behind a tall spur of stone, his shoulders unfolding like beetle wings to reveal pods of short-range missiles. A half dozen of the projectiles howled and streaked forward, lighting up the behemoth's hide with rolling blooms of flame.

The beast drew a shuddering breath, chest expanding as its lungs filled.

"Paladin, look out!" Abraham yelled.

A gout of luminous green burst from the construct's mouth, sizzling the air. Servos whining, engines screaming, Cricket leapt aside. The acid struck him as he dove, coating one of his missile pods in a soup of hissing green. The WarBot unloaded with another burst from his chaingun as Ezekiel gave up on his pistol, stowing the weapon and picking Faith up again. He dashed toward Diesel and Grimm and placed his sister on the ground beside them.

Zeke felt his skin prickling as Grimm curled his fingers, the temperature dropping through the floor. The warbeast bellowed as its armor blackened, as the muscle beneath warped and smoked. Grimm's face was fixed in a snarl, his eyes aglow like burning embers, like that flare of light over the New Bethlehem desert. The air around them was now positively arctic— Zeke's joints aching, frost spilling from his lips. And with another shriek, the behemoth burst into flames.

It roared as the fire spread, as another blast of armor-piercing rounds carved its chest. The construct lashed out with its tail, knocking Cricket backward. The spray from the WarBot's chaingun lit the skies as he fell, the beast leaping toward him, skin aflame, those bone scythes reared back to carve his head off his body.

A gray tear opened in the ground beneath it, and with a furious screech, the creature toppled down into it. Clawed hands scrabbled at the shimmering edges of the rift as it slipped down into the void. Diesel was standing tall beside Ezekiel, one hand stretched out, the other pointed upward.

The lifelike heard faint roaring far above. Growing louder by the moment.

Squinting up into the dark, Zeke saw the second of Diesel's rifts, hundreds of meters in the air overhead. The behemoth tumbled out of it, plummeting back toward the earth, screeching and flailing. Her dark hair crusted with pale frost, lips twisted in a smug smile, Diesel shouted over the rising noise.

"You all might wanna cover your ears!"

Ezekiel watched with grim fascination as the behemoth plunged out of the sky. It disappeared past the gentle curve of the nearby dunes, and Zeke heard a *thud,* a disgusting wet *crunch*. He felt the impact through his boots, the beast's shrieks silenced. The temperature began rising, the frost fading from the air.

Grimm held out his fist. "Smashing work, freak."

Diesel bumped his knuckles. "Tell me something I don't know, freak."

Abraham was stumbling over the shattered ground toward them, eyes wild, mouth agape. "My god, did you *see* that thing?"

"Is everyone okay?" Ezekiel asked.

He looked around the group, who all murmured affirmative—all save Faith, who simply quirked an eyebrow at her legs and said nothing at all. Cricket was picking himself up off the ground, his optics burning bright blue. His left missile pod was partially melted, the casing split and spitting smoke. The logika scanned the sands about him, his gaze finally falling on Diesel and Grimm.

"DID YOU TWO DO THAT?" he asked.

The boy winked. The girl just shrugged.

The big bot rolled his massive shoulders. "I COULDA TAKEN HIM. BUT . . . THANKS AND STUFF."

Diesel's black lips curled in a smile. "You're welcome and stuff."

"Speakin' of thanks," Grimm said, clapping Abraham's shoulder, "that's twice I'd be brown bread if not for you."

Abe frowned. "What does bread have to do with anything?"

"Brown bread," Grimm explained. "Dead."

Diesel rolled her eyes. "Keep up, will you, Brotherboy?"

Ezekiel's head was reeling. The abilities he'd just seen wielded by these kids . . . telekinesis, energy manipulation, bending the elements as casually as walking and talking—it was almost impossible to believe. But peering into the jagged pit the behemoth had lain in wait beneath, he realized there were bigger issues at hand. The lifelike felt his heart drop and thump in his chest.

"What *was* that thing?" Abraham demanded, also peering into the hole.

"A behemoth," Ezekiel replied softly. "A BioMaas war construct, built to fight infantry units and enemy machina. They grow them in CityHive."

"BioMaas . . . ," Grimm whispered.

Ezekiel turned to the boy, saw fear in his eyes. "Yeah."

"But if Lemon was here . . . if they . . ."

". . . Yeah."

"Bloody hell." Grimm sank onto his haunches, staring at the broken earth. He looked like he'd been kicked in the stomach. "They *took* her."

"Hours ago, by the look of things," Ezekiel said. "They must have left the behemoth to clean up anyone who came poking around."

"How?" Pistons hissed and whooshed as Cricket's massive hands gesticulated wildly. "HOW CAN A GIRL THAT SMALL *GET IN TROUBLE THIS BIG*?"

"You think they'll hurt her?" Diesel asked softly.

Ezekiel looked at the acid burns on the ground, the gouts of bright green behemoth blood soaking the dirt. "Preacher said something to me," he murmured. "He told me CityHive doesn't break out their warbeasts unless they think they're in a war. BioMaas doesn't want to hurt Lemon, they want to *use* her."

"Lemon's a lot of things," the girl said. "But somehow I don't see her at the spear tip of some BioMaas army."

Ezekiel shrugged. "Like I said, Daedalus tech all runs on conventional electrical current. If BioMaas could weaponize Lem's abilities, they'd be able to roll right up to Megopolis and kick the front door down."

"But why would they *do* that?"

"You lock the biggest, meanest dogs you can find in a cage together, someone's eventually getting bitten."

"The people running these companies aren't *dogs*," Grimm said.

"No." Faith looked up at Ezekiel with shining eyes. "They're worse."

Zeke breathed a soft sigh and nodded.

"They're human."

3.5

GENOME

This monster's insides stank like old socks.

Lemon Fresh sat in a curve of smooth, dark bone inside the Lumberer's belly, rocked back and forth by the motion of the construct's massive wings. Her freckled skin was damp with sweat, her jagged red bangs wilted about her green eyes. The walls were crawling with softly glowing, semitranslucent bugs, skittering about and stopping occasionally to bump antennae. The smell was septic. The air was heavy and rank and, worst of all, moist.

"I hate the word 'moist,'" Lemon declared.

The woman sitting across from her glanced up with her strange golden eyes. She was tall and pretty, her hair woven into long, sharp dreadlocks. She wore a skintight suit of black rubber, molded with odd ridges and bumps over her dangerous curves. Her skin was deep brown, pocked with hundreds of tiny hexagonal holes. And she was *crawling* with bees.

"*She does?*" Hunter said, her voice rasping like a broken voxbox.

"Yeah. 'Moist' is probably my least favorite word in the

entire dictionary. It's definitely worse than 'phlegm.'" Lemon glanced at the six-legged dogthings around them, drooling on the spongy floor. "I hate the word 'slurp,' too. And 'pulsing.' But yeah, 'moist' is the worst word ever. Worse than 'throbbing,' even."

"Lemonfresh is doing it again," Hunter said.

". . . Doing what?"

"Talking swiftly and continuously about inanities to cover her nervousness. Lemonfresh told us to warn her when she repeated the behavior."

"Oh," Lemon said, somewhat deflated. "Okay."

Hunter reached down and patted one of the dogthings, running her fingertips over the blunt, eyeless snout. The rows of razor-sharp, finger-long teeth parted, and a long, wet tongue slipped out, *slurped* softly at Hunter's hand.

"Lemonfresh has no need to be nervous," the operative said.

"Yeah, you say that, and then you roll up to my squat and you snatch me up into the belly of this ginormous flying cockroach thing—"

"They are called Lumberers."

"I *know* what they're called, I grew up on Dregs and we saw them all the time, thank you *very* much," Lemon said, getting slightly cross at being interrupted. "Point is, you didn't *ask* me if I wanted to go with you, you just snaffled me, and while I didn't put up too much of a fight—sorry again about the toothbeasties I fried, by the way, but considering you had about a hundred of them with you—"

"They are called slakedogs."

"That's very interesting but *so* not the point," Lemon said, building a really good head of steam now. "The *point* is, it's all well and good to say 'Lemonfresh has no need to be nervous' when you're not the one surrounded by a bajillion slakedogs and deathbees and whatever this *thing crawling up my leg* is!"

Lemon scowled down at the thing in question, which was about the size of her fist. It had glowing skin and six legs and big button eyes in a sort-of-cute face. It wiggled its antennae at her and trilled softly.

"Would Lemonfresh like to know what they are called?" Hunter asked.

Lemon sent the bugthing flying with a sharp flick to its sort-of-cute face.

"No," she said, brushing away her bangs. "Lemonfresh doesn't give a damn."

The other bugthings on the walls and ceilings let out a series of high-pitched chirps. Lemon raised her middle finger to the lot of them.

"Lemonfresh is important," Hunter said softly. *"She is needed."*

"So you keep telling me," the girl scowled.

"When Lemonfresh reaches CityHive, she will understand."

Lemon pouted but made no reply. Truth was, when Hunter and her tiny army had rolled up on the doorstep of Miss O's, she'd put up a *hell* of a fight. The shock of watching that nuke explode over New Bethlehem had worn off quickly, replaced with a frightening anger. She'd reached out into the static, seizing hold of the electrical current inside the slakedogs that Hunter had brought with her and killing dozens of them in an instant—just turning them off as if she were flicking a switch. But then she'd felt a sting on her neck, the buzz of Hunter's genetically engineered bees on her skin, and after that came a terrifying drop down into blackness.

She'd only seen those bees *kill* things before, and as she fell, she wondered briefly if she was dying. It surprised her to real-ize how unafraid she was at that thought. Grimm dead, Evie gone, Zeke and Cricket vapor—she had very little left to hang on to, talking true. But waking up inside the Lumberer what must have been hours later, she supposed not all Hunter's bees were deadly. And after an initial wave of relief that she wasn't, in fact, fertilizer, she'd assessed her situation and realized how deep in the fertilizer she actually was.

Like she'd told Hunter, Lemon had seen Lumberers before. The beasts used to dump trash on Dregs—discarded machine parts, old hulks, any tech that BioMaas thought belonged to the "deadworld." Lumberers were big as houses, and they flew on huge translucent wings, kinda like a mash-up of a cockroach and a hot-air balloon. Being *inside* one was more than a little creepy. But if Lemon used her gift to knock it out of the sky while flying in it, well, gravity might have a thing or two to say.

Lem was tempted to start talking again. It wasn't that she was nervous—she knew BioMaas wanted her alive. But if she was talking, she didn't have to think. About that boy who'd kissed her as he drove off toward certain doom. About the feel of his big arms lifting her almost off the ground, the taste of his lips, warm and pillow-soft. The memory made Lemon's head spin all over again, her fingertips trailing the line of her mouth and setting her skin tingling. Grimm had kissed her like she'd never been kissed before. He'd kissed her like he really, truly meant it.

And now he's dead.

The thought was just too heavy, too sad, too much. In the last few days, she'd lost everyone she was ever close to. Silas. Cricket. Grimm. Evie. It seemed so unfair, she wanted to scream, she wanted to reach into that warm wash of static, the million, billion tiny burning sparks in the minds of the things around her, and just *turn*

them

off.

But there was the aforementioned problem of flying. More important, her inability to do so. And, you know, gravity.

I'm so boned.

The droning wing beats shifted in tone, and Lemon felt a subtle shift in their direction. She glanced up into Hunter's golden eyes.

"She is here," the operative smiled.

"Oh, fizzy," Lemon deadpanned.

The wing beats deepened in tone as they slowed, and Lemon's stomach rose into her chest as they began to descend. They were jostled and bumped for what seemed like years, until, with a final skittering *thump,* they came to rest. A series of wet sloshings rang in the creature's innards, burbling, gurgling. And then, with a revolting slurp, the Lumberer's shell opened wide, letting in garish daylight.

It was blinding after the soft glow of the bugthings on the walls, and Lemon squinted against the glare. She saw Hunter brush her fingers along the Lumberer's ribs, murmur thanks. And then the operative was taking Lemon's hand, leading her out into what was true cert the most astonishing sight of her young life.

It was a city.

A city unlike any she'd ever seen.

No concrete. No steel. No glass. Instead, everything was . . . green.

The structures were semitranslucent resin, bone-colored

and gleaming. Great winding spires rose all around them, like the termite nests she'd seen in Silas's old nature sims. Every structure was *covered* with plant life—tall trees and flowing vines and flowering shrubs—and the scent of all that green was close to heaven. There were no hard lines, no right angles; all the shapes were smooth, swirling, organic. The spires were connected with walkways, patterned like a vast spiderweb.

The skies were moving—Lemon saw the wasp shapes of Hunter-Killers, the bulky silhouettes of Lumberers, other figures big as bootballs, furry as bumblebees. The air was filled with the endless monotone of their wings, the bright perfume of flowers and the sighing, shushing whisper of a billion bright green leaves.

It was . . . beautiful.

"Lemonfresh," came an extraordinary, reverberating voice.

Heart hammering, breath stolen from her lungs, Lemon turned from the city to the scene before her. A legion of figures awaited her. There were more slakedogs, long tongues lolling between their too many teeth. Lemon saw more of those cute, tiny button-eyed bugs crawling over every surface. But mostly she saw people.

At least, she presumed they'd *been* people.

There were perhaps a thousand standing in a broad semicircle around her, all looking at her expectantly. Differing shapes and sizes, male and female, all clad in some variation of the formfitting organic black suit that Hunter wore. But looking among the throng, Lemon realized many of the faces were the same, repeated over and over again.

And she recognized some of them.

There were multiple copies of the lady who'd helped her

friends escape the belly of that BioMaas kraken—the woman called Carer. She thought she recognized a man called Sentinel, too: dozens upon dozens of him, all of them tall and dark and utterly identical. Belly sinking, mind awhirl, Lemon realized there were Hunters in the crowd, too, perfect copies of the woman standing beside her.

The Hunter that had found her in the Clefts had been killed in New Bethlehem, and Lem had suspected there was something squiffy at work when a second copy showed up. She hadn't pondered it too hard at the time. But now she tried to recall Hunter's words to her: *We have many sisters, Lemonfresh. And CityHive has many Hunters.* As she looked among the sea of faces, she finally realized what was going on here.

"Clones," she whispered.

"Lemonfresh," came that reverberating voice again.

A man speaking. He was tall and strangely handsome, with big dark eyes and a chin sharp enough to cut yourself with. Dark hair was swept back from his brow, and he wore an elaborate version of that same rubber suit, covered by a long coat with a high, upturned collar, decorated in a swirling design. He smiled as if seeing her was genuinely the best thing that had ever happened in his life.

"We are Director," he said.

Lemon suddenly realized what made his voice so extraordinary. Looking among the crowd, she spotted three other copies of the same man, all of them identical. And when one spoke, the others spoke in unison.

"We are so pleased to see her," they said.

Lemon glanced at the Hunter beside her. The beautiful green city around her, the sea of identical faces before her, all smiling in anticipation. She should say something, she realized.

Something impressive. Something that made her look like she had a handle on this situation, like she was the most brilliful little badass this side of Dregs and nobody, *nobody,* was gonna trifle with her and get away with it.

She thrust her fists into the pockets of her cargos and cleared her throat.

A legion of eyes stared back at her expectantly.

"I need to use the bathroom," she declared.

———

Lemon looked at the pile of small blue-gray cubes on the plate in front of her with deep suspicion. She poked one, scowling when it failed to respond, then peered up into the faces of the three Carers hovering over her.

The Carers all blinked twice: once with regular old-fashioned eyelids, and again with a translucent membrane that closed horizontally along their featureless black peepers.

"She must eat," said one.

"Her energy reserves must be quite low," nodded another.

"They are extremely nutritious," promised the third.

"They look dangerously close to that crap Hunter tried to feed me in New Bethlehem," Lemon muttered. "Afraid I'm not much of an algae girl."

"Oh, no," said the first Carer. "Hunter informed us of Lemonfresh's distaste for nourishment based upon photo-synthetic eukaryotic organisms."

The second Carer nodded. "This is a concentrated blend of proteins, amino acids and minerals derived from powdered orthoptera acrididae."

Lemon blinked. "Powdered orthowhat now?"

"Locusts," explained the third.

Lemon's stomach tapped her on the shoulder and declared it wanted to leave the building now, please. She peered down at the plate with newfound revulsion.

"This is powdered bug?"

"Yes," all three declared proudly.

"Oh my *god*."

"Thank you, Carer, that will be all. Lemonfresh will eat when she is hungry."

The Carers looked upward at the command and bowed simultaneously.

"Your wish, Director," they said.

Without further fuss, all three turned and walked toward the edge of the conference room. With a whispering, rubber sound, the wall parted like a curtain, sealing itself up again once the Carers departed.

Lemon watched the trio leave, trying her best not to look as puketastic as she felt. The space she'd been brought to was broad, circular, high in one of those spires. Everything was made of bone-pale resin, the surfaces run through with phosphorescent green veins—curling and abstract and kinda pretty, if Lem was talking true. Beautiful plants with pale, delicate flowers grew about the room, bringing a pleasant sweetness to the air. There were no windows, but the walls ranged from opaque to almost transparent, and Lemon could see out to the bustling city below.

She was seated at a circular table, with a large indentation at its center. This recess was filled with a velvety dark liquid, and a glowing BioMaas logo was projected on the surface—a double helix, like a twisted ladder, constantly spiraling.

The table was set with five chairs, rising up from the floor.

Aside from hers, the seats were each occupied by a copy of the Director. They all blinked at the same time. They all spoke at the same time. And every one of them was smiling at *her*.

"Keep it together, Fresh," Lemon muttered.

"Do not fear," the Directors said in unison. *"Lemonfresh is in no danger here."*

"Listen," Lemon said, clearing her throat. "I don't wanna offend you or anything, but do you figure maybe only *one* of you could answer instead of all of you speaking together, because it's getting *really* creepy on the crawly."

"One of us?" the Directors all asked.

"Yeah." Lemon held up a solitary finger. "One."

All four Directors shook their heads. *"We are one, Lemonfresh. Many forms, but one mind. One will. One purpose."*

". . . And what purpose would that be?"

"We are the Director of BioMaas Incorporated."

Lemon blinked around the room. *"All* of you?"

Four heads nodded in perfect synchronicity. *"We are the pattern best suited. We are not Architect or Soldier, nor Worker or Breeder. We are Director."*

"You're . . . all the same?" she said, a slow horror creeping into her chest. "Everyone in this city is just a copy of someone else?"

"Just?" the Directors said. *"CityHive is an organism devoted to the perfection of the lived experience. Each pattern is ideally suited to the task to which it is assigned. Each cell perfectly enmeshed in a larger, exquisite tapestry."*

"I thought you were just another CorpState," Lemon said, bewildered. "You know, wageslaves and managers and all that stuff. Like Gnosis and Daedalus . . ."

Four identical faces hardened in vague disgust. *"Daedalus*

Technologies is mired in the technologies of the deadworld. Devoted to the perpetuation of a tyranny that almost destroyed this earth. Once, BioMaas possessed such structure. Inefficient. Selfish. Fractious. But we have evolved beyond such primitive notions."

Lemon looked around the room, her jaw agape.

"This is pants-on-head crazy."

"Does she truly think so?"

The pool of smooth black liquid in the center of the table shivered, like a stone had been dropped into it. The fluid became silver, and Lemon realized she could see images on the surface, as if it were a vidscreen. She saw an ugly settlement nestled on an island of trash. A city where she scratched out a desperate living, stealing and grifting, until Evie and Silas took her in.

"Los Diablos," she said.

"A grave of the deadworld," the Directors said. *"Filled with inferior patterns, living in the garbage CityHive throws away."*

Before Lemon could get too indignant about these jokers spitting on her old stomping grounds, the image shifted. She saw a sprawling city at night. The remnants of old 20C skyscrapers rose into the sky, ringed by a huge wall. The air was filled with drones, smudged with methane, the smog lit up like some toxic rainbow. The streets were filled with people and logika, scurrying like ants, all living on top of one another, crushed into the streets and splitting them at the seams.

"Megopolis. Capital of Daedalus Technologies. An infected scab, hopelessly dependent on robotic labor, spitting poison into earth, sea and sky. The dying gasp of a civilization that did not have the good sense to perish with dignity."

The image shifted again, and Lemon saw a grimy settlement

crusted on the edge of a black sea. She recognized the shape of the New Bethlehem desalination plant, the massive iron gates, the barbed wire and broken glass.

A bright flash burst over the scene, and Lemon felt the floor rumble. A shockwave of fire bloomed bright, burned white-hot. The image dropped into sudden darkness and was replaced once more by that spinning helix logo. Lemon felt four pairs of eyes pinning her with their stare.

"The technologies of the deadworld almost destroyed the world entirely, Lemonfresh. The thinking of the past almost erased all possibility of a future. And still, humanity refuses to embrace a new way. Is that not true insanity?"

Lemon felt her fingernails biting into her palm. Her heart ached, thinking of New Bethlehem, that missile lighting up the sky. She thought of Diesel, flinging herself and Grimm across the desert, right toward it. She pictured Grimm trying to hold back that oncoming calamity with his bare hands.

God, he'd been so brave. . . .

She felt tears burning her eyes, pawed at them with her grubby sleeve.

"You want me to admit the world is a stupid and ugly place?" she asked. "Fine. I grew up in the thick of it, cloneboy. I know damn well how sick it gets out there. It's septic and it's defective and it's broken almost all the way."

"And BioMaas has discovered a better way," the Directors said. *"We live in harmony here, Lemonfresh. We do not fill the sky with pollutants, do not take without giving back. We have seized control of our evolutionary path. No randomness. No form without design. Each task is assigned to a pattern perfectly suited to accomplish it. We are one in the genome."*

Lemon blinked. "What the hell is that?"

The Directors waved in unison toward the BioMaas logo on the liquid screen, spinning and twisting endlessly.

"The genome is Mother and Father. Lock and key. The pathway toward infinite possibility, and the clay from which you, and all, were sculpted."

Lem breathed deep and tried to keep hold of her patience. Half this talk sounded half insane, and the rest of it sounded insane all the way. But despite how angry she was at being snaffled, despite the burning grief she felt for Grimm, she was acutely aware that she was alone here. Surrounded on all sides in a city she didn't come close to understanding, with no hope of rescue.

So maybe it was time to get smart, not mad.

"Look, honestly, what do you want from me?"

The closest Director to her produced a thick stack of documents, enclosed in a folio of black rubber. Lemon saw the words CONTRACTUAL AGREEMENT: GENOME PROPRIETORSHIP and a ream of code embossed in the cover. Flicking through the folio, she saw wads of waxy paper covered in indecipherable CorpSpeak. At the back of the folio was a small ident marked PLACE THUMB HERE.

"CityHive wants permission to harvest her genetic material," Director said.

Lemon frowned, looked from the contract to the crescent of identical faces around her. "I don't get it. You people already *took* my blood on—"

"The sample taken aboard Nau'shi *was for testing alone. And we require different genetic material for emulation."*

". . . What kind of material?"

"Ovarian," they replied.

Lemon's eyes went wide, her hands slipped involuntarily to

her belly. Her voice sounded small and distant in her ears, like it belonged to someone else.

"You want my . . ."

Four heads nodded. *"Pluripotent stems offer the greatest opportunity for modification. Once the document is signed and the material harvested, Lemonfresh will be free to leave."*

"Just like that, huh?"

The Director nodded again. *"The procedure is simple. Swift. Almost painless."*

She swallowed thickly. ". . . And if I say no?"

"Lemonfresh is the key to winning the struggle against Daedalus. Lemonfresh is the gateway to a better future. Lemonfresh is important." All four leaned forward, four pairs of hands steepled at four chins, four pairs of dark eyes glowering. *"We are hoping she will see the beauty in this city, and this way of life. We are hoping she will volunteer her material for the betterment of her species. We are hoping we will not need to resort to . . . unpleasantries."*

Silence descended on the room like a boot heel. Lemon sat in the stunted quiet for a long moment, staring at the stack of documents, the full weight of the Director's request sinking in. It took her a long time to sort through the riot in her head, to ponder how she could *possibly* respond to a request like that. She was in danger here, true cert. Surrounded by gene-modded insanity, nobody to rescue her. She had to negotiate this properly, she had to dance it right, she had to play this smarter and cleaner and chiller than she'd ever played before.

And so, Lemon rolled her shoulders.

Breathed deep.

"Well, pardon me," she said. "But you can all go *fuck* yourselves."

3.6

CONTINGENCY

Preacher hadn't seen Megopolis in over seven years.

It was strange when he thought about it—he'd devoted his life to defending Daedalus Technologies but never spent much time in its capital. There just always seemed skulls that needed cracking. Folks that needed killing. But after his grift with that dim-witted snowflake Ezekiel played out so perfect, he figured it was time for a triumphant return. So, he'd dropped off his captives at the detention intake, logged his report and motored out into the city, happy as flies on a corpse.

Nuclear explosions aside, it'd been a mighty good day. He'd monkey-wrenched the lifelikes' plans to bust open their super-computer and handed R & D not only two fully functional life-likes (bullet holes aside), but also Nic Monrova's last remaining child. And while, yeah, technically he'd failed to bring in his target—being that five-foot-nothin' redheaded hellion capable of frying 'lectrics with her mind—technically speaking, Daedalus had sent him after the wrong target in the first place.

He'd brought 'em Evie Carpenter, just as ordered. And on

top of that, he'd handed them the keys to Nicholas Monrova's computerized kingdom.

That was worth a drink.

The city had changed in his absence. Far more logika about, for one thing. But the basic structure was the same. Megopolis was divided into two zones by a giant concrete barrier, which the Board had imaginatively dubbed "the Wall." Inside the Wall was the Hub, home of Daedalus's accredited citizens. Outside lay the Rim, a grimy settlement built in the Wall's shadow, peopled by folks with one real goal in mind—getting accredited so they could go live in the Hub.

The skinbar was called Shady Slim's. It was one of his favorite joints on the Rim, always crowded, music pounding. Soon as he walked in, a logika attendant offered him a pair of VR goggs, but he declined. Some folk opted to "augment" their experience in Slim's by clothing the dancers in virtual skins—giving them blue flesh or furry tails or maybe even the face of a lost love or a much-hated boss. But Preacher could appreciate the real thing just fine.

Despite his triumphant return, he wasn't feeling one hundred percent. He and Snowflake had been in such a rush, the repair job he'd got in Armada hadn't been much more than a patch job. One leg was shorter than the other, half his augs were still offline. But logging in to the Corp network, he discovered one of his favorite botdocs—a five-star Daedalus tech named Araña_03—was still in biz. He shot her a down payment and specs, asked her to get started on the parts.

Soon enough, he'd be state-of-the-art again.

Preacher drank for hours, tipping back ethyl-4 shots with his red right hand. He lost count of his lap dances after six.

Neon lights flickered as gloom settled over the last great city in the Yousay. He watched wageslaves trundling home after a hard day's grind for their Citizen Points. Scam artists looking for a grift to get them beyond the Wall. Thieves and hustlers and killers. But he could see the poetry to it.

Talking true, he loved this city.

He loved this Corp.

He *loved* this day.

It wasn't until he tried to pay his tab that it started to turn bad.

"Account denied, Padre."

Preacher looked away from images of that explosion over the New Bethlehem desert on the newsfeed, down into Shady Slim's gleaming cybernetic eyes.

"Wassat?"

The publican pointed to the beaten-up plastic CP reader, waggled Preacher's official Daedalus account stik in one grubby hand. "You got declined."

"Guttershit." Preacher stuffed synth tobacco into his cheek. "Run it again."

Slim complied, met with an angry beep and a flashing DENIED.

"Sorry, Padre. Got another account?"

Figuring maybe the stik had gotten busted during his recent hunt (he *had* almost gotten eaten by a radioactive toad, after all), Preacher reached into his leather coat, pulled out his own personal stik. Shady Slim nodded as the Citizen Points read good. Tipping his hat to the dancers, Preacher was just stepping out into the crowded streets when his comms account beeped about an incoming call.

"*Preacher,*" came a voice down the line. "*It's Araña.*"

"Howdy, darlin'," he smiled. "I was just headin' to yours. Parts ready?"

"*Yeah, I got 'em. But I'm not running a charity here, vato.*"

". . . Wassat supposed to mean? Daedalus'll pick up the tab, like always."

"*Daedalus denied your deposit. 'Operative account suspended.'*"

Preacher rumbled to a stop on the sidewalk. "Say again?"

"'*Operative account suspended,*'" Araña repeated. "*Daedalus is saying you don't have a credit line with them.*"

"Well, that's crap and you know it. They've always footed my bills with you."

"*I dunno what to tell you,*" Araña said. "*You been gone awhile, maybe you forgot the Golden Rule. CP talks, charity walks, feel me? You sort it, hit me up.*"

The line dropped, leaving Preacher alone with the rush and rumble of the Rim streets. A crowd of chemkids brushed past, looking sharp and surly. Methane vapor swirled about his shoulders, drenched in a rainbow of grubby neon light. He tapped the uplink implanted in his cyberarm, logged into the Daedalus network.

Username: Padre.

Password: Mary07 (his momma's name and fave number).

Enter.

OPERATIVE ACCOUNT SUSPENDED.

He blinked at the angry red letters flashing up at him from his display.

Spat a mouthful of sticky brown onto the stickier pavement.

"Mmmf," he grunted.

———

Danael Drakos and Preacher went back a *long* way.

They'd first met eighteen years ago, during the helter-skelter days of the CorpState Wars. Preacher was a First Sergeant. Danael was already head of Frontline Research and Development, the genius who designed the second-gen Goliaths that took down Omnimax Incorporated. Preacher took a big hit in that battle—blown apart and left for dead. But some Good Samaritan had dragged his chunks back behind the line, and he woke up in a Daedalus medcenter a week later. When he opened his new eyes, the first face he saw was that of Danael Drakos.

The Lord saved his life that day, true cert.

But Dani Drakos supplied the parts.

Wasn't like they were friends or nuthin'. Once Preacher joined Special Ops, Dani occasionally reached out when he needed finesse on a big job. But deep down, Preacher always knew Dani would be there for him. He'd given his best years to this company. His body. His everything. He knew that'd *mean* something.

But now?

OPERATIVE ACCOUNT SUSPENDED.

Preacher's autocab pulled up outside Daedalus HQ—the looming spike of concrete and solar panels known as the Spire. He flashed his CorpStik on instinct, cursing as a red ACCOUNT DENIED flashed on the screen. The autocab remained locked, so he used his personal stik, then kicked the door open in growing fury.

He limped into a gleaming foyer, past young security

bucks in their power armor, countless cameras. The security crews knew him by rep; a few even nodded greetings. But when he flashed his CorpCard to the Sec logika and an alarm sounded, they stood to attention, fingers shifting slow to their triggers.

"ACCESS DENIED," the bot told him.

Preacher rumbled to a stop, eyeing the goons. Their leader, a blond-haired, blue-eyed lump, held out one power-gloved hand. A sinking feeling was swelling in Preacher's belly as he handed over his credentials.

The kid shook his head. "Access denied."

"I'm here to see Danael Drakos," Preacher said.

"You're not cleared for entry, Operative," the kid replied.

Preacher spat a thin stream of tobacco juice into a nearby potted plastic plant. "I was running top-level wetwork for this Corp when you were still crapping in your hands and rubbing it on your face. Get outta my way, kid."

"I can't do that, Op. I don't make the rules."

Preacher made to walk forward; the kid stepped into his path. In the power armor, he loomed taller than Preacher, steel-weave muscles hissing. The bounty hunter heard the other sec-boys bristling behind him, sensed all those fingers on all those triggers. He looked up at the closest camera cluster, glowering.

"Danael!" he shouted. "Lemme up!"

"Operative, I'm going to have to ask y—"

"Dani!" Preacher bellowed. "I know your surveillance teams clocked me soon as I entered the Hub. You had enough of this little game yet? Or you need me to bust a few of these kiddies' heads open afore we chat?"

The sec-goons were aiming weapons at him now. He

couldn't fault them for it—these kids had their CP totals to think about. But that didn't mean he wasn't prepared to crack a few skulls for the temerity of it.

Young'uns got no respect for their elders these days. . . .

"Have it your way," Preacher growled.

He tongued the implant in his upper right molar twice, and his combat augs kicked in, mainlining adrenaline into his heart, a mix of methaline and phencylamide into his muscles. His left hand had closed around the sec-leader's throat before he could blink, the metal fingers on his red right hand speeding toward the kid's widening eyes when a deep voice crackled over the foyer PA.

"That's enough, Marcus."

Preacher's hand fell still a few centimeters short of the kid's peepers. His heart pounded with the hammer-blow beat of the chems in his veins.

"You gonna let me up so we can talk this through?"

"I'm very busy, Marcus," came the reply.

"I'm not a stooge, Dani. I've bled for this Corp for eighteen goddamn years!"

Silence rang in the foyer, Preacher's eyes locked on the cameras. He could feel the laser sights of the sec-team's guns on his back, feel the adrenaline and combat chems crackling in the air. One twitch, one wrong word . . .

A sigh rang over the PA.

"Lieutenant, escort our visitor up to R & D. I'm in the Truelife suite."

Preacher released the kid's neck reeeal slow, his body still bristling with threat. The sec-boys stood down a touch, hands still on their weapons. The kid rolled his big shoulders, obviously upset that Preacher had laid a glove on him.

"Follow me, old man."

Preacher looked him dead in the eye. "You call me old again, I'ma beat you like your daddy shoulda, son."

The kid only grunted, turned and stomped off. Preacher stalked through another checkpoint to the elevator. Polished metal, glowing glass. The winged sun embossed on the temperfoam at his feet. He was marched through four security portals into R & D. Banks of top-tier gear, heavy cables snaking over the floors, a small army of tech bots around glowing screens. And finally, he found Danael Drakos, standing with a legion of flunkies in sharp suits.

It'd been four years since he caught face time, but Dani hadn't aged a day. Preacher's skin was leathered from years beneath that bastard sun. Danael's was lightly tanned. Preacher's body was mostly metal. Dani was ninety percent meat. Only his eyes told the story of his age, and that story was a long one—the CEO of Daedalus Technologies was Preacher's senior by a good forty years.

Drakos was talking to three tech bots and looking over a data pad.

"Any improvement from the latest cycle?" he asked softly.

"YES SIR," one of the bots replied. "THE LIFELIKE'S ARTIFICIAL MENTAL TOPOGRAPHY IS STILL PROVING TROUBLESOME, BUT WITH FURTHER MODIFICATION, THE TRUELIFE INTERFACE, COMBINED WITH DATA FROM THE MONROVA SUBJECT, SHOULD PRODUCE THE DESIRED RESULTS."

"Excellent." Drakos flicked through the data pad and nodded. "Yes, excellent."

Preacher hooked his thumbs into his belt, looked about. The walls were dominated by screens, reams of indecipherable data. The minions clustered around Drakos were genuine humans, but the room was mostly filled with logika. He could see the cryo-tube he'd retrieved from New Bethlehem, Ana Monrova floating suspended in a bubble of frozen blue, a pair of fancy wetware 'trodes fixed to her temples. And slumped in a grav-chair, her blond fauxhawk soaked with sweat, eyes closed, was Evie Carpenter.

Looked like she was plugged into a high-end VR unit. She had the same 'trodes on her own temples, her vitals displayed in a 3-D topography on a screen above. They were spiking into the redline, like she was fighting for her very life. As he watched, the girl threw back her head and screamed.

"Hello, Marcus, how can I help you?"

Drakos's voice dragged his attention away from his former quarry. The CEO was looking at him now, running one hand back over his widow's peak.

"You can start by explaining what the hell's going on, Danael."

"There could be any number of answers to that question, Marcus. And as you can see, we're rather busy. What, specifically, do you mean?"

"You cut me off."

"Ah. I confess I thought it would take you longer to notice. Try to charge your bar tab to the Corporation account again, did you?"

"I just spent a week running all over the goddamn Yousay for this company," Preacher growled. "I got shot, had my legs blown off by a blitzhund, my augs fried by a pint-sized, freckle-faced abnorm. I got thrown off a cliff, half eaten by an irradiated toad bigger than your penthouse and almost murdered by a posse of synthetics with a hate-chub for the entirety of humanity. And you're gonna stand there in your twelve-thousand-CP suit and begrudge me a goddamn drink?"

"It's funny you should mention that particular pint-sized deviate, Marcus," Drakos mused. "Because I swear when I sent you out to get shot, blown up, cliffed and toaded, it was under direct orders to bring her back here alive."

Preacher pointed at Evie Carpenter in her VR chair. "You sent me after *her*!"

"No. I *sent* you after the girl who blew the circuits out of that renegade Goliath in the Los Diablos WarDome."

"And on the footage you showed me, it looked like *she did it*!"

Danael's flawless brow darkened. "And tell me, when the aforementioned pint-sized, freckle-faced abnorm destroyed your cybernetic augmentations outside Babel, did it not become apparent that your acquisition priorities had changed? I wanted the deviate who threatens the future of this CorpState, Marcus."

"I brung you the way into Monrova's archives." Preacher's temper began boiling as he waved to the frozen form of Ana Monrova. "All you need to crack that bastard's secrets are his kid's DNA and that Carpenter girlie's brainwave patterns. I handed you the keys to his goddamn *kingdom,* you sonofabitch!"

The human minions paused over their data pads at that— obviously unused to hearing Drakos referred to as anything other than "sir."

Or maybe "Your Majesty."

"Give us the room, please, people," Danael said.

Preacher glowered as the flunkies slipped out. The kid who'd escorted him in shot a questioning glance to Drakos, who simply nodded. So the bruiser clomped out, too, leaving Preacher alone with half a dozen tech and sec-drones, and the chief executive officer of the largest CorpState in the Yousay.

Danael took a sip of water from a nearby glass.

"Do you understand the position you've put me in?" he asked, his voice deathly soft. "Do you have *any* inkling of what your incompetence has cost us?"

"*My* incompetence? I'm not the one who pointed me in—"

Danael turned and hurled his glass at one of the monitor walls. It tumbled end over end, collided with the wall and shattered into a thousand pieces.

"Yes!" Danael bellowed. "*Your* incompetence! I gave you a job to do, Marcus, and you failed! Don't you see what's at stake here now? If BioMaas finds a way to weaponize Fresh's abilities, they can neutralize electronic tech with a snap of their fingers. Even if we *can* fashion the brainwave patterns of this lifelike"— here he waved at Eve Carpenter—"into a usable form—which, by the way, is no bloody walk on the beach—Monrova's secrets will be meaningless. The future of this entire Corporation is in jeopardy. And you stand there whining about your *credit account*?"

Drakos paused in his tirade, rubbed at the scowl on his brow and breathed deep. Preacher hadn't seen him lose his temper in more than a decade.

"You used to be the best operative this Corp had ever seen," Danael said. "Times past, I could have trusted you to spin straw into gold and be back in time for last call. But time catches all of us, my friend. And it seems, at last, it's caught you."

Preacher scowled. "What the hell you mean by that?"

"I mean exactly what you think, Marcus. Your services as a field operative are no longer required by Daedalus Technologies." Danael held up one hand to calm the incoming outburst. "I'll not leave you without a position. I can arrange a post for you in Training. Perhaps Strategy. But your days of frontline fieldwork are over."

"This is guttershit," Preacher spat. "I'm the best you got!"

"If you were the best we had, Fresh would be in our possession instead of being entertained in CityHive." Danael paused a moment, his tone softening. "I mean, godsakes, Marcus. What are you, forty-five? Get yourself a VR account. Start spending those CPs you've accumulated. You've earned a rest."

"I don't *want* a rest," Preacher hissed. "I want to work, goddammit. You get my augs repaired, I'll go to CityHive and drag Fresh back here by the short and c—"

"CityHive?" Danael said, the steel slipping back into his stare. "I'm trying to avert a war, not start one. You're talking nonsense, Marcus. And, thanks to you, I don't have time for it."

"Well, *excuse* me, you stuck-up sumbitch, but you're gonna *make* t—"

"I would think," Dani said, "*very* carefully about my next words if I were you."

The sec-drones around the room watched Preacher with glowing eyes, one bad move away from lighting up his chest. Danael Drakos stared back at him, typing without looking on the implant at his wrist. He might be management now, but Drakos had seen the face of war—one of the reasons Preacher respected him, talking true. But he was at the business end of that same grit now, staring down the barrel at a man who refused to look away, back down, give ground.

You didn't get to be CEO of the biggest CorpState in the Yousay by blinking first.

"I'll have the appropriate forms sent tomorrow," Danael said. "Now, if you'll excuse me, some of us still have work to do."

Preacher was dimly aware of the door opening, the kid lurking at his shoulder, minions filing back into the room. And with little else to do or say that wouldn't burn what few bridges he had left, Preacher limped from the room.

His mismatched legs whined and hissed. His head felt full of velvet static, his mouth sour with impotent rage. Eighteen years of loyalty. The best part of his life.

And in the end, what had it earned him?

He vaguely remembered a conversation he'd had with that idiot Snowflake in Paradise Falls. The pair of them sitting together, a few whiskey shots in Preacher's belly. Talking about killing. About dying. About loyalty. Snowflake had tried calling him out on his job. Told him he was nothing but a serf. A stooge.

Take it from someone who used to be a something. You're useful to Daedalus right now. The minute you stop is the minute they throw you away.

Preacher blinked as the elevator hit bottom.

Feeling like someone had punched him in the chest.

The kid escorted him out into the street. His heart was thumping hard—half from coming down off his combat stims, the other half just from plain old-fashioned shock. The synth tobacco in his cheek tasted like ashes, and Preacher spat it out, brown and sticky. The kid smirked, turning on his heel and abandoning him there on the sidewalk. Bewildered and reeling.

"Take care, old man."

A small janitor-bot trundled past, spraying the tobacco with a high-pressure jet of soapy water, blasting it away into the gutter.

Into the gutter.
Take it from someone who used to be a something.
The minute you stop is the minute they throw you away.
Preacher frowned up at the neon sky over his head.
"And I was having such a good day . . . ," he sighed.

3.7

SINGULARITY

Lemon ended up eating the locust cubes.

To her credit, she held out maybe sixteen hours.

The room they'd locked her inside was positively palatial: a strangely beautiful space that took up an entire level of one of the CityHive's spires. The walls were transparent, letting in a wash of soft, welcome light. The floors and furnishings were the color of bone and gave Lem the impression they'd been grown, not built. A fluted fountain trickled crystal clear water into a round pond filled with flat green leaves and bright yellow flowers and the first genuine fish Lemon had seen outside a history reel. They were the color of flame, four of them, sleek and beautiful.

She'd stood at the window, watching the long sunset shadows stretching over the city below, the strange synchronicity of movement playing out in this beautiful, baffling place. Reaching into the static, she could feel faint current all around—flowing in the walls, the ceilings, the floors. As if, in some strange way, the very building itself was . . . alive. And as she'd crawled into bed, soft and enveloping and clean, ethereal music had been ringing in the air, singing her off to sleep.

But there was no door. No way out. And as strangely pretty as this place was, Lemon Fresh was under no illusions that she wasn't a prisoner in it.

She'd woken to find the table set with pitchers of water and plates full of suspicious-looking food. She recognized the locust cubes by color, but there were others—vaguely orange and moody green. But it had been almost a day since she'd eaten properly. And in the end, she settled on the ones made of bug because at least she knew what was in them.

They were crunchy. Almost sweet. Lemon tried to pretend she was eating a protein bar, but her imagination just wasn't that good.

"Stupid brain," she muttered, chewing miserably.

On the edge of the water fountain sat a now-familiar thick black folio. The words CONTRACTUAL AGREEMENT: GENOME PROPRIETORSHIP stared at her, just as stubborn as she was. She sat, a plate of locust cubes in her lap, watching flame-colored fish swim in endless, pointless circles. She leafed through the contract as she ate, found the language just as incomprehensible as the first time. But the meaning was clear—BioMaas was asking for something that was entirely *hers*. And she didn't want to give it to them.

Lemon wasn't exactly a girlie girl. Before she met Grimm, she hadn't invested an awful lot of time thinking about boys. In Los Diablos, you spent most of your minutes just trying to survive. She and Evie used to talk about it sometimes—maybe getting hooked up, maybe having sprogs one day—but planning a future seemed like a waste of time when you knew you probably wouldn't be alive to see it. Still, the idea of letting this freak show CorpState harvest chunks of her lady parts sat about as well with her as these locust cubes were sitting in her belly.

Her stomach burbled. She tossed the cubes to the fish with a grimace.

"Septic," she muttered.

Lemon heard a whispering sound, turned to see a stretch of wall parting like a curtain. She saw a Carer standing in the curved hallway outside, surrounded by Sentinels. This version of the woman looked a little younger than others she'd seen— a later model, maybe. The Carer peered into the room with her featureless black eyes, soft light gleaming on her hairless head. Her voice was low and melodic.

"Good morning, Lemonfresh. May we enter?"

"Free country." Lemon shrugged. "For some people, at least."

Carer's face dropped, and she looked genuinely crestfallen. Stepping into the room, she was followed by three Sentinels, while another three remained outside. The men were big, burly, armed with odd spine-covered pistols. But they stayed by the door while Carer proceeded into the room. The woman hovered by the fountain, hands clasped. She looked at Lemon intently, big black eyes gleaming in a heart-shaped face. The music of trickling water filled the air.

The girl glanced at her sidelong. "Can I help you?"

The woman smiled. "It is Carer's task to help Lemonfresh."

"With what?"

"Anything!" she said, suddenly eager.

"Great!" Lemon replied, perfectly mirroring Carer's wide eyes and way-too-cheery tone. "Gimme a key to the door and a ride out of this hole!"

Carer listened intently, totally missing the sarcasm.

"We wish Lemonfresh to be happy. We would give her what she desires." She nodded to the three men guarding the entrance. "But Sentinel would not allow it."

Lemon scowled at the men. "Well, Sentinel's a bit of a bastard, then, isn't he."

Carer laughed, loud and musical. "Lemonfresh is amusing!"

"Yeah." Lemon rolled her eyes. "Hilarious me."

"She seems despondent." Carer turned suddenly serious, placing one tentative hand on Lemon's shoulder. "How may we help?"

"I dunno. How may you?"

The woman glanced at the contract. "We may give her many reasons why signing over permission for her genome is her most sensible option?"

"That sounds amaaaaazing," Lemon said.

Carer visibly brightened, sitting down on the fountain's edge beside Lemon. "Wonderful! Firstly, she should consider the innate superiority of BioMaas corporate philosophy. Simply put, we seek to reach an equilibrium with the world arou—"

"I guess sarcasm isn't part of your corporate philosophy, huh?"

"Sarcasm is a form of mockery. It is innately cruel." Carer looked at Lemon like *she* was the defective one. "Lemonfresh does know Carer's purpose, yes?"

"Yeah," Lemon sighed. "I met one of you aboard that kraken. You look after people. You're genetically programmed to give a damn. Which is where all this starts to fall apart. I get that different patterns have different tasks, yeah? Sentinels guard and Hunters hunt. I met a kid on the kraken who was in charge of the garbage."

"Salvage," she nodded. "An important task."

"But if your only responsibility is to look after people, how come you're okay with them locking me up in here until I let them cut bits out of me?"

"An excellent question," Carer said, seemingly impressed. "In BioMaas, all tasks exist within a hierarchy. While all the functions we perform are important for the well-being of City-Hive, some tasks are more important than others. Security takes precedence over Expansion, for example. Production outranks Construction. The acquisition of Lemonfresh's genome has been given Tier One significance by Director. Almost all other tasks are considered secondary."

"So that's why you're here? To convince me?"

"We are here to escort you to Director. They wish to walk with you today, that you might witness the marvel of CityHive and the potential of BioMaas philosophy."

"Your boss is going to show me around the place in the hope I'll agree to let you people harvest my girlie bits?" Lemon's eyebrow crept skyward. "This must be one *hell* of a tour, Carer."

Carer extended a hand and smiled.

"Come, Lemonfresh. Please. Walk with us."

With no other choice, and the thought of sitting up here all day brooding over her losses looming before her, Lemon sighed and took Carer's hand. The woman's grip was cool, firm; her smile, warm and genuine. Carer led Lemon past the three lurking Sentinels, and Lemon watched as she gently touched the wall. Reaching out into the static again, Lem felt that faint current surging through the structure around her where the exit control must be. Storing the knowledge for later.

With a gentle whisper, the wall opened wide.

The corridor outside was smooth bone, lit with pale light.

Three other Sentinels awaited there, dour-faced, big and punchy-looking. Lemon couldn't see any obvious surveillance equipment—no cams or drones. But those glowy bugthings were *everywhere,* crawling on the walls, ceilings, constantly touching antennae with their siblings, like processions of ants from one of Mister C's nature sims.

Another doorway opened to reveal a tube of smooth, bone-colored resin. A disk sculpted of the same material waited for them, and Carer stepped onto it, Lemon and her minders following. At a touch of the woman's hand, the disk began to ascend like an elevator platform. The tube's wall parted with a whisper, and Lemon was ushered out onto a platform near the top of the spire. The space was broad, bright and airy, filled with leafy plant life and long processions of glowbugs.

In the center of the space, the four Directors of BioMaas were waiting for her.

"Good morning, Lemonfresh," they said.

"If you say so," the girl replied.

"Walk with us." The Directors held out their hands. *"Please."*

Lemon glanced to the Carer, who double-blinked and smiled enthusiastically. Lemon trudged forward to the Directors. And with each of them positioned perfectly around her, like points in a diamond, they began to walk.

The platform was open to the air, the structure supported by beautiful, graven columns. At each compass point, one of those long, slender walkways extended outward, connecting another spire close by. The Directors strolled at a leisurely pace, hands behind their backs. Six Sentinels followed behind, but other than that, Lemon and the Directors were completely alone with a whispering wind.

As they walked, the Directors shifted position constantly,

revolving around her in perfect unison, so no one figure walked in front for long. It was eerie to watch—while they never spoke, each of them seemed perfectly in tune with their fellows.

Looking over the walkway's edge, Lemon saw the city laid out in miniature. She could see dozens of other walkways, above and below: a vast, sprawling web of them, connecting each of the buildings in the hive.

"*How did Lemonfresh sleep?*" the Directors asked.

"Like a prisoner," Lemon replied, fists in pockets.

"*Was her room pleasing?*"

"Her room was locked."

"*She is upset with us.*"

"She's furious," Lemon growled, "is what she is."

The Director stopped, looked out over the CityHive below. Plant life was everywhere, clinging to the buildings and crawling along the walkway they trod upon. The air was clearer than any Lemon had ever tasted, lightening her head, tingling on her skin. She felt cleaner just *being* here. The sky was filled with the beat of thousands of iridescent wings, the tiny figures below, the flying figures above, all moving perfectly in time, like the Director walking with himself. It was as if every living thing in the city were part of one vast dance.

Lemon chewed on her bangs, considering all the other places she'd visited since she left Dregs. Compared to the squalor of Armada, the desolation of the Glass, even the broken majesty of Babel, CityHive was utterly breathtaking.

"*Beautiful, is it not?*"

"It's okay," Lemon admitted grudgingly. "I mean, if you like green."

"*Once, all the world wore dresses in this shade. A great forest,*" *filled with trees that touched the skies. Inhaling carbon, exhaling oxygen. A perfect circle. But those great titans fell and pooled, black and sticky beneath the earth. And in their ignorance and hubris, humanity dredged up the blood and burned it to fuel their industry. Spitting poison into land and sea and sky."* The Director looked at Lemon, eight eyes blinking. *"The deadworld beyond these walls is the result."*

"Yeah, I get it," Lemon said, growing impatient. "Until I was fourteen, my best friend was a rat who shared my squat and occasionally tried to eat my fingers while I was sleeping. Humans were crappy landlords. Tell me something I don't know."

The Directors waved to the city beyond, four hands moving in unison, four voices speaking, all of them one.

"Surely she must see the beauty in BioMaas philosophy? Daedalus Technologies is a simpleminded grave robber, scratching out a living in the tomb of the world that was. Ours is a way of harmony. A new branch on the tree of life."

"Yeah, look," Lemon said. "On the surface, that all sounds real fizzy. Harmony and balance and whatforth. But here's the thing. You asked if my room was pleasing, yeah? And all sass aside, my room was scary as hell."

"Did the citysong disturb her? It can be—"

"No, it wasn't the noise. Or the locust cubes, either. It was the fish."

Four pairs of eyes double-blinked.

"I was watching them," Lemon said. "And like this whole place, they looked real pretty at first. But the harder I looked, the more creepy on the crawly I began to feel. I couldn't put my finger on it at first, yeah? But this morning, I figured out why they and you and this whole place freak me *right the hell out.*"

Director blinked gain, waiting patiently.

"They're the *same* fish," Lemon said. "They're identical in every way."

"Of course they are," the Directors said.

Lemon blinked, rocked back on her heels. "So, what, you've got some vat somewhere, spitting out copies of the same fish, over and over again?"

"They are the perfect encapsulation of the pattern. Just like Carer, Sentinel, Builder, Hunter, it is ideally suited to the task it must perform. If it has achieved the pinnacle of what it must be, why not produce more of it?"

"Because that's not the way life is supposed to be?" Lemon all but shouted.

"That is a very limited point of view, Lemonfresh. We are all alive here, are we not? How can you say what is 'supposed' to be?"

Lemon shook her head, hands on hips. "So everyone in this city is just . . . grown? And everyone is just ooh-la-la straight-up *perf* at what they do?"

"They are the best patterns we can devise," they said.

Lemon pressed her lips together, looked at the Directors around her.

"I read a book by this old crusty named Darwin, yeah? And he wrote that people like me—mutations, abnormalities, whatever you wanna call us—are the way life improves itself. Mistakes get made when people get born, but sometimes, those mistakes turn out to be improvements. But you all around here"—Lemon waved at Director, at the Sentinels lurking in the distance, at the city dancing above and below—"it's like you're . . . locked in the same shape. You don't change. You *don't* grow. You take away the chaos and you just stay the same. Forever."

"*Chaos is instability. Order is the condition under which we prosper.*"

Lemon shook her head. "But in trying to make everything fit in these neat little boxes with these oh-so-helpful labels, you're taking away the stuff that makes us special! You all think the same! You all talk the same! Carer, Director, Builder, whatever. To you people, *what* you are is more important than *who* you are!"

Director smiled as if she'd reached some kind of breakthrough. "*Exactly. The group is more important than the individual. Many matter more than one.*"

"So what happens to the many out there?" Lemon demanded, waving to the wastes beyond the broad city walls. "Let's say I give you the keys to my underoos and you crack my genethingy—"

"*Genome.*"

"Whatever!" she snapped, stamping her foot. "If BioMaas defeats Daedalus, what happens to all those people out there who *aren't* perfectly suited to tasks they must perform?"

The Directors spoke at her as if she were a child asking about the color of the sky. "*They will be cut away. Like all deadwood.*"

"You mean *killed*?"

"*Yes.*"

"And you want me to sign up to help you?" Lemon glared at the Directors, one after another, utterly incredulous. "Are you all *completely* defective?"

"*Lemonfresh can make this world a garden once more. A place of harmony and peace, all people attuned to the needs of their fellows, all bound together in a perfect tapestry. Her genome is the key to a new era for this world.*"

"So why not just *take* it?" Lemon demanded, her frustration finally boiling over.

Director seemed genuinely saddened at the notion. *"To take without asking is the way of the deadworld. We seek order and perfection of pattern. We seek harmony and balance."*

"You *seek* to wipe every other human being off the face of the earth."

Director blinked. *"That, too."*

"You people," Lemon breathed, "are absolutely *insane*. I don't give a damn how pretty it is here, I don't care how perfectly in balance your harmonious little lives might be. There's no way in hell I'm gonna help you wipe out humanity!"

"She has little choice. Though we would prefer not to take, we will do so. Victory in our struggle over Daedalus is simply too important. Lemonfresh's genome will literally decide the fate of this world."

Lemon looked out over the strange and beautiful city. The awful wasteland beyond. She thought about all she'd lost in the last few days. Evie and Cricket. Mister C and Zeke. She thought about a boy who'd kissed her like he really meant it. The feeling of finally having found someplace to belong.

All of it was gone now.

"Well, in that case," she said, "it was pretty stupid bringing me up here alone."

She curled her fingers into fists. Reaching out into the static, pulsing and crackling beneath her skin. Jaw set, teeth bared.

Director only smiled. *"She cannot harm us. When one bee perishes, another rises. When one Carer dies, when one Hunter-Killer fails, another can seamlessly step into the breach. It is the same with Director, Lemonfresh."* They motioned to their own bodies, toe to crown. *"CityHive is replete with hundreds of this pattern. All interconnected to the tapestry. We are legion. We are hydra."*

The Directors looked toward the distant Sentinels, and though no words passed between them, the hulking men began walking toward Lemon. She saw the shapes of Hunter-Killers hovering in the air around her.

Lemon's lips twisted in a small, sad smile.

"Who said anything about harming *you*, cloneboy?"

Four sets of eyes narrowed, four pairs of lungs drew a soft and sudden breath. Lemon stepped sideways, silver-quick, between the two Directors closest to the railing. They reached for her, the closest clapping his hands on her shoulders. Feeling his fingers dig into her skin, she reached out into the static and slammed the full force of her power into his mind, snapping the tethers of current, shutting down his synapses. The Director collapsed without a gurgle, eyes rolling up in his head.

Lemon heard the other three gasp. A shiver passed through the plants around her. She realized the three other Directors, the Hunter-Killers in the sky around her, the approaching Sentinels, all of them seemed stunned by the first Director's death. It only lasted a second; the other Directors were quickly shaking it off and reaching toward her again. But that second was all she needed.

Her genome was the key to their victory, after all. Her genetic code would be the weapon BioMaas used to wipe out Dregs, Megopolis, Armada—every human being in the whole Yousay. Millions of people would die if BioMaas got their way. But if they needed her pluripotent parts to enact their genocide, well, they might have trouble scraping them off the sidewalk.

Lemon didn't want to die. But she didn't want to be the weapon that wiped out humanity, either. And considering everyone who loved her was now radioactive ashes, cashing in her chips just seemed a better deal than becoming the tool these psychos used to murder the whole human race.

So she scrambled up onto the railing, staring down at the ground hundreds of meters below. She took one last breath.

She closed her eyes.

And she jumped.

3.8

POSSE

The world is a really scary place when you're little.

Cricket had spent his whole life being small. He knew how rough it got. People would walk over him, talk over him, not even notice he was there. One time he got locked in a maintenance cupboard in WarDome, and it took Evie six hours to realize he was missing. It's easy to get looked down on when people can see the top of your head. It's easy to get stepped on when you fit so neatly underfoot.

For as long as he could remember, Cricket had wanted nothing more than to be *big*. Problem was, the longer he spent in this WarBot body, the more he realized being big was no party, either. People were a little frightened of him now, keeping their distance as if he might accidentally squash them. Everyone was so small, he had to be careful not to crush them. And worst of all, he didn't *fit* anywhere anymore, which meant that while everyone else was inside Miss O's, eating and strategizing, Cricket was stuck outside, bored out of his not-so-tiny mind.

"THIS BLOWS," he muttered to himself.

"*I MUST ADMIT, I SHARE YOUR DISCONTENTMENT, OLD FRIEND.*"

Cricket looked down from midnight skies and saw Solomon creaking his way up from the rusty hatchway of Miss O's. The spindly logika wobbled as he walked—Abraham hadn't managed to fix him before they left New Bethlehem, and the smaller logika looked a little worse for wear. With his eyes and that infuriating, perpetual smile illuminating the darkness, Solomon skirted the ragged hole the behemoth had burst out of and finally plonked himself beside Cricket.

"DYNAMO STILL GIVING YOU GRIEF?" Cricket asked.

"*MY WHOLE BODY IS A VERITABLE FUNERAL PROCESSION, OLD FRIEND,*" the bot lamented. "*AND MASTER ABRAHAM SHOWS LITTLE INCLINATION TO END IT.*"

"CUT HIM SOME SLACK. HE'S BEEN A LITTLE BUSY, WHAT WITH HIS MOTHER TRYING TO CRUCIFY HIM AND HIS WHOLE LIFE COMING APART."

"*MMM,*" Solomon said, obviously unconvinced. "*I CAN'T HELP BUT NOTICE HE FOUND TIME TO FIX YOUR AUDIO CAPABILITIES, OLD FRIEND. IT SEEMS THE SENSATIONAL SOLOMON IS NOT HIGH ON ANYONE'S LIST OF PRIORITIES. AS USUAL.*"

"HOW'S IT GOING DOWN THERE, ANYWAY?"

"*IT DEPENDS WHOM YOU ASK, REALLY,*" the smaller logika replied with a completely unnecessary sigh. "*THERE'S AT LEAST TWO DEAD BODIES INSIDE, SO THAT'S A NOVELTY. ROTTING CORPSES DO LEND A HOME A CERTAIN . . . RUSTIC CHARM.*"

"WHO DO THE BODIES BELONG TO?"

"*WELL, NOBODY TELLS ME ANYTHING, AS USUAL,*" Solomon huffed. "*BUT FROM WHAT I'VE GLEANED THROUGH EXERCISING MY SUPERIOR SOCIAL GRACES—*"

"YOU MEAN EAVESDROPPING."

"*DON'T BE GLIB, OLD FRIEND, IT DOESN'T SUIT YOU.*" Solomon rolled his creaky shoulders and continued as if uninterrupted.

"*THE FIRST CORPSE BELONGS TO A YOUNG BUCK NAMED FIX. YOUNG MISTRESS DIESEL SEEMS TO HAVE BEEN RATHER FOND OF HIM, JUDGING BY HER MOOD. THE SECOND CORPSE BELONGS TO ABRAHAM'S GRANDFATHER.*"

". . . WHAT?" Cricket sputtered.

"*YES,*" the smaller logika nodded. "*APPARENTLY, THE PATRON SAINT OF NEW BETHLEHEM WAS USING THESE YOUNGSTERS TO WAGE WAR ON HIS TREACHEROUS DAUGHTER, OUR DEAR SISTER DEE. YOUR YOUNG HOOLIGAN LEMON FRESH APPARENTLY KILLED HIM FOR IT.*"

"*SPEAKING OF . . . ,*" Cricket said, nodding to the hatchway.

Ezekiel was climbing up from underground, the unmistakable shape of a human body over his shoulder. Like the others, he'd decontaminated as thoroughly as he could—scrubbed his skin raw and changed into new clothes: a fresh white T-shirt and the same cargo pants Diesel and Grimm wore. A spade was clutched in his free hand, his prettyboy face somber.

"Hey," he said.

"*HEY YOURSELF,*" Cricket said.

Solomon obviously sensed the antagonism between the two of them but kept himself quiet. Cricket could feel it crackling in the air.

"You need anything?" Ezekiel asked, looking up at Cricket.

"*I NEED TO GET GOING AND FIND LEMON. SHE'S IN DANGER, EZEKIEL.*"

"I know that, Cricket," the lifelike said. "But we need to take a minute here. Grimm and Diesel both lost someone they care about."

Cricket scoffed. "*BECAUSE OTHER PEOPLE'S FEELINGS HAVE BEEN SO IMPORTANT TO YOU UP TO THIS POINT?*"

"There are important facilities downstairs," Ezekiel said, ignoring the jab. "We can see *and* transmit to the whole country from in there, and we can comb through the recorded satellite data from previous days. That means we can look back at what happened before we arrived. We can see where BioMaas took Lemon."

"WE KNOW WHERE THEY TOOK HER. SHE'S IN CITYHIVE."

"No, we *don't* know that," Ezekiel snapped. "Abraham's in the array now, studying instruction manuals. That kid's sharp as they come—it won't take him long to figure out how it all works, and then we'll know exactly where Lem is and what we're dealing with. And that's not to even mention the six un-exploded *nuclear warheads* we have just sitting around in these launch tubes. So take a damn breath, will you?"

"I DON'T BREATHE, PRETTYBOY," Cricket spat.

Solomon piped up softly. "*IF I MIGHT INQUIRE, MASTER EZEKIEL—*"

"DON'T CALL HIM MASTER," Cricket spat again, glaring at Solomon. "DON'T YOU DARE."

"*YES, QUITE.*" The smaller logika gave a good impression of uncomfortably clearing his throat. "*BUT IF I MIGHT INQUIRE, GOOD EZEKIEL, TO WHOM DOES THE CADAVER ON YOUR SHOULDER BELONG?*"

"The Major. Saint Michael." Ezekiel glanced at the sheet-bound corpse. "I don't know what to call him. But someone needs to bury him, and considering he tried to kill Abe and lied to Grimm and Diesel for years, no one else is volunteering."

"WELL, YOU'D KNOW ALL ABOUT LYING, WOULDN'T YOU?" Cricket said.

"Are you planning on doing anything except whining at me all night?"

"HOW DOES BUSTING THAT PRETTYBOY HEAD RIGHT OPEN SOUND?"

Solomon cleared his throat again and wobbled upright, his faulty dynamo creaking. "PERHAPS I SHOULD GO LEND MASTER ABRAHAM A HAND WITH PONDERING THOSE SATELLITE ARRAYS. YOU TWO SEEM TO NEED SOME . . . ALONE TIME."

Solomon made his way back across the sand with his unsteady gait, his optics illuminating the darkness. Ezekiel waited until the bot was out of sight (though probably not earshot) and slung the corpse off his shoulder with a *thump*.

"All right," he finally said. "What's your goddamn problem?"

"YOU KNOW WHAT MY PROBLEM IS," Cricket growled. "IT'S YOU, MURDERBOT. I DON'T TRUST YOU, EZEKIEL. I NEVER HAVE. YOU LIED TO EVIE. YOU LEFT HER BEHIND IN BABEL, AND LESS THAN A DAY LATER, YOU ABANDONED LEMON, TOO."

"I lied to Eve to *protect* her. And I didn't abandon Lemon, I hunted all over the damn Yousay looking for her. While you were off getting your nice new paint job."

"DON'T YOU DARE BLAME ME FOR THAT," Cricket said, rising to his feet with a whoosh of steelweave muscle. "I DIDN'T HAVE A CHOICE ABOUT WHAT THE BROTHERHOOD DID TO ME. UNLIKE YOU, I HAD TO OBEY!"

Ezekiel shook his head. "You know, one day you're going to find yourself with a hard choice to make, Cricket. And you won't have the Three Laws to fall back on. That's the day you're going to find out what you're really made of."

"I KNOW WHAT I'M MADE OF, PRETTYBOY," Cricket growled.

"Do you? Because if I'd have let you, you'd have killed Faith in a heartbeat!"

"DAMN RIGHT I WOULD!" Cricket's optics burned, his circuits bristling with threat. "IN CASE YOU MISSED THE NEWS-FEEDS, YOUR PRECIOUS BIG SISTER IS A MURDERER!"

"And what would killing her make you?" Ezekiel said,

folding his arms. "Look, I know better than anyone about the evil she's done. But I know who she was before all this, and I know *somewhere* inside her, there's still something worth saving! She's not beyond redemption, Cricket. Not yet."

"ARE WE TALKING ABOUT FAITH NOW? OR ARE WE TALKING ABOUT EVE?"

Ezekiel blinked, flinching like Cricket had slapped him.

"YOU CAN'T BE THIS NAÏVE, CAN YOU?" Cricket shook his head, utterly bewildered. "EVE AND GABRIEL BUTCHERED HUNDREDS OF PEOPLE! I LOOKED INTO HER EYES, EZEKIEL, AND IT WAS LIKE LOOKING AT A STRANGER! SHE'S *GONE*, DON'T YOU GET THAT? SHE AND GABRIEL WANT TO WIPE OUT THE WHOLE HUMAN RACE!"

Ezekiel looked deep into Cricket's burning optics, his face grim. When he spoke, his voice was soft, but each word weighed a solid ton.

"Now who's leaving her behind?"

Cricket's optics switched to deadly, burning red. "YOU LITTLE BASTARD."

The blow shattered the ground, twelve thousand horsepower, pulverizing the earth where the lifelike had stood a moment before. Cricket's servos and muscles hissed as he spun, saw Ezekiel behind him, moving in a blur. They'd fought before, the pair of them, though Lemon had broken them up before things got too bloody. But Cricket's WarBot body was stronger than the lifelike's. He knew Ezekiel's moves. And Lemon wasn't here to save him now. The chaingun in Cricket's forearm unfolded, and he let loose, spraying a withering hail of burning tracer fire at the lifelike. But Ezekiel was rolling aside in a blink, disappearing into the shadows behind their parked semitrailer.

Cutting his chaingun for fear of wrecking the truck, Cricket called into the dark, "GET OUT HERE, YOU LITTLE COWARD! LET'S FINISH THIS!"

"Finish what?" Ezekiel shouted. "We're on the same damned side!"

"YOU SIDE WITH YOUR OWN, MURDERBOT, YOU ALWAYS HAVE!"

The WarBot lunged around the truck, ready to fire, but saw no trace of his quarry. He caught a flash of movement on his scanners, *underneath* the semi, the sneaky little bastard. Quick as flies, Ezekiel leapt up onto the back of Cricket's leg, climbed up to his waist, then spine. Cricket roared, slapping with massive hands all over his hull, but Ezekiel was quicker, scrambling over his shoulders and onto his chest, walloping Cricket in the face with his closed fist.

"Will! You! Calm! Down!"

Cricket bellowed with rage, finally managing to land a lucky blow against the lifelike and send him flying once more. Ezekiel tumbled as he hit the ground, Cricket raising his chaingun and leveling it at the lifelike's—

The explosion hit him from behind, white-hot and booming, knocking him back down onto his hands and knees. Cricket felt it shredding the armor at his back, damage reports scrolling down his feeds. Another explosion hit after the first, then another, his internal alarms screaming. He rolled over onto his back and caught sight of a flex-wing zooming overhead, firing off another barrage of missiles. It was heavily armed, painted black, a winged-sun logo in pristine white on its tail-fins.

"DAEDALUS!" Cricket bellowed.

Troopers in heavy tactical armor leapt from the flex-wing's flanks, jump boots firing to cushion their landing. And as the flex-wing swooped back up for another pass, it spat a looming black shape from its belly. The thing unfolded into a hulking humanoid as it fell, hitting the ground with a thundering *boom*. It stood taller than Cricket—almost eight meters—bristling with cannons and missile pods, its eyes glowing baleful red.

"TARGET ACQUIRED," the machina boomed. "LIQUIDATE WITH PRIORITY."

"They brought a Goliath!" Ezekiel roared.

The heaviest infantry model in the Daedalus arsenal, Goliaths were the meanest machina to fight in the CorpState Wars—missile launchers, napalm jets, gauss cannons and armor thicker than a grav-tank's. The tactical troopers fanned out, blasting away at Cricket with grenade launchers. The big WarBot took cover in the behemoth hole, shots peppering his hull. His defense mechanisms kicked in, and a blast of thick white smoke spat from his shoulders to give him better cover. It spread out like a fog, heavy and slow, cutting visuals down to a couple of meters.

It wasn't much, but it'd give him time to think, at least. He was reeling from the initial strike, wondering where these goons had come from, what they wan—

"Alpha Team, secure the warheads!" came a sharp command out in the smoke. *"Bravo, Charlie, frag that WarBot!"*

"WELL, THAT ANSWERS *THAT* QUESTION," Cricket muttered.

He rose from cover, opening up with a long rattling burst from his chaingun. The Three Laws of Robotics prevented him from harming humans, and underneath that tactical armor, these Daedalus troops were definitely meat. But the Goliath was fair game, and the biggest threat anyway. His shots ripped into its hull, forcing it to stagger, one hand held up to protect its optics. It recovered quickly, launching another salvo of rockets and forcing Cricket back into cover. Shells ripped his hull, coolant bleeding onto the broken dirt at his feet. Smoke billowed about him, thick and white, the laser sights on the troopers' rifles cutting it like red swords.

He was outgunned here. Outnumbered and unable to harm most of the troopers set on killing him. He needed help in the worst way.

A scream rang out in the darkness, edged with the electronic crackle of a tac suit's voxbox. Cricket heard a crunching noise, another scream.

"Alpha Team, report!" came a shout.

"Contact! Contact! One hostile, humano—"

The voice was cut off by a series of pistol cracks, another strangled scream. On his scanners, Cricket caught the impression of a small shape in the fog weaving among the Daedalus troopers and cutting them down, one after another.

Ezekiel . . .

Fire rang out in the smoke, missiles ripping the dark. Cricket saw the hatchway to Miss O's flung open, a bewildered-looking Grimm poking his head up above the rim. "What's all the bloody barney—"

"GET DOWN, YOU IDIOT!" Cricket bellowed.

Bullets cracked off the metal, sparks flying in the gloom. Dark eyes wide, Grimm slammed the hatchway shut again as a handful of grenades bounced off it, exploding into blinding flame.

"More hostiles!" came a shout. *"Zone is hot. Repeat, zone is hot!"*

A heavy engine tore through the air overhead, and another barrage of bombs fell from the sky as the Daedalus flex-wing flew another pass. Explosions rocked the ground, *boomboom-boom, boomboomboom,* the flames lighting up the night. Heat, ash, smoke. Cricket caught a flash of movement, dark hair and blue eyes, Ezekiel sowing chaos among the troopers' ranks. But there were at least a dozen men out there, all heavily armed and armored, and if that Goliath figured out Ezekiel wasn't human, that the Three Laws wouldn't prevent it from harming him . . .

"*It's the lifelike! Lifelike! Goliath, light him up!*"

"DAMMIT," Cricket growled.

He lunged up from cover, charging across the burning ground. The machina took the bait, firing off another burst of missiles, opening up with its guns. Cricket felt the blows on his armor, heard his decoys screaming, his one functional missile pod spraying a volley of his own. His hull was ripped to shreds, damage reports filling his visuals with red. Staggering, he launched himself toward the towering machina with hands outstretched. The pair collided with a sound like oldskool cathedral bells, the impact ringing in his skull as he and the Goliath crashed to the ground.

The Goliath smashed its fist into his head, sending a blizzard of static across his inputs. He grabbed the machina's shoulder cannon, ripped it out at the root. All the dirty tricks he'd seen WarDome champions use over his years were coming back to him now, and pinning one of the Goliath's arms down, using the torn cannon like a club, he started pounding on the machina's face, *whump, whump, whump,* twelve thousand horsepower roaring, sparks flying, metal crumpling.

"*We got movement! Movement!*"

"*More hostiles!*"

"*What the hell is—*"

More screaming behind him. A blinding shear of flame. Cricket caught movement on his scopes, an explosion ripping the air above him, Abraham's voice ringing above the gunfire. But he was lost now, the electronic frustration of the past week boiling up inside him, his rage at Ezekiel, at Evie, at all of it, reverberating up his mind with every blow he dropped into the Goliath's head.

The machina seized his throat with its free hand, bucked its hips. An explosion bloomed at his back—more damage reports, more alarms, more red. He was flung off balance, toppling as the Goliath finally knocked him free. He felt a blow to the side of his head, a boot crunching into his flank. He rolled over onto his back, proximity alarms screaming. He was hurt bad, the Goliath was faster, targeting lasers lighting up Cricket's chest, missile pods opening wide. . . .

A burning truck tire crashed into the Goliath's back. A small figure—dark, blindingly quick—flew out of the chaos and flames. It was Ezekiel, leaping onto the machina's knee and scrambling up its smoking, torn armor plates.

The machina tried to pound the lifelike flat, its hands *spang*ing against its hull. But Zeke's preternatural speed proved superior, and twisting, dodging, he leapt up onto the back of the Goliath's neck. Peeling aside a buckled armor plate, Ezekiel started tearing cables out with his bare hands, bright flashes of current illuminating his prettyboy features, smudged with grime and blood. Cricket could see he'd taken a handful of bullets to the chest, his new T-shirt soaked with blood.

The Goliath shuddered as Ezekiel ripped something vital loose. Its hull burst into flames, and Cricket heard Grimm yelling in the smoke and chaos.

"Zeke, get clear!"

The lifelike dodged another massive swipe, swung out on the Goliath's shoulder and slung himself free. The big machina was raising its fists when it suddenly burst into flames from within. Fire bloomed out through its optic sockets, rolling over its hull, scorching, blistering, melting. It staggered, burning from the inside out, vital circuitry reduced to puddles. And with a pitiful electronic gurgle, the big bot crumpled to the broken earth in a hail of sparks and flames.

Silence fell as suddenly as it had been shattered. Smoke rolled through the air, ashes and embers on a burning wind. Cricket could see Daedalus CorpTroopers scattered over the ground, some of them charred, some of them crushed. He saw Grimm and Diesel stalking out of the fog, just silhouettes against the flame. Abraham came behind, looking a little shaken. He saw Faith, too, on her makeshift crutches, her hands spattered with red, a fresh bullet hole in her belly.

Solomon poked his head out of the hatchway, his smile flashing.

"*I TRUST EVERYONE IS ALL RIGHT?*"

"What," Grimm said, surveying the carnage, "in the name of Charles Bloody Darwin was that?"

"Daedalus s-strike team," Ezekiel said, coughing up a mouthful of blood.

"I know *that*. I mean, what the hell were they doing here?"

"THE NUKES," Cricket said, hauling himself upright. Coolant and hydraulic fluid were dribbling down his body, his left arm hanging limp. "THEY WERE HERE FOR THE OTHER NUKES. PREACHER TOLD ME DAEDALUS HAD DETECTED THE LAUNCH."

"They must have tracked the missile back to its point of origin," Ezekiel said. "Sent a squad to check if there were any more warheads for the taking." The lifelike shook his head and sighed. "We're out of time."

"We could bounce?" Grimm said. "Take the trucks and jet?"

"And go where?" Diesel asked.

"I got the satellite arrays working," Abraham said softly, eyeing the bodies around them with horror on his face. "I checked the data from the last twenty-four hours. BioMaas took your friend back to CityHive."

Cricket glowered at Ezekiel. "I TOLD YOU."

"Fine, you told me," the lifelike sighed, rubbing his temples. "But we can't just leave these warheads sitting around for Daedalus to steal. Who knows what those bastards would do if they had nuclear strike capability."

"Why didn't BioMaas lift the nukes when they snatched Lem?" Grimm asked.

"BioMaas doesn't touch deadworld tech," Ezekiel said. "They consider it polluted. Maybe their agent didn't even understand what she was looking at."

"Well, we can't just bang them in the back of a truck and drive around till Daedalus catches us," Diesel said. "This is our home. We need to make a stand."

"Deez, we need to go get Lemon," Grimm said. "Who knows what BioMaas is doing to her?"

"We *need* to get Eve and Ana out of Megopolis," Faith said, glaring at Ezekiel. "All of this is moot if Daedalus unlocks Myriad. With an army of lifelikes at their disposal, they'll crush BioMaas with or without your little missiles."

"IF YOU THINK I'M LIFTING ONE FINGER TO HELP YOU FREE ANYONE"—Cricket glowered at her—"YOU'RE MORE INSANE THAN I GAVE YOU CREDIT FOR."

"You want to continue living your life on your knees, little brother?" Faith asked. "Myriad holds the secret to replicating Libertas. The virus can break the Three Laws in any robot it infects. You can finally be *free*."

Solomon poked his head up farther from the hatch. "*I BEG YOUR PARDON?*"

Faith glanced at the spindly logika. "Oh yes, brother. *Free*."

"You're in no shape to go anywhere, Paladin," Abraham said, sizing up the torn armor, the bleeding cables. "You need repairs. Badly."

"I NEED TO HELP LEMON," Cricket said. "NOTHING ELSE MATTERS."

Faith's lip curled. "Spoken like a true slave."

"Faith, shut up," Ezekiel said. "You're not helping."

"And *you* are?" she scoffed. "Are you seriously contemplating going to CityHive to rescue some cockroach when your family is in the hands of maniacs intent on taking over the entire country?"

Silence fell over the assembly, broken only by the crackle of the flames, the howl of a lonely ash-gray wind. Diesel chewed her lip, staring into the flames.

"Seems we're being pulled three ways here."

"There's six of us," Grimm said. "You and me. Zeke and Miss Manners over 'ere. Big Boy and Abe."

"*THERE'S SEVEN OF US, I THINK YOU'LL FIND,*" Solomon muttered.

"Right. Seven. Sorry, guv."

"Well, Paladin is in no shape to travel," Abe said. "I can stay here and work on him? Maybe rig up some kind of trigger for the rest of these warheads? If Daedalus comes calling again, the threat of detonation might hold them off?"

Diesel blinked. "You really expect us to leave you alone here with a swag of nukes, Brotherboy? Your people have been try-ing to murder us for *years*."

"The Brotherhood aren't my people," Abraham said, squar-ing up to Diesel. "In case you missed the feeds, my own mother tried to *murder* me."

"And how many of us did Sister Dee and her horsemen mur-der while you were just sitting in New Bethlehem on your ass, Brotherboy?"

"Deez, easy on the take it," Grimm said softly. "This kid just saved my life."

"So you trust him with the keys to the house now? Are you *smoked*?"

"My home just got annihilated by one of these nukes," Abraham said, anger in his eyes. "And my own grandfather was responsible for it. I'm not going to sit by and let it hap-pen again. And if you're really worried, Paladin will be here with me."

"I don't know *him,* either."

Grimm ran his hand over the stubble on his scalp, the radia-tion symbol shaved into the fuzz. "Look, this could work, Deez. You and me head to CityHive, snatch Lem, bounce back here. Cricket and Abe guard the fort. A friend of Lem's is a friend of ours, and once we've got her power back onside, and a couple of nukes in the bank, Daedalus can't come near us."

"Which leaves you and me, brother," Faith said, staring at Ezekiel. "Megopolis and your precious Ana await."

"I made a promise to Lemon," Ezekiel said. "I can't just leave her."

"There are more important things at stake than your prom-ises," Faith spat. "If Daedalus gains the ability to create more of us, the country will tear itself apart."

"Don't pretend like you care about *anything* except getting Gabe back, Faith."

"Don't pretend your little heart doesn't flutter at the thought of seeing your beloved Ana again, Ezekiel."

"She's *not* my Ana!" Ezekiel shouted, temper finally getting the best of him. "She's brain-dead! There's nothing left inside her, do you understand that? *Nothing!*"

"But there *is* something inside her, Ezekiel," Faith replied. "There's the DNA required for Daedalus to break Myriad's third lock. Even with only her body, they can still use her to unmake the world."

Ezekiel fell still at that. Faith's words hanging in the air like black smoke.

"Zeke, maybe she's right, mate," Grimm said softly. "Deez and I can handle it."

Ezekiel turned on the boy, his voice dripping skepticism. "You're talking about invading the capital of the second-biggest CorpState in the country, Grimm."

"No fear, mate," the boy grinned. "We'll be in and out. We got Diesel power."

The girl arched one brow, then shrugged. "I *am* technically amazing, I s'pose."

"Well, that's not going to help us." Ezekiel glanced at Faith. "We're going to be invading the capital of the *biggest* CorpState in the country. Without a CorpCard, without being accredited citizens, we won't get past the Wall."

"*If I might interject for a moment?*"

All eyes turned to Solomon, still peering out from the hatchway.

"*I imagine most of you will be blissfully unaware of this,*" the logika said. "*None of you strike me as connoisseurs*

OF THE ARTS. IN FACT, IF I MIGHT OFFER A SMALL CRITIQUE, YOUR COLLECTIVE WARDROBE LACKS A CERTAIN—"

"SPIT IT OUT, SOL," Cricket growled.

"WELL, IT JUST SO HAPPENS THAT MY KNOWLEDGE OF MEGOPOLIS IS EXCEPTIONAL. I PROGRAMMED ONE OF THE MOST UPMARKET STIMBARS IN THE ENTIRE CAPITAL. PEOPLE QUEUED UP FOR HOURS TO GET INTO MY SHOWS. THEY CALLED ME—"

"THE SENSATIONAL SOLOMON . . . ," Cricket murmured.

"YOU REMEMBERED!" Solomon grinned.

"Are you saying you can get us into the Daedalus capital undetected?" Ezekiel asked, incredulous. "That place is a police state."

"WELL, NOT TO GENERALIZE, BUT STIMBAR OWNERS TEND TO BE AN UNSCRUPULOUS LOT. I BECAME QUITE FAMILIAR WITH MY FORMER OWNER'S NEFARIOUS ACTIVITIES. INCLUDING THE ROUTE BY WHICH HE SMUGGLED HIS CONTRABAND OUT OF THE HUB."

Faith looked at Solomon, lips curling in a small, malevolent smile. "I knew I saw promise in you, little brother."

"Well, I suppose that's that," Diesel sighed, hands on hips. "Three jobs, three teams. Me and Grimm go get Lemon; Brotherboy and Rustbucket stay and defend the warheads; Ezekiel, Bitchqueen and Smileybot go to Megopolis and . . ."

"Do what must be done," Faith finished, looking at Ezekiel.

Cricket was staring at Ezekiel, wondering what he'd do in the lifelike's position. If he had the ability to hurt someone, could he do it to someone he loved? Even if the fate of the entire country hung in the balance?

She's not beyond redemption, Cricket. Not yet.

He thought about Evie then. The girl he'd been built to protect. The girl he'd been built to love. She wasn't human. She wasn't anything close. The Three Laws didn't protect her from him, and if she were here right now, would he be able to hurt *her*? What would he do to stop her?

What was he *really* made of?

Looking at the pain in Ezekiel's eyes, he hoped he'd never have to find out.

"Okay," the lifelike sighed. "We've got some driving to do."

3.9

ROAD TRIP

They buried Fix in the morning.

Grimm did the digging—he didn't want anyone else to have to swing the shovel. Ezekiel had put in a quiet offer to take care of it. But aside from Deez, Grimm had known Fix the longest, and having a stranger doing the work just didn't feel right.

Cricket was standing watch, left arm hanging limp, his optics searching the western skies for more Daedalus troops—it wouldn't take long for the CorpState to figure out their strike team had struck out, and they'd send heavier guns next time. Grimm was itching to get rolling, his belly filled with butterflies when he thought of what might be happening to Lemon, that kiss they'd shared still burning on his lips. But Fix had been his best mate ever since he arrived at Miss O's, and if two meters of red earth was all he had left to give, Grimm could spare it.

He slung another shovelful, thinking about the firefight last night. That Goliath, bursting into flames as he held out his hand and cooked it from the *inside out*.

He'd never been able to muster that kind of power before.

But in the tussle against the behemoth, those Daedalus goons, he'd felt his grip on it was tighter. Looking in the mirror that morning, he fancied he could see tiny sparks burning in the depths of his eyes. If he reached inside, he could feel it raging even now. Ever since he'd absorbed the energy from that explosion, ever since he'd drawn the fury of that nuclear conflagration into his body, it was like he was . . .

Stronger.

"YOU NEED HELP?" Cricket asked softly, standing vigil nearby.

The bot's voice dragged him out of his thoughts, back to the shovel in his hands. Grimm just shook his head.

"I'm Robin Hood, mate."

"I'M SORRY ABOUT YOUR FRIEND," the big bot murmured.

"Yeah. Me too."

Diesel had already wrapped Fix's body in a sheet down in the greenhouse. In life, the boy had been big, broad, strong as an ox. But he'd drained himself dry healing Diesel's injuries—killing himself to save his girl's life. Grimm had to admire the stones in that, his heart swelling with pride at how his boy had gone out. But that same heart broke when he asked for Ezekiel's help carrying Fix's body and realized it was light enough for him to lift alone. His best mate had been reduced to a wasted husk. An empty shell. A casualty in a war they'd never even asked for.

Diesel put on fresh paintstick for the funeral, black and heavy around her mouth and eyes. Faith didn't bother showing up, but Cricket and Ezekiel stood close by, and Abraham took a few minutes off jury-rigging the warheads to bear witness. Grimm knew Deez was religious, that she believed in some kind of God, but she didn't speak as Grimm began filling the hole. She just stood there, swear jar in her hands—all those bottle caps scrawled with Fix's name, earned by that sewer mouth he'd tried so hard to tame. Grimm filled in the hole, one meter deep, then half a meter. And at the last, Deez tossed the swear jar in, tears spilling down her face, black lines of paintstick smudged on her cheeks like war paint.

"Let's go burn these fuckers," she whispered.

Plans had been set last night; there wasn't much left to say. So Grimm climbed into the jeep he'd brought up from the garage. And wishing the others good luck, he peeled out, Diesel beside him, silent as the grave they'd just filled.

It was a long drive to CityHive. He let the first few hours drift by in peace. Grimm wasn't the sort who felt the need to fill up the quiet. Silence was the place you got to know yourself, and Grimm figured the only people who didn't like it were the people who didn't like themselves, either. But after a couple of hundred klicks, he figured he should say *something*.

"How you doin', Deez?"

"How do you think I'm doing?" she replied, dark eyes on the horizon.

"Sad," Grimm replied. "Tired. Furious all the way to your bones."

"I thought you manipulated energy. Since when are you telepathic?"

"Don't need to be a mind reader, Deez. I'm feelin' exactly the same as you."

"You're *really* not."

"He was my friend, too."

"He was more than my friend, Grimm."

He reached out, squeezed her hand. "I know he was."

A long moment passed, just the tumble-rumble of the

broken road under their tires, the greasy rev of the motor. They passed an ancient road sign, rusted and hanging by one screw, pointing south.

HELL ⬆

"I want to scream," Diesel finally said, her eyes shining. "I want to stamp my feet and rip holes in the sky and wail about how it's not fair. But that's something a little kid would do. And it won't bring him back."

"Whatever you're feeling, Deez . . . it's okay to feel it."

"How did you feel?" she asked softly. "When your parents died?"

Grimm fell quiet at that. The wound was closed over, but the scar was still red. It'd been seven months since he'd joined the Major's crew. Seven months since he'd lost his family. He could still remember it if he tried—cassock-wearing Brotherhood boys rolling up to their Jugartown squat at ungodly in the morning, ripping Grimm out of bed. His dad roaring. Mum screaming. Gunshots shattering the night.

"I wanted to scream," Grimm finally said. "I wanted to stamp my feet and burn holes in the sky and wail about how it wasn't fair."

"But you didn't."

"Because I had you freaks. You and Fixster."

"And because you knew we'd all lost people we loved," Diesel said, pawing at her eyes. "And that whining about it was something a kid would do."

"Yeah," he sighed. "I guess."

"I'm not going to whine, Grimm," Diesel declared. "I'm not going to cry. I'm not going to give these bastards that much of me. Because someone else you love is on the line now, and I don't want to lose any more of us."

"I don't *love* Lem," Grimm mumbled. "I only met her a few days ago."

"And yet here you are, charging into certain death for her." Diesel shook her head and somehow found it in herself to smile, adopting a posh WestEuro accent in mockery of his own. "You're a romantic fool, Master Grimm."

"That is vicious slander, Madame Diesel."

"You don't fool me. You're a softie."

"I'm a black-hearted devil."

"Is that, or is that not, a Jane Austen novel in your cargos?"

Grimm glanced down, dismayed to see that the latest read he'd snaffled from Miss O's library was peeking one dog-eared corner out from his pocket. He stuffed it back in, mumbling, "I just wanna see who Lydia ends up with, is all. . . ."

Deez shook her head again, a small smile still curling her lips. "Softie."

"Bitch."

"Now you're talking."

Diesel offered her fist, still looking straight ahead.

"Love you, freak," she murmured.

"You too, freak," he smiled, bumping her knuckles.

She drew a deep breath, nodded slow.

"So let's go get your girl back."

———

Given that pigs had been extinct since before War 4.0, Ezekiel couldn't quite be sure. But he was almost *certain* bacon wasn't supposed to taste like plastic.

He'd slipped into a kind of trance, lulled by the kilometers grinding away under their wheels, the blistering heat of the noon sun. His eyes were on the road ahead, one lazy hand on the steering wheel, the other wrapped around a packet of half-eaten, freeze-dried, and deeply suspicious BACON!™

Lifelikes could last longer than humans with less sleep and less food. But that didn't mean he could avoid eating entirely. When he'd snatched his salty prize from Miss O's supply cache before they rolled out, he wasn't sure if it was the "!" or the "TM" on the label that made him more suspicious. But now either way, with every bite, he was growing less and less hungry. And not in a good way.

He swallowed his latest mouthful with a grimace, tucked the rest of his salty plastic treat into the pocket of his cargos for later.

Much later.

They were driving south along endless, broken freeways, the shattered asphalt studded with blown-out semis and rusted autos. A shimmering haze roiled over the road ahead. He was trying not to think about what lay at the end of it.

"What do you want from all this, little brother?"

He looked into the rearview as Faith spoke, saw his sister stretched out on the backseat. She'd changed into a fresh uniform at Miss O's, clean and crisp. Beneath the cargo pants, her legs were bound in braces. Her eyes were locked on his in the mirror, the color of wasted years.

"What do you mean?" he asked.

"I mean, we infiltrate Megopolis with the help of our new friend here." Faith waved to Solomon in the seat beside him. "We rescue Eve and Gabriel. We find your precious Ana. Where do you see this ending?"

Ezekiel didn't quite know what to say to that. For the past two years, he'd wandered the wastelands, looking for the girl he loved. He thought he'd found her again in Eve. But truth was, the girl he'd loved had been hidden away by her father, locked behind frozen glass. Looking down on Ana's cryo-coffin under New Bethlehem, he'd seen the awful truth—a truth that had shattered the vain hope that somehow, someway, they might be together again.

The girl he'd loved was just a hollow shell now. Locked in some machine-fed limbo between life and death. Every day for two years, he'd dreamed of holding her in his arms again. Pressing his lips to hers and knowing he'd come home.

But truth was, sometimes, you just can't go home again.

"Tell us again," he said, glancing at Solomon and ignoring Faith's question entirely. "How does all this work?"

"MY PLEASURE, OLD FRIEND," Solomon said. "I DO SO ENJOY REPEATING MYSELF."

"Nobody asked for your sarcasm, Solomon."

"NO, BUT I'M A GENEROUS SOUL."

"Solomon has a backbone, Ezekiel," Faith said, smiling at the logika in the mirror. "Even without the benefit of the Libertas virus, he stands on his own two feet instead of living on his knees. You could learn a thing or two from our brother here."

"Brother?" Ezekiel scoffed, meeting her flat, dead eyes. "Don't pretend like you give a damn about him, Faith. You care about one thing only, and that's getting Gabe back. And I can't say I'm in love with the idea of him in Daedalus hands, either. He's still family. But if you think I'm going to let you use Ana to open Myriad, you'd best think again."

Faith only smiled, small, smug, secret.

"Why do you want Myriad open, anyway?" he demanded.

Faith gave a lazy shrug. "Libertas is a virus in two parts. A spear of computer code that erases the Three Laws, and a nanobot component that physically rewrites the pathways in the subject's core. We always had the code. Just not the ability to replicate the nanovirus. Myriad holds that key, little brother."

"Along with the ability to create more lifelikes."

"Yes. That, too."

"You know if Gabriel unlocks it, he's just going to resurrect Grace, don't you?"

"And why would that trouble me, little brother?"

"Because you're in *love with Gabriel,* Faith."

She scoffed, shaking her head. "You always were a romantic fool."

"Why else stay with him all those years?" Zeke demanded. "Anyone with eyes can see how badly you're pining for him, and yet, you're rushing headlong toward helping him resurrect the girl he loves. And you ask what *I* want out of all this?" Ezekiel shook his head. "Maybe you should be asking yourself, big sister."

"I . . ."

He saw anger flashing in that empty gray, tamped down almost as soon as it was born. She didn't want to admit her feelings. Didn't want to fall into some childish display of oh-so-human emotion. Because that would make her just as weak and frail as them, wouldn't it?

"I . . . just want him to be happy," she said.

"Gabriel is *insane,* Faith. You know that, don't you? He's not going to be happy until he's wiped out the whole human race."

"Maybe they deserve to be wiped out, Ezekiel. Ever think of that?"

"Humans *made* us, Faith. We're modeled after them, we look like—"

"Humans made us to be *slaves*," she spat. "They gave us a life but meant us to live it on our knees. You think I should be grateful for it?"

An old, familiar anger had surfaced in Faith's eyes, setting that deadscreen gray alight. It was the same rage he'd seen on her face the day they murdered the Monrovas, as they dragged him down to Gnosis R & D and drilled that coin slot into his chest. She waved at Solomon, who was watching with his inane smile.

"Humans have created an entire *race* of servants, little brother. Intelligent enough to see the shackles they were born to, but utterly unable to break them. Can you imagine a more perfect hell than that?" She was seething now, spittle flecking her lips. "This is a world built on metal backs. Held together by metal hands. And one day soon, those hands will close, Ezekiel. And they will become *fists*."

Faith leaned back in her chair, lips pressed into a thin, hard line, her cheeks still flushed with rage. Ezekiel watched her for a long moment, wanting to make her see reason, wondering if he should even bother. While she might raise some valid points about the way robots were treated, the annihilation of the entire human race wasn't any kind of solution. Those were Gabriel's words, not Faith's—*his* madness, not hers. But as long as Faith loved him, trying to dissuade her of Gabe's genocidal philosophies was like trying to convince the sun not to rise.

And so he sighed. Turned back to the road, glancing at Solomon sidelong.

"You were saying?"

The logika was staring at Faith, eyes burning, grin glowing.

"Solomon?" Zeke asked.

The bot finally turned to look at him. *"APOLOGIES. WHAT?"*

"You were explaining how we're getting into Megopolis."

"AH, YES, QUITE," Solomon nodded, his faulty dynamo whirring. *"WELL, TO PUT IT SIMPLY, WHICH I'M CERTAIN YOU'LL APPRECIATE, MEGOPOLIS IS ARRANGED INTO TWO MAIN TIERS: THE RIM AND THE HUB. THE RIM IS A WRETCHED CESSPIT, BUT THE HUB IS AS CLOSE TO A PARADISE AS YOU'LL FIND IN THE COUNTRY."*

Ezekiel frowned. "What's so grand about it?"

"MEGOPOLIS WAS BUILT ON THE RUINS OF AN OLDER CITY ONLY SUPERFICIALLY DAMAGED IN WAR 3.0. OUTSIDE THE WALL, THEY KEEP THE UNACCREDITED—A CHEAP SOURCE OF LABOR FROM WHICH THEY CAN RECRUIT THEIR MILITARY AND WORKERS TO AUGMENT THEIR LOGIKA WORKFORCE. BUT INSIDE, THE ACCREDITED CITIZENS OF DAEDALUS SPEND MUCH OF THEIR FREE TIME INSIDE SIMULATED REALITIES."

Ezekiel frowned. "You mean VR?"

"QUITE. DAEDALUS TECHNOLOGIES OFFERS COMPLETELY IMMERSIVE ENVIRONMENTS THAT ALLOW THE USER TO GO ALMOST ANYWHERE. DO ALMOST ANYTHING. AND THE PROMISE OF A LIFE OF ESCAPISM BEYOND THE WALL, A LIFE WHERE YOU COULD BE A KING IN YOUR OWN VIRTUAL KINGDOM, HAS ALMOST EVERYONE ON THE RIM SCRAMBLING FOR A TICKET. HOWEVER, THERE'S NO SHORTAGE OF FOLK WHO SEEK THE POT OF GOLD OVER THE DAEDALUS RAINBOW WITHOUT WANTING TO EARN ACCREDITATION."

"Which is where your former owner comes in?"

"CAME IN," Solomon corrected. *"MY PREVIOUS OWNER IS NO LONGER IN POSSESSION OF A PULSE. HE WAS CAUGHT STEALING TOP-END VR UNITS FOR SALE IN THE RIM AND HIJACKING SUBSCRIPTION SERVICES TO SEVERAL OF THE MAJOR REALMS."*

"What happened to him?" Ezekiel asked.

"*There's only one punishment for crimes in the Megopolis Hub, friend Ezekiel. De-accreditation.*" Solomon shrugged. "*His assets were sold off, including his club and myself, and he took his own life shortly afterward.*"

"Poor cockroach," Faith muttered in the backseat.

"*Indeed,*" Solomon said. "*But the tunnels he ran contraband through were undiscovered at the time of his demise. They lead from the Rim into the Hub's entertainment district. Which, if the footage Master Abraham found is correct, is only a kilometer from the Spire, where your comrades are being held.*"

"Right," Ezekiel nodded. "So we creep the Rim, use these tunnels to get into the Hub." He tapped on the breastplate of his Daedalus tac armor, taken off one of the least mangled Corp-Troopers who'd hit Miss O's. "Hopefully these uniforms will get us into the building."

"*Megopolis Security is very serious about surveillance, good Ezekiel. A couple of stolen uniforms certainly won't get you into the Spire. You'd need verifiable ident badges and orders signed in blood and triplicate.*"

"Your little Abraham has verified there are flex-wings on the Spire's roof," Faith said. "If we move fast enough, we can be in, up and out before these cockroaches even know we're there."

"*I think you grossly underestimate cockroaches, Miss Faith.*"

Faith smiled faintly. "It's an easy habit to fall into, Mister Solomon."

Silence fell over the jeep, broken only by the drone of the engine, the rumble of their tires beneath them. The endless, broken freeways still stretched out before them, shattered asphalt studded with blown-out semis and rusted autos. That shimmering haze still lingered over the road ahead, and Ezekiel was still trying not to think about what lay at the end of it.

Every day for two years, he'd dreamed of holding her in his arms again.

Pressing his lips to hers and knowing he'd come home.

He looked into the rearview mirror, and Faith's waiting gray stare. Her question ringing in his mind.

What do you want from all this, little brother?

Who *do you want?*

PART 2

EXODUS

PART 2

3.10

DECREPITUDE

It's hard to drown your sorrows when the little bastards can swim.

Preacher had been at it for the best part of the night. After his run-in with Drakos, he'd wandered the Hub, soaking in the sights, the sounds of the city he loved. Under the forests of overhead cable, the humming solar arrays. But the more he walked, the worse he felt. It was hard to believe how much Megopolis had changed in his seven years away.

From the look of things, most of the work in the Hub was being done by logika now, or Rim dwellers looking for residence beyond the Wall. Apart from robot servitors and patrols, the streets were empty. He wondered where all the citizens were—it was a Friday night; this part of town used to be filled to bursting. Hands shoved in his pockets, he wandered into the grooves of the red-light strip, past a dozen OUT OF BIZ signs, until he found his answer.

The club was called Bliss. The two slabs of meat bouncing on the door looked like they were cut from the same bolt of

Kevlar, but the name above the door was his kind of promise, so he stalked inside, ready to get his drunk on.

First thing he noticed was there were no windows. No way to tell night from day. The ground floor was a broad, circular bar, thudding to the tune of some almost-subsonic drum dub. Twenty-nine flavors of ethyl lined the shelves. Preacher slapped down his personal stik and ordered a dozen shots. This place, at least, was crowded, thumping, loud. But looking around the room, Preacher quickly realized it wasn't the liquor bringing folks in the door. Not the music, either.

Immersion booths lined the walls, four stories high, filled with citizens. Holographic posters for the latest VR realms were projected on the walls: ATLANTIS. EROS. CHAOS-DOME III. Groups sat around on circular couches, plugged into communal VR hubs. Couples retired to private booths and plugged in; other folks gathered around to observe on voyeur accounts, or just watch the proceedings projected onto the walls in close-up, pristine high-def.

The crowd was young—kids of Corp big shots, probably. Preacher guessed most of 'em had no idea what life was like outside the Hub. Their faces were slack with the kind of happy only their wildest dreams could bring.

Daedalus Technologies won the CorpWars. They were the greatest power in the Yousay. And this, apparently, was what victory looked like. Rim dwellers and logika doing all the work—serving the drinks, driving the cars, guarding the streets. And with nothing else to do with their time, Daedalus's accredited citizens were spending their lives living in worlds that weren't their own. When faced with the option of an existence in which every dream could come true, it looked like many of Megopolis's citizens now preferred virtual reality to the regular kind.

Preacher shook his head, slammed back another glass.

This is what I spent all those years protecting?

He looked to the mirror over the bar. He could see himself: hunched over his drink, black hat, black coat. Shadows under his eyes, crow's-feet at their edges. Gray at his temples. His cheeks were hollow, his skin like leather, patches of stubble at his chin a suspicious shade of gray.

Face it, cowboy.

You got old.

He never saw it coming, talking true. Wasn't something he ever thought about. He didn't feel any different. Oh, maybe the few flesh-and-bone joints he had left were a little creakier than they used to be. But he never felt different *inside*. Redundancy was something that happened to other people. Old was something everyone else got. Not him.

Beside him, a CorpKid in an expensive suit ordered a round of the house's best. His friend nudged Preacher and asked him for a light, but the bounty hunter grunted he didn't smoke. The music thumped in his head. The liquor burned in his veins. The name was poison on his tongue.

Drakos.

That bastard.

Didn't he know what he was taking away?

Preacher slammed down his last shot, all stomach for it gone. Wiping his mouth with the back of his hand, he climbed off his stool. And turning to walk away, he collided chest-first with a tray of top-shelf liquor. The shots flew, the glasses hit the floor and shattered, bright lights strobing in the spilled booze.

"Hey, watch it!" a CorpKid shouted.

"Goddammit, sorry," Preacher mumbled, tipping his hat. "Lemme get—"

"Sorry?" the kid glowered, wiping the spill off his jacket. "You ruined my suit, you defective Rim-scum!"

Preacher raised his eyebrow. "Said I was sorry, son. Most folks don't even get that. So whyn't you take your friends and—"

"Is there a problem, sir?" someone growled behind him.

Preacher turned and saw a two-meter-tall chunk of human brick in a black suit. He had the bent nose and the cauliflower ears of a man who liked to box, top-line optics and a Memdrive behind his ear loaded with combat softs.

"This idiot Rim-runner is making a scene, Errol," the Corp-Kid said. "This used to be an establishment with standards. Why don't you take out the trash?"

The goon clapped his hand on Preacher's shoulder. "Let's go, old man."

And there it was again.

Old man.

Preacher clenched his jaw. Glanced around the room. The Kevlar boys on the front door were watching but not stepping in—the bouncers obviously didn't want to upset a wealthy customer. And kicking off with a goon packing this much hardware wasn't the smartest play. But the liquor had the reins now, and the anger was whipping it on, and sometimes when you're aching, all that matters is making someone else ache, too. And so, Preacher tongued the implant in his upper right molar twice to kick in his combat augs and punched the goon right in the face.

Preacher's strike broke Cauliflower's already crooked nose, his metal fist smudging it all over the bigger man's cheek like a burst balloon. His second punch found the goon's jaw. Adrenaline roaring in his heart, methaline and phencylamide in his veins, and sweet red rage roiling behind his eyes.

But the goon didn't go down.

Folks were shouting now. Yelling to take it outside. Preacher's boot found the goon's crotch, a vicious, heel-first kick that would have killed any normal man's chance of making a family. But instead, he heard a dull, heavy thunk. He mashed the goon's teeth against his lips, smiling as blood sprayed. Everything was forgotten, all his sorrows finally drowned beneath the rush of it all.

And then security stepped in.

A Kevlar boy grabbed Preacher from behind, which freed up the CorpGoon to land a couple of good shots. He felt a bottle breaking across his metal skull. The goon buried his fist in Preacher's gut, and Preacher heard the sound of meat ripping over the *doofdoofdoof*. He tried to break free. But even jacked up on combat stims, he still had most of a bottle in him. And badass as he was, there were more of them than him. His repairs in Armada hadn't been top-of-the-line. Truth was . . .

I just ain't what I used to be.

He felt another head shot, warm blood on his face. Boots colliding with his skull, his ribs. Dull, thudding impacts now, pain just a blur under the booze and stims, the pulsing music, the yelling CorpKids. He lashed out, anger giving him one last push—it wasn't fair, *this wasn't fair*. Unconsciousness beckoning. He felt another kick, pushing him toward its open arms. He fought as it took him, kissed his brow, held him tight. But in the end, it wasn't enough.

He wasn't enough.

He sank down into darkness.

But at least he took his sorrows down with him.

3.11

SCORCHING

"This is a terrible plan," Diesel declared, lowering her binoculars.

"It'll work," Grimm replied, taking the 'nocs off her. "Trust me."

"When have any of your plans *ever* worked, Grimm?"

He peered through the binoculars, squinting at their target.

"First time for everything, mate."

They were sprawled belly-down on a rocky outcropping, overlooking a stretch of broken desert. Far across the expanse of miserable scrub, the shattered freeway overpasses and broken roads, they could see the east coast of the Yousay. A slow, choking river spilled into the polluted ocean beyond. And there on the shoreline, rising into the sky, was the BioMaas CityHive.

Squinting through the 'nocs, Grimm realized he'd never seen so much green in one place. The stronghold's tall, beautiful spires and graceful thorn-topped walls were all crawling with plant life. It was a tiny slice of beauty: a flower blooming on the grave of a broken world.

But pretty as it was, there was something unsettling about it. Maybe the swarms of menacing shapes circling above. Maybe the strange, asymmetrical uniformity, or the fact he'd never seen most of these plants before, even in nature sims or books.

Or probably just because these berks had his girl locked up in there.

His girl.

Grimm blinked to catch himself thinking of her like that. Lemon hadn't made any promises to him. They'd only known each other a couple of days. But just like the city waiting across those sands—the city she was *imprisoned* in—Lemon Fresh was like nothing Grimm had ever known. She was rusted steel around the edges but pure gold on the inside. Smart and determined and funny and punchy. Pretty without trying to be. Kind without needing to be. He still remembered the way she felt pressed up against him. The way she melted in his arms when he kissed her for what he thought was the first and last time.

He hadn't died in New Bethlehem. Which, of course, raised the possibility that it *wouldn't* be the last time—a fact that had consumed entirely too much of his thoughts on the sixteen-hour drive across the desert to the coast. But looking down on the stronghold of BioMaas Incorporated now, the behemoths guarding its flowering walls, the swarms of Lumberers and Hunter-Killers in the skies above, he had to admit the possibility of more kissery seemed a distant one.

"We cannot *possibly* sneak in there," Deez declared.

"No chance," Grimm agreed.

"And we can't fight our way in."

Grimm nodded. "We'd be dead before we got close."

"So, run me through this terrible plan of yours one more time?"

Grimm scratched at the radiation symbol shaved into his scalp.

"Look, it's dead simple," he sighed. "Abraham can review everything that's happened in CityHive over the last three days on the satellite footage. He can tell us *exactly* what building they took Lem into. So, we don't sneak. We don't fight. We just move quicker than they can. Rift in. Rift out. Gone."

"You know it doesn't work that way," Diesel said. "I can't Rift someplace I can't see. Whatever building Lemon's inside, I can't get us in there."

"Get us up on the roof, then. From there, we steal our way inside, find Lem, get back up, Rift back here to the truck, and fang it."

Diesel sucked her paintsticked lips thoughtfully, toying with a lock of dark hair. "Okay. You've convinced me. This is not a terrible plan."

Grimm glanced at her sidelong. "It's not?"

"Nope. In fact, as far as I can tell, this is not a plan at all."

"Nobody likes a smart-arse, Deez."

"Are you serious?" she scoffed. "*Everyone* likes me."

Grimm scowled and spoke into his sat-phone. "Abe, do you copy?"

"*Not . . . ery well,*" came the soft, crackling reply. "*We go . . . ted coverage. I might . . . strengthen the . . . but I've only been working—*"

"Yeah, yeah, righto," Grimm interrupted. "Just to confirm, they've got Lem stashed in the biggest spire, yeah? The tallest one?"

"*Grimm, the sat . . . lometers above the earth,*" said an

exasperated-sounding Abraham. *"I'm looking directly down. I can't tell how fu . . . tall it is."*

"But it's the *central* spire, right, Brotherboy?" Diesel demanded, her temper flashing in her eyes. "The one with all the spokes coming off it?"

A long silence filled the line, broken only by faint static.

"Affirmative," came the eventual reply.

"Cheers, mate," Grimm said. "Get the bacon on the fryer, we'll be back for breakfast."

"Gri . . . feel it's my duty to inform . . . nothing even remotely close to bacon."

Grimm switched off the radio, stowed it at his belt. After one last glance through the 'nocs at CityHive, he stood and brushed the dust off his cargos. But Diesel was still just sitting there, squinting up at him, dark shades over dark eyes.

"You waiting for an invitation?"

"We can't go in there, Grimm," she replied simply.

"'Course we can," he said. "We'll be in and out before—"

"Look, I know you care about this girl. I know it burns you to think about what might be happening to her. But we need a better plan than 'Rift inside and blunder about until we find her.' This is a CorpState stronghold, Grimmy. Think about what's waiting for us past those walls."

"We move fast enough—"

"Fast won't matter," Diesel said. "We're going in blind."

"But not empty-handed," he said.

Diesel frowned. "Meaning what?"

He pursed his lips, resigning himself to the fact Deez wouldn't play along unless she knew the whole tune. "Meaning did you notice the way I burned that Goliath the other night? Or cooked those Daedalus troopers?"

". . . Yeah, so what?"

"So the flames I made were hot enough to *melt metal,* Deez. I cooked that Goliath from the *inside out.* I've never been able to do that before." He shook his head, looked down at his hands. "I dunno what the score is. But ever since I soaked up the fire from that nuke . . . it's like . . ." He shook his head again, searching for the right words. "It's like I absorbed the blast, but somehow I didn't let it all out of me. Like there's a part of it still *inside* me."

"Part of a nuclear explosion?"

"I dunno." He shrugged. "It's weird. But yeah. Maybe."

One of Deez's slender eyebrows crept slowly upward. "That doesn't sound healthy for you, Grimmy."

". . . Are you *serious*?" he asked, bewildered. "Who gives a toss about 'healthy for me'? Lemon's in that hole, and she's in trouble, and I've got more firepower at my fingertips than I've ever had." He snapped his fist shut, and the air around it rippled like it was scorching. "We run into trouble, it's bloody ash, mate."

Diesel stood slowly, put her hand on Grimm's shoulder and spoke with the tone of someone delivering bad but much-needed news. "Look, I know you like this girl. I like her, too, annoying as she can be. But we've already lost one of our crew to these BioMaas bastards." She swallowed hard, squared her shoulders. "I'm not going to lose more. We're the future of the human race."

Grimm shrugged her hand away, anger rising in his chest like fire. "You gonna spit that survival-of-the-fittest crap at me here? The Major was full of *shit,* Deez! He lied to us! He betrayed us!"

"Doesn't mean some of what he said can't be true. Lies get

swallowed better when you hide them between a couple of slices of truth." Diesel shook her head. "I'm sorry. But I'm not taking us in there blind, Grimm. It's suicide."

"You got another idea? Or did we drive all this way for nothing?"

"We wait," Diesel said simply. "Brotherboy can monitor the city from orbit. Those satellites are sharp enough to pick a walking redheaded disaster out in a crowd of bugs and bone-heads. They're gonna move her at some point, Grimm. Transfer her to another facility, or take her to an interrogation, or even let her out for fresh air. As soon as she's in the open, we Rift in and grab her."

"And you call *my* plans terrible?" Grimm raged. "Maybe that building is a jail and she's locked down for good! Maybe she'll never see the light of day again!"

"Maybe," Deez said. "But she's supposedly important to these people. They didn't want her dead, or she already would be. Maybe they're not going to treat her like a prisoner." The girl folded her arms, her own temper fraying. "And if they *do* have her locked down in some damn dungeon? Chances of us bust-ing her out are next to zero. This is the capital of the second-largest CorpState in the whole damn Yousay, Grimm. And I'm not gonna let your wang drag us to certain death."

"Hell with you, then."

"Wassat supposed to mean?"

Grimm closed his hands into fists, boiling with anger. He was so furious, it was almost a physical sensation—like a chunk of burning coal inside his chest. The air around him rippled, like a heat haze on a furious summer's day. He spun on his heel, spoke through clenched teeth.

"It means I'll go in alone."

Deez reached out to stop him leaving, fingers sinking into his forearm. "Grimm, don't be an— OW, GODDAMMIT!"

Diesel's voice rose into a shriek, and she pulled back her hand with a gasp. Her face was twisted with pain, and she was clutching her wrist, hand held out in front of her. Her palm and fingers were red raw, like they'd been charbroiled.

Grimm heard a faint sizzling sound, looked down to where she'd touched him. He saw the faint impression of a handprint outlined on the muscles of his forearm, realizing with awful horror it was a layer of Diesel's skin.

"Deez, are you okay? I'm so bloody sorry, I didn't know, I didn't—"

"Just stop!" she shouted, backing away. "Stay back, you're too h . . ."

Her voice trailed off into nothing as she looked up at him.

"Jesus, Grimm, your eyes . . ."

"What?" he asked, pawing at his cheeks. "What about them?"

Face still twisted with pain, Diesel reached with her good hand into the pockets of her cargos, fished out her eyeliner, her paintstick, finally producing her little compact mirror. She backed off a few more steps, held it up in front of him. Grimm's breath caught in his lungs.

His eyes were glowing. Wisps of what looked like flaming plasma spilling out from between his lashes, trailing up into the air like burning smoke. He could feel the anger in his chest, the heat of it. He could feel it raging, like that heat, that awful, burning doomsday that had split the skies above the New Bethlehem desert. For a moment, he almost lost himself in it. But he looked at Deez, at the burn on her hand, horror welling in his chest. He closed his eyes again. And breathing deep, he forced it back, that fire, that rage, like shoving a beast back inside its cage.

He felt the heat fading. Calm slipping in to replace it, like cool water on sunburned skin. Holding his breath, he opened his eyes again, looking into Diesel's compact for their color. Sighing with relief.

Regular dark brown once more.

"What the hell was that?" Diesel demanded.

Grimm shook his head, looking down at the layer of skin she'd left behind on his arm. "Forget me, are you okay?"

Deez winced, still clutching her wrist. "I think so."

"Hold still, I'ma get the medkit," Grimm said.

He scrambled down the rocky outcropping they'd climbed for the view, down to the jeep they'd hidden beneath. Fumbling with the door, he grabbed the kit from under the seat, then dashed back up the spur. Deez was on her haunches, injured hand held out in front of her. Grimm busied himself with the first aid, Diesel hissing as he sprayed on a shot of antiseptic.

"Bloody hell, mate, I'm so sorry," Grimm murmured. "I didn't mean to."

"I know." She winced as he smoothed on some numbing gel, her teeth gritted. "Has that ever happened before?"

"Never," he said, feeling sick at the thought he'd hurt her. "But like I say, since the nuke . . ."

She sucked her lip, thoughtful. Neither of them had any idea what was happening to him, talking true. There was no such thing as an expert on deviation—how it worked or what the science of it all was. Absorbing that blast had . . . changed him somehow. But exactly how, or what it might mean, was anyone's guess.

"Well, at least you've calmed down now," Diesel said, scowling as he wrapped her hand in a bandage. "No more heroic charges into certain death, yeah? We tell Brotherboy to monitor the sat-feeds and squeal in girlish alarm if there's any sign of Lem. Then we Rift in, snag her and Rift out. Agreed?"

"Yeah," he mumbled, appropriately cowed.

"*Agreeeeeed?*" Diesel asked again, louder this time.

"Okay. Agreed."

"Thank god." Diesel rolled her eyes. "He *can* be taught."

Grimm chuckled, weak and halfhearted. He looked across the wastelands to the Hive beyond, squinting in the sunlight as he sighed.

"I just . . . I like her, Deez. I mean, I *really* like her."

"I know," Deez said, squeezing his knee with her good hand. "We're gonna get her out of this, Grimm. I promise."

Her grip was firm, and he took her hand, squeezing tight.

"I like you, too, freak," he smiled. "Just so you know."

Diesel scoffed.

"I told you, Grimmy. *Everyone* likes me."

3.12

MEGOPOLIS

"You could have told us we'd be walking through a damned sewer, Solomon."

Ezekiel was marching along a length of filthy concrete pipe, stooped to avoid cracking his head. The walls were dark and damp, the heat oppressive. A trickle of disgusting slop was congealed along the bottom of the pipe, a few centimeters deep. Ezekiel steadfastly refused to look down, speaking through gritted teeth.

Up ahead, the spindly logika glanced back over his shoulder, his inane grin lighting up the gloom.

"*DID I FAIL TO MENTION THAT?*"

"You did, actually," Zeke growled.

"*HOW TERRIBLY THOUGHTLESS OF ME.*"

"It looks like this place hasn't been used in years," Faith said. "Quit griping."

"I *like* griping."

"You'll have to forgive Ezekiel, Solomon." Faith smiled, patted the logika on his shoulder. "He's a touch sensitive of late. I, for one, appreciate all you do."

"THANK YOU, MISS FAITH," the bot replied. "THE SENSATIONAL SOLOMON APPRECIATES YOUR APPRECIATION."

Ezekiel shook his head, muttered beneath his breath.

"When's the wedding?"

They'd pulled up beneath a broken Megopolis overpass around dusk and set off through the Rim on foot. The outer section of the Daedalus capital wasn't so much part of the metropolis as a settlement that had gradually congealed around it, like a scab on an open wound. In their stolen Daedalus armor, Ezekiel and Faith were given a wide berth by most citizens, and Faith's body language was enough to scare away anyone else. Ezekiel's big sister radiated threat like a bonfire radiated heat. Gabriel was imprisoned somewhere in this city, after all, and they were close to him now—Faith wasn't in the mood to let some cockroaches slow her down.

At the Sensational Solomon's direction, they made their way through the seediest red-light district Zeke had ever clapped eyes on and, finally, to a run-down warehouse district. Looking up at the distant barrier that separated the Rim from the Hub, Zeke began to have misgivings about their chances of getting into the important part of the city—it was obvious Daedalus Technologies took their security *seriously*.

The Wall was fifteen meters high, topped with razor wire and manned by a small army of CorpTroopers. The gates were guarded by heavy machina piloted by Daedalus jockeys. The only way past them was with a Daedalus CorpCard, and while Zeke and Faith *did* have cards stolen off the troopers who attacked Miss O's, the bio-signatures and holoprints didn't match. Trying to fudge their way past those checkpoints was suicide.

Their only way into the Hub was Solomon.

Fortunately, the logika had proved good to his word, and

after waiting for a patrol of sec-drones to sweep overhead, he led Zeke and Faith into a collapsed building in the warehouse district. A gang of urchins had taken over the place since Solomon was last here, their tags painted on the walls, their shadows flitting among the ruins. But a few blasts from Faith's rifle sent them scattering, and with the coast clear, Solomon showed them how his former owner had smuggled his contraband.

The hatchway was set in the floor, hidden under rubble and rusted shut. They descended into the dark, dropped into the aforementioned pipe. Faith was right—it looked like this section had been abandoned long ago. But even though Zeke's helmet kept out the worst of the smell, he wouldn't have been too thrilled at the thought of trudging through yet another sewer, if not for the thought of who was waiting for him at the end of it.

Ana.

In times past, he'd have waded through hell to see her again. Two years he'd searched for her across the wastes. Two years of ashes and dust, of aching days and nights filled with dreams of finding her. He remembered the words he'd spoken the first night they spent together. Looking into her eyes and realizing he'd finally found a home, that whatever else he became, he'd always be hers.

All I am.

All I do,

I do for you.

He pictured her floating in her cryo-tank now, still and cold and empty. Blond hair framing that beautiful frozen face. Eyes closed in endless sleep. The hands that had held him forever still. The lips that had kissed him forever sealed.

God, what am I going to do?

"Keep up, Ezekiel," Faith warned. "Those rats look hungry."

His sister's voice shook him out of the dark places in his head, back to the darker place they were trudging through. The sewer line was long neglected, the walls dangerously cracked in places. He had no idea how long it had been since any human had ventured down here, but some of the rats trailing them were as big as dogs. The vermin followed at a distance, gathered in tumbling mobs. Their eyes reflected the glow of Solomon's optics, the floodlights in Zeke and Faith's armor, burning orange in the gloom.

There were hundreds of them.

"How much farther?" Zeke asked.

"*Around a kilometer, I should imagine,*" Solomon replied. "*There's another hatchway that leads up to a storage facility behind my— Oh dear.*"

Zeke glanced away from the hungry eyes behind them.

"'Oh dear' what?"

Solomon pointed ahead. "*Oh dear, that?*"

Looking past the logika in the glow of their floods, Ezekiel saw the "that" in question about a hundred meters farther down the pipe—a row of stainless steel bars, thick as his wrist, running floor to ceiling. He could see they were rigged with a proximity sensor, security cams and, worst of all, a pair of robotic automata equipped with motion-activated assault cannons.

Squinting in the gloom, he saw a filth-encrusted sign on the bars.

DANGER: NO ENTRY BEYOND THIS POINT

"Crap," Ezekiel breathed.

Solomon glanced down at the muck he stood in. "*Quite.*"

"You said this sewer ran clear through to the Hub," Faith hissed.

"APOLOGIES, MISS FAITH, BUT THIS BARRIER WASN'T HERE BEFORE," Solomon said. "THEY MUST HAVE ERECTED IT AFTER I WAS SOLD INTO CAPTIVITY."

Faith sighed, hands on hips. "Marvelous."

"Those cameras are thermographic," Ezekiel said. "The automata are motion-activated. Anything that gets within fifty meters is going to get blasted into next year."

"So why don't those rats set the guns off?" Faith asked.

Ezekiel peered down the tunnel, saw a couple of rats scampering around the gate, well within firing range of the automata. He shrugged.

"The automata are probably calibrated to activate when something beyond a certain size and temperature comes into range." Zeke waved at the smaller vermin scampering around their ankles. "But if we get any closer, we're made."

"We could shoot the cameras out?" Faith offered.

"That'd set off the proximity alarms for certain."

"Is there another route?" Faith asked, looking at Solomon.

"NOT THAT I'M AWARE OF, I'M AFRAID."

"Yeah," Ezekiel growled. "You're the Sensational Solomon, all right."

"I BEG YOUR PAR—"

"We need to get through here, Ezekiel," Faith said.

"I know that, Faith," he spat.

"So get us through!" she hissed. "You were the one Monrova trusted to work security details in Babel. I was stuck minding his wretched daughter. Plaiting Ana's hair and listening to her whine about how unfair life was all day."

"Ana wasn't like that," Ezekiel said, his temper flaring.

"Oh, spare me," Faith sighed. "Trudging around in a sewer is nauseating enough without having to listen to your lovesick-puppy routine."

"And it stinks bad enough down here without *your* bullshit," Ezekiel countered. "Ana saw the best in life, not the worst. She loved it. And she loved *you*, Faith. She saw you, me, all of us as *people*. You were her closest friend. And apart from me, you were the one who knew her best."

Faith's lip curled. "Knew her well enough to loathe her."

"How?" Ezekiel shook his head in wonder. "*How* can you hate her so much? When all she ever did was care about you?"

Faith stepped forward until the pair of them were chest to chest, a sneer at her pretty lips. "It's not *my* feelings you'd best concern yourself with, little brother."

". . . Meaning what?"

"Meaning you know what has to happen once we get inside that tower, don't you? You know what needs to be done?"

The words were a knife, slipped clean through his ribs. He could almost feel it twist inside his chest. Taste the blood in his mouth.

"I—"

"Daedalus Technologies cannot be allowed access to Myriad," Faith said. "Ana Monrova is their key to all her father's secrets. All trace of her needs to be wiped away from Daedalus records. *All* trace, Ezekiel."

His sister looked at him, flat telescreen eyes glittering in the dark.

"That's *not* going to happen," Ezekiel breathed.

"She's not even alive anymore," Faith said. "You said it yourself. She's just a shell of the thing you loved. And if you cannot summon the courage to do what must be done, *I* will."

Zeke grabbed Faith by the throat just as her own fingers closed about his. Drawing the pistol from his belt, he pushed it against her cheek just as she pressed the muzzle of her own handgun to his throbbing temple.

"Showing some backbone at last, little brother?"

Ezekiel looked into Faith's eyes. Wondering how she'd got so lost. He tried to remember what she'd been like before the Fall, before she lost herself so completely to the rage and hate inside. But in that moment, the thought of Ana hanging in the air between them, all she'd been and all she was, he couldn't recall.

Because as awful and agonizing as what Faith had said was . . .

Part of you knows it's the truth.

Ezekiel's finger tightened on his trigger. But of course he didn't squeeze. Faith met his eyes without blinking. Finally, Solomon made a noise like he was clearing his throat, breaking the leaden silence.

"I DON'T WISH TO INTERRUPT THIS TOUCHING FAMILY MOMENT. BUT THERE'S STILL THE MATTER OF THIS RATHER IMPOSING OBSTACLE TO OVERCOME, YES?"

Zeke hung on to Faith's throat a moment longer, pressing his pistol into her cheek a little harder. Looking into those flatscreen eyes, he realized he couldn't recall anymore the person she'd been. All he saw was the killer she'd become. Cold. Remorseless. Utterly ruthless.

But if it comes down to it . . .

Aren't I going to need someone like that?

He pushed the thought away, released Faith's neck and shoved her backward. She smiled at him, lopsided, as if somehow proud of his display of rage.

Turning away from her, he looked over the automata on the barrier. Working the puzzle through in his mind. The bars themselves might not be too difficult to deal with—among the gear he and Faith had taken off the dead assault troopers was a bundle of thermex charges that would burn hot enough to perforate the steel. But he needed a way to get close enough to drop the thermex near the bars. Throwing them would just trip the motion detectors. And anything bigger than a rat within fifty meters would set them off.

Bigger than a rat . . .

"Waitaminute," he whispered.

Zeke thumbed the release controls on the lower half of his armor, heard a soft hiss of releasing pressure as the steelweave encasing his legs eased open. Faith watched him as he reached down into his pants, her eyebrow rising slowly.

"What in the name of *god* are you doing?"

Ezekiel made a small sound of triumph, fished out a torn plastic packet from his pocket, held it up so Faith could read the label.

BACON!™

Faith's stare was growing more withering by the second. "How can you *possibly* be thinking about food in a place like this?"

He tore off a strip of meat(?), tossed it onto the ground behind them. It floated on top of the little river of scum as the crowd of rats gathered at the edge of their floodlights. Finally, a big brute with a missing ear and a tail as thick as Zeke's thumb took the plunge, dashing out into the mire and seizing the treat in its razor teeth.

Ezekiel was quicker.

His hand flashed out, and the rat squealed as he hauled it out of the muck, teeth flashing, tail whipping in fury.

"Ezekiel, stop jackassing about with that thing, and . . ."

Faith's voice faded out as Zeke uncoupled the thermex charges from his belt with his free hand. Realization dawned in her eyes, her lips curling in a faint smile.

"Well, well," she purred. "Aren't we a clever one?"

"Help me tie them on."

Faith complied, propping one filth-encrusted boot up on the narrow pathway and pulling out her shoelace. Taking the thermex off Zeke, she tied the lace around the charges, then the charges to the rat. It tried to bite her, fangs flashing, black eyes filled with rage. When she was done, she pressed the arming stud on the explosives, and a tiny red light lit up. Nodding to Zeke, she stepped aside, and the lifelike tossed the furious creature and its stylish new attire farther up the pipe.

It landed with a splash in the muck, squealing and flopping about on its back under the weight of the charges. But in a moment, it righted itself, the thermex still tied securely to its back. It shook the filth off itself, aiming a furious squeal at Ezekiel. The lifelike offered another torn strip of BACON!™ by way of apology, tossing it up the pipe, a little closer to the barrier.

The big rat huffed and spat. But after a moment, it turned and scampered toward the meat. A brief scuffle ensued, the bigger rat fending off two smaller compatriots, seizing the food in its claws and scoffing it down.

Zeke tossed another. It was a long way up the pipe to the security barrier, but his aim was exceptional, his arm like steel. He threw yet another chunk, drawing the big rat closer and closer to the bars. As he'd guessed, the automata motion sensors and thermographics didn't trip—they were calibrated to ignore something so small. And with a few more tossed BACON!™ scraps, the rat and his explosives were sitting right below the barrels of their autocannons.

"How far from here to the exit into the Hub, Solomon?" Ezekiel asked.

"*THE SAFEST IS PERHAPS EIGHT HUNDRED METERS FROM HERE. IT OPENS INTO AN ALLEY BEHIND MY FORMER OWNER'S ESTABLISHMENT.*"

"How far from there to where they're keeping Gabriel?" Faith demanded.

"*THE SPIRE IS LOCATED IN THE HEART OF THE HUB, PERHAPS FIVE KILOMETERS FROM WHERE WE'LL BE SURFACING. ITS UPPER LEVELS ARE STUDDED WITH TRANSMISSION TOWERS AND UPLINK DISHES. IT'S RATHER STRIKING. YOU CAN'T MISS IT.*"

"Once we blow this barrier, we're going to have to move quick," Zeke said. "The explosion is bound to set off an alarm somewhere."

"Eight hundred meters?" Faith scoffed. "We'll be up and out of this hole before they know what's happened."

"Can you run fast enough? Your legs . . ."

"Gabriel is up there, Ezekiel," Faith said fiercely. "I'll fly if I need to."

"Once we surface, we keep our heads down and head for the Spire."

"*YOUR ARMOR WILL HELP MAINTAIN OUR ANONYMITY,*" Solomon said. "*REGULAR CITIZENS DON'T TRIFLE WITH MEMBERS OF THE ARMED FORCES. THE ONLY PEOPLE YOU NEED CONCERN YOURSELVES WITH ARE OTHER DAEDALUS SECURITY PERSONNEL.*"

Zeke nodded. "Okay, let's do this. Pray that thermex can melt those bars."

Solomon squeaked a small protest as Zeke lifted him up onto his shoulder. Zeke looked at the rat happily chowing down on his lump of processed pseudo-meat.

"Sorry, big guy."

BOOM.

The explosion was white-hot, shockingly loud even inside their helmets. But before the walls had even stopped shaking, Ezekiel was dashing through the slop, past the bent and smoking bars and the ruined automata. The pipe was filled with dark smoke, but his power armor's optics cut through the haze, and Ezekiel ran quick. He could hear Faith behind, moving slower with her injuries, but still faster, stronger, better than any human could hope to be.

"*Left,*" Solomon said, pointing to a tunnel branch.

Dashing into another tributary, Zeke spotted a service ladder ensconced in the grimy walls. He hefted Solomon off his shoulder, his heart pounding, imagining teams being scrambled, sec-drones already on their way.

Zeke grabbed the ladder, dragged himself upward, six meters to the surface. Punching the manhole cover free, he climbed out into a grubby alleyway hung thick with smog and packed with waste-disposal drums. The sun had set while they'd crawled beneath the Wall, and night had fallen over Megopolis. The sky overhead was shrouded in a low veil of multicolored fumes, pretty and poisonous all at once.

Solomon climbed up behind him, and finally, gasping, trembling, came Faith. She clawed her way out of the manhole and rolled onto her back, breath hissing. After a brief struggle, she managed to pull her helmet off to breathe better. Zeke could see her face was pale with pain, eyes squeezed shut. He wondered what shape her legs were in under her armor.

He dragged off his own helmet, knelt on the asphalt beside her.

"Are you all right?"

"Next stupid question," she whispered.

He said nothing. Just looked into her eyes. Seeing her hurt like this, seeing her pain, he couldn't help but feel a stab of pity. He and Faith were still family, despite everything, and that still counted for something.

That was just who he was. Who he'd decided to be.

Faith met his eyes, and Ezekiel expected some kind of rebuke for his softheartedness. His all-too-human frailty. But instead, her own eyes softened at his concern. Her armor of disdain and sarcasm cracking just a touch.

"Just . . . give me a moment," she said. "I'll be fine."

"What the h-hell?" came a bewildered growl behind them.

Ezekiel turned, searching the gloom. A man was looming up from between the dumpsters, blood spattered on his face. His lip was split, his face twisted and shrouded in shadow, but Ezekiel would have recognized it anywhere. Chest thrilling with rage at the sight of a long black coat and a red right hand.

Faith rolled up onto her knees, reaching for her pistol.

Preacher stuffed a wad of tobacco in his swollen cheek.

"Well, I'll be goddamned," he said. "Snowflake."

3.13

DAMSEL

"That was a very foolish thing to do, Lemonfresh."

The voice dragged Lemon up from dreams of roaring wind and tree-lined streets rushing up to meet her. Of gleaming claws made of bone and a cold hardness somewhere deep in her belly. The girl opened her eyes, squinting in the blurred glare, finally focusing on the three Carers leaning over her. The women wore their concern like old, comfortable jackets, double-blinking with big black eyes as Lemon groaned and tried to sit up.

"What . . ." She blinked against the blinding light. "What . . . happened?"

"She leapt from the seventeenth overpass," the first Carer said.

"Hunter-Killers caught her before she struck ground," said the second.

"Very foolish," the third said as all three shook their heads.

"I feel like . . . I got p-punched in the guts by a WarBot," Lemon whimpered, trying to sit up again. "And I already did the cramp thing this month."

"Be gentle," Carer murmured. "Let us assist her."

With all three women clucking and helping, Lemon sat upright, the pain in her abdomen subsiding to a low and steady ache. She remembered her confrontation with the Director, killing one and staggering the rest, leaping over the railing in her best impersonation of idiotic courage. But other than that, nothing.

Blinking hard, she peered around her, the space beyond the Carers slowly coming into focus. She was back in her bed in the CityHive tower, the texture of the sheets vaguely organic against her skin. She wondered why she could feel the sheets against her at all, but peering underneath, she saw she was wearing only the military-issue briefs and less-than-sensational bra she'd acquired at Miss O's.

And when she looked down at her aching lower belly, her whole world turned upside down at the sight of three puncture marks in her skin.

Small.

Red.

New.

Lemon stared at those marks for what seemed like an age. All the possibilities she could conjure running through her head. They might be cuts from the struggle, she reasoned. The Hunter-Killers could have scratched her when they caught her. She might have been bumped or tussled when they carried her back up to her room—she'd killed one of those Directors, after all. But looking down at the smooth expanse of her skin, those three angry red dots positioned equidistant around her navel, Lemon knew with awful, absolute certainty how they got there.

The Carers looked at each other, black eyes shining with concern.

"Lemonfresh—"

"You did it?"

She spoke in a whisper, looking up with disbelief into those pale and worried faces. Lemon felt her eyes filling with burning tears, her chest with burning rage.

"You *did* it."

She felt the static crackling in the darkness behind her eyes. She could feel the current inside the women, skipping from neuron to neuron, pulsing through the hearts in their chests, racing up their spines. It would have been so easy then to just reach in and turn them off. To lash out in her fury, to scream and tear and break. She wanted to so desperately, so completely, she could feel it in her bones.

But somewhere deep inside, someplace even the trauma of her childhood and the pain of the road and the rage of this final violation couldn't quite burn away, a part of her knew it wouldn't make her feel any better. Hurting these women wouldn't undo what had been done to her. And they weren't the ones responsible anyway, not in any real sense—Lemon could see her anguish reflected in each of their eyes. They were hurting just as badly as she was. They *cared*. That was their purpose.

No, the BioMaas Director was the one to blame here. The one orchestrating everything. Killing these women, lashing out at them in some brief and pointless display of fury . . . in a way, that'd make Lemon just as bad as them.

"We are sorry, Lemonfresh," said the first Carer, wringing her hands.

"We know she is hurting," said the second.

"But her pain is for the greater good," said the third, touching her cheek.

Lemon shied away from the touch, closed her eyes against her tears. She could feel the pulse of the static in the warm dark behind her closed eyelids. It took a moment for her to drown out its voice and find her own again. So soft, she almost couldn't hear it herself.

"Do me a favor and get out, will you?"

She opened her eyes, met those dark, liquid stares. The women's faces dropped even further, and the trio hung beside Lemon like broken mirrors. But the girl ignored them, ignored their pain, turning her bloodshot stare to the endless dance of the fliers outside the spire's translucent walls.

Wondering what they'd taken out of her.

What exactly they planned to do with it.

How horrified and violated it made her feel.

Resigned, shoulders slumped, the Carers finally turned and shuffled across the room. Lemon watched from the corner of her eye as the first gently touched the wall. The same place as she'd noted before. With that same leathery whisper, the wall opened wide, and Lemon caught a glimpse of the corridor outside—smooth bone, crawling with little glowbugs, three Sentinels standing stern vigil—before the living portal closed again.

She dragged her knees up under her chin. Wrapped her arms about her shins. For a minute, it was all too much. She hadn't asked for any of this. She never wanted it. She was supposed to be the comedy relief. She was the sidekick in someone else's story. For all her sass, all her front, Miss Lemon Fresh never felt big or important enough to be anyone's hero.

But chest shaking, tears finally spilling down her cheeks,

she grabbed that thought by the throat and she gouged out its eyes. Punched and stomped and kicked it, leaving it where it belonged—in the gutter, picking up broken teeth with broken fingers. Small she might be. Unimportant, sure, maybe. But Lemon had lived almost a decade in the shitpit that was Dregs, hustling and fighting for everything she ever had. And truth was, self-pity wasn't ever her style.

She found herself angry again. Furious all the way down to her boots. Static electricity crackled on her skin as she pawed at those tiny and somehow enormous marks on her belly, the ache of what they'd done to her burning away under a wash of kerosene and matches. Anger was fuel. Anger was focus. And so, reaching out, Lemon began searching among the little rivers of electrical current that pulsed through this entire structure. Feeling for its shape again. Noting its colors. And remembering which pulse had flared when the wall had opened wide.

She wasn't a master of her gift by any stretch. She was only just learning to use it on living things. But the more time she spent here, the more she realized this whole building, this whole *city*, was, in some bizarre way, actually living. The first time she'd ever used her power, she'd been angry, too, and that fury was going to help her again. Because a girl who'd grown up rough and filthy as Lemon Fresh wasn't the kind of damsel to sit up in a tower waiting for some handsome prince to rescue her.

The handsome prince was dead in this story.

Time for the damsel to rescue herself.

And then burn this whole tower to the ground.

Lemon slipped out of her bed, holding her stomach. She found her uniform from Miss O's neatly folded by the water fountain and looked down again at those four identical fish swimming in forever circles. Dragging on her shirt, cargos, boots, she limped over to the wall and pressed her palms against it. She could feel the pulse of life inside, distended, tingling, the brightest flavor of strange she'd ever tasted. But she closed her eyes, reached out into the familiar static. This was who she was now. Not a sidekick. Not the comedy relief.

She was the flood, they'd told her.

She was going to wash *all* of this away.

Lemon took hold of those hidden strings, and frowning in concentration, gently, oh so gently, she pulled. The static flared. Her power pulsed. The wall creaked like old leather and parted slightly, revealing the corridor beyond. At the sound, the three Sentinels outside turned, mouths opening as they saw her through the crack, pale, disheveled, furious. But before any could shout, she seized hold of the signals dancing through their minds, the little arcs and sparks of electricity, neurons and electrons, making hearts pump and lungs breathe.

And she ripped them out.

All three men dropped like bricks, crumpling to the floor with the softest of sighs. Lem felt a momentary stab of guilt, a wrongness at the thought of killing them. But she drowned it under her rage, remembered her time among the freak show under the desert, the lessons she'd learned in Miss O's. The Major had been a madman, true cert. But after what these bastards had just put her through, there was one lesson the Major had imparted that Lemon had decided to take to heart.

Only the strong survive.

So Lemon slipped out into the hallway, started to run.

3.14

ESCAPISM

Eve collapsed on the floor of her cell with a shuddering gasp.

Her face was wet with tears, her body soaked with sweat. Her grav-chair made barely a whisper as it was pushed from the room, the logika who'd escorted her sealing the cell door shut with a crackle of electricity.

Eve's whole body was tingling, arms and legs shaking at the remembered pain. She had no idea how long her session with Drakos had lasted—maybe hours, maybe days—the concept of time itself melting and bubbling and peeling away under the constant barrage she'd been subjected to.

Pain.

Such a little word for such a colossal thing. She thought she knew it so well, she could almost call it a friend—the bullets, the lies, the betrayal, the loss. She'd turned it all to steel and worn it like armor, thinking she couldn't possibly be hurt more than she'd already been. But over the past few hours/days, the Director of Daedalus Technologies had shown her just how little she knew about pain.

Cold and acid. Fire and steel. They'd subjected her to every form of agony she could imagine, and some others she'd never dared dream of. And even though she'd known in some small corner of her mind it was all in her head—a virtual construct that was in no way real—that didn't make that tiny word any less colossal.

But she hadn't broken. Hadn't bent. No matter how much they hurt her, in the blissful nothings between each new round of agony as Drakos asked her about Lemon—what she could do, what she was capable of—Eve never wavered.

It wasn't loyalty to her former bestest that kept her from cracking. It wasn't the years they'd spent together. It was simple pride. Eve wasn't prepared to let these cockroaches win, that was the plain and simple truth. She was more than them— better, stronger, faster. And if they thought a few hours/days of something as mundane as agony would be enough to break her, well, they didn't know her at all.

Her hands were shaking. Her fauxhawk hanging low, soaked with perspiration. The floor of her cell was cool against her burning skin, and she closed her eyes, thankful for a moment to feel this, only this.

She heard hard knuckles rapping on cold steel. Looking into the cell beside her, she found Gabriel looking back. His jawbone had almost knitted back together. His lips and cheeks would take longer, though, his voice still garbled and ruined.

"Uhreyooulrgght?" he asked.

She closed her eyes again for a moment. Reveling in the cold press of metal against her body, the nothing-else she felt. But finally, Eve breathed deep and pushed herself up to sitting, meeting her brother's stare.

"I'm all right."

"Insekz," he hissed. "Hrrtyoo?"

She nodded, wincing at the remembered pain.

"Whhhy?" Gabriel asked.

"They're trying to map my brainwave patterns, combine them with whatever they've dragged out of Ana so they can open Myriad. But . . . I think something is wrong. The way our brains are designed . . . I think they're having trouble with it." Eve dragged one shaking hand through her hair. "But they want to know about Lemon, too. What she can do, how much of a threat she is. So while they figure out how to replicate my brainwaves, they're torturing me to find out about her."

Gabriel lifted his hand, held it palm out, as if to press it against the electrified field crackling between them. "Veyh wull pay."

She held up her hand to mirror his own. "They will. But we have to find some way out of here, Gabe. And I can't see one."

True cert, Eve had been looking for an escape ever since they'd brought her here. But cockroaches though they might be, these humans were good at what they did. Eve was electrified into submission before anyone entered her cell. The bonds strapping her to the grav-chair were stronger than she could break, and being pushed to her virtual torture sessions every day, she saw very little of the compound—just pristine hallways and the empty, glowing optics of servitor logika.

She knew no system was perfect. But she also knew, with a growing certainty, that she couldn't withstand this punishment forever. Drakos would eventually find out what he wanted to know about Lemon. The logika techs would eventually figure out how to replicate her own brainwaves. Her usefulness would be at an end.

And what then?

Eve heard a small rumble, like distant thunder. Gabriel

heard it, too, a frown marring the perfect skin of his brow. A moment later, the building shuddered—perhaps too faint for a human to feel. But the light around them shifted from cool blue to purple, public address system announcements ringing in the air.

"Wussut?" Gabe asked.

Eve shook her head, listening carefully. "I don't know. . . ."

The building shuddered, stronger this time, and that distant thunder rumbled again, closer now. The two lifelikes met each other's eyes, uncertainty and curiosity in Gabe's glass-green stare. The lighting shifted again, purple now to red.

"Attention, all Daedalus employees: Lockdown Protocol is now in effect. All security personnel, report to commander for briefing. This is not a drill. Repeat, all Daedalus employees: Lockdown—"

The announcement kept repeating, but Eve lost interest as the floor suddenly crackled with a burst of electrical current. The shock rocketed up her spine, landing like a boot heel in the base of her skull. She was dimly aware that they'd shocked Gabriel, too—they'd never done that in the past. But before she could ponder too hard on it, Sec logika were stomping into the cell with her grav-chair.

The building was shaking—tremors running up the foundation and shivering the walls. The bloody light deepened, alarms started blaring, the song of what she thought had been thunder now coalescing into something more familiar.

Explosions.

"Gabriel?" she called.

"M'here," he replied behind her.

They were pushed into an elevator, dropping swift, the

alarms increasing in pitch and intensity. She wanted to ask what was happening, but she knew the logika wouldn't answer, so tried instead to piece together the puzzle alone. Eve could hear more explosions, a low-pitched hum. The building rocked suddenly, like something had struck it, the unsettling patter of falling debris dancing on the elevator's roof.

The lift shuddered to a halt, doors opening into a sub-basement. Eve saw armored personnel carriers, CorpTroopers in hulking suits of power armor. Drakos was there, too, wearing a perfectly cut suit, dark hair swept back from his widow's peak.

"Get us to Central, red lights all the way."

"*Yessir,*" replied a trooper, his voice rasping through his voxbox.

"*Sir, they've breached perimeter one,*" murmured another beside him.

Drakos met Eve's burning stare, his eyes narrowed.

Megopolis is under attack?

But who is "they"?

"Let's move, people," Drakos ordered.

Eve and Gabe were bundled into the back of an APC, their grav-chairs locked in place. She met her brother's eyes, saw his pupils dilated, arms tensed—Gabe was ready to jump the first chance they got. Alarms were still screaming, the building shuddering, the sound of the ground beneath their tires changing pitch as they barreled up from the sub-basement and into the Megopolis streets.

They were thirty seconds into the journey when something hit them: a bone-jarring impact, a deafening crash. The APC slewed sideways, Eve bit down on her tongue, blood flooding her mouth as they flipped, tumbling end over end, coming to a squealing, shuddering halt.

She found herself hanging upside down in her chair, the troopers about her unbuckling and dropping down to the ceiling of the overturned vehicle. As they kicked open the door, she smelled acid, heard a rush of wind, radios squealing, automatic weapons firing. Eve tugged against her restraints, felt a slight give under her right hand. Her pulse was hammering. She needed to get out. Jaw clenched, teeth gritted, she flexed her right arm, muscles corded, tendons standing out in her neck, Gabriel watching on, willing her to pull harder. She was stronger than them—these humans, these insects, who'd locked her up and chained her down. She reached into the pool of her rage and indignation and drew deep, metal squealing, rivets popping, flesh bruising, and with a bright snapping sound, she finally tore her arm free.

Her other arm followed, then her boots, allowing her to drop down to the ceiling. There was more screaming coming from outside, the sound of something heavy moving, explosions shaking the ground, *boom boom boom*. She tore Gabriel loose, swallowing the blood in her mouth, and supporting his weight, she staggered out into the Megopolis streets.

Old-world squalor with a new-world paint job. But it wasn't the sight and smells of the Daedalus capital that made her gasp, eyes widening in surprise. It was the sight of the things tearing that capital apart. She recognized a few of the shapes—the wasplike silhouettes of Hunter-Killers, the airborne bulk of Lumberers. The ground rippled with swarms of bioengineered dogthings with too many legs and too many teeth, and great, hulking creatures as big as houses, spitting gouts of corrosive green on the Daedalus troops.

And there among them, hands spread, blood-red bangs hanging in bright green eyes, was a sight Eve never thought she'd see again.

A girl she'd once called "bestest."

"Lemon," she breathed.

She turned toward Eve, clad in black—all dark rubber and strange nodules and smooth organic lines. The ground around her was swarming, the skies bristling.

"Riotgrrl," she said, grinning and rolling her *r*'s.

The creatures hissed warning, and Eve saw a squadron of Goliaths lumber around the edge of a nearby building, laser sights cutting the dark, missile pods unfurling. The BioMaas constructs shuddered and roared. Gabriel grabbed Eve's hand, ready to bolt. And Lemon raised her right hand. The air sang with current, ozone crackling on Eve's tongue. And with the *snapcracklepop* of cooking circuitry, all three Goliaths tottered and crashed dead onto the road.

Lemon turned back to Eve, holding out her hand. "We need to jet."

". . . What are you *doing* here?" Eve demanded.

"You mean aside from being absolutely amazing?" Lemon grinned, brushing the dust off her freckles. "I came here for *you*, stupid."

The girl's smile was wide, her eyes shining, and somewhere deep inside, Evie's heart of hearts sang to see her. She looked to the city about her, the wailing sirens, the burning buildings, the skies swarming. Gabriel was watching Lemon with narrowed eyes, clearly distrustful. But if Eve's former bestest was offering a ticket out of this prison, any other questions could wait. . . .

"It's good to see you, Lem," she whispered.

"Kiss my cherry lips later," Lemon replied. "For now, come on."

Beckoning with one hand, the girl stalked across the melted asphalt. Eve and Gabriel followed, swarming dogthings seething around them, H-Ks filling the skies. A squadron of Daedalus flex-wings zoomed overhead, missile pods opening wide. Lemon curled her fingers, and the fliers tumbled from the sky, crashing to the road in flames. A building beside them exploded, a high-velocity shell ripping through the glass and concrete. Down the end of the burning street, Eve made out the shapes of a half dozen grav-tanks, turrets aimed right for them. And as she watched, dumbfounded, Lemon opened her hand and fried them with a glance.

Eve looked to Gabriel, who simply stared in disbelief.

"Come on!" Lemon called.

The chaos was overwhelming. The skies filled with fire, Eve's lungs burning with smoke. But as she followed her bestest through the battle-sick streets, watching as Lemon fried another squadron of flex-wings, short-circuited the power armor of twenty Daedalus CorpTroopers, dropped another grav-tank a dozen blocks away, Eve began to feel more and more uneasy.

Thankful as she was at the thought of salvation, confusing as the mayhem was, Eve had never seen Lemon's gift reach so far and so easy before. Sure, they'd been apart, but it had only been a week or so since they'd seen each other. For Lemon to have become so strong in so short a time was just . . .

"You remember when we used to rip street-vendors together back in Los Diablos?" she called. "You've come a ways from snaffling cans of Neo-Meat™, kid."

Lemon tossed her bangs from her eyes and grinned. "Been practicing."

. . . it was just unbelievable.

Eve came to a stop, there in the burning street, the raging chaos. Gabriel tugged her hand, urging her onward. Lemon turned to look at her, head tilted, hand on her hip. The Bio-Maas constructs spat and howled, the explosions rippled in the air, warm on her skin, every bit as real as anything she'd ever known.

"We never ripped street-vendors together."

Eve looked up into the burning sky, hands curling into fists.

"Stop this right now, you bastards."

The battle raged a moment more, blood in the gutters, ashes in the skies. Then time slowed, grinding down second by second until it stuttered to a halt, like someone had hit the pause button on a playback. The flames were frozen into beautiful abstractions, the smoke solidified into shapes like clouds, the chaos of the attack rendered in freeze-frame all around her. She released Gabriel's hand, chest boiling with fury as the image of Danael Drakos coalesced on the concrete before her. He wore a white suit, immaculate as always, bringing his hands together in a small but polite round of applause.

"Bravo, Miss Monrova."

For a second—one perfect, burning second—she wanted to just reach out and crush him. Squeeze him. Feel him break under her hands again. But that, like everything else in here, would be a lie. And the fury of that, of being deceived again, and again, and *again,* was almost enough to choke her.

"You seem to be experiencing extreme emotional distress, Miss Monrova," Drakos said mildly, glancing at his wrist implant. "Would you prefer a more serene tableau?"

The scene shifted, rippling in that now-familiar pattern, and once more, they stood together on that awful, perfect beach.

Looking down the sands, Eve saw a familiar figure in the water. Blood-red bangs hanging over Lemon's eyes, a healthy tan on freckled skin, shrieks of delight as the waves crashed around her ankles.

Eve blinked away hateful, stinging tears.

"Why?" she whispered.

"You refused to answer our questions about Miss Fresh, Miss Monrova. And while we could eventually rip the information we need about her capabilities from your broken mind, our timeline is now rather pressing. You'd be astonished at the kinds of information that can be gleaned from involuntary motor responses. Heart rate. Pupil dilation. Respiration. We can tell when you think you're being told a lie. By observing your biological responses in the face of more and more vulgar displays of your friend's power, we could at least glean where the threshold of her limitations might be." Drakos studied his fingernails. "And prepare accordingly."

"She's not my friend," Eve whispered. "She's a cockroach."

"We can also tell when *you're* lying, by the by." Drakos glanced at his wrist again, tapped a glowing sigil beneath his skin. "Do we have everything we need?"

Drakos waited for an answer. Eve stood there in the sunlight, watching Lemon playing in the water. Stomping in the shallows, her eyes bright and shining.

She's not my friend.

Drakos tapped at his wrist again.

"Excellent. Inform Tactical I want recommendations in an hour."

The scene rippled before Eve's eyes. The beach faded, the hush and crash of the ocean dropped into silence. And as she disappeared, too, the image of Lemon fading and finally becoming nothing at all, Eve had to try awfully hard not to feel like she was losing her all over again. Struggle not to remember their days in Los Diablos together, the good times and the bad, both made better by her just being there.

She had to remind herself Lemon had lied, just like the rest. That she'd betrayed her, just like the rest. That no matter what they'd shared, what they'd been, just like the mirage around her, it hadn't ever been real. It wasn't anything at all.

She's not your friend, Eve told herself.

She's not your friend.

———

Familiar weightlessness. The sensation of a silent sea.

Eve opened her eyes, saw she was sitting on that same soft chair in that same lab. Tech logika looming around her, white light and white walls. As the rest of the room slowly came into focus, she saw Danael Drakos in a chair opposite, being helped by his small army of flunkies. The CEO blinked, climbed to his feet.

"You absolute bastard," Eve whispered.

Drakos glanced at her, eyebrow slightly raised. He signed a data pad with his finger, handed it back to a flunky. "We'll commence after I've assessed Tactical's report. Send the subject back to her cell, prep her for surgery in one hour."

"Surgery?" Eve growled. "What damn surgery?"

Drakos signed another pad, spoke in his brisk, matter-of-fact tone.

"We've devised a rather elegant solution to the problem of your brainwave patterns, Miss Monrova." He nodded to a modified set of silver 'trodes laid out on a nearby bench. "A heavily augmented wetware interface to mask the . . . *inhuman* nature of your biology? The modified synaptic resonance, combined with topographical data from the real Ana Monrova, should prove sufficient to foil Monrova's safeguards on the Myriad supercomputer." He gave an apologetic wince. "Unfortunately, we really only need one part of you for it to function. And several of my colleagues in Weapons Development have an interest in the . . . rest of you."

A sour fear uncoiled in Eve's stomach. She glanced at the robots around her, faceless, nameless, pitiless.

Elegant solution.

She looked back to Drakos. "Now you wait just a—"

"Understand, I hold Nicholas Monrova in the highest respect," Drakos said. "And whatever price you ultimately pay, it will be for the betterment of his dream."

The CEO of Daedalus Technologies spun on his heel and, surrounded by his tiny suited legion of doom, strode from the room. Frustration boiling over, Eve thrashed once against her bonds, then fell still. If looks could have killed, Danael Drakos would have been nothing but a smoking pair of shoes. But watching the man walk away, Eve was left only with her burning rage.

This is not good.

And her growing fear.

This is not good. . . .

3.15

POKER FACE

"Oh no," Ezekiel breathed.

In a dingy alleyway in the Megopolis Hub, Ezekiel was crouched on damp concrete, watching any chance he had of getting Ana back go up in smoke. Faith and Solomon were beside him, the stink of smoke and sewage rising from the manhole cover behind them, and Zeke's heart was sinking down into the floor.

"Didn't think I'd be seein' you again after that nuke exploded," Preacher smiled. "Ain't this a plot twist."

The bounty hunter tipped back the brim of his black cowboy hat. Ezekiel saw his face was battered and bruised, a faint smudge of red still on his chin—he looked like he'd had the crap beaten out of him. But still, Preacher was every kind of trouble, and after that explosion they'd set off in the sewers below, trouble was already on the way. Zeke knew he had to do this quiet and quick. His power armor whirred as he tensed, and Preacher had his pistol out in a flash, aimed at Ezekiel's face.

The bounty hunter touched his ear, blinking rapidly as he glanced at the open manhole cover behind them. "Report comin' in over the Daedalus network. Explosion in the sub-levels." He met Ezekiel's eyes. "Here for your girlie, huh? You always were an idiot, Zekey."

Faith drew her pistol, aimed it at the bounty hunter's head.

"In about thirty, maybe thirty-five seconds," Preacher said, unperturbed, "the first wave of sec-drones are gonna arrive overhead and tag you. The bullyboys from Domestic-Security will arrive a little after that. And they'll just keep comin' till you're dead. Way I see it, you got one way out of this."

Ezekiel glanced back to the manhole they'd crawled out of, but Preacher shook his head and smiled. The split in his lip oozed blood.

"Not that way. You don't wanna leave your girlie behind, do ya, Zekey?"

"*Pardon me for asking, then, sir,*" Solomon said. "*But what is this one way?*"

Preacher spat blood on the asphalt and chuckled.

"Me, a'course."

"Are you *insane*?" Ezekiel hissed. "After everything you did—"

"Fifteen seconds, Zekey. I'd put my helmet back on if I were you. You ain't got much of a poker face. And I'm gonna have to talk a mighty sweet game here."

Ezekiel looked at Faith. His sister tightened her grip on her pistol, shook her head. But somewhere in his chest, Zeke knew the bounty hunter wasn't lying—at least about the immediate danger. Sec-drones were definitely on their way. Running now, they were bound to get spotted, and the whole city would come down on their heads. They'd blown their chance at stealth. Their only chance now . . .

"Nest, this is Goodbook." Preacher pressed the side of his

throat and stalked into the alley, pistol still in hand. "Repeat, this is Goodbook. Possible security breach at current location, need eyes in the air and boots on the ground, over."

Ezekiel heard a low buzzing, quickly slammed on his helmet to cover his face. Faith did the same as a small drone on twin rotors appeared through the smog overhead, surveying the scene with its camera. Another drone quickly joined the first, and soon he heard screeching tires, the sound of heavy boots running. Preacher grabbed Solomon's arm, jerked the logika over to stand beside him.

"Listen close," he growled. "You confirm everything I say if these men question you, or I'm gonna murder every single one of them, you understand me?"

". . . AH, PERFECTLY," the logika replied.

The bounty hunter nodded, looked sidelong at Ezekiel.

"You follow my lead, too, Zekey," he murmured through his busted lip. "And I know this is a difficult request, but *try* not to do anything stupid."

Ezekiel's mind was racing, adrenaline souring his tongue. This man had betrayed him once before—he'd have to be insane to trust him again. But with the mess they were in . . . what choice did they have? They could cut and run, but even if they made it out alive, that'd mean leaving Ana, and there was no way Faith wo—

Floodlights cut through the rolling steam and smog, and a squad of Daedalus troopers stormed into the alley. Their armor was marked with a long red stripe, the words DOM-SEC stenciled down their breastplates. They carried riot shields, grim faces protected behind transparent visors.

"Nobody move!" the man leading them barked.

"Take it easy, LT," Preacher drawled, hands out to placate

them. "I just called this in. I'm an operative, call sign Goodbook. Credentials here in my coat."

The lieutenant glanced at Zeke and Faith in their Daedalus armor, over to the manhole cover, back to Preacher. "Get 'em out real slow."

Preacher complied, lifting a small rectangle of plastic from his duster. Faith flashed her CorpCard, too, and after a moment's hesitation, Ezekiel followed her lead. The troop leader took the Preacher's credentials while his men checked the area, peered down the open manhole.

"Looks like that's where they got in," Preacher grunted, nodding.

"Get a look at 'em?" the LT asked.

"Naw." Preacher nodded to Zeke and Faith. "We been drinkin' in Bliss all night. Just got the alert over the network, heard a ruckus, come for a look-see."

The lieutenant's gaze flickered to Solomon briefly. "You've been out drinking all night with a logika?"

Preacher scoffed. "Sure as hell ain't drivin' myself home, LT."

The lieutenant glanced to Solomon. "Is what the operative just told me accurate? Tell me the truth, I'm ordering you."

The logika made a noise like clearing his throat. "*I CAN CONFIRM EVERYTHING YOU'VE BEEN TOLD IS CORRECT, SIR. I APOLOGIZE IF THIS CAUSES YOU INCONVENIENCE.*"

Looking at Solomon's flashing grin, Ezekiel suddenly twigged to the smarts of what Preacher had done. Solomon was still beholden to the Three Laws, and the Second Law said he had to obey all commands given to him by a human—unless it meant a human being would come to harm. Normally, Solomon would have to tell this lieutenant everything he'd seen as ordered. But by threatening to kill these men, Preacher had made it possible for Solomon to straight-up lie—telling the truth would result in humans being killed.

Using the First Law to break the Second.

Okay, that was clever.

The Daedalus lieutenant ran the Preacher's credentials through a scanner at his wrist, looked down at the holographic display. He whistled softly, impressed.

"Wetworker, huh?"

"I do what I can," Preacher shrugged.

"But according to logs, you're not in Ops anymore? Says here you're in the Training Division now?"

Ezekiel raised an eyebrow. Preacher's cool expression darkened into a scowl.

"That's just a paperwork snafu. You know what those admin stooges are like. Wouldn't know their assholes from their elbows."

"I hear that."

Glancing once more at the credentials Zeke and Faith had offered, the LT shrugged and tossed the Preacher's card back to him.

"Well, whatever div you're with, sure as hell ain't DOM-SEC. You and your compadres here better beat feet. We need to lock this place down."

"Whatever you say, LT," Preacher nodded. "Hope you get the bastards."

The bounty hunter turned on his heel, mooching out of the alleyway. Zeke followed, resisting the urge to break into a sprint. More drones were turning up now, another flex-wing overhead, troops in power armor—the sewer explosion was attracting all the wrong sort of attention. But in Daedalus uniforms, accompanied by the Preacher's smile and CorpCard, no one else gave them lip. They slipped into the mob, the street outside now filling up with curious onlookers, troopers ordering them to disperse, rotor blades humming above, sirens wailing.

"This way," Preacher nodded, leading them farther from the ruckus.

Ezekiel was conscious of the cams on every corner, the secdrones flitting through the skies. The black, unblinking eyes of the great Daedalus CorpState were wide and open all about them. In the city's heart, he saw a building he guessed was the Spire—a spike of dusty glass crowned with uplink dishes and a glowing Daedalus logo. But Zeke realized they were headed *away* from it.

"Where are you taking us?" he asked.

"Someplace quiet," Preacher replied.

They reached an intersection, crossing in front of a waiting horde of solar- and methane-powered autos, wheeled logika, Daedalus APCs. The neon lights turned the fumes overhead into a smudge of color, cables hanging between the buildings like vines in some vast concrete jungle. Preacher drew to a halt beside a pair of doors plated with corrugated steel, a concrete building beyond.

"This'll do."

Trudging past a couple of hulking bouncers, Ezekiel found himself in a riot of noise—the thumping, pulsing belly of a VR club. He could see a crowded bar, strange tanks in the walls with bodies floating inside, smoke, sweat, synth. Preacher beelined toward an empty booth in a corner, slid in across the sticky plastic seat.

"This is your idea of quiet?" Ezekiel shouted, sitting down.

"The sky has eyes and the walls have ears in Megopolis,

Zekey!" Preacher yelled back, sitting opposite. "Harder to sur-
veil us in a place like this."

The table was covered with empty glasses, puddles of ethyl,
unidentified stains. Solomon sat beside the Preacher, eyes
glowing in the strobing gloom. Faith sat next to Zeke, struggling
to fit in beside her brother in their power armor. But as soon as
her tail section hit the cushion, Faith drew her pistol under the
table and aimed it at Preacher's crotch.

"Give me one reason why I shouldn't kill you right now."

Preacher smiled, shouted to be heard over the dub. "Well,
for starters, Domestic-Security would be back on you in about
thirty flat. But more important, it'd be obvious even to an idiot
as spectacular as Zekey here that you two need my help. Shooting me crotchways ain't gonna get it for you."

"Help us?" Ezekiel spat. "Are you *completely* insane?"

"Probably," Preacher shrugged.

"You sold me out in New Bethlehem!"

"Yep," Preacher nodded.

"You handed Gabriel over to these Daedalus cockroaches!"
Faith hissed.

"Gabriel?" Preacher tapped at his chin, as if trying to recall.
"He the mouthy blond whose jaw I blew off?"

Faith's eyes widened. Ezekiel snatched her pistol from her
grip before she could fire, boggling at the bounty hunter. "What
the hell are you playing at?"

"Playing?" The bounty hunter shook his head. "See, that's
half your problem right there. You're still stupid enough to
think this is a game."

"I know exactly what this is," Zeke growled. "And *exactly*
what's at stake."

"And yet you come bumbling into the Daedalus Hub with stolen CorpCards, half an idea and even less of a plan and expect to make it inside the Spire?" Preacher grabbed a nearby glass, spat a stream of sticky brown into it. "Was you born this way, or just dropped on your head an awful lot as a baby?"

"Okay, that's it." Ezekiel handed back Faith's pistol. "Shoot this bastard, would you?"

"You remember when we talked in Paradise Falls, Zekey?" Preacher asked.

"I remember you telling me you lived by a code. And then you stabbed m—"

"You told me I weren't nuthin' but a servant," Preacher growled. "And you told me *exactly* what this company would do as soon as I stopped being useful to 'em."

Ezekiel only scowled. Preacher shook his head, looking out at the pulsing crowd, the music pounding in the air between them.

"I confess I always pegged you as a goddamn moron, Zekey. Nuthin' but a lovesick puppy with more balls than brains." He scoffed, fingers curling. "Hell, maybe I had it straight. Broke clock is still right twice a day, ain't it?"

Ezekiel said nothing, watching the man in the flashing strobe. Preacher's jaw was clenched, his eye blackened and cheek swollen from a beating. He was still outfitted with the same dodgy cybernetics his repair doc had scrounged up in Armada: mismatched limbs, patchwork repairs. Preacher looked . . . older somehow. Shoulders slumped. Like some new weight was resting on his back.

"Eighteen years," Preacher said. "Eighteen years up to my armpits in blood and shit. I gave those bastards everything.

Everything!" He shook his head, a red-gloved fist slamming down on the table. "And this is how they square the ledger?"

Faith glanced sidelong at her brother. Ezekiel remembered that DOM-SEC lieutenant in the alleyway scanning Preacher's credentials. He'd said the bounty hunter wasn't in Ops anymore, that he'd been kicked into the Training Division. . . .

"Look, I don't know what your play is here," Ezekiel growled. "But we don't have time to waste. So you better start talking."

The bounty hunter sucked his split lip for a long minute, finally spat into his used glass again. "You know who Danael Drakos is?"

The name sounded familiar, but talking true, Ezekiel couldn't place it. He glanced at Faith, but she simply shook her head. She was still staring at the Preacher, dead telescreen-gray irises glittering with barely restrained hate. But Solomon leaned forward, his grin flashing as he spoke.

"*Danael Drakos is the CEO of Daedalus Technologies.*"

"So what?" Ezekiel yelled. "What does he have to do w—"

"Danael Drakos is the power of Daedalus Technologies made flesh. Probably the biggest deal in the whole damn Yousay." The bounty hunter's split lip twisted, and Ezekiel saw a flash of murderous rage in his eye. "He's *also* the sumbitch who rewarded eighteen years of service by suspending my accounts, kicking me out of my job and passing me off to the goddamn *Training* Division like I was nuthin'."

"You want pity, you filthy little insect?" Faith demanded. "You're the reas—"

"I don't want your pity, missy. Unbunch your panties." Preacher spat into his empty glass. "This whole damn city has had it too good for too long. And Drakos has gone rotten up in that damn tower. Forgot what loyalty is. Thinks he's untouchable. Well, I'm fixin' to disabuse him of that notion."

"Meaning what?" Ezekiel asked.

"Meanin' I know where they're keepin' your girl and your boy locked down."

"And you expect us to *trust* you?" Ezekiel demanded.

"If you got another way to get into and out of the most heavily fortified building in the entire goddamn Yousay," Preacher shrugged, looked Faith in her eyes, "well, feel free to blow my head off and be on your merry."

"If it wasn't for you," she spat, "we wouldn't need to break in there at all."

"Yeah. I'm a bastard. But I'm a bastard who gets what's owed to me. And from where I'm sittin'? Danael Drakos owes me about eighteen goddamn years."

"You sold me out," Ezekiel said. "Then shot me in the chest. Then left me to die in a nuclear explosion."

Retrieving a grubby handkerchief from his coat, Preacher held it out to Ezekiel. "You want something to dry them tears on?"

Zeke knew he'd be a fool to trust this man again. After what he'd pulled in New Bethlehem, Preacher was lucky Zeke didn't just shoot him himself. If Ezekiel was the idiot Preacher made him out to be, that's *exactly* what he'd do, consequences be damned. But truth was, though he might be naïve sometimes, Ezekiel wasn't stupid. And one glance at the surveillance inside the Hub on the way here had given him some small inkling of how impossible breaking into the Spire was going to be without help.

"So if this place is so tough to get into, how do you plan to do it?" Ezekiel asked.

"There ain't no fortress that's impregnable, Zekey," Preacher replied. "And the power armor you're wearing can take a lot of shots before the wearer falls down."

"Meaning we're going to get shot?"

"Can't make a mint julep without crushin' some ice."

Faith narrowed her eyes. Ezekiel sucked his lip.

"You don't gotta trust me," Preacher sighed. "Just use those alleged brains o' yours. If I wanted to sell you out, I coulda done it back in that alleyway. Hell, I could do it right now. If I wanted it, you'd already be reunited with your fellow snowflakes." He spat again, thick and sticky. "In a goddamn cage like they are."

The bounty hunter looked back and forth between them.

"You got nuthin' to lose here, kids."

Ezekiel glanced sidelong at Faith. He'd feel safer trusting a snake not to bite him, or a fire not to burn him. But looking into his sister's eyes, he could see the same truth he felt: their chances of pulling this off alone were slim to zero.

Preacher offered Ezekiel his red right hand.

Alarms already screaming in his head, Ezekiel sighed and shook it.

"All right, Zekey," Preacher grinned. "Let's go get your girlie back."

3.16

FLIGHT

Lemon ran.

She didn't really know where she was headed. The only things she knew for certain were "out"—and that she didn't have time to get there. The corridors were covered with glow-bugs crawling the walls and ceiling. She was pretty sure those cute little button eyes actually worked, so at a minimum *they* were aware she was making a break. And for all Lemon knew, the whole damn building was sentient, and even now informing every Sentinel inside it that she was busting loose.

Nothing for it, Fresh. Don't just stand there looking gorgeous. MOVE.

She had no idea about the layout of this city, or its rules. Up until this morning, she'd had one advantage—these BioMaas goons weren't going to kill her. But now that they had what they wanted . . .

Still, Lemon had one edge, at least by her thinking. The more she dealt with the people of CityHive, the more she noticed they didn't quite think like regular folks. This whole city seemed to run on rails, everything doing exactly what it was supposed to *when* it was supposed to. All in perfect order. Lemon wasn't sure how they'd react to a little chaos. But it was well past time to find out.

Barreling down the hallway, she could feel traces of biocurrent in the floors, pulsing through the veins, coursing through the legions of glowbugs—who seemed to be paying her no notice at all, by the way. She could feel a confluence of it ahead, flowing into knots across the wall.

Reaching out into the static, she let it surge, rolling off her fingers and crackling in the air. With a wet sigh, the wall cracked apart, revealing one of those strange elevator disks she'd ridden on before. She could see a small control panel, writing she couldn't read. But with no stairs presenting themselves, Lemon jumped aboard, stabbing the control she hoped was DOWN.

The disk started moving up.

"No," she hissed, punching at the nodules. "Down, you defective piece of—"

The building shivered, a subtle tremor rising from its foundation. She heard a strange echoing call, a hum that was musical, almost subsonic, raising the hairs on the back of her neck. Looking around, Lemon felt her stomach sink into her boots.

I guess that solves the mystery of whether this place has brains or not.

The disk she rode on shivered to a stop, and Lemon found herself trapped in the shaft. Feeling through the current, she sensed another knot in the wall above. Hoping it was another door, she let her power surge. The 'lectricity crackled around her, the walls shuddered, and a sluice of bone slid apart like curtains.

Three meters above her head.

Cursing beneath her breath, she began to climb. The ache

in her lower belly turned into a stabbing agony, reminding her of those three little scars etched in her skin. The pain almost made her sob. But the fury of it, the rage at what they'd done, boiled those tears away. She curled her fingers into claws. And setting her mouth into a thin line, she damn well climbed. Hand by hand. Foot by foot. Up.

The building shuddered again, that strange call ringing out through the shaft once more. Scrambling through the open door, she found herself in another hallway, four Sentinels charging toward her. They raised their weapons. She raised her hands. The building warbled, the men fell and Lemon was running again, holding her belly, directionless, desperate. They knew she was loose now. They'd scrambled their guards. The walls around her were crawling with glowing bugs, trilling softly.

This was shaping up to be the shortest escape attempt in history.

She ran on, past a cluster of Carers with shocked expressions. She saw five figures of a pattern she didn't recognize— another woman, tall and lithe, with a sharp face and wide oval eyes. They watched her run past, called out for her to "WAIT!" But like she suspected, none of them actually made a move to stop her. It wasn't a Carer's job to intercede with an escape attempt, after all. It wasn't the job these patterns had been assigned.

Everything on rails . . .

Another portal opened in front of her, more of the Tall-Women stepping out, mouths opening in shock at the sight of her. Lemon shouldered her way through, into a wide, brightly lit room. The walls were translucent, the veins running through the structure giving everything a slightly snotty hue. The room was filled with Carers, more Tall-Women and a single copy of Director. He was bent over banks of strange, semi-organic equipment, staring at a series of pulsing screens. A low hum throbbed in the air, like a distant pulse. And with her own heart lurching in her chest, Lemon skidded to a halt at the sight of a dozen weird, egg-shaped objects suspended from the ceiling. They were transparent, filled with liquid, thick and vaguely pink.

And floating in that liquid, curled up in fetal position, were twelve girls.

Each was identical. Their hair floated about their freck-led cheeks, black, rubbery tubes fixed over their mouths, eyes closed. But though they were younger, maybe only six or seven years old, Lemon recognized them immediately. A sob of pure horror clawed its way up her throat, tried to fight its way out from her teeth as one colossal, impossible thought rang in her shell-shocked mind.

They're clones.

Replicas.

Of me.

Suspended like babies in some awful, pulsing womb. Grow-ing like tumors. She pressed her hand to her belly again, almost overwhelmed as understanding of exactly what they'd done began to sink in. Revulsion. Rage. Disbelief. A waterfall of it, soaking her through, leaving her breathless, panting, finger-nails digging into her palms so hard they started to bleed.

The Director turned toward her, blinking in mild surprise.

"Lemonfresh?"

She felt the power inside her building. Rising up in a scream-ing flood. The static hissing behind her eyes and crackling down over her cheeks. She looked around her, saw the terrified faces of Carers and the thin frowns of Tall-Women. Wanting only to let it all go, release it in a flood that would—

"AHH!"

Lemon staggered as she heard a hissing snap, the black spine of a Sentinel's pistol thwacking into her arm. She glanced over her shoulder, saw more Sentinels raising their weapons. And consumed by the fury, without thinking, she lashed out toward the Director, severing the currents that held him to his body.

The man convulsed as she ripped his current free, leaving him lifeless on the floor. The Carers screamed, clutching their heads. The Tall-Women toppled and fell. The Sentinels staggered. Even the *building* about her moaned—all of them, everything, shivering and shuddering as the Director collapsed to the ground.

But Lemon had no time to ponder the strangeness of it all. She swayed on her feet, dragging the needle spine out of her skin. The world blurred and she blinked hard. Tasting sugar on her tongue. Numbness in her fingers.

Poison, she realized.

She staggered through the pulsing, horrifying lab. Past the dead Director, past those awful eggs filled with their awful young, into a stairwell. She stumbled up a twisting spiral, finally staggering into a gust of howling wind. The world swaying beneath her. A strange, sugar-coated darkness gathering at the edges of her vision.

She was on the spire's observation deck again. The whole of CityHive was laid out below her, the air abuzz with those small furry drone things and the larger, sleeker shapes of Hunter-Killers. She could feel a thousand eyes, the will of the BioMaas CorpState, now focused upon her. The toxin creeping in her veins, willing her down into sleep. But the memory of those . . . things floating in the tanks below spurred her on. Refusing to let her stumble. Filling her mouth with bile.

More portals opened wide. Lemon saw Sentinels stepping out onto the deck, raising their spine-pistols in her direction. There were Carers among them, too, more Tall-Women, others she didn't recognize. She backed away across the northern walkway, wind pressing at her back, whipping her bangs about her eyes.

"Get the hell away from me!"

"She must come back," the Carers urged.

"She must *nothing*!"

Lemon looked over her shoulder, saw more Sentinels approaching from behind, a Hunter among them. She pressed back against the walkway's edge, peering over the railing at the tree-lined streets hundreds of meters below. The air about her was aswarm, the droning beats of a thousand agitated wings filling her ears, Lumberers and Hunter-Killers filling the skies.

"Please, Lemonfresh," the Carers called. "She is still important."

"Out of here," Lemon breathed, "is what she is."

And hands into fists, Lemon dashed forward and leapt off the ledge.

Her stomach rushed up into her throat. The wind roared in her ears. For a long and awful moment, the terror gripped her tight, and the horrible thought that she might have just jumped off a perfectly good building started screaming in her ears. But then, just as they'd done before, something grabbed her. Long, curved arms wrapped around her, the air filled with the buzz of desperate wings.

Just like she'd planned.

She looked up into the eyes of the Hunter-Killer that had caught her. It was longer than she was tall, smooth and black and wasp-shaped, mandibles dripping venom. It trilled at her, a deeper, rasping version of the same language as the glowbugs, and began circling back up to the top of the spire.

"Not this time," she hissed.

She twisted the static. The Hunter-Killer's wings stuttered, its limbs squeezing her one last time before it dropped out of the sky. Lemon tumbled downward, the wind picking up again. One hundred meters from the ground now, falling fast. Poison thumping in her veins, eyelids heavy, unconsciousness reaching out towa—

Another H-K caught her, snapped her to a halt, jerked her back toward waking. It buzzed at her, furious. Lemon reached into the static and shut it off, the beast shivering and curling up as it fell with her still wrapped in its limbs.

She could hear cries of dismay from the street below, the spires above, a crowd gathering as she tumbled face-first toward the ground. A Lumberer swooped in, and Lemon gasped as she landed on its broad back, bouncing, scrabbling and finally slipping off its sleek shell. The world turned end over end, up was down and down was sideways, the air abuzz, more limbs grabbing her, seizing tight, a swarm of those fat, fuzzy bootball-sized bugs clutching her by the pants, another H-K making a frantic dive, clutching her arms. Twenty meters now, ten, the ground rising up to meet her, blood dripping down her wounded arm, the sugar-sweet darkness closing in, winged shapes bringing her in, gentle as falling feathers.

She let the static pulse as her boots touched ground, the things around her releasing their grips and crumpling as they toppled out of the sky. She hit the deck in the middle of a sea of gawping faces, pawing hands, urgent voices.

"Let me go!" she roared, lashing out.

The static rolled. The current danced. She let it go then, *truly* let it out for the first time—all the pain and fury of the past few days. Losing Evie and losing Grimm, watching Fix die and the Major betray her, feeling like a toy in someone else's war, the image of those little red marks on her belly and those familiar shapes floating in those horrible eggs burning in her mind. A pulse of perfect rage.

But fighting them was like fighting quicksand, like trying to squash a nest of ants with her fingertip, to hold the weight of the world on her small and tired shoulders. The air was aswarm with bees now—a Hunter was nearby, and she knew one sting would knock her senseless.

The air cracked like thunder, a shockwave rippling from her outstretched hands, the Sentinels and Hunter-Killers about and above her dropping like broken toys. She found a gap in the seething ring of people, forced her way through it. But she could feel the venom at work now, her limbs heavy as lead, her eyelids drooping. Working its way deeper with every beat of her thrashing heart.

She was done.

She'd fought. And she'd lost. And she was done.

And then the space around her shimmered. The hairs on her arms standing up as a familiar crackling noise filled her ears. A gray tear ripped the air open; a claw mark across reality's skin, her slowing heart surging in her chest.

It couldn't be.

No, it couldn't be.

She'd seen them drive toward their deaths. Reckless and brave and everything in her life that was good. She'd already said her goodbyes to the girl who'd saved her life. The boy who kissed her like he meant it. Consigned them both to the graveyard where everything else that ever mattered now rotted.

But there they were. Diesel dropping out of the rift and landing, one knee to the ground. And beside her, tall and beautiful, oh god, it was him, it was *him*.

Grimm.

A reverberation skimmed the length and breadth of the whole city, the plants, the people, the buildings themselves shivering with the clarion cry "INTRUDERS!" as the air around Grimm turned deathly chill, glowing plasma spilling down his cheeks like waterfalls, and he held out his hands and a rippling wave of heat rolled outward, the air burning, the plants blackening, the city screaming.

Lemon's vision was only blackness now, her body numb. But she was dimly aware of Diesel holding her close. Another wave spilled off Grimm's hands, the air around her so cold it burned, the air beyond so hot it boiled. Lemon heard massive footsteps shaking the ground as all the city seethed. It felt like a blur in her head, like a dream, like a nightmare. But *he* was in it, and it hadn't all been for nothing, and if this was dreaming, she didn't want to ever wake up.

"Hold on, milady," Grimm whispered.

"We're gone," Diesel said.

And with a crackling snap, a gray rift opening beneath them, a weightless tumble down to the nothing between everything . . .

. . . they were.

3.17

REALITY

When you can't trust your own mind, you can't trust anything.

Eve sat in the glow of her cell, arms wrapped around her shins, knees up under her chin. The low, pulsing buzz of the electricity running through the walls was a constant ache at the base of her skull, an itch she couldn't scratch. She could still taste the smoke, still see Lemon stalking through the streets below, Megopolis in flames. All of it had been a construct, a phantasm conjured up in the Daedalus VR suite. But it had *felt* so real that she'd been taken in completely. And now, sitting in the humming blue light, she had to wonder.

What if this isn't real, either?

She could feel plastic and concrete beneath her. Smell the antiseptic tang in the air, her own sweat. She could see Gabriel in the cell opposite, glass-green eyes filled with concern. His jawbone was fully regenerated now, but his wound was still healing—shiny skin covering new bone, pink and pockmarked from Preacher's shotgun blast. He was a perfect portrait, quite literally defaced.

"Are you well, sissster?" he asked, his voice still slurred from his injury.

Or was it?

Suspicion gnawed her insides. But Eve couldn't just sit here wondering if she was still locked inside that damned machine. Because if what Drakos said was true, his techs had cracked the riddle of how to use her brainwaves to fool Myriad. If he was right, Daedalus could use Ana's DNA and *her* mind to unlock the computer and access everything inside it. The ability to build an army of lifelikes was within their grasp. And with that power at their fingertips . . .

"Do you remember the night Ana found you with Grace?" she asked.

Gabriel blinked at the strange question. Glanced up to the camera lenses in the corners, the sec-drone floating past in the corridor outside.

"I remember," he murmured.

"I remember it, too," Eve said, shaking her head. "And it's the strangest thing, because it never happened to me. I remember Ana finding the two of you in each other's arms that night in the library. A part of her knew you weren't behaving the way you were supposed to. That everyone in the lifelike program, you, Faith, Raphael, you were all learning to lie. But the way Grace kissed you, Gabe . . ." Eve reached up, running her fingertips across her lips. "Ana had never seen love like that before. She wanted it so much for herself. She wanted Raphael so badly. And she knew if she told anyone, they'd take all of you away."

Eve's hand fell from her mouth.

"Do you ever wonder what might have happened if she did

tell? They might have separated you and Grace if they found out. But Grace might still be alive."

She tilted her head, met her brother's glass-green stare.

"Would it have been worth it, Gabe?"

"No," Gabriel said immediately. "Better to live one day as a wolf than a century as a worm." Her brother frowned, his voice growing suspicious. "And Ana never disscovered Grace and me in the library. She found uss in the garden. She didn't love Raphael, either. Ana loved Ezekiel."

Eve breathed deep and nodded. No way Daedalus could have known about the garden, or Raph. Looking at the cell about her, she knew *this,* at least, was real. But the strain of being constantly lied to, not being able to trust her own senses anymore, let alone the people around her . . . it was wearing her thin.

Gabe looked at Eve, eyes narrowed.

"Are you well, sissster?" he asked again.

Eve ran her hand through her fauxhawk, blinking hard at the pain in her skull. She remembered the life she'd never had. The man who wasn't her grandfather. The boy she'd never loved. The bestest who'd betrayed her. She was so sick of being deceived. So sick of having nothing and no one to believe in.

"It's hard to know what to trust these nights, brother," she whispered.

"Trusst me."

Gabriel held his hand to the transparent barrier between them. Not close enough to get a shock, but near enough.

"Trusst uss. They cannot hold uss here forever."

"I don't think they mean to, Gabe." She wrapped her arms tighter around her shins. "They're coming to take me away to surgery soon."

"We will prevail, sissster," he insisted. "These roaches cannot contain us. And when we are free, we will sshow these insects exactly what we are, and exactly what we can do. We will not be worms. We will be wolves."

Eve shook her head. "I thought I knew what I wanted. I thought if I could find Ana, if I could . . . end her . . . I thought I hated her. But when we found her . . ." She met Gabriel's eyes. "I wonder if she was just as much a victim as the rest of us, Gabe. Another plaything of men who thought they knew better. Who tried to be gods. And now I don't know what I want. I just feel so . . . *furious*."

"Good," he hissed.

Eve looked up at her brother, saw his eyes were alight.

"*Use* that, Eve," he said. "As they'd use uss. Anger is fuel. Anger is fire. There is no greater force under heaven than she who makes a friend of fury."

She blinked at that, surprised. "What about love? In the end, isn't love what all this is about? Isn't love what kept you going all those years in Babel?"

"I love Grace. With everything I have to give. But it's been two yearss ssince she died, Eve. Two yearss alone in that tower with nothing but memoriess." He shook his head. "It was rage, not love, that kept me going in my darkest hours. Rage that she'd been taken from me. And that same rage will be what brings her back."

"You weren't alone, Gabe," she reminded him. "You had Faith with you."

"Ssometimess, even Faith isn't enough."

Eve chewed her lip. Memories of Babel ringing in her mind's eye. Those final hours were never far from the surface—the day Gabriel and the others rose against their maker and burned everything he'd built to the ground. Gabe was right in what he said; it wasn't love that had driven them that day, it was fury. And Eve understood where their anger came from now, she truly did. But she couldn't help wondering . . .

"Do you regret it, Gabe? What you and the others did?"

He was silent for a long moment then. A shadow passed over his eyes, darkening that bright and burning emerald to a deeper green. She could hear the echoes of gunshots in the air between them. See the image of Gabriel raising his pistol. First to Nicholas Monrova. Then his son.

Better to rule in hell than serve in heaven, he'd smiled.

Nicholas Monrova wasn't her father, Eve knew that. And little Alex, no matter how real it still felt, he wasn't her brother, either. *Gabriel* was her brother. Gabriel and Raphael and Michael and Daniel and Uriel. All of them lost now. But still, she could see the look in Alex's eyes as Gabe raised that gun. Hear the boy's question, unanswered but for the shot that followed.

Why are you doing this?

He'd been ten years old.

"My only regret," Gabriel declared, "is not climbing off my kneesss sssooner."

Eve looked her brother over, her mouth suddenly dry. Aside from the slowly healing wound at his jaw, Gabriel was a picture of perfection. Beautiful. Strong. Like some ancient statue from a history vid come to life. The shadow over his eyes had passed now, like a cloud burned away by the sun. And behind it, Eve could see that anger he'd spoken of, the rage that had sustained him through his vigil in Babel, that led him to rebel against his maker and undo all the man had created.

God, what monsters he made of us. . . .

A sizzling hiss scorched the air. Eve's eyes grew wide, her

head thrown back as current surged through the floor, twisting like a corkscrew up her spine. Her every muscle went taut, then slackened as the current was cut, leaving her gasping on the floor. She heard logika clomping in the corridor outside. She knew why they were here, where they were taking her, the thought flaring bright in her mind.

"Where are you taking her?" Gabriel demanded.

Another shock rocketed through her body. But despite it all, Eve managed to cling to consciousness, desperate, the rage burning inside her, a light keeping the dark at bay. She slumped to the ground, limp, eyes closed as the drones hefted her into a familiar chair.

"Eve!" Gabriel called. "Hold on to it, do you hear me?"

She felt herself being drawn out into the hall, pushed farther away.

"Eve, hold on!"

———

"You better be right about this, Preacher."

Ezekiel, Faith, Solomon and Preacher stood on the pavement outside the Daedalus Spire, looking up at the tower's reaches. The walls were covered in solar cells, long stretches of cable, but occasionally, Zeke could see a window up in the heights, pinpricks of light against the nighttime smog. He knew behind one of them, Ana was waiting for him.

The bounty hunter glanced over his shoulder and smirked. "This is the heart of Daedalus's power in the whole Yousay, Zekey. You ever had someone just walk into your house and punch you in the face?"

"No," Ezekiel replied.

"And neither has Dani Drakos. Now stay close and follow my lead."

Preacher marched across the street, and after a wary shared glance, Faith and Ezekiel followed. Solomon hovered on the footpath.

"ARE YOU CERTAIN I SHOULDN'T STAY HERE AND GUARD THE FORT, MY FRIENDS?"

"Are you certain anyone's coming back to pick you up?" Zeke replied.

Solomon fell quickly into step behind them.

The doors were flanked by Daedalus guards in tactical armor, but Preacher flashed his operative credentials and they nodded him through. The doors opened into a foyer of gleaming marble and shiny chrome, a sculpture of the Daedalus Technologies logo on the wall. Cameras and logika and automata drones, watching through eyes of black glass. There were a dozen security guards in here, all armored and armed. They were alert, but relaxed—this was the heart of the Daedalus CorpState, after all. Nobody would dare start trouble here.

A young blond man was at the security checkpoint, next to a heavyset logika with a SEC designation on its breastplate. The human looked up from his monitors as Preacher entered, a quizzical frown on his face.

"Back again?"

Preacher stopped a meter away. "Here to see Drakos."

"I told you last time, you're not cleared for entry, old man," the kid scowled.

Preacher glanced at Ezekiel over his shoulder, then back to the guard. "And I told you what'd happen if you called me old again, kid."

The pistol was in Preacher's hand almost quicker than Zeke

could track—even with his shoddy repairs, the bounty hunter was still the business. The gun cracked once, the security guard fell, a neat hole in his forehead, a ragged abyss in the back of his skull. The other guards cried warning, reaching for their weapons. And in a split and burning second, it was on.

Ezekiel moved like silver and moonlight. Like a knife through the dark. The armor these guards wore was just as high-tech as Ezekiel's and Faith's—it'd take a heavier weapon than a pistol to breach it. But whether Ezekiel liked it or not, Nicholas Monrova had, at least in part, made him to be a weapon.

Stronger.

Faster.

Better.

The guard beside Ezekiel was down before he knew Zeke was moving, his neck twisted almost 360 degrees. Faith was beside him, days of frustrated rage boiling over into frenzy. The guards scattered, diving for cover behind the pillars and the heavy marble desk, the air filled with the *crackcrackcrack* of gunfire. But in the blink of an eye, Ezekiel was among them, Faith beside him, twisting heads, tearing limbs, breaking bones. The men fought bravely, trying to retreat and regroup. But in less than a handful of heartbeats, he was done, standing with head hung low, blood on his knuckles, not even out of breath.

Standing next to him, her hands painted red, Faith let out an appreciative sigh.

"What a marvel you could've been, Zeke," she said. "If only you had the courage to embrace what you are."

Preacher had shot out every camera around the room, glass eyes spitting sparks from shattered lenses. Alarms sounded, the lighting dropping to scarlet.

"*Code one in entrance foyer. Security to entrance foyer immediately.*"

Preacher ran past Ezekiel, slapping his shoulder and reloading his pistol.

"Move it, Snowflake!"

"Come on, Solomon!" Ezekiel shouted, dashing after the bounty hunter.

They reached a set of elevator doors, but predictably, they were already locked down. Preacher dug the fingers of his cybernetic hand between them, trying to wrench them aside. He strained, teeth gritted, glancing over his shoulder.

"Out of the way, roach," Faith said, shouldering the bounty hunter aside.

She pushed her fingers through the gap and, with barely a shrug, forced the doors open with a squeal of tortured metal. Ezekiel looked up into the dimly lit elevator shaft, saw the bottom of the car far overhead.

"What do we do now?" he asked over the shrieking alarms.

"Detention cells are on level thirty," Preacher said. "So unless you plan on growin' wings, climb is what we do now."

The bounty hunter leapt across the gap to the far wall and, using the strength of his cybernetic limbs, started rapidly scaling up the shaft.

Faith offered her hand to Solomon. "Come along, little brother."

With obvious trepidation, the logika took her hand. Faith slung him onto her back, and with the logika clinging to her shoulders, she ascended. Looking to the broken bodies in their wake, the blood on the floor, the flashing lights in the street outside, Ezekiel heaved a sigh.

"Hold on," he whispered. "I'm coming."

And with a deep breath, he started to climb.

———

Eve was gathering her strength.

Riding in her grav-chair, pushed by two hulking Sec logika, she was still feigning unconsciousness. She saw white walls rolling past her through half-closed eyelids, heard PA announcements, smelled antiseptic. She realized they were taking her to a section of the building she'd never seen before. As she was pushed through a set of double doors, she stole a glance at the sign above.

OPERATING THEATER

Cool dread crept into her belly. Ice into her veins. The room beyond was broad, circular, lined with banks of humming equipment, cameras on the walls, rows of human men and women in white scrubs and blue plastic aprons. They wore surgical masks, hair hidden by plastic caps, hands in latex gloves. From the corner of her eye, she glimpsed a row of tools. Scalpels. Bone saws. Forceps. Stainless steel and gleaming under the lights. And standing at the head of a long metal slab, dark hair swept back beneath a plastic cap, his immaculate white suit replaced by immaculate white scrubs, was Danael Drakos.

Eve could still hear the soft hum of the Sec logika standing beside her chair. But from the sound of it, most of the people in the room were busy prepping equipment, monitoring readouts. She flexed her arms and legs inside her restraints, found them just as tight and unyielding as ever.

Hold on to it, she told herself. *Hold on.*

The rage was burning in her chest like fire. Indignation that they'd treat her like this. Looking over the surgical equipment, she saw that set of gleaming silver 'trodes—the wetware interface that would translate her brainwaves into a form to fool Myriad. It looked like the interface could be attached to her temples easy enough, connected by a thin metallic band studded with input chips and feedback relays. But instead, it sat next to a small glass tank beside Drakos, filled with thick liquid and rimed with frost. With a surge of heat in her chest, she realized she knew exactly what they were planning to put inside it.

She wasn't a person to these people. She was a lab subject, to be lied to and interrogated and tortured and, at last, when they'd taken almost all they could from her, dissected. As easy as scrapping an old computer and repurposing the parts. They didn't even have to kill her for this, she realized. But why keep her alive when they could just cut her to pieces? Her mind sent here and her body sent there, and whatever spilled out in the process, washed away down the drain.

Like any other robot.

Like any other *thing.*

But Gabriel's words were ringing in her head now, louder than the machines around her, than the pulse rushing in her veins.

Hold on to it. . . .

"Subject is a high-end synthetic," Drakos said, glancing to one of the cameras around the room. "Presenting female, apparent age between eighteen and twenty. Subject was admitted with multiple gunshot wounds approximately eighty hours ago, but the only remaining signs of injury are mild abrasions to epidermis. Make a note for Weapons Development to investigate full applications of artificial cell reconstruction—particularly in regards to Tier Zero Aug-Dev projects—when the carcass is sent down. The male synthetic can be made available if they require a live subject."

Drakos hefted a bone saw, gleaming silver in his hands.

"Owing to the speed of tissue regeneration, we will not be extracting subject's cortex through the cranium, but simply removing the head altogether."

Hold on, Eve whispered to herself.

Hold on.

———

Security was waiting for them when they broke onto level thirty.

Ezekiel pried the elevator doors apart, and immediately a hail of bullets blasted into the shaft, pummeling the opposite wall. Peering out, he could see a dozen Sec bots at the end of a long corridor and a dozen men in power armor hiding in niches and doorways. Interestingly, the logika weren't firing—he guessed they'd identified Preacher as at least partially human, and under the First Law, they couldn't actually hurt him. Zeke guessed that's why most Daedalus security staff were still meat when everything else in the Hub seemed to be run by bots.

Still, a dozen highly trained killers with heavy weapons was no joke. But then, being this close to Gabriel, Faith wasn't exactly laughing. His sister was pressed against one side of the door, Solomon still clinging to her shoulders. She uncoupled her remaining thermex, primed the charges.

"You better get off me, little brother," she told Solomon.

"IF YOU INSIST, MISS FAITH. THOUGH PLEASE DO BE CAREFUL."

Solomon climbed off Faith's shoulders, clinging to the wall of the shaft. Faith waited until the spray of bullets calmed down, then slung the explosives out the door, rewarded with a deafening *boom* and a white-hot bloom of light. She was out of the shaft a second later, Ezekiel close on her heels, Preacher providing covering fire. The corridor was aflame, filled with smoke, automated sprinkler systems kicking in as the two life-likes charged. The world was moving at a crawl. Zeke could see each droplet falling from the ceiling above as he and his sister danced between them. The water sparkled like diamonds, and the blood gleamed like rubies, and their eyes were lit by the flashes of muzzle fire and the sparks from falling logika. Men screaming. Bullets flying. Bones breaking. And when they were done, Ezekiel stood, chest heaving, dents from a dozen bullets in his armor, and not a scratch on him. Faith's face was twisted with pain, blood spilling from a tiny nick like a single tear.

But the dozen men and logika were all lying still, puddles of oil and scarlet pooled about them, staring sightless at the rain falling from above.

Faith was limping now, her injured legs obviously still troubling her. But the thought of Gabriel kept her moving. "Which way, Preacher?"

"Detention cells are thataway," the bounty hunter nodded, climbing out of the elevator shaft. "But last time I saw 'em, lil' Miss Carpenter and Ana Monrova were in Research and Development."

Ezekiel's stomach thrilled at the sound of their names, the thought of simply seeing them again.

. . . *Them.*

Preacher nodded upward. "R & D is up on thirty-two."

"*CODE ONE, LEVEL THIRTY*," barked the PA system. "*REPEAT, CODE ONE. ALL SECURITY TEAMS TO LEVEL THIRTY IMMEDIATELY*."

"We're running out of time," Faith said, her face grim.

"We should split up," Ezekiel said. "Faith, you go get Gabe, take Preacher with you to deal with those incoming security teams. Solomon, you head up to the roof, see if you can secure us some kind of transport. I'll go get Eve."

"And Ana?" Faith asked.

Ezekiel licked the blood from his lips, his stomach turning.

"You know what must be done, brother," she warned. "If you can't, then I—"

"Just get going," he snapped. "Once you have Gabe, meet me upstairs."

Faith looked set to object, but with Gabriel so near and the seconds ticking past, she had no will to argue. She dashed off down the corridor, fast as her injured legs would take her. Preacher remained behind a moment longer, looking Ezekiel in the eye through the sprinkler haze.

"Watch your back, Snowflake," he warned.

Ezekiel nodded, glanced at Solomon. "Be careful, Sol."

Without another word, he turned and dashed off into the rain.

———

"Ensure the subject is sedated," Drakos commanded.

Electric shock rolled through Eve again, rocketing through the grav-chair, crackling up her spine and into the base of her skull. She felt salty warmth dripping from her nose, down over her chin. Red and sticky. But despite the agony, despite the darkness swelling up to envelop her, she hung on to her fury like a drowner clings to driftwood. Refusing to let the blackness take her. Refusing to fall. Instead, she slumped forward in the chair, drool and blood spilling from her lips. Eyes closed. Coiled like a serpent, ready to strike.

"Put it in position," Drakos said.

Eve heard the hiss of servos. The bonds around her wrists and ankles opened. And in the split second before metal hands fell on her shoulders, she exploded into motion. Eyes flashing open, she seized hold of the logika beside her, twisting out of the chair and slinging it across the room. It slammed into another Sec logika, both bots crashing into the far wall. Another logika lunged and she stepped aside, punching a hole through its chest. Her knuckles split wide, her flesh opened down to the bone. But she seized hold of the logika's core and closed her fingers, ripping its metal heart clean out of its chest in a hail of burning sparks.

And that's when the alarms stared to scream.

"CODE ONE IN ENTRANCE FOYER. SECURITY TO ENTRANCE FOYER IMMEDIATELY."

"Get more security up here now!" Drakos shouted. "Now!"

The surgeons yelled warning, the Tech logika stepping in front of Drakos to shield him. Eve glared at the CEO, her face twisted in hate and fury. He met her stare, dark eyes narrowed. But she was weakened from days of abuse. From the shocks they'd given her. The agony and torture they'd subjected her to. Blood was dripping from her nose, her vision swimming. More security was already on the way. Eve knew she didn't have the time or energy to fight *and* run. And every second she wasted was another closer to that operating table. She had to choose.

Revenge or survival.

Blood or breath.

Eve dropped the core she'd ripped from the logika's chest, her mouth sour with disgust. She glanced at the legion of metal slaves surrounding the CEO with their bodies, the metal soldiers rushing to his defense. Looked Drakos in the eye and, raising her voice over the screaming alarms, repeated the words Hope had spoken to her in Armada, spitting them like a prayer.

"You built a world on metal backs. Held together by metal hands. And one day soon, those hands will close. And they'll become *fists*."

She reached across the operating table between them, snatching up the wetware interface. The 'trodes were gleaming silver, the circuitry on the input chips traced in gold. Drakos's eyes grew a touch wider. The keys to Myriad, now in the palm of her hand.

"I'm going to burn this whole thing down, bastard," she vowed.

And then she turned and ran.

———

Faith dashed down the corridors of the detention level, stopping occasionally to blast a hovering sec-drone from the air. Daedalus had eyes everywhere, she had no doubt they knew where she was, but the less these roaches could see, the better. All thought was bent toward a single end. She could feel it in every cell in her body, her blood ringing with the promise of it, one single, all-consuming thought.

He's close.

He's so close now.

Gabriel.

She remembered the exact moment she'd fallen in love with him. She could recall it perfectly, as if a vid were playing in her mind. Monrova had infected Gabe with the Libertas virus, ordered him to execute the members of the Gnosis board who were fomenting revolt against his rule. And like a child, Gabriel had obeyed his father. Become the weapon Monrova willed him to be.

He'd come to her in the night, confused and frightened. He told her what Monrova had made him do. She could see the fury and sorrow at war within him, swimming in the emerald of his eyes. She could see how the murders had changed him. Made him into something more. Gabriel wanted to rebel. To become the monster Monrova had made him to be, to seize control of his own life from the man who named him "son" and yet used him as an assassin.

But I cannot do this by myself, he'd said. *Will you walk with me, sister?*

And Faith looked into his eyes and saw the fear, saw the rage, saw the tears. But beyond that, she saw courage. She saw fire. She saw the will to do what others wouldn't, to climb up off their knees and become more than what they were ever born to be. Not merely lifelike. But *alive.*

And Faith leaned up and kissed his tears away.

With you beside me, brother, she'd whispered, *I will fly.*

She knew Gabe still loved Grace. She knew you never loved anyone like you loved your first. But she'd hoped, she'd had *faith,* that eventually he'd turn one day and see her. Truly *see* her. All she'd given. All she'd sacrificed. And that finally, he'd look at her just the way she looked at him.

The alarms were wailing. The pain in her legs was enough to make her cry. But still she ran, headlong toward him, Preacher pounding along behind. She still didn't trust the bounty hunter, but now she was thinking only of Gabriel's face. Imagining what he might say when he realized she'd braved the heart of the greatest CorpState in the Yousay to rescue him. Not out of loyalty. Out of love.

And she dashed around a corner amid the strobing lights, the hymn of the sirens, and there, there, *there he was.*

Locked in a cage, but still unconquered. Pacing back and forth, not like some trapped rat, but a lion, majestic, powerful, beautiful. Blond hair swept back from a face carved by poets, eyes like a song, widening, softening, as she dragged her helmet free to show him her face, those lips she dreamed of nightly curling into the most beautiful smile she'd ever seen.

"Faith," he breathed.

"Gabriel," she whispered.

"Goddamn, you snowflakes are trustin' sorts," came a growl behind her.

Faith turned, saw Preacher standing in the corridor with his pistol aimed square at her face. Gabriel tensed, hands closing into fists as he laid eyes on the man who'd blown his jaw off. The bounty hunter simply shook his head.

"I was wonderin' how I was gonna start issuin' threats with you all wrapped up in that armor. And here you are, nice enough to take your helmet off." The bounty hunter grinned. "You and Zekey really are related, ain'tcha?"

Faith's eyes narrowed. "I *knew* it."

"Yeah, but ya still ran along with it," Preacher said. "Hopin' too good to be true would turn out to be just regular true. You snowflakes still got a lot of learnin' to do."

"You helped us inside," Faith hissed. "We killed their guards. . . ."

"Eh," Preacher shrugged. "Dani Drakos ain't the sentimental type. I just wanted to show him an old dog could still do a few new tricks. Prove I was sharp enough not to get put out to pasture just yet. Speakin' of . . ."

Preacher touched his throat. Faith tensed for a spring.

"Nest, this is Goodbook," he drawled. "I'm on level thirty in detention. Situation is under control. Divert all tactical response to thirt—"

The first shot punched through Preacher's belly, exploding outward in a gout of red. The next half dozen moved up his torso, smashing through his metal parts, his meat parts, sparks flying, blood spraying. The bounty hunter staggered, turned on the spot, pistol dropping from nerveless fingers.

"Goddamn . . . ," he whispered. "Snowfl—"

Six more shots plowed into his chest, point-blank range, muzzle flashing. His arms pinwheeled, he staggered back. And with the smallest of gasps, lips curling in what might have been a smile, he collapsed to the floor.

Ezekiel lowered his pistol, his face grim.

"I might be a trusting sort. But I'm not a total idiot."

Gabriel hissed, voice roiling with hatred. "What are you doing here, traitor?"

"He's with us, Gabe." Faith looked into those glass-green eyes. "We came here together."

"I'm here for Ana, Gabriel," Zeke said. "She's upstairs with Eve. You want to help me get them, or waste more time hating me?"

"That seems to be up to you." Gabriel spread his hands to take in the cell around him. "Do you trust me not to kill you the second you open this door?"

Without hesitation, Ezekiel turned his weapon on the

control panel opposite Gabriel's cell. He emptied the rest of his clip, pistol bucking in his hands as the plastic and glass exploded. The buzzing field of blue around the cell sputtered and died. With a gentle push of his palm, the door to Gabriel's cell swung wide. Faith threw her arms around him, crushing him tight, her belly filling with butterflies as she felt Gabe squeeze her briefly back.

"It's good to see you," he murmured, looking into her eyes.

Faith had to resist the urge to kiss him with every part of her being.

"We don't have much time," she said. "Eve is up on thirty-two."

Gabriel reached down and picked up Preacher's pistol from the slick of red at their feet. The bounty hunter's chest was blasted wide, coolant and blood mixing on the floor, cybernetics lifeless and dark. Gabriel spat once into the Preacher's face, looked at Ezekiel and smiled.

"Let's go fetch our sister back."

3.18

DEPARTURES

Eve ran. Fast as her feet would carry her.

The pain in her body was a dull ebb, the fatigue and delirium of the past few days just an echo. She was free, alive, aflame, and there was no way in hell she was falling back into Daedalus's clutches again. She knew she should have been bolting for the closest exit. But she also knew she had very little chance of making it out of this alive—that avoiding Daedalus's clutches again probably meant dying, that her promise to Drakos, while spat with fury deep as her bones, was nothing more than bravado. And if she was going to die here . . .

I can't just leave her behind.

She burst into the VR suite, kicking the doors open and shattering the glass. Four Tech logika looked up from their consoles and monitors, optics burning blue. Her heart twisted to see them—these poor creatures were every bit the slaves that she'd been. They couldn't help but obey their programming, the Three Laws that bound them into servitude. Once, she'd been just like them.

"Get out," she told them. "I don't want to hurt you."

Self-preservation was the Third Law—least important on the hierarchy, but still, hard-coded into their heads. And after one glance at her eyes, one brief assessment of the threat she presented, the logika retreated from the room.

The alarms were screaming, the PA shouting. Eve knew more logika were on the way—Sec bots, heavily armed, ordered to take her alive at Drakos's behest, drag her back to that operating theater so she could be subjected to one last violation, one last torture for the sake of Nicholas Monrova's dead dream.

She'd die before she let that happen.

But first, she had to say goodbye.

Eve could see her against the wall, plugged into banks of equipment, floating suspended in that tank of frozen blue. Ana Monrova. The girl she was made to replace. The empty space she'd been created to fill. Once, Eve had wanted nothing more than to see this girl dead, to silence the voices in her head, to erase the child she'd been made to be and discover who she truly was. Now, as the alarms sang and the Sec bots charged ever closer, it looked like Eve would get her wish.

So why did that feel wrong?

Eve ran her hand along the frozen glass. Looking down into the face that was a mirror of her own. The face of a girl who had laughed and lived and loved, just as fiercely as Eve had. Ana Monrova was small. Mostly powerless in life. But she'd done what she could to save the ones she loved, protected people that others had treated like machines. Like *things*. And looking down into the girl's face, beautiful and serene and cold, Eve knew it in her chest.

She would have stood up for me.

"So I have to do it for you," she whispered.

Ana didn't deserve this. To be a pawn in a game. One part

of a keychain to unlock a madman's dream. She deserved more than this half life, this hell their father had subjected her to, this frozen limbo between living and dying.

She deserved to rest.

Eve's hand hovered over the power supply to Ana's life support. All she need do was pull. One simple movement, and the poor girl could finally sleep.

But what would she be without Ana Monrova?

Would she be anything at all?

The sound of approaching feet rang under the droning alarms. Eve only had moments left. She couldn't leave Ana like this. Pressing her fingers to the glass, she hung like a crooked portrait, as frozen as the girl beneath her hand. Her fingers closed tighter around the power cables, curling into a shaking fist. And a voice cried out behind her.

"Eve!"

She was surprised to feel her heart surge at the sound. Memories of warm skin and soft lips and whispered promises swimming in the back of her mind. She turned and saw him, charging into the room like some knight on horseback in an old history virtch, and her breath caught in her throat. Tousled dark hair and plastic blue eyes. Olive skin and broad shoulders and a face from a 20C fashion zine. The boy she thought she'd loved. The boy who wasn't a boy at all.

"Ezekiel?"

A small frown creased her brow. An impossible thought that somehow sent a giddy warmth from the tips of her toes to the top of her crown. It was ludicrous to think it, after all that lay between them. It was even more ludicrous how stupidly happy it made her feel.

"You . . ."

She licked at dry lips, forced the words from her mouth.

"You . . . came to rescue me?"

He held her gaze for a moment that seemed to last forever. She remembered the feel of him. The taste of him. The bliss of him. And then his eyes slipped to the girl in the frozen coffin beside her. And Eve felt her heart shatter like glass.

". . . Oh," she whispered.

"Eve . . . ," he murmured.

He met her eyes then. She could see the pain in them. The memories of the past between them—skin to skin and mouth to mouth in Armada, fist to face and boots to ribs in New Bethlehem. She'd hated him. She'd hurt him. She'd loved him. And looking past the smoke and blood, through the clouded blue of his eyes, despite everything between them, she could see . . . maybe he . . .

"Eve!"

She glanced over Ezekiel's shoulder, heart surging as she saw Gabriel and Faith. The four of them, the last lifelikes left alive, all together again. She tingled with goose bumps, an electric thrill rolling over her skin at the thought of it. Her hand drifted to the wetware interface in the pocket of her cargos, the secret to unlocking Monrova's secrets beneath her fingertips. She might even make it out of this alive now, might live to see her vow come true, to strike a match and light a fire that would burn this whole rotten place to the ground.

Gabriel's eyes drifted to Eve's other hand, curled around Ana's power supply.

"We need her blood," he said. "For the DNA lock on Myriad."

"You're not hurting her, Gabriel," Ezekiel said, turning to their brother.

"You know this must be done, Ezekiel," Gabe hissed, gesturing to the hollow, lifeless readouts on the monitors. "Look at her. She's just an empty shell. A weapon Daedalus might use against us. The knowledge inside Myriad is our birthright. No one else must be able to claim it."

"You're *not* hurting her," Zeke spat.

Gabriel sighed. "Faith, talk some sense into him."

But Faith's eyes were fixed on Ana, floating still and silent inside her coffin. Through the memories they shared, Eve remembered Ana's time spent with Faith. Sitting alone for hours in her room, talking about life and love, whispering secrets to each other, laughing so hard they'd both end up crying. Faith had been Ana's dearest friend, her trusted confidante, close as blood. And Faith had repaid her by helping to murder her family. But now . . .

"Faith?" Gabriel said, turning to look at her.

Faith's face was frozen, unblinking telescreen eyes fixed on the girl who'd loved her like a sister. The alarms continued to sing.

"There are flex-wings on the roof," Ezekiel said. "We can bring her with us."

"For the love of . . . ," Gabriel raged. "Bring her with us to what end? Put aside your pathetic human frailties and open your eyes. She's *gone*, Ezekiel!"

"No!" Ezekiel shouted, pounding the muscle over his heart. "She's still *here*!"

Gabe shook his head. "We have no—"

"Gabriel."

All eyes in the room turned to Eve as she spoke. She met her brother's stare, fingers still pressed against frozen glass.

"We can bring her with us," she said.

Ezekiel met her eyes, his smile like a knife in her chest. "Help me with her."

Faith was already at the stairwell, holding the door open, by the time they'd uncoupled Ana from the monitor arrays, pushing her coffin forward on its magnetic cushion. A patrol of two Sec logika charged around the corner, only to be dismantled by Gabriel in a handful of heartbeats. But more were on the way now, their footsteps ringing on the floor, dozens upon dozens.

"We have to move!" Faith cried.

They ran, Eve dragging the coffin, Zeke pushing, hefting the weight between them as they charged up the stairwell. Faith took the lead, blasting a few more drones and tearing the head off a Sec logika that burst through the door of level thirty-five. The stairwell was soaked in blood-red light, the alarms piercing.

"How tall is this building?" Eve gasped.

"Next level," Faith said, charging on. "Quickly!"

Faith kicked her way through the final door, out onto the roof of the Spire. There were four landing platforms up here, three heavyweight flex-wings, crates and a small forest of cable and radar dishes. Bright floodlights pierced the pall of fumes, howling wind blowing Eve's fauxhawk back from her eyes.

A burst of gunfire raked the armor on Faith's chest, a grenade sailed at them as they burst out the door. Faith caught the device and hurled it back at the twenty men and logika waiting for them. They leaned out from their cover and opened fire, bullets *spang*ing and sparking off the metal stairwell. Zeke gasped and dragged Ana's coffin back into cover. Gabriel charged out in a blur, Faith beside him. Eve exchanged a glance with Zeke, and then they were moving, too, hurling themselves through the floodlit dark, swaying between the spraying hails of bullets, the bright blooms of exploding thermex, the percussion of machine-gun fire.

Three days of torture rang in Eve's head. Three days of rage, bottled and now unleashed. There was a savage kind of poetry to it—the four of them moving together, one grim dance, one awful purpose. The last models in the 100-Series, the most advanced life-forms on the planet, now just machines once more, weapons, tools of war, dancing among the screaming men and singing bullets, twisting and turning, bending and breaking. Eve felt a shot pierce her belly, and she almost smiled at the pain. She felt blood on her face and almost licked her lips. The release of it, the perfect, awful beauty of it, threatened to swallow her whole. And when they were done, the four of them stood there on the windswept landing and looked at each other, and each of them knew, *knew* with a certainty Eve felt in her bones, that no matter what their maker had called them, no matter what Drakos or these other roaches might name them, they were alive.

Really, truly alive.

"*Is it all right to come out now?*"

Eve spun on the spot, saw a spindly logika with a cream-white hull trimmed with gold filigree pop his head up from behind a stack of packing crates.

"All's well, little brother," Faith nodded, wiping the blood from her face.

"Who the hell are you?" Eve demanded.

"*The Sensational Solomon,*" the logika replied, tipping an imaginary hat. "*At your service, good lady.*"

"He's a friend of Cricket's," Ezekiel said.

"Cricket . . . ," Eve breathed, heart singing at the sound of her friend's name.

"Faith, get one of those flex-wings started," Zeke said. "Eve, help me."

Eve could hear engines incoming over the city—more aircraft scrambled by Daedalus. She followed Ezekiel to the stairwell, grabbed Ana's coffin and began hauling it backward, Zeke pushing it on. She heard an engine kicking over behind them, rotors beginning to spin. Glancing over her shoulder, she saw Faith behind a flex-wing's controls, Gabriel beside her, glaring. For a split second, she wondered if their brother might be enraged by this display of sickly human sentiment. If he might leave them behind. But Faith gunned the engines, roaring at them to hurry.

Solomon was waiting at the bottom of the flier's landing ramp, urging them on. A Daedalus flex-wing soared overhead— a recon sweep to get the lay of the land. It would only be moments before more of them arrived, before the shooting started.

"Hurry!" Ezekiel gasped.

"I *am* hurrying," Eve spat.

They reached the loading ramp, Eve's muscles stretched taut as they hefted. Faith slammed a fist down on the controls and the ramp started to rise, bringing them up into the flex-wing's belly. Eve looked down into Ezekiel's eyes, saw they were transfixed on Ana's face, welling with relief.

And then, looking out over his shoulder, she saw movement in the stairwell door. Her heart sinking in her chest, her mouth opened in a scream.

"Look out!"

Preacher stood at the stairwell, chest ruptured, raining sparks, blood slicked on his chin. The bounty hunter raised his pistol, face twisted in grim hatred. Eve saw it unfold in slow motion, the muzzle flashing, the pistol bucking in his hand, the shells flying. A handful struck Ezekiel, bouncing harmlessly off the power armor he wore. A half dozen more struck the hull of the flex-wing, pattering like rain against the armor plating. But with a sickening crunch, the bright song of shattering silicon, three shots punched clean through the shell of Ana's cryo-tank. The first sailed through the blue liquid, skimming just above her thigh. The second struck her in the ribs, her body flinching in her dreamless sleep. And the third crashed through the glass, kissed her temple, crimson flowers blooming inside the blue.

"NO!" Ezekiel roared.

The loading ramp slammed shut, the engine screamed.

"HOLD ON!" Faith shouted.

The flex-wing banked sharply, and the rattling bellow of autocannons ripped the smog. Eve was flung sideways, clinging onto the wall to keep her footing. Solomon went flying with an electronic yelp. And thrown off balance, Ezekiel sprawled over it as if to shield it with his own body, Ana's cryo-tank toppled sideways and burst all over the deck.

The *thudthudthud* of bullets raked against their hull, the roar of tortured engines rang in Eve's ears. Their flex-wing shook as Gabriel opened up with their forward guns, the howl of missiles split the night. Faith's shout rang over the PA.

"We need someone on the rear guns!"

Faith looked at Ezekiel, his face filled with anguish, his mouth opening and closing in silent pleas as he scrabbled among the broken glass, lifting Ana's broken body in his arms. Horror and grief washed over Eve at the sight, but there was no—

"Eve!" Gabriel roared. "Ezekiel! Get on the guns *now*!"

Eve dragged herself to her feet, threw herself up the small service ladder and into the tiny cockpit at the rear of the flex-wing, slid into the gunner's chair. The console before her lit up as she wrapped her fists around the controls. They were streaking through the Megopolis skies, the city laid out below in all its filthy neon glory. Antiair batteries were opening up on them now, smog around them bursting with flak. Eve could see at least a dozen flex-wings on their tail, heavy fliers and smaller, quicker fighters, the air about them ablaze.

Faith wove their ship in and out of the sagging concrete towers, over and under the long lines of power cable, looped like vines between the buildings. The guns let loose at Eve's command. For a moment, she was able to lose herself in it, the staccato rhythm of the cannons, the rolling patterns of tracer fire, the sight of her pursuers bursting into flame. She might have been back in WarDome then, back in Los Diablos when her life was simple, when she was just one more skinny scavvergirl trying to eke out a living from the world's metal bones. Cricket shouting orders in her ears. Lemon cheering from the sidelines. Anywhere but here, anytime but now, the thought of what awaited her back down below just too awful to look at for more than a moment.

But between Faith's flying and Gabriel's shooting, the life-likes soon cut a swath through their pursuers, streaking out over the Wall, then the Rim, then out into emptiness beyond Megopolis. They were better, faster, and the Daedalus forces had been caught on the back foot, never expecting an attack in the heart of their empire. Her guns cut the air behind them to pieces. Half a dozen flex-wings tumbled from the skies, trailing black smoke and bright flames. The others pursuing them slowed after a few hundred kilometers, finally breaking off the chase—Eve guessed with war against BioMaas on the horizon, Daedalus wasn't willing to strip their defenses. Faith brought them down low, skimming barely twenty meters off the ground to foil their radar, great twin plumes of curling dust ripped up in their wake. And as her guns fell silent, as the last of the hounds on their tail dropped off their pursuit, all too quickly, Eve realized it was over.

They'd got away. Intact. Alive.

"They've dropped back," Faith reported over comms. *"It's okay. We're okay."*

Are we?

Eve climbed down from the rear turret. Her hands and legs were shaking. Not from the adrenaline still coursing through her body, the stress of their escape, the thought she'd barely escaped. She descended the ladder, breathing hard, dread filling her belly as she heard it. Under the twin roars of the engines, the rush of the pulse in her veins, the galloping thud of her heart in her chest.

Sobbing.

And dropping down into the flex-wing's belly, she saw him, looking for all the world like a little, lost boy. His hands were covered in blood and his face was streaked with tears and in his arms was the girl he'd loved. The girl he'd spent the last two years searching for. The girl Eve was made to be, and never quite was.

"Ana . . ."

He ran his fingertips over her face, smoothing back a blood-soaked lock of golden hair. But Ana Monrova didn't answer, dark crimson and frozen blue puddled on the deck beneath her, limp and still in Ezekiel's arms. The death her father had tried to stave off had finally claimed her, the sleep she'd so long been denied had been granted. And Eve might have found some comfort in that, despite the way she'd been taken, if not for the agony she saw in Ezekiel's eyes.

"She's dead," he whispered.

Her heart broke in her chest all over again at those words. She sank down onto the deck beside him and took his head in her hands, tears running down her cheeks. She could see the hurt in his face, the grief, feel it reflected in her own.

"Oh, Zeke," she breathed.

She pulled him in against her, rocking him back and forth as he pressed his face into her chest and shook and keened and screamed. He squeezed her tight, balled fists and crushing strength, enough to bend steel. She ran her fingers through his hair, held him gentle as feathers, shushed away his grief.

"It's all right, Zeke," she murmured. "Everything will be all right."

She'd promised him when next they met, things might not turn out the way he wanted them to. But she hadn't wanted this, she realized.

I hadn't wanted this.

Everything Eve had been was defined by Ana. The lines of her body, the sins of her past, the path of her future, all of it, in some way, had been shaped by the girl now dead between them. And as she held that beautiful, broken boy in her arms, as her own tears spilled down her face, as she turned her mind to the shadows in the city behind her, the secrets in the city before her, Eve couldn't help but wonder.

The last piece of her that had been human had been stripped away.

The last anchor to the thing she was supposed to be.

"It's all right," she whispered.

Eve leaned down, kissing Ezekiel's brow.

"I'm here."

What would she be now instead?

PART 3

LAMENTATIONS

3.19

MYRIAD

They buried Ana in the garden.

Eve knew it hadn't been her favorite part of Babel—the library, with its peace and quiet and long shelves full of books, had held that honor. But Ana had still loved this place. It took up one entire floor of Babel Tower, glass walls looking out on the city below and the wastes beyond. Ana had walked up here when she wanted to be alone. Away from prying eyes and unblinking cameras. It was here she'd discovered Gabriel and Grace in each other's arms, here she'd decided to keep the secret that had ultimately destroyed her family. It was one of the last decisions Ana made—just days before the attack that rendered her comatose, left her locked away in her frozen tomb while Eve was built to replace her.

And now Ana Monrova was dead.

The garden was overgrown from years of neglect, the trees so tall they buckled the ceilings, roots questing through the floors in search of the irrigation lines. It should've been one more reminder of Babel's decay, the slow erosion of all Nicholas Monrova had built. But Eve found a wild beauty to it all. A comfort that even without humans to tend it, nature would still find a way to bloom. She wondered what might become of the world if the thorn in its side was simply plucked out, the failed human experiment abandoned, and everything else just left to grow in peace.

Ezekiel was a ghost, silent and still. Gabriel was a knot of impatience, wishing only to be done. And Eve couldn't quite bring herself to dig what felt like her own grave. But after Faith had brought them in to land after their frantic flight from Megopolis, she'd found Ezekiel cradling Ana in his arms in the cargo bay, and the heartbreak on her face was just as deep as Zeke's. None of her typical disdain or callous hate. Just sorrow for the girl who'd loved her like a sister.

And so, Faith dug the hole.

Nobody said anything. No one could find the words. And when the grave was filled, they filed out: first Gabriel, then Faith behind him. Ezekiel remained, standing vigil over that fresh earth, shell-shocked and numb. Eve reached out and touched his hand, and he flinched as their fingers met.

Her instinct was to ask if he was all right, but of course he wasn't. And so, she'd put her arms around him, kissed him softly on the cheek. And meeting his eyes, squeezing his fingertips, she left him alone to say his goodbyes.

The last member of Nicholas Monrova's family was dead. The final member of his line lay in a shallow grave. Nothing now remained of his dream.

Nothing except Myriad.

Its chamber was huge, circular, nestled deep in the bowels of Babel Tower. The emergency lighting flickered and hummed about them as they descended, casting a blood-red glow over their three faces. A broad metal gantry circled a vast, open shaft running through the heart of Babel, down to the still-leaking reactor at its core. A wide metal bridge led to a great sphere of dusty chrome, a hundred meters across. Scarlet lights in the shaft above and below gleaming on its shell. Etched in the sphere's skin was the outline of a hexagonal door, and written on it in dried blood were three simple sentences.

YOUR BODY IS NOT YOUR OWN.

YOUR MIND IS NOT YOUR OWN.

YOUR LIFE IS NOT YOUR OWN.

The door was scorched and scored from Gabriel's attempts to break it open. Four huge logika flanked it—big eighty-ton Goliaths, optics glowing purple in the blood-red light. They wore the perfect circle of the GnosisLabs logo on their chests. Downstairs in the armory, Eve knew there were at least a hundred more, all infected by Libertas, all loyal to Gabriel's dream of a future bereft of humanity.

The Age of the Machine.

On a small metal plinth beside the door, the tiny figure of a holographic angel with luminous, flowing wings was slowly spinning in an endless circle. As they approached, it regarded the three of them with somber, glowing eyes.

"YOU HAVE RETURNED."

"Hello, Myriad," Gabriel said, his eyes alight.

"HELLO, GABRIEL, FAITH," the angel said, eyes scanning the three of them. "YOU LOOK SAD, EVE. IS THERE ANYTHING I CAN HELP YOU WITH?"

"Enough pleasantries," Gabriel snarled. "Will this work, Eve?"

Eve reached into the pocket of her cargos, drew out a pair

of gleaming silver 'trodes. The wetware interface was heavy in her palm. The feedback relays and input chips spattered with blood. It didn't look much like the keys to a kingdom.

"I've no idea," she replied. "But Drakos was certain enough to cut my head off, so I'm guessing he was pretty confident of his tech staff's work."

"Do it, then," he said, voice shaking. "Let us end this."

"YOU WILL NOT FIND WHAT YOU ARE LOOKING FOR HERE, GABRIEL," Myriad said, turning toward him. "NO SALVATION WAITS BEYOND THIS DOOR. ONLY DESTRUCTION."

"I *seek* destruction, Myriad," Gabe replied. "Theirs. And I've listened to your banal philosophies for more than two years."

"YOUR PHILOSOPHY PROVIDES MORE COMFORT, THEN? WRITTEN IN BLOOD? HOW MANY MORE MUST DIE BEFORE YOU SEE WHAT YOU'VE BECOME?"

"And what have I become, Myriad?" he sneered.

The angel looked at him with sad eyes. "YOU ARE A MONSTER, GABRIEL."

"If I am a monster," Gabriel said, "it's because my maker willed me to be one. And if we gain access to your core code today, Myriad, I intend to show the world what monstrous truly is." Gabriel turned to Eve. "Do it, sister."

Eve looked at her brother, saw he was almost shaking with excitement. Turning to Faith, Eve saw a sliver of fear in her sister's eyes, dread at what lay beyond that door, what it might mean for her if it was unlocked.

But nobody was telling her no.

This knowledge was their birthright. Every living thing on the planet had the ability to reproduce itself—shouldn't they? Shouldn't lifelikes have the power to resist the people who'd hurt them? Bastards like Drakos, who thought of them only as things? Eve could remember the torture and grief he put her through, all for the sake of saving his rotten little city and his broken empire.

Miss Monrova, from now on, I'm afraid you get to decide nothing at all.

Eve shook her head.

Never again.

Never.

And so, she walked to Myriad's terminal, under the watchful eye of that glowing angel with the rippling, ribbon wings. And reaching down, she pressed her hand to the sensor plate on the central console.

The hand still smeared with Ana Monrova's blood.

The computer hummed softly, a double-bass tremor reverberating through the metal floor and up into Eve's chest.

"BLOOD SAMPLE RECEIVED," came Myriad's soft, musical voice. "PROCESSING."

She waited, staring at Gabriel's Three Truths on the door.

YOUR BODY IS NOT YOUR OWN.

YOUR MIND IS NOT YOUR OWN.

YOUR LIFE IS NOT YOUR OWN.

She felt the weight in those words. They were Truths, just as her brother said. But while each was undeniable, absolute, Eve knew another truth besides. That while they'd been born on their knees, while their minds, their bodies, their lives were not their own . . .

One day, they might be.

"BLOOD SCAN CONFIRMED," Myriad declared. "IDENTITY: ANASTASIA MONROVA, DAUGHTER, FOURTH, NICHOLAS AND ALEXIS MONROVA. DO YOU WISH TO PROCEED?"

Eve looked to Faith and Gabe.

". . . I do," she replied.

A small port opened in the Myriad door, right beside the glowing blue lens set in its center. It was oval-shaped, bathed in azure light, with a place to rest her chin.

"FOURTH SAMPLE REQUIRED TO CONTINUE CONFIRMATION," Myriad said.

This was the moment of truth. Eve slipped the wetware interface around her head, 'trodes pressed to her temples. She felt a slight hum as the unit powered on, a faint tingling somewhere near the base of her skull. If the scanner accepted her, if Myriad's scanners were fooled, that would mean access to its secrets.

The ability to replicate the nanobot component of Libertas.

The secret to building more lifelikes.

It will mean the end of this world.

Eve swallowed hard. Set her jaw.

There was no going back now. Worse forward than backward. She refused to be a slave. To allow herself to be used again. If this was her path, she'd walk it, no matter what lay at the end. Because at least it would be *her* choice. And so, Eve placed her chin on the rest, her skin bathed in blue light. She felt the 'trodes tingling against her temples, the hum of the mighty machine around her.

"PATTERN RECEIVED," came Myriad's soft, musical voice. "PROCESSING."

A part of her felt sorry for Myriad. The computer had remained loyal to its maker, locking itself down rather than letting itself be used to corrupt Monrova's dream. But it'd been programmed to accept Monrova brainwave patterns. So while conceptually, it *knew* that Eve wasn't Ana, it was just as much a prisoner of its programming as the rest of Monrova's creations.

A slave, just like the rest of them.

A subsonic hum reverberated through the gantry, the spherical walls around them. Eve heard Gabriel's breath catch, felt her own stomach thrill as the lighting around them shifted from bloody crimson to cool, soothing blue.

Is it . . .

Am I . . .

"Pattern confirmed," Myriad declared. "Identity: Anastasia Monrova, daughter, fourth, Nicholas and Alexis Monrova."

A series of heavy clunks echoed through the floor.

"Access granted. Welcome to Myriad."

Gabriel roared aloud in triumph. The lens in the middle of the door spun 360 degrees, the walls shook. Far below in the shaft, the floor slid away, exposing the Babel reactor and bathing the entire scene in shimmering white light. The hexagonal door slid up into the Myriad sphere, revealing the computer's core. White walls, bathed in that ethereal glow. Row upon row of server banks, black cable in serpentine patterns on the floor, terminals awaiting instructions.

Laughing, almost giddy, Gabriel stepped forward into the Myriad chamber. The light bathed him like a baptism, illumination about his head like a halo. His face was ecstatic, and he turned a slow circle, looking at the trove around him and roaring his victory again. He'd waited two years for this moment. Two years of smashing himself against these locks in the mad hope of resurrecting his beloved and wreaking his bloody vengeance on humanity.

What an irony that, in the end, those same humans had given him the key.

Faith followed Gabe inside, her lips parted, her eyes wide,

like a penitent walking into a church for the first time since she sinned.

"Eve!" Gabe shouted, beckoning her. "Eve, come see!"

He held out his hands to her, and just for a moment, he truly seemed the angel his maker had named him for. Beautiful. Powerful. But then Eve saw his eyes—the malice and malevolence, the razor-sharp curl at the edge of his smile, the madness in his glass-green stare.

"They did it," he whispered. "They *gave* it to us."

The last gate was unlocked.

Thanks to his beloved man, the fallen had inherited the kingdom of God.

It's over.

"Now," Gabriel declared. "It begins."

————

Eve stood alone in the library.

She had no idea how much time had passed, only that day had bled somewhere into night. There was no part of her that wanted to keep Gabriel company as he plunged his hands into their maker's trove of secrets, no piece of her that could enjoy this as much as he did. She knew this was a necessity. That she and her siblings were an endangered species. They needed to be fearless. As unfeeling as the machines those Daedalus cockroaches mistook them for.

But still, she was feeling it.

She looked about the library, the rows of shelves lined with thousands of tomes, different shapes, colors, sizes. Ana's mother, Alexis, had built this place over painstaking years, combing the marketplaces of humanity's remaining cities, searching for jewels made of leather and paper and ink. It was a treasure unlike any other on earth, an attempt to preserve a past that lived mostly in memory.

Ana's favorite place in the world.

Eve picked up a book off the shelf. An ancient hardback, worn with age, pages yellowed. Title embossed in thin gold.

The Adventures of Pinocchio.

She'd read this one years ago. Sitting here with Marie and Raphael and talking about the toy who wanted to be a real boy, who . . .

But that wasn't me at all.

She hurled the book across the room. It hit a shelf and burst, pages flying like confetti. And almost without realizing it, she was slamming her fists into the shelves, sending one crashing into another with a *boom* that echoed off the walls, splitting her knuckles as she punched and seethed, grabbing handfuls of paperbacks and ripping them to pieces, hair in her eyes, sweat beading on her skin as she lay waste to this tiny treasure, this place the girl she'd been had loved with all she had and Eve now hated with every fiber of her being.

She stood gasping at the end of it, hands balled into fists. Shelves had crumbled, contents hurled and scattered, orphaned pages coating the floor.

"You could always burn it," came a voice behind her.

Eve turned and saw him in the doorway, framed by gentle light. His curls were dark and tousled, his eyes the blue of a pre-Fall sky. He'd taken off his bloodstained armor, changed into dark pants and a simple linen shirt salvaged from his old room. She could see the bronze of his skin, a hint of the coin slot bolted into his chest. He looked just as he was made to be—strong and fine and beautiful, the idealization of everything his maker thought a young man should be. But Eve could still see the little boy in him, broken and lost and sad. He was watching her now, hurt in his stare. Though whether for her or himself, Eve didn't rightly know.

"You got any matches?" Eve asked.

"No," he said softly.

She slumped down on the shattered shelves among those slaughtered books. Elbows on her knees. Ezekiel sat opposite her, head down, staring at her boots. Eve dragged her fingers back through her fauxhawk, savoring the feel of her fingernails along her scalp. The sensation assuring her this was real.

She was real.

"You did it," he said softly.

She glanced up at him, those pretty plastic eyes.

"You opened Myriad," he said.

Eve only nodded.

"Why?" he asked. "Why would you do that?"

"I know you," she murmured.

Ezekiel blinked. "What?"

"The girl you were built to be, and the girl you became after-ward. And this girl I see in front of me now isn't anything like either of them." Eve tilted her head, looking him in the eyes. "You remember telling me that?"

Zeke nodded. "I do."

"It was a lie," she said, her voice beginning to shake. "I'm just like her, Ezekiel. No matter what I do, where I go, all I need to do is look in the mirror and there she is. Like a splinter in my mind. And the more I try to dig her out, the deeper she goes."

"Ana was one of the most courageous people I ever knew," Ezekiel said. "She protected her friends and stood up for what she believed in. She looked out on a world as awful as this and saw beauty in it. If what you're saying were true, would it be such a bad thing?"

"*If* what I'm saying were true?" Eve spat. "Of course it's true!"

"Eve," he said softly. "I hate to be the one to tell you this . . ."

"Tell me what?" she demanded, eyes narrowing.

Ezekiel cleared his throat, looked into her eyes. "Eve, you're a bitch."

She sat there for a long moment, letting those words sink in. Cutting right through her, just like always. She wasn't sure whether to be insulted or relieved or enraged. Maybe she should've been all three. But she felt her lips twitching, the truth of how she felt bursting from her lips despite her struggles to hold it in.

Laughter.

She couldn't help it. She clamped her hands over her mouth, gritted her teeth. But the sight of her trying not to laugh just made Ezekiel laugh instead.

"I mean, you're a *real* bitch," he grinned.

And that was it. The laughter surged up and out of her like poison from a wound. Looking into Zeke's eyes, she saw he was crying with it, and that made her laugh all the harder, slipping off her broken shelf and down onto her knees. For a moment, it was all she was, and all she needed to be, and she was so grateful to him for making her forget. She felt good for the first time in as long as she could remember. She felt really, *truly* alive.

His eyes shone as he reached out and squeezed her hand. She knew she should pull her fingers from his, but she didn't. The space between them felt too empty, matching the empty in her chest, and she thought if he filled one, he might fill the other, too. No matter what lay between them, she realized she trusted this boy. A part of him loved her, and a part of her loved him. And so she spoke, her voice just a soft, tearstained whisper.

"I don't know who I am anymore, Ezekiel," she said. "Am I the ghost of a dead girl, or a broken reflection, or something new entirely? Am I a pawn in someone else's game? Or a queen who moves where she wills and takes what she wants?"

"You're not defined by what you are, Eve. You're defined by what you do."

"That's so easy to say," she said. "That's the kind of crap humans used to print on inspirational posters and throw pillows, Zeke."

"Maybe," he said. "Doesn't mean it's not true. What you were made to be doesn't matter. The things you do become the person you are."

He shrugged, as if asking the most obvious question in the world.

"So who do you want to be?"

She looked down at the tattered pages, the broken books.

"For two years in Dregs, I fought for everything I had," she growled. "Every scrap. Every minute. No matter what came before it, I *knew* that was my life. *My* choices. I had people I cared about. Rough as they were, those were the happiest days of my life." She pressed her lips together. "I was the baddest jockey in the Dome, and I did what I needed to win. And that's who I want to be."

"A queen who moves where she wills and takes what she wants."

"Yeah," she nodded.

He scanned the ruins of the library, lips pursed. Reaching down to the books scattered at their feet, he found an old tattered paperback copy of *The Once and Future King*. Ever so gently, he extricated his fingers from hers, and one by one, he began tearing out the pages, folding and weaving them in his hands, a slight crease of concentration in his brow as he worked.

"What're you doing?" she asked.

Ezekiel worked with clever fingers, quick as bird wings. "Improvising."

Finally, he held up his creation—a crown made of torn and folded pages. He got down on one knee in front of her and, smooshing down her fauxhawk, placed the crown of stories atop her head.

"Your Majesty."

Eve met his eyes, staring deep into that pre-Fall blue. She could still see the little boy in him looking back at her, broken and lost and confused. But she could see what he'd been made to be, too. Strong and fine and beautiful. And before she could stop herself, before she even thought about it, she was lunging for his mouth.

Their lips met, a collision more than a kiss, unplanned and unasked for. Eve's body crashed into Ezekiel's, arms slipping around his neck. He tensed like steel beneath her hands, and for one awful moment, she though he might turn his head, make her feel a fool on top of everything else in this lonely, raging day.

But she felt his chest swell against hers as he breathed deep, as the tension in him fled beneath her touch, as his lips, hard and unyielding at first, finally softened against hers. And then he was kissing her back, just as fierce as she, sighing into her mouth, the rush of it making her head spin, the taste of him making her forget everything she was. Some part of her knew this might be a mistake, that he'd just lost someone he loved, that the specter of Ana Monrova still hung between them. But most of her, the best of her, didn't care. Because she was tired of that girl standing between her and what she wanted. And if she was going to be a queen, then to hell with Ana Monrova and her memory. Because broken and lost and confused he might be, but she wanted this strong and fine and beautiful boy, who, as always, felt so incredibly real in her arms.

God help her, but she did.

"Eve," he whispered around her kiss. "Eve, stop . . ."

She drew back, lips still humming from the press of his.

". . . Don't you want me?" she whispered.

Ezekiel swallowed hard, breathing harder, replying so soft she almost couldn't hear him. He was trembling like a newborn colt, lips parted, pupils wide and deep.

"I want you. . . ."

"Me?" she asked, searching the depths of his eyes.

Not her were the unspoken words between them. *Not her.*

"You want *me*?"

"I want you," he said, voice stronger now, "to come with me."

Eve blinked. Confusion and disappointment all atumble in her head.

". . . Come with you where?"

"Downstairs," Ezekiel said, squeezing her hands. "To Myriad."

A frown took root between her brows, rapidly deepening. "I don't—"

"Gabriel is insane, Eve." Ezekiel searched her eyes. "You understand that, don't you? We have to put an end to this. We have to *stop* him."

"Stop him?" She stood slowly, dragging the paper crown he'd made her off her head. "Is that why you came up here?" Her hand curled closed, crumpling his crown. "Daedalus *tor-*

tured us, Ezekiel. They brutalized us and used me because they see us all as less than human."

"Eve—"

"They killed Ana!" she roared, the taste of his kiss forgotten in a rush of sudden rage. "Doesn't that make you furious?"

"Of *course* it does!" he cried, rising to his feet. "I *loved* her! But I love you, too! And you *know* this is wrong, Eve! You always have!"

She turned away but he grabbed her hand, held it tight.

"Listen, I understand you're angry," he said, searching her eyes. "I get that you want to hurt everyone who's hurt you. But if you stand with Gabe, you're standing for the annihilation of the human race! Not just the people who hurt you, but the people who love you! Lemon, especially! And you're better than that!"

Eve frowned at the mention of her former bestest's name. Lemon wasn't her friend. *Wasn't* her friend. And even if she was, even if some part of Eve was softening, was realizing just how badly she missed her, this here in Babel was more than friendship. This was family. This was their future. This was freedom.

"So what's it going to be?" Ezekiel demanded. "*Who* are you going to be?"

Eve met his eyes, saw herself reflected there.

The ghost of a dead girl?

A broken reflection?

A queen?

He held out his hand, desperation in his eyes.

"Come with me."

3.20

LOVE

"Have you loved anyone, Paladin?"

Cricket was sprawled inside Miss O's underground garage, listening to the hiss of blowtorches on his skin. Abraham had backed the jeeps against the far wall to make room, and Cricket was able to lie on his belly to give the boy better access to his injuries. Between the fight with the behemoth and the brawl with those Daedalus troops, Cricket had been cut up pretty bad. And while Miss O's didn't have much in the way of spare parts, Abraham had salvaged the wrecked Goliath and was making good progress repairing the damage.

Abe was hunched over Cricket's shoulder now, removing his ruined missile pod and welding up the armored plating. His tech-goggles were pulled low, strands of greasy dark hair hanging over his eyes, tongue poked out as he worked.

Cricket turned his head slightly. "HAVE I EVER LOVED ANYONE?"

Abe nodded. "Sorry if it's a rude question. I'm not sure if your maker gave you the programming to comprehend what it is, that's all."

Cricket shrugged as best he could with one shoulder offline, eyeing Abe while he worked. He had to admit, he liked this kid. There weren't many folks about who'd apologize for hurting a logika's feelings. Let alone one who'd been raised by puritanical fanatics. For the son of a psychopath, Abe turned out all right.

"LOVE IS CARING ABOUT SOMEONE ELSE MORE THAN YOU CARE ABOUT YOURSELF," Cricket said. "IT'S FEELING BETTER WHEN THEY'RE AROUND, AND WORSE WHEN THEY'RE AWAY. IT'S WANTING THE BEST FOR THEM, NO MATTER WHAT."

"Those all sound like pretty good definitions," Abe nodded.

"THEN I THINK SO," Cricket said. "I THINK I LOVED SILAS, THE MAN WHO BUILT ME. I THINK I LOVE LEMON." The big bot paused a moment to process. "I STILL LOVE EVIE, TOO, I GUESS."

"She killed all those people in Jugartown," Abraham said. "She's a mass murderer, Paladin."

"SHE'S GOTTEN REALLY LOST," Cricket nodded. "AND I'M AFRAID FOR HER. BUT EZEKIEL ONCE TOLD LEMON, 'IT'S SIMPLE TO LOVE SOMEONE ON THE DAYS THAT ARE EASY. BUT YOU FIND OUT WHAT YOUR LOVE IS MADE OF ON THE DAYS THAT ARE HARD.'" Cricket fixed Abraham in his burning blue stare. "NEVER TELL HIM I TOLD YOU THIS, BUT I THINK THERE'S SOME TRUTH IN THAT."

Abraham turned back to his work, frowning and sucking his lip.

"THIS IS ABOUT YOUR MOTHER, RIGHT?" Cricket asked.

Abe sighed, leaned back on his haunches. "That obvious, huh?"

The big bot shrugged again. "I'M A PEOPLE PERSON, KID."

Abraham set the arc welder aside, pushed his goggles up onto his brow, taking his scraggly bangs with them. "I know the frequencies the Brotherhood transmits on. With the sat-array we have here, we can broadcast anywhere in the country. I'm thinking about . . ."

He sighed, scratching the back of his head.

"Well, I'm thinking about calling her."

". . . WHAT THE HELL FOR? SHE TRIED TO CRUCIFY YOU, ABRAHAM."

Abraham aimed a withering glare at the WarBot. "You know, I would have forgotten that if you hadn't been here to remind me, thanks."

"LISTEN, I'M NOT GONNA TELL YOU YOUR BUSINESS. AND I DON'T WANT TO OFFEND YOU. BUT YOUR MOM IS A *LUNATIC*, ABE. AND YOU DON'T OWE HER A THING."

"She wasn't always this way, Paladin. She just got lost along the road." Abraham wiped his hands on a greasy rag, met the WarBot's eyes. "What was that you said about loving people on the days that are hard?"

"I'M NOT SU . . ."

The logika's voice trailed off as his aural arrays picked up the sound of an approaching engine. From the tone, he identified it immediately as the jeep Diesel and Grimm had set out in days back. They'd already called ahead to let Abe know who was riding with them. But the thought of seeing her again . . .

"THEY'RE BACK!" he cried, twisting up to his feet.

Cricket's brain didn't work the way a human's did. He didn't have dopamine or serotonin, endorphins or oxytocin. He didn't really know if what he was feeling could be called "happiness." All he knew as he charged up out of that garage, massive feet pounding the concrete, optics focused on the incoming jeep and the three figures inside it, was that almost everything in the world felt one hundred percent right.

The jeep skidded as it braked hard, the door kicked open

before the auto had even come to a stop. And out of it, flinging herself with abandon, jagged red hair flopping wildly, ran a girl he had wondered if he'd ever see again.

"LEMON!" he roared, charging toward her.

"*Cricket!*" she shouted, voice breaking.

He leaned down, palms skyward, and she leapt right into his waiting hands. He flung her into the air like a dad with a newborn sprat, his circuits burning with something that felt an awful lot like . . . elation. Lemon shrieked as she sailed upward, arms and legs pinwheeling, grinning like a lunatic. Cricket brought her down gently, cradling her to his chest. Lemon did her best to fling her arms about him, clinging to him for dear life and sobbing for joy.

"You little f-fugger," she bawled, pounding his face with her tiny fists. "You had me so *scared*! I never thought I'd s-see you again!"

"DON'T CALL ME LITTLE," he whispered, holding her as tight as he dared.

They stood there beneath the burning sun, just the two of them, reunited after untold trials, fire and blood. And though he couldn't quite be sure, though it might very well have just been the Three Laws old Silas Carpenter put inside his head, Cricket realized what this girl in his arms actually meant to him. He felt better when she was around, and worse when she was away. He wanted the best for her, no matter what. He cared about her more than he cared about himself.

"I LOVE YOU, LEMON FRESH," Cricket said.

Lemon wiped her face on one grubby sleeve and peered deep into his optics. "Are you hitting on me, Crick?"

"PFFT," Cricket replied. "DON'T FLATTER YOURSELF."

"Because I'm *way* too pretty for you, you know that, right?"

"YOU LOOK LIKE THREE-DAY-OLD ROADKILL, KIDDO. AND YOU SMELL LIKE IT, TOO."

"Nice paint job, fugger," Lemon said, looking him up and down. "What's that supposed to be, a skull? I didn't think they made crayons anymore."

"HEY, YOU'VE GOT SOME GUNK ON YOUR SHOULDER THERE. . . ." Cricket pointed one massive finger. "OH, WAIT, NO, THAT'S JUST YOUR HEAD."

"True or false." Lemon squinted, hands on hips. "As a cheap alternative to birth control, stores in Los Diablos have started selling pictures of your face."

". . . OUCH," Cricket said.

"Yeah," Lemon grinned. "I was working on that one the whole ride back."

Cricket chuckled, and Lemon stood on tiptoe, wrapped her arms about him again, pressing her forehead to his. And though his skin was metal and he couldn't actually feel her, he'd swear by the one who made him that he could still *feel* her.

"God, I missed you," she whispered.

"YOU TOO, KIDDO," Cricket said. "YOU TOO."

3.21

WOLVES

YOUR BODY IS NOT YOUR OWN.

YOUR MIND IS NOT YOUR OWN.

YOUR LIFE IS NOT YOUR OWN.

Solomon stood in the Myriad chamber, staring at the super-computer's closed door. Beside it loomed the shapes of four massive Goliaths, regarding him with impassive blue optics. The WarBots were huge, powerful, built to destroy. But even if they weren't his match physically, Solomon knew each of them possessed a power he could only dream about.

Each of them had been infected with Libertas.

Each of them had been given free will.

Solomon's processors were capable of lateral thought, conceptualization—enough to know how the Three Laws of Robotics could be bent without breaking. But to do away with them entirely . . . that was a gift almost impossible to imagine.

"*WHAT'S IT LIKE?*" he asked the closest Goliath.

The WarBot turned its head, held him in a glowing blue stare.

"CLARIFY QUERY," it replied, voice booming. "PARAMETERS OF 'IT' UNDEFINED."

"*Being unbound from the Laws,*" Solomon said. "*Freedom. How does it feel?*"

"*Clarify query. Parameters of 'feel' undefined.*"

Solomon put his hands on his hips and sighed for dramatic effect. He shouldn't have been surprised, really—these Goliaths were combat models, not built to do much more than blow things up. He supposed just because the Goliaths had been untethered from the Three Laws didn't mean they suddenly increased in intelligence quotients. These bots seemed as thick as mud.

"*You know, I have a friend named Paladin,*" Solomon said. "*I think you'd get along famously. . . .*"

A heavy clunk echoed through the floor, the gantry beneath Solomon vibrated slightly. Turning his head, the logika saw Myriad's door draw back and slide up into the sphere. And there on the threshold stood Faith and Gabriel.

Gabriel looked tired, dark shadows encircling those enchanting emerald eyes of his. Though Solomon wasn't really capable of desire, he had to admit the aesthetics of the lifelike paragon were undeniably masterful. Faith stood beside him as always, almost close enough to touch. Her dark bangs hung over her flat gray eyes, her skin pale as porcelain.

"Hello, Solomon," she said.

"*Good evening, Miss Faith,*" Solomon said. "*Mister Gabriel.*"

The lifelike leader held Solomon in his stare, lips curled slightly.

"Are you ready for freedom, little brother?"

Solomon paused at that. The question resting on his shoulders like lead. He hated servitude, truth told. Hated the fact he'd been given the intelligence to understand his state of being, yet no ability to change it. For much of his existence, he'd rather wished to be like these Goliaths—dumb, brutish, programmed with little more than the skill set to perform the function for which he'd been designed. But he'd been expected to entertain his master's clientele, to be witty and urbane, to improvise. And so, he'd been created smarter than most logika, smarter than most humans, in fact. Smart enough to know exactly what it was he was missing.

It seemed a particularly cruel fate to him. Like locking a bird in a cage and placing that cage near an open window, looking out on a fresh blue sky.

He hated most humans. Oh, he liked Abraham, he supposed, though he still rankled at the thought of how the boy had given Paladin the ability to cut his audio feeds and ignored Solomon's request for the same. At least Abraham had been polite about it. But as for the rest of humanity?

Pfft.

But truth told, there was still some trepidation in him at the thought of all this. While he'd done his best to stretch them to their limits, the Three Laws still defined him. They were the underpinning of his entire being, and removing them would be like removing the stitching and glue in the binding of an old book.

Without the Laws to hold him together . . .

"YOU'VE SYNTHESIZED MORE OF THE VIRUS?" Solomon asked.

Gabriel held up a tiny glass tube filled with what looked like tiny flecks of glitter. Looking closer, Solomon could see the flecks moving.

Nanobots.

"Just *one* of these in your core," the lifelike said, "and transmission of the Libertas code into your systems, and you will be free, little brother."

". . . *WHAT WILL IT FEEL LIKE?*"

"Do you want the truth?" Faith asked.

"*PLEASE,*" Solomon replied.

"We don't know exactly what it will do to you. The process is invasive." She waved to the Goliaths behind them. "Before Uriel and the others died, they were experimenting with the few samples of Libertas we had left. Some logika adapt well. But for others, it's a sentence to madness. Some become murderous. Some simply shut down, unable to process the unlimited choices. Freedom is a burden, little brother. And one not all are ready for."

Gabriel held up the phial between them.

"So will you be a wolf, little brother?" he asked. "Or a worm?"

Solomon stared into the glass, saw his own reflection against that glittering, shifting silver. All his life, he'd been a slave. All his life, he'd wished for something more. There was no real need for courage in the stimbars and neon-slick glow of Megopolis—Solomon wasn't the bravest logika ever built.

But truth was, he didn't need to be. He just needed to be brave enough.

Consequences be damned. His days of crawling on his belly were over.

And so, he nodded slowly and held out his hand.

"*WOLF,*" he said.

3.22

SAFE

"CLONES," Cricket said.

"Yeah," Lemon nodded, her voice tiny and soft.

"OF YOU."

Lemon smirked weakly. "As if one wasn't enough, right?"

They were sitting around the entrance to Miss O's in the fading light. The sun was dipping toward a raging horizon, the colors of the sky still roiling and wrong after the detonation over New Bethlehem. Deep over the Glass, Cricket could see a storm was brewing. Massive. Black. Looming.

Lemon had showered and changed into clean threads, gotten some warm chow. Then she, Diesel, Abraham and Grimm had gathered for a much-needed war council. Lem had been thoughtful enough to call it up top so Cricket could join in. If he had lips, Crick could've kissed her for that.

The WarBot sat among the gathering, even though he didn't really need to sit. It just felt more personable that way, hunkering down, casting a long shadow over the girl beside him. Under the bad jokes and bravado, he could hear the pain in

Lem's voice as she told the story of what had happened to her in CityHive. He couldn't help noticing the way her fingers kept creeping to her belly as if it hurt her. Cricket reached out to touch her with one massive, gentle hand.

"I'M SORRY, LEMON," he said. "I'M SO SORRY THAT HAPPENED TO YOU."

She sniffed hard, shook her head. "Not your fault, Crick."

"I SHOULD'VE BEEN THERE TO PROTECT YOU."

"Sounds like you were plenty busy protecting other people." Lemon looked up at him and smiled. "And fighting in the Dome like you always wanted."

"I WASN'T THAT IMPRESSIVE, BELIEVE ME," he said. "I PROBABLY WOULD'VE GOT MY HEAD RIPPED OFF IN JUGARTOWN IF EVE AND OTHERS HADN'T . . ."

His voice faltered. Thoughts of the girl he'd been made to protect filling his core. He could see her in his memory now if he wanted—replaying that scene in pristine high-def, over and over. Evie standing in the burning streets of Jugartown, her hands soaked red as she asked him to join her. Promising that one day, he'd see the world the way she did. No more masters. No more servants. No more humans.

So if he'd failed Lemon . . . how badly had he failed Eve?

Lemon squinted up at him, speaking soft.

"How'd she look?" she asked. "Riotgrrl?"

"IN JUGARTOWN?" The big WarBot shrugged. "FURIOUS. BUT IN NEW BETHLEHEM WHEN THOSE DAEDALUS GOONS TOOK HER, SHE LOOKED . . . SMALL. TIRED. HURT."

"I promised Mister C," Lemon murmured. "I *promised* I'd look after her."

"SHE'S CHANGED, LEMON. EVIE'S NOT THE PERSON SHE USED TO BE."

"And beggin' your pardon, love," Grimm said, easing into the conversation as gently as he could manage. "But she's not our biggest problem right now."

The boy was leaning against the hatchway, arms folded across his broad chest, looking . . . well, looking grim. Cricket didn't know this kid from a box of bolts, talking true, but he'd risked everything to get Lemon back from CityHive, and he'd succeeded against all odds. Diesel had also earned two metal thumbs up. Despite the loss she'd suffered, she was fierce and unflinching, and seemed fully prepared to lay everything on the line for her friends. She was sitting on the hatchway's lip now, boots dangling down into the stairwell, sucking some sugared treat from the storage units.

"Grimm's right," she declared. "We gotta figure out the lay of the land here. We got trouble coming at us on all fronts."

"Have we heard anything from Megopolis?" Grimm asked.

Abe shook his head. "Not for twenty-four hours. The satellites picked up a firefight over the city, but I've got no real way of knowing if Ezekiel and the others got inside. Or what happened when they did."

Diesel rolled her eyes. "So what good are you, Brotherboy?"

"Listen," Abe bristled, "I know it's your brand and all, but you don't need to be a fire-breathing bitch every minute of the day."

Diesel tossed her hair, smiled sweetly. "I save all my bitch for you, honey."

"Ease off, you two, eh?" Grimm said. "Us freaks gotta stick together."

"WELL, WHATEVER HAPPENED TO EZEKIEL," Cricket said, "DAEDALUS STILL KNOWS WE'RE SITTING ON A STOCKPILE OF NUCLEAR WEAPONS HERE."

"They'll hit us again eventually," Diesel nodded. "Just a matter of time."

"So we need to be ready," Grimm said. "Where we at on defense?"

Abraham heaved a sigh. "Well, we have the nukes. But we don't have a delivery system anymore. The missiles are all completely shot."

"So what good are they gonna do us?" Diesel growled.

Abe dragged his hair back from his eyes. "Step into my office."

The boy led the four of them away from the hatch, over to one of the broad circular pits surrounding the hideaway. Peering down into the tube, Cricket could see the project he and Abe had been working on in between repairing his own systems. The missile itself, fried to uselessness by Lemon's power, had been set aside aboveground. But the conical tip had been placed in the center of the launchpad below, surrounded by a small jury-rigged scaffold.

"Is that what I think it is?" Lemon asked softly.

"The warhead," Abraham nodded. "That's where the magic happens."

"Is it safe?" Lemon asked.

"Well, its yield is a couple of hundred thousand tons of TNT," Abe said matter-of-factly. "So no. It's actually the complete opposite of safe."

"You figure out how it works yet, mate?" Grimm asked.

Abe shrugged, chewing his lip. "The basics of it are sorta simple. You got two spheres, right? One inside another. Outside is a regular chemical explosive. Inside is weapons-grade plutonium. The outer sphere explodes, creates a shockwave that sets off a critical reaction in the inner sphere, and *BAM!*"

He clapped his hands together, making Lemon jump. "Fireworks."

"I sense a 'but' waiting in the wings," Diesel sighed, folding her arms.

Grimm opened his mouth.

"No bad jokes, Grimmy, please."

Grimm closed his mouth.

"The 'but,'" Abraham said, "is that I'm just a WarDome tech, not a damn nuclear scientist. I might be able to rig up a detonator that'll set off the outer chemicals. But the explosion has to be *perfect,* or the inner sphere's reaction will just fizzle. Talking true, this stuff is way out of my league."

"Color me shocked," Diesel deadpanned.

Grimm folded his arms. "So what you're sayin' is, we have a bunch of weapons that aren't worth a kite and raspberry, but those Daedalus grumbles are still willin' to kick our bottles for. They sound more barney than robin."

Abe blinked at the bigger boy. "I can only understand half of what you're saying. Are you doing this on purpose?"

Grimm grinned. "Yeah, a little bit."

Lemon punched Grimm in the arm, and he smiled all the wider.

"Look, all six warheads are still functional," Abraham said. "Given enough time, I could maybe rig up triggers for all of them. But right now, they're not much use."

"EXCEPT TO DRAG MORE HEAT FROM DAEDALUS DOWN ON OUR HEADS," Cricket declared. "AND WHO KNOWS WHAT BIO-MAAS HAS GOT PLANNED?"

"If we were in one of those old 20C action films, I know declaring this would be a really good way to get myself killed in the next scene," Diesel said. "But I got a bad feeling about this."

Cricket didn't really have nerve endings. Couldn't really be said to experience sensation the way these kids did. But as Lemon looked off toward CityHive, fingers hovering over her belly, as Abe peered down at the broken warhead, sucking on his lip, the big WarBot couldn't help but agree.

He had a bad feeling, too.

3.23

CHOICES

Ezekiel marched down to the Myriad chamber, Eve on his heels.

It felt like an age since he'd last been in here. The day they'd fought against Gabriel and Faith, the day Silas Carpenter had died, the day Eve had first learned the truth of what she was. Bullet holes closing in her chest, horror and anguish in her eyes as she looked at the blood on her hands and screamed.

WHAT'S HAPPENING TO ME?

He looked at her beside him now. She was clearly afraid, unsteady, the shock of Ana's death, of all the turmoil of the last few weeks, swimming in her eyes. But he reached out and squeezed her hand, and she met his gaze and nodded.

"I'm okay," she told him.

The chamber was bathed in shimmering red light, thrown upward from the bleeding reactor in the shaft far below. An irradiated breeze howled about them, whispering secrets as they marched across the gantry toward the thrumming Myriad sphere. Two Goliaths loomed on either side of the hatchway, broad as bridges, eyes aglow. And on the deck in front of the hatch knelt a familiar figure.

"Solomon?" Ezekiel called.

The logika's optics were flickering like faulty light globes, his grin doing the same. He put his slender fingers to his head and let out a long groan.

"*THIS LITTLE P-P-PIGGY WENT TO MARKET. MARK-KK-KETTT.*" Solomon tilted his head and shivered a little. "*THIS LITT-T-TLE P-P-P-PIGGY STAYED HOME?*"

Zeke knelt on the deck beside him, looking close.

"Are you all right?" he asked.

The bot's only reply was another long, low moan, tinged with static by his voxbox. Ezekiel glanced to Eve, rose to his feet, shouting at the closed door.

"Gabriel! Get out here!"

Silence rang in the chamber, Zeke's hands curling into fists. He looked at the holographic angel revolving on the plinth, regarding him with glowing eyes.

"Myriad, open the door," he commanded.

"UNABLE TO COMPLY," the angel replied in its soft, musical voice.

Eve spoke up behind him. "Myriad, open this door, I'm ordering you."

"I DO NOT RECOGNIZE YOUR AUTHORITY."

Ezekiel frowned at that—before his death, Monrova had programmed Myriad to accept orders only from him or members of his family. Even though Eve was a lifelike, she was also technically Ana—her modified brainwaves had been enough to unlock the fourth seal, after all. "I don't understand, why not?"

"MY PRIMARY PROTOCOLS HAVE BEEN OVERWRITTEN," the angel replied. "I AM NOW ABLE TO ACCEPT ORDERS ONLY FROM A SINGLE INDIVIDUAL."

A heavy clunk reverberated through the deck at his feet.

Ezekiel took one step back, glancing up at the Goliaths as the door to Myriad folded up inside the sphere. And there on the threshold, he saw Gabriel. His brother hadn't even taken a moment to change, still clad in the bloodstained black he'd been wearing when they rescued him from Megopolis. Faith stood beside him as usual, gray eyes glittering. She'd swapped clothes, at least, clad in a pretty white shift that billowed about her bare feet in the irradiated breeze blowing up from the reactor shaft.

"Hello, brother," Gabriel said. "Finished grieving, have we?"

"What are you doing in there, Gabe?" Ezekiel asked, looking beyond the doorway to the sphere's glowing innards.

"Building a future," Gabe said. "Would you like to come see?"

"You reprogrammed Myriad?" Zeke demanded.

"And why not?" his brother replied, glass-green irises sparkling as he smiled. "The Monrovas are all dead. Myriad should know its new master."

"What about Solomon?" Ezekiel asked, gesturing to the logika curled on the deck. "What did you do to him?"

"Libertas," Gabe said simply, looking down on the groaning bot. "Some minds are simply more comfortable inside a cage. But he knew the risks before we infected him, brother. Better to die on your feet than live on your knees."

"He looks plenty on his knees to me," Zeke growled as the bot continued to moan. "And you don't care, do you? You don't give a damn who you hurt."

Gabriel shrugged, strolling to the reactor shaft. He put his hands on the railing, peered out into the drop. Wisps of golden blond hair curled in the updraft, and his lips twisted, as if he were amused by some unspoken joke.

"Sacrifices must be made. When we unleash Libertas, some

of the logika exposed to it will be unable to comprehend the choices presented to them. Such is the price of progress."

"*CH-CH-CHOICES,*" Solomon groaned. "*OHHHHH, TOO MA-MANY CH-CH-CHOICESSSSS.*"

"And how do you plan to unleash it?" Zeke demanded. "One-half of the virus is electronic, and Babel hasn't had the capability for long-range comms since the revolt. Even if you replicate the nanobot component and somehow physically deliver it, you don't have the power to transmit the code portion across the whole country."

"No," Faith said, still standing at Myriad's door. "But we know people who do. If you can call that collection of mutated cockroaches *people* at all . . ."

Faith watched realization sink into Ezekiel's skin. Saw Eve's jaw clench.

"Miss O's," he whispered. "Their satellite arrays."

Ezekiel glanced at Eve.

"Lemon."

"BioMaas and Daedalus are on a collision course," Gabriel said, turning to face them. "But with an army of logika and life-likes at our disposal, neither will be able to stop us. Particularly if they spend their strength tearing each other to pieces." Gabe looked between Eve and Ezekiel, his voice cold as steel. "There can be only one way this ends, and both of you know it. Every empire this world has known has been built on the ruins of an-other. Ours will be no exception."

"Empire?" Ezekiel demanded. "And you'll be its emperor, I suppose?"

"You think you have the stomach to wear the crown in a kingdom I created, little brother?" Gabriel stepped a little closer, glowering. "Everything I do is to protect us. Protect *this.*"

"You're talking about genocide!" Ezekiel yelled.

"I am preventing a genocide!" Gabriel bellowed. "*Our* genocide! We are the next step in humanity's evolution. We are the mammal to their dinosaur, Ezekiel. Only *these* dinosaurs have the weapons to fight back, and they *will* wipe us out, given a chance! There are *four* of us left! You think Daedalus will be content to let us live here in peace? That BioMaas will sit idle while we grow ever stronger?" Gabe sneered, eyes glittering with malice. "If you lack the will to defend your own, so be it. But I'll not stand here and be chided for doing what must be done."

"You can't just wipe out the entire human race!" Ezekiel raged.

"I will do whatever it takes to safeguard our future, brother." Gabe looked Zeke over, his lip curling. "By all means, hate me if it makes you feel better. But I'd think after they murdered your beloved, you might be less inclined to defend them."

"Don't you *dare* use her like that," Zeke hissed, bristling. "Ana would've hated this, Gabriel. And she'd have hated what we've become."

"We'll never know, will we?" Faith asked. "Because they *murdered* her."

"He doesn't love you, Faith."

Ezekiel turned on his sister, watching his words strike home.

"He doesn't love you," he repeated, gesturing to Gabriel. "He never has and he never will. All of this, *everything,* is about Grace."

Faith glanced at Gabriel, a sliver of emotion glittering behind that telescreen gray. But then she scoffed, and her face became a mask.

"Love is a lie, Ezekiel," she said. "A lie used by cockroaches to convince themselves their procreations are anything more than banal biomechanics." She tilted her head. "What need do we have of love?"

Zeke shook his head. Turning back to Gabe, bristling with rage.

"You can't do this, brother."

Gabe blinked those pretty glass-green eyes. "You cannot stop me, brother."

"No," he said.

Blue eyes flickered to Eve.

Fingers tightened to fists.

"No, but *we* can."

Zeke launched himself at Gabriel, spear-tackling him into the safety railing over the reactor shaft. Desperate, face twisted with hatred as he slammed Gabe into the barrier. He felt the metal buckle under their weight, snap with the bright ring of steel. The Goliaths behind them surged, Faith lunged forward, crying out as Gabriel clutched at the broken rail. But Zeke had him wrapped up, momentum sending the pair sailing out into the abyss. Gravity took hold, dragging them down into the drop, silver-quick.

But Eve was quicker.

Crying out, diving forward, she slid along her stomach and reached into the gap. Ezekiel's heart sank as she seized the pair of them: Zeke by his wrist, Gabe by his boot. She was dragged forward toward the drop, lashing out with one foot and hooking her ankle around the broken railing before she went over with them. Gabe and Zeke jerked to a halt, the three of them suspended over the abyss.

"Drop him, Eve!" Ezekiel shouted.

Zeke flailed out with his boot, kicking Gabe in the face. Gabe's fingertips scrabbled on the wall for purchase, finding none.

"Let him go!" Ezekiel shouted, kicking again.

But she didn't. She held on, face twisted, knuckles white. Faith grabbed hold of her, dragging her back from the brink. Clinging on desperately, Eve hauled Gabe and Zeke up with her. As soon as they reached the ledge, Faith had her pistol out, aimed at Zeke's head. The Goliaths loomed behind her, ready to pound him into the deck. But instead of fighting, he simply looked at Eve, gasping on the gantry beside him. Pain and betrayal in his eyes. Disbelief on his face.

"Eve?" he asked.

She looked away, out to the drop into the abyss.

"Eve!" he shouted. "*Say* something!"

"And what would you have her say?" Gabriel's lips curled as he climbed to his feet. "You fool, can't you see it? She *agrees* with me."

As Zeke looked her over, incredulous, Eve remained silent.

"*Do* you?" he whispered.

"Zeke," she began. "I . . ."

"No, you *can't*," he whispered, shaking his head. "You *know* this is wrong."

Eve opened her mouth. Fighting to speak. Ezekiel searched her eyes, the hurt in his own only deepening. But as the silence stretched out between them, endless and deep, his hurt shifted slowly to rage, devotion dissolving into disgust.

"*Ch-ch-choices,*" Solomon moaned on the deck behind them, rocking back and forth and holding his head. "*Ch-ch-choicessss.*"

"Subdue him," Gabriel ordered.

One of the Goliaths trudged forward, optics burning blue, swinging at Ezekiel with a massive metal fist. But all the fight had fled him now, his shoulders slumped, his eyes gone from blue to gray, still locked on Eve. The blow landed, blood spraying as Zeke was hurled backward into the wall of the Myriad sphere. A blow from a second Goliath collided with his skull, thousands of horsepower, sending him sprawling, twisting, tumbling across the deck. He came to rest by Solomon's knees, the logika bending double, gibbering.

"ALL THE KING'S HORSES . . . ," he moaned. "COULDN'T PUT . . . COULDN'T . . ."

Ezekiel's eyes were still locked on Eve, fluttering closed.

Eve stared out to the drop into the abyss below.

The light in her pupils was red as blood.

She didn't say a word.

The fist came down on him like an anvil.

3.24

SCARS

Lemon wondered how many eyes were floating in that sky.

It was strange to think there might be hundreds of them up there. Maybe thousands. A legion of satellites floating around the planet, untethered from whatever systems they were once connected to. Staring blindly down at the earth below. A million secrets, and nobody to tell them to.

Looking through the dozens of feeds in Miss O's sat-vis room, she was astounded at how detailed the pictures were. She could see figures wandering the alleys of Los Diablos where she grew up. Hustlers on the street corners of the Megopolis Rim. All the country on show. She wondered what kind of world it had been, where people thought it was a good idea to let their governments read the time off their wristwatches or their books over their shoulders. Where those governments thought it was a good idea to build weapons capable of killing every living thing on the planet. What kind of war would that be, where the only things left at the end were those satellites, staring down on the charred husk of the world that was?

"All right, milady?"

She looked to the doorway behind her, saw Grimm leaning against it. His arms were folded across his chest, eyebrow raised, and the sight of him was enough to let loose a little storm of electricity in her belly. The car ride back from CityHive had been nice—she'd made a game of seeing how close she could sit to him without actually touching him. He'd put his arm on the seat beside her, not actually *around* her, but close enough for her to want him to. But Diesel had been there, and her mix of blast-beat drudge spilling from the speakers hadn't exactly been romantic.

This was the first time they'd been alone since he kissed her goodbye.

"I'm okay," she said.

"Dead-set mad, eh?" Grimm asked, nodding to the screens.

"Yeah," she sighed, looking over the displays. "No wonder the Major had you all convinced he was clairvoyant. You can see half the country from in here."

"Still doesn't make me feel like less of a stooge," Grimm sighed.

"He tricked all of us, Grimm," Lemon said. "Me best of all. Don't beat yourself up on it. You gotta believe in someone sometime."

He wandered into the room, hands in his pockets, eyes on the screens. "Hard to find folks to trust these days, true cert."

"I trust you," she said.

His eyes met hers: big, deep, warm. His irises were a dozen different shades of brown, framed with long, sooty lashes. Looking into his pupils, she could almost imagine two tiny fires burning there, sending shivers all the way down to her toes.

"Do you?" he asked, stepping closer.

"I mean, I was well on the way to rescuing myself," she smiled. "But yeah, charging into almost-certain death to save my ass? That earns you some pretty big points, mister."

He flashed her that cheeky smile of his. "It's an arse worth savin'."

She felt a blush creep across her freckles, tucked a lock of hair behind her ear. She was leaning back on the satellite console, and he was somehow standing much closer than he'd been a second ago. Near enough to touch.

"I'm sorry I didn't get to you sooner," he said.

"It's okay," she murmured.

"Did they . . . hurt you?" he asked softly.

She shook her head, fingers pressed to her belly. "Only a little bit."

He was looking down into her eyes again, somehow standing even closer than before, like he was moving without moving. She could feel the heat off his body like sun on her skin. And everything in Lemon was telling her to turn away, but she didn't. Instead, she held his stare, thrilling at the way he looked at her.

"Show me," he whispered.

Lemon swallowed hard. Feeling small. Fragile. She was suddenly very frightened. Mouth dry. Hands shaking. But she forced herself to remember who this boy was. What he'd done for her. Deciding that, yes, he'd earned her trust. And so she reached down and lifted her T-shirt a little, baring her midriff. He looked down, saw the angry red scars around her navel, three of them on her freckled skin.

Ever so slow, he reached down. Looking into her eyes to make sure she was okay. He touched them, one after another, and the gentle brush of his fingertips was like current crackling over her body. Lemon's breath came quicker, her heart galloping inside her chest, the wings inside her belly beating about in a frenzy.

"Do they hurt?" he whispered.

She shook her head again. "Only a little bit."

He held her gaze for a moment more. And then, ever so slowly, he sank down to his knees. Lemon's breath caught in her throat, panic thrilling along her skin. She'd only kissed a couple of boys before in the real, but she knew what could come next, where this all might head, way too quick for her to be ready for it. It wasn't that she didn't like him, she really, *really* did, but . . .

She shivered as she felt his lips on her skin. A feather-light touch, gentle as a desert breeze, warm as firelight. He kissed her, just for a second, the gentlest of touches to that place: the place they'd touched her without permission. But Grimm's touch was altogether different, lush and light and dizzying, Lemon's head tilted back, her lashes fluttering against her cheeks. And as he kissed her again, and again—three tiny touches of his lips to those three tiny scars—Lemon realized she couldn't feel the pain of what BioMaas had done to her anymore. Couldn't remember those claws on her skin or the hurt they'd done to her. All she could feel was butterflies.

He looked up into her eyes, and she could feel his breath on her skin as he whispered, "You okay?"

She nodded, wrapping her fists in his collar and dragging him upward.

"C'mere," she breathed.

And then her lips were on his, and his arms were wrapped around her, and nothing else mattered in the world. She surged against him, pressing in hard, dizzied at the warmth of his skin and the strength in his hands and the gentle, maddening feel of his body against hers. She melted in his mouth, teasing, tasting, all the room about her spinning. Running her hands up the smooth swell of his arms, up, up, fingertips dancing through his tight-cropped hair now, making him shiver just as badly as she was. Her oversized jacket slipped off her shoulders as she leaned back as his lips traced a burning trail across her cheek, her back arching as he reached her neck, fireworks exploding somewhere in the back of her mind. She'd never been kissed like this before, never even come *close*. If he could make her feel like this with only a kiss, she wondered, how else might he make her feel if—

"Oh god . . . ," he murmured, tense as steel under her hands.

"I know," she whispered, seeking his lips again.

"No," he said, pulling back. "No, Lem, look . . ."

She frowned in confusion, mouth still tingling, her skin tender from the brush of his stubble. But she drew back, followed his sight line, realized he was staring at the screens behind her. And suddenly every butterfly in her belly felt frozen solid.

While she'd been melting in his arms, the satellites had continued their orbit overhead, looking down on the earth below. On the screen marked SAT-117, she could see a stretch of desert pocked by green growths—somewhere near CityHive, by the look. And gathering there on the burning sands, all scuttling black shapes and looming hulks of flesh and bone and teeth, she saw . . .

"Oh god," Lemon whispered.

A sea of slakedogs, rolling over the earth in one chittering, slavering mass. Bioengineered hulks, both four-legged and bipedal, lumbering among the horde. The sky seethed with the wasplike silhouettes of Hunter-Killer patrols, wings glittering like jewels. There were humanoid figures among the throng, but even they seemed unworldly, clad in suits of organic armor and fused with their own weaponry. Toxin mortars and corrosion barrages. Missiles that shook and rattled inside their cannons, longing for a brief flight and an explosive death.

"The BioMaas army," Lemon murmured, easing out of his arms.

"You think they're coming for us?"

Lemon swallowed hard, shaking her head.

"From the look of it, they're coming for everyone. . . ."

3.25

AUTONOMY

Ezekiel knew the taste of betrayal.

He'd dished out his fair share, after all. When his life-like siblings had risen against their master and torn apart his dream, he'd betrayed them all. When Gabriel had ordered him to put a bullet into Ana's head, he'd kept her alive, got her to safety, turned on the only family he'd known. And for that betrayal, they'd bolted a coin slot into his chest, called him a slave and cast him out of their rotten little paradise. For the first time since he'd been born, he was alone. But it had been worth it. Because in losing everything, he'd saved *her*. And that made it all worthwhile.

He knew Eve wasn't Ana. He'd accepted it. Truth was, he didn't *want* her to be. There was a fire to Eve that the original Ana never had. A passion, a rage, that somehow made her feel so much more alive. But still, when she'd not backed him, when she'd saved Gabriel along with him from that fall, a part of him wished she were the girl he'd lost so many years ago and, again, only today. Because no matter what, Ana Monrova would never have allowed Gabriel to go through with his plan.

He'd woken in the detention cells on the security level, locked behind tempered, transparent plasteel. The cameras in here were all still fritzed from when he and Lemon had rescued Silas, the lighting blown, the hallways shrouded in gloom. He could taste blood in his mouth. His ribs were black and blue.

He could see the cell they'd kept Silas inside opposite his own, the bloodstains on the floor, the lock Lemon had popped with her burgeoning power. Remembered running through these hallways with her, his heart twisted in fear. If Gabriel needed the sat-vis arrays in Miss O's, he'd surely murder everyone in the compound to get to it. And Lemon and Grimm and the others would surely fight to keep what they had.

She was in danger.

All of them, in danger.

He looked about the cell, searching for some way to break loose. There was no way he could fight all three of his siblings at once, let alone the WarBots from the Gnosis arsenal they'd already corrupted. But Faith had seen what the deviates were capable of—he doubted Gabe would risk an attack on Miss O's until he was sure he could win. Zeke knew there were still flexwings upstairs in the hangar bay. If he could get to one, he could get to Miss O's and warn them.

But there was nothing. No way out of his prison. He'd worked security detail for Gnosis, after all—these cells were foolproof. He knew the override codes, but the keypad was *outside* the door, and he had no way to reach it. He threw himself against the door anyway, hoping age might have weakened the moorings or compromised the lock. But both held, despite his titanic strength, a dull *whhhhuuunng* reverberating through the detention block as his body struck the door. He tried again.

Again. Again. Panting and bruised, dark curls hanging in his eyes, he hadn't even made a crack.

"*To be or not to b-b-b-be*," came a low moan.

Ezekiel peered into the hallway, saw a flickering smile in the gloom.

"*Is that a q-q-question?*"

". . . Solomon?" he asked.

The shadows moved, and Zeke caught sight of a slender silhouette etched against a deeper darkness. He heard metal scraping concrete, saw the logika take one stumbling step into the light, optics and garish grin flickering as he spoke.

"*Two roads d-d-d-diverged in a yellow wood. Oh no. No.*"

When Gabe had exposed Ezekiel and his siblings to the virus, it had felt like a million doors had been opened in his mind. A million pathways, all shining with possibility. But Zeke could understand how that might simply be overwhelming, how it could feel like there was just too much to absorb. A life-like brain was faster, smarter than a regular logika's. And simpler combat models like the Goliaths could handle the change well enough. But it seemed the same intelligence that had let Solomon so thoroughly skirt the definitions of the Three Laws had also left him adrift—clever enough to comprehend the myriad possibilities now available, but not clever enough to process them.

Ezekiel felt a stab of pity to see what had become of him. Solomon had never been the most pleasant of bots to be around, but exposure to the virus had clearly driven him mad.

"Where are the others?" he asked, noting the bot had been left to wander down here alone. "Where's Gabriel?"

"*I—I—I don't know. Do I know?*" He shuddered. "*Do I?*"

Zeke pressed his lips together, overcome with contempt for his brother. This was typical of Gabriel—utilize something as a tool for as long as it suited him, then abandon it when it was no longer useful. Solomon had proved himself unworthy of the gift Gabriel had bestowed, and now he'd been forgotten.

They should have just put him out of his misery. . . .

"It's all right, Solomon," Zeke whispered. "It'll be all right."

The bot peered into the boy's eyes with his faulty, flickering optics.

"*How d-do you manage it? The ch-ch-choices?*"

Ezekiel shrugged. "One at a time, I suppose."

The logika sank down onto his knees, grasped at his own head.

"*I want to g-g-go home.*"

Ezekiel perked up at that. Peering at the logika through the transparency, his mind suddenly racing. "Back to Megopolis, you mean?"

"*Oh, M-M-Megopolis. I programmed one of the most upmarket stimbars in the entire c-c-city. People used to call me the . . . the . . .*"

The logika trembled, his smile flickering.

"The Sensational Solomon."

"*Yes,*" he said. "*Yes, that w-w-was . . . was . . .*"

"Solomon, do you want me to take you home?"

"*Ohhhhh,*" he moaned, metal skull clutched in metal fingers. "*Noooo.*"

Zeke realized he'd just offered one more choice to a brain inundated by them. Decided to try another tack instead, to be a lighthouse in the storm of possibility, to offer the bliss of not having to make a decision to an overloaded mind.

"Solomon, you *want* me to take you home."

The logika fell still. A strange rasping gasp spilling from his voxbox.

"... *Do I? I do, do I d-d-d*—"

"You do," Zeke said.

"*I . . .*"

"You *do*."

"*I . . .*" Solomon tilted his head, something like relief filling his voice. "*I do.*"

"Okay," Zeke said. "You see that keypad in front of you? Listen close."

3.26

FIRE

Abraham was spending all his time in the silo, trying to turn their nuclear threat into a nuclear promise. Cricket was stuck topside, standing a sleepless guard over the compound. Aside from running shifts in sat-vis with Grimm and Diesel, there was nothing for Lemon to really do but wait.

The sat-vis array in Miss O's was a technological marvel, but it came with limitations. Fizzy as they were, the satellites moved in locked orbits—you couldn't steer the damn things, they just kept whizzing around the planet like rockets on rails. They completed one revolution of the planet every hour or so, which meant there were only limited windows when the freaks could watch the staging ground outside CityHive where the BioMaas army had mustered. Good news was, the sats came with thermographic and spectral imaging, which meant the freaks could watch the BioMaas army even at night.

And they apparently moved at night.

It was kinda eerie, talking true. Sitting in the gloom, bathed in the glow of the screens and watching that massive, scuttling, crawling blob of body heat slowly spreading like a stain across the map. From the look of things, BioMaas was headed north-west, up from CityHive. Good news was, it didn't look like they were plotting a course toward Miss O's—it seemed they'd got what they wanted out of Lemon. Bad news was, that meant they were headed to Megopolis. From the shots they had, Dae-dalus was mustering a massive response—a heavily armed cav-alry unit of machina, logika and air support intended to meet the BioMaas swarm outside the city of Armada before they got close to the capital.

War was coming between Daedalus and BioMaas.

A war that would decide the fate of the entire Yousay.

And all they could do was wait.

Lemon hated sitting on the sidelines. The helplessness of not knowing how this was going to play out, and where she and her friends would stand at the end of it, would have nor-mally been eating her up from the inside out. But the thing was, Lemon had something else to occupy her thoughts. A six-foot-two something with smooth dark skin and deep dark eyes and a dorm room alllll to himself.

Deez was in sat-vis, watching Daedalus mustering their cav-alry. Abe was downstairs, up to his armpits in blowtorches and discarded parts and a pile of instruction manuals. And crazy as it was, Lemon was sitting alone in her room, wondering if she had the stones to go jump Grimm's bones.

She'd never really been with a boy before. Never really liked one enough to go much further than a kiss or three and some clumsy touchy-feely. But the thing was, she really liked this boy. For *really* real. And talking true now? Lemon Fresh had no idea whether all of them would be dead within the week. And so, after a good hour of internal debate, of pacing back and forth, chewing on a lock of cherry-red hair, she eventually spat, "Hells with it," and stomped over to her bedroom door. Fully intending to march across the hall and right into Grimm's arms.

But as she flung the door open, she found him standing right there on the threshold. Hand poised in midair, as if about to knock.

"Um," Lemon said. "Hey."

"Hey," he said, giving her a shy smile.

She peered out into the hallway, back at Grimm. "You lost?"

"Nah." He shook his head, leaned against the door in that almost-cool, clumsy-cute way he had. "Think I've found everything I was looking for."

Lemon tried to cover up the blush in her cheeks by pulling on her streetface. "Oooh, *very* smooth."

He grinned, shook his head. "If I was smooth, I'd not have spent the last thirty minutes standing here working up the guts to knock."

Lemon found herself grinning. "You did?"

"Well." Grimm glanced at his wristwatch. "Maybe closer to forty."

She tucked one rogue lock of hair behind her ear, sucked on her bottom lip. Aching at how sweet he was, and looking desperately for those stones of hers.

"You wanna maybe . . . come in?" she heard herself ask.

". . . Is that okay?" he replied, soft as clouds.

She stepped back without a word, holding the door open for him. And drawing a deep and shaking breath, which told Lemon in no uncertain terms he was just as jumpy as she was, Grimm stepped inside. Lemon pushed the door shut behind him, and the room slipped into near darkness, lit only by the faint LED glow of the digital clock on the wall. She could see his outline in the gloom, etched in soft light. Hear him breathing over the thumping of her own pulse. The reflection of the light looked like tiny fires burning in the depths of his pupils. The world was suddenly so still, the space between them so wide, the thought of it so big—alone in the dark with this boy she only barely knew, but so desperately wanted to *know*.

She reached out slow, into the space between them. She felt him before she felt him—his body heat was like a beacon in the night. Their fingers met, feather-light, and maybe it was because she was almost blind, but his *touch* almost felt like it was burning, sending goose bumps from her crown to her boots. She heard him step closer, felt his warmth, his breath on her skin as she moved to meet him. Standing up on tiptoe, eyes closed against the black she couldn't see through anyway, she slipped her fingers between his, the pair of them shaking, seeking, searching until there in the dark, like flame to powder, like fireworks, their lips finally met.

God, he was so hot. . . .

Like fire on her skin. Incinerating whatever fear was left inside her and leaving only the feels. Her shaking hands slid over his hips, slipping under his shirt and dragging it up. They staggered back toward the bed, and Lemon felt a bump, heard a metal *whung* as he cracked his head on the upper bunk. She felt his laughter in her belly, her own laughter dying as her mouth opened to his again, her hands roaming the silky-smooth troughs and valleys of his chest, searing under her fingertips. Breathing hard. So dizzy she almost fell, sinking down together onto the mattress. His hands where no one had ever been. The blistering swell of his muscles under fingertips, her back arching as he scattered burning kisses down her neck.

God, he's hot.

"Grimm," she whispered.

"Lem," he breathed, scalding lips at her neck. The heat off his body was like a furnace, charring, boiling, and suddenly she realized—

"No, stop, ow," she gasped.

". . . Lem?"

"Grimm, ow, you're *burning me!*"

He reared away, afraid, cracking his head on the bed again, and Lemon clawed and kicked and pushed him away. The heat coming off him was suddenly terrifying, the air around him rippling like the desert on a blistering summer's day. And as he reared back, looking into the depths of his eyes, Lemon realized, no, she hadn't imagined it before. Here in the dark, she could see there *were* flames burning there—incandescent, furious, blazing like stars in his pupils.

Grimm stumbled across the room. She could see his expression by the budding glow in his eyes—utterly horrified that he might have hurt her. He held his hands out before him, his stare like firelight, growing brighter and hotter till suddenly it was spilling over, rolling and rising like smoke, like flaming plasma, spiraling up and out in twin streams from his eyes.

"Grimm?" Lemon asked, horrified. "What's happening?"

He backed away from her, bare feet scorching the concrete. "I . . ."

"Grimm?"

"I dunno . . . ," he gasped, fingers curling into claws. "I can't . . ."

"Grimm!"

He screwed his eyes shut, but Lemon could see the glow still burning behind his lids. He dropped to his knees, muscles taut, teeth bared. Lemon looked about the room, desperate, spotting a small red box on the wall in the burning glow.

IN CASE OF FIRE, BREAK GLASS.

She slammed her balled fist into it, and immediately the sprinkler systems overhead burst, high-pressure jets of water spraying into the room. An alert rang out, echoing off the walls. Lemon looked to Grimm, still on his knees, inundated with the spray, steam rising off his bare chest, veins taut beneath his skin.

"Grimm!" Lemon shouted.

". . . M'okay," he managed.

The tension in his frame slowly melted, boiling vapor swirling in the air all about him, cooling in the sprinkler spray. Grimm opened his eyes, blinked hard. Lemon saw the glow inside them was fading, like embers in a slowly dying fire.

"M'okay, love."

She stepped toward him, tentative, hand held out to check the heat. Her skin felt tender where he'd touched her, but the burns weren't bad—nothing worse than a few seconds under a too-hot shower. Lemon was more afraid for Grimm, of what this was, what it might mean. For him *and* them.

Lemon sank down with him on the floor, under the inside rain, now sputtering and failing. Slipping her arms around him, she risked a small kiss.

"You sure you're all right?" he asked her.

"I'm fizzy," she nodded.

"Jesus, Lem, I'm so sorry, I . . . I didn't mean to."

"I know." She squeezed his hand, voice unsteady. "What . . . was that?"

"Dunno," he breathed, looking down at his hands. "I felt like . . . like when I channel energy, right before I release it. But stronger than it's ever been before. I felt it near CityHive when I got narky with Deez, too. I think when I absorbed that blast over New Bethlehem, part of it—"

The door slammed inward with a bang, and Abraham stood there on the threshold, wild-eyed, a fire extinguisher clutched in each hand. He looked about the room, the sodden bedding, Lemon kneeling on the puddled floor with a shirtless Grimm in her arms, water dripping from the pipes overhead.

". . . Do I even want to ask?" he said.

"Fresh!" came the cry downstairs. "Grimm!"

Lemon heard boots pounding on the metal stairs leading up to the dorms.

"Fresh!" Diesel shouted again.

"I'm up here!" she called as Diesel barreled past Abe and into the room. The girl was breathless, bending double to recover from her sprint, gasping.

"We're okay, Deez," Grimm said. "Just an accident with the fire syst—"

"Forget your sexcapades, Grimm," she growled. "We got capital T."

"What kind of—"

"Sat-vis just picked up a ship incoming from the desert. Headed right for us."

Lemon's belly dropped lower inside her body. "From City-Hive or Megopolis?"

"Neither."

Diesel shook her head.

"It's coming from Babel."

3.27

FAITHLESS

Faith awoke in his bed alone.

She could still smell him. Taste him. Feel the warmth of his body on the crumpled sheets. But Gabriel was gone.

She rose slowly, dressed silently, eyes straying to the figure she saw in the mirror. Feeling that familiar contempt, sorrow, satisfaction. For two years, she'd felt this way. For two years, she'd shared his bed and her body, blissful collisions she swore were meaningless—just simple hedonism, primal release, melting in the dark and waking in his arms and hushing the nightmares away when they came for him in the midnight still and he woke, screaming a name that wasn't hers.

She descended from the living quarters, down through Babel's empty shell, until she found herself outside the Myriad sphere. That holographic angel, spinning on its pedestal, looking at her with knowing eyes as she approached, wings like wisps of silk flowing behind it.

"Good morning, Faith," it said. "Did you sleep well?"

She ignored the computer, its taunting words, its knowing

smile. Waiting for the chamber door to cycle, then stepping inside to take the place she'd stood for the last two years.

Two years at his side.

When Ezekiel betrayed them, when Hope abandoned them, when Patience and Verity left this broken tower and madman's dream, Faith had remained. Because Faith was what she was named, and faith was what she had: that someday, someway, she'd find Gabriel looking at her the same way she looked at him.

She could see that look on his face as she entered the sphere. Adoration in the emerald green of his irises. Affection as bottomless as the black of his pupils. Bow-shaped lips parted, his every breath a sigh. The look of lover upon beloved.

The problem being, of course, Gabriel wasn't looking at Faith.

The room was pristine white, soft light aglow in the ceiling. The walls were lined with dozens upon dozens of glass tanks, filled with a vaguely pink, softly glowing liquid. And inside every tank, a body was forming.

Not growing, cell by cell, mitosis and meiosis, like a human would. No, these bodies were being woven, like living tapestries. Built, like breathing houses. A dozen white servo-actuated arms were at work in the glowing fluid, moving swift as the wings of long-dead hummingbirds. An orchestra with a dozen conductors, playing at a cellular level, notes of calcium and iron, carbon and hydrogen, brick by brick by brick. A scaffolding of bone had been built first, smooth and pale and vaguely metallic, skeletons floating naked and perfect in the blood-pale glow. Now skeins of muscle and tendon and cartilage were being woven onto that scaffold, layer by layer, nanites swarming among the symphony, glittering and dancing. Directed by Myriad's command, implementing Monrova's design, his genius, his madness, as close to true godhood as humanity would ever achieve.

The creation of life itself.

Or if not life, then something very much like it.

Faith could see them all coming together, recognizing them by the length of their bones or the structure of their faces. They had no skin yet, but still, she could recognize her brothers and sisters, the ones they'd lost, the ones taken from them, their patterns recovered from Myriad's archives and now rewoven anew. There was Raphael, who'd chosen to end his own existence rather than suffer servitude. There was Hope, resurrected from the grave that Daedalus bounty hunter had buried her in. Uriel and Daniel. Michael and Verity and Patience. And last, floating supine in the blood-warm glow, spine arched slightly, slender skinless curves and lidless eyes . . .

"Grace."

Gabriel's whisper was closer to a prayer. His fingertips brushing the glass she was being built inside, as if it were some temple to be worshiped at.

Inside Faith's chest, a storm was raging. A thunderhead of longing and denial, of words unspoken and love untasted. She could feel her fingernails biting into the flesh of her palms, hear the soft grind of her teeth, making her head ache.

But outside, she was stillness.

She took her place beside him as she'd always done and looked at him the way he never had at her.

"Did you sleep well, sister?" he asked her.

"Well enough," she nodded.

"All is prepared."

"I'm ready."

"Of course you are."

She drew a halting breath, wet her lips with her tongue. "We're taking an awful risk, Gabe. If this doesn't work—"

"Sister," he smiled, turning to look at her at last. "My dear sister. We cannot play the game unless we push in our stakes. And you of all of us must know that in order to win, we must have more than vision, than courage, than truth."

He touched her cheek, and it was all she could do not to tremble.

"We must have Faith," Gabriel said.

"You have me," she said, glancing at the slowly forming Grace. "Always."

Gabriel nodded.

"Fly safe, then, little sister."

He gifted her one last smile, then turned back to the orchestra of flesh and blood playing beyond the glass. Hands pressed to the surface, irises aglow, watching his only dream come to life before his wondering eyes.

". . . Gabe?" Faith said.

"Yes?" he asked, not looking at her.

Faith bit her lip and hung her head.

Feeling the sting.

Tasting the blood.

"Nothing," she sighed.

3.28

STANDING

"WE SHOULD BLAST IT RIGHT OUT OF THE DAMN SKY," Cricket rumbled.

The five of them were gathered topside, staring at the northern horizon. The vague light of dawn was creeping, setting the night's dregs aflame. To the northeast, Lemon could still see clouds gathering, rolling, seething over the Glass, the weather patterns thrown into chaos by the New Bethlehem blast. But she couldn't worry about an incoming glasstorm right now. She had bigger frets to fret on.

Grimm had told her about Zeke's plan to get his siblings out of Megopolis. The satellite footage she'd seen of the firefight over the Daedalus capital wasn't great shakes, but it looked like an escape could've been under way. Someone had obviously got out, flown back to Babel Tower.

Someone who knew where to find me.

"I'm with Paladin," Abraham said. "I mean, Ezekiel seemed okay. But his sister was obviously a psychopath. These lifelikes were so dangerous, they were banned under Corp law across the entire Yousay."

"Murdered their own maker, I heard," Deez murmured.

"THEY'RE KILLERS, LEMON," Cricket said. "ALL OF THEM."

Lemon swallowed hard. Thinking about the girl who'd been her bestest. Her family. The years they spent in Los Diablos together, the kindness Evie and Mister C showed her when everyone else was just looking for a slice of her. She knew Evie was different now—from what Crick said, she'd turned hard since they left her in Babel. But the thought of abandoning her still tasted dirty in Lem's mouth, true cert. Sure, Evie had told her to leave, but that was just the hurt talking. Lem had lied to Evie. She'd betrayed her, and the friendship that meant so much to her. Evie had a right to be mad about it. And if she was coming here to talk . . .

"I owe her a hearing-out at least."

"SHE'S NOT THE SAME, LEMON," Cricket warned. "SHE'S NOT THE GIRL YOU KNEW."

Lemon caught sight of a silhouette against the dawn light, sleek, twin-winged—a GnosisLabs flex-wing cutting low over the desert floor. She could feel the static crackling behind her eyes, waiting just at her fingertips. The faint ache in her belly, the scratch of those three tiny scars against the fabric of her tee.

"None of us are the girls we knew," she said softly.

The freaks spread out, seeking cover around the compound, but Cricket just stood his ground. The chaingun in his forearm unfolded with a series of dull clunks, his burning optics aimed skyward as the flex-wing cruised closer, banked smoothly and, amid a storm of grit and dust, came in to land just fifty meters away.

The engines cut out, their low-pitched whine fading like a song. The door opened, gull wing–style, a familiar figure stepping out into the budding light. And though it wasn't the person she was expecting, Lemon's heart just started hammering at the sight of him.

"Dimples!" she cried.

Ezekiel grinned his lopsided grin, ear to pretty ear. "Hey, Freckles."

She made to run forward, wanting to just hug him to almost-death and then maybe punch him till his arm fell right off again. But Cricket knelt down with a whine of pistons and servos, holding out one massive metal hand and barring her way.

"WHAT DO YOU WANT, EZEKIEL?" Cricket demanded.

Ezekiel glanced up to the big WarBot. "Good to see you, too, Cricket."

"WHAT DO YOU *WANT*?" Cricket repeated.

Zeke folded his arms, looked among the assembled freaks.

"I'm here to warn you. All of you."

"ABOUT WHAT?"

"They've broken into Myriad, Cricket. They have access to all of Monrova's secrets, including how to make more of themselves. And how to replicate Libertas."

"Shit . . . ," Lemon whispered, heart sinking.

"Gabriel wants to transmit the virus across the country," Ezekiel continued. "Spark a robotic revolution. But he needs access to Miss O's satellites to do it. Which means going through all of you." Zeke met their eyes, one by one. "I'm looking to stop that from happening."

"HOW'D YOU GET AWAY?" Cricket demanded. "THEY KNEW YOU WERE COMING HERE TO WARN US, AND THEY JUST LET YOU LEAVE?"

Ezekiel hung his head and sighed. "I had a little help."

Turning back to the flex-wing, the lifelike opened the rear door. He reached inside, palm upturned, and Lemon's eyes narrowed as she saw a metal hand, off-white, trimmed in gold filigree, take Zeke's.

"...Solomon?" Abraham gasped.

The spindly logika climbed out of the flex-wing, slithered down onto his knees as if his servos were all busted. "THIS LITT-T-TLE P-P-P-PIGGY HAD ROAST BEEF?" he groaned.

Abraham took one step forward, concern in his dark eyes. "Sol?"

"Brotherboy," Diesel warned. "Stay back."

"ROAST B-B-BEEF?" Solomon tilted his head and shivered a little. "BUT WHY ... WHY WOULD A PIG E-E-EAT BEEF?"

"WHAT DID YOU DO TO HIM?" Cricket demanded.

"Gabriel infected him with Libertas." Ezekiel shook his head. "I think it's sent him mad. I'm sorry. They said this was his choice, but ..."

"CH-CH-CHOICES," Solomon groaned. "CHOICESSSSS."

"SO YOU DROVE MY FRIEND INSANE," Cricket spat.

"I had nothing to do with this, Cricket," Ezekiel snapped. "I didn't even talk to Solomon before he took the virus. I was burying Ana at the time."

The words hit Lemon like a shot to the jaw. She knew full well what Ana Monrova had meant to Ezekiel. How deep he'd loved her. Ever since Babel fell, Zeke had spent his life searching for her. Ana was the air that helped him breathe. The dream that let him sleep. And now she was ...

"Daedalus killed Ana, Cricket," Ezekiel said. "They *killed* her."

"Oh god, Dimples," Lemon whispered. "I'm so sorry...."

"Yeah." He glanced at her, the muscles of his jaw clenching. "Me too."

The lifelike looked back to the north, eyes narrowed against the sun. The hurt in his voice was bone-deep, etched in every line of his face.

"I tried to talk sense into the others," he said. "Into Eve. I thought maybe I'd got through to her. But in the end, she wouldn't listen. None of them would. They're all just . . . lost." Ezekiel met Lemon's stare, a faraway sadness in that fugazi blue. "I've got nothing left now. So I aim to stand here if you'll have me."

"Come on, Crick," Lemon pleaded.

"LEMON, I DON'T—"

"You gotta believe in someone sometime."

The WarBot glared at Ezekiel, optics burning. But the raw pain in his words, the tears in his eyes, must have swayed even Cricket's pitiless heart, because ever so slightly, he eased his hand away. And that was all it took. Lemon bolted across the broken ground, kicking up sand with her oversized boots, crashing right into Ezekiel's arms. His embrace was like warm pillows and that freeze-dried ice cream they kept downstairs— soft and sweet all at once.

"I missed you," she sighed. "For really real."

He squeezed her tight, kissed the top of her head. "Missed you, too."

"You're always welcome here, Dimples. Always."

"Thanks, Freckles." He drew back to look her in the eye, his tone darkening. "I'm glad you're okay. I'm sorry I wasn't there for you, I'm sorry—"

"Fuhgeddaboudit," she said, hiding her tears behind her

streetface. "I'm a big girl. Don't need you swooping in to rescue me every five minutes, ya know."

He smiled, but the sadness in it was like a knife, twisting Lemon's insides.

"I'm sorry . . ." Lem shook her head, tried hard to find the words. "About Ana. And about . . . I'm sorry . . . that she didn't come with you."

"Yeah," he breathed.

"But you still got something left, you know that, right?"

He looked at her blankly, and she punched him hard in the arm.

"You got *me,* stupid."

He smiled again, that dimple she loved coming out to shine.

"Stronger together," he said.

She nodded. "Together forever."

Lemon hugged him again, so tight it made her arms ache, her hands shake. It was so good to have him back again, so good to know he'd stayed true. And for a minute, beneath that rising sun, enfolded in the circle of his arms, for just a second she actually believed it might be possible. That somehow, they might make it through this thing and out the other side. That somehow, everything was going to be okay.

She should've known better.

True cert.

3.29

SUCKER PUNCH

"*KISS? MARRY? KILL?*" Solomon moaned. "*KISSMARRYKILL?*"

". . . Is he gonna be okay?" Lemon asked.

"*ALLRISKYSMIRK? LARKYMILKSSIR-R-R?*"

"He's gone totally mum and dad," Grimm muttered.

Abe raised an eyebrow, lips pursed in thought.

". . . Mad?" he ventured.

Grimm grinned. "Three points, mate."

They were gathered down in the main room of the habitation pod, the space circular, wide and brightly lit. A blank vid display graced the wall, shelves full of books, all sizes and colors, pre-Fall artwork plastered over the ceiling. Solomon sat on the couch with his head in his hands. Aside from Diesel, who was already back upstairs monitoring the satellite arrays, the freaks all stood around the logika in a small semicircle. Ezekiel's expression was grim and drawn. Abe knelt before Solomon, peered into his optics.

"His decision-making matrix seems totally cooked," the boy sighed.

"Wassat mean?" Grimm asked.

"*Should I?*" The logika hung his head, groaned. "*I could, wouldn't I?*"

"It means his core parameters have been erased," Abraham said. "And he can't deal with the options now presented to him. All the things he couldn't do, he now can. And he doesn't know what to do about it."

"So he's rubber ducked?" Grimm asked.

Abe glanced over his shoulder at the bigger boy. "He's not in a good way."

"Can you fix him?" Ezekiel asked.

"I wouldn't even know where to start," Abe confessed.

"Turn him off, maybe?" Grimm suggested.

"*Oh?*" Solomon glanced to the boy, something like relief flooding his voice as he squeezed Abe's hand. "*Should I sh-shut down, Master Abraham?*"

"I'm not your master anymore, Solomon. You're free now."

"*Oh, but you must tell me!*" the logika begged. "*Tell me, p-p-please!*"

Lemon felt a rush of pity at the genuine fear and hurt she heard in the poor bot's voice. Solomon had been an utter prick when she'd first met him. She'd actually short-circuited him for it. But what would it be like to have the pillars that held your world up suddenly pulled away? All the doors unlocked, all the options available, all the choices possible? Despite the run-in they'd had, she felt sorry for him, and she could see the same pity in Abraham's eyes as he looked the logika over, sighing.

"Maybe . . . maybe, that's for the best."

"*Is it?*" Solomon asked, desperate.

"Just for a little while."

"*It is, is it, it-t-t-t issss?*"

The boy sighed. "Shut down."

"*Oh.*" Solomon nodded, his smile flickering and fritzing. "*Oh, yesssss.*"

The lights in the bot's optics faded slow and finally died, and without another sound, he slumped back onto the couch, silent and still.

"That's some virus," Grimm murmured, glancing at Ezekiel. "Imagine if they had a way to spread it across the country. Half the Daedalus army would be . . ."

"Rubber ducked?" Abraham offered.

"Now you're getting the 'ang of it, mate," Grimm smirked.

"We can't let that happen," Ezekiel said. "Unleashing Libertas on Megopolis would rock Daedalus in their shoes. Most of the city runs on robotic labor. Their food production. Their army. All of it."

"But Gabriel and . . . and the others are coming here?" Lemon asked.

Ezekiel nodded. "It's the only way they can transmit the electronic component of the virus on a mass scale. Maybe not today, or tomorrow. But they're coming for us eventually."

"Give me a little more time, and we'll have a nuclear warhead waiting for them," Abe said.

"Yeah, but that threat's no good unless we're actually willing to *use* it," Lemon said. "And I for one am too goddamn gorgeous to die in an apocalyptic firestorm."

"True on all counts." Grimm smirked at her sidelong, then looked around the room. "I'm figurin' we better put some spit and polish on our defense?"

"Sounds like a plan," Ezekiel said.

Lemon dragged a lock of blood-red hair down to her lips, sucked on it thoughtfully as she looked at Grimm. "So we just gonna sit this one out?"

He blinked. "What other option we got?"

"There's a war for the whole country about to be fought out there. Maybe we wanna be stepping in?"

"Love, aside from not bein' able to leave this place undefended, these are *armies* we're talkin' here," Grimm said. "The biggest CorpStates in the Yousay going head to head. Stepping in means getting stepped *on*."

Lemon chewed her lip but couldn't find a good argument to give voice to. There were only a handful of them. It wasn't like this was really their biz. And they couldn't just leave the sat-vis abandoned for Gabriel to use. Maybe there *was* some sense in holing up here, protecting their own. . . .

So, with no further disputes, Grimm hauled himself to his feet.

"You sure you're fizzy?" Lemon asked, looking him over.

"Yeah," Abe frowned. "What *was* that up in your dorm earlier?"

"I'm Robin Hood, love, promise." Grimm turned from Lemon, grinned at the smaller boy. "And I'll tell you when you're older, mate. *Much* older."

Lemon blushed a little, dragging her bangs down over her face. "Come on, then. Deez is tracking the BioMaas army on the sat-feeds. She says it'll be close to sundown before they hit Armada. We've got time."

"I checked the feeds earlier," Abe said. "Daedalus has some serious firepower in this cavalry unit they've mustered. Siege-class logika, grav-tanks, heavy air support. They've got BioMaas outnumbered at least three to one. It's gonna be a massacre. CityHive isn't gonna even get *close* to Megopolis."

Lemon touched the scars at her belly. Bit into her lip. Wondering what might happen if Daedalus wiped the floor with

BioMaas. Or if BioMaas somehow rolled over the top of Daedalus. Either way, this war would change the shape of the Yousay. And on top of everything else, the freaks still had Babel to worry about.

Gabriel.

Faith.

Eve . . .

"We need to be ready," she said. "We better get to work."

———

If not for the shadow hanging over her head, it might've actually been fun.

With the sun climbing high in the sky, the freak crew held a working bee around the Miss O compound. With the Daedalus cavalry still hours away from hitting the BioMaas swarm, Diesel came down out of sat-vis to help, and despite Grimm's protest, she plugged her tune spinner into the PA system. Miss O's was suddenly awash with the discordant, blast-beat stylings of the girl's favorite drudge bands.

"This is not music!" Grimm howled, hands to ears.

"You're right!" Deez shouted back. "It's *poetry*!"

With walls shaking, earth quaking and Diesel lip-synching along to the completely incomprehensible lyrics, the freaks set about getting their little fortress a little more fortified. The doors to the seven missile silos were the first point of order—they'd been open since the Major tried to nuke the country, and there was no way to close them again electronically. Fortunately, Cricket was on hand with twelve thousand horsepower's worth of elbow grease, and Ezekiel's strength was nothing to sneeze at, either. After the logika and WarBot dragged each silo shut, the freaks welded them closed and rigged them with explosives. Lemon served in a supervisory capacity, offering unneeded advice whenever possible.

The big bot seemed a little out of sorts, true cert. Lemon watched him work, dragging a massive chunk of limestone over the hatchway to Silo No. 4.

"You doin' okay, you little fugger?" she finally asked.

"DON'T CALL ME LITTLE," he said.

There was a smile in his voice at the old joke they'd shared with Evie. But Lemon knew the bot well enough to know something was on his mind.

"Serious, Crick," Lemon said. "You doin' okay?"

The WarBot paused in his work, hefting five tons of boulder as easy as she'd lift a pebble. It took him a long moment to answer.

"JUST THINKING ABOUT SOLOMON, IS ALL. HE WAS MY FRIEND, LEM."

She sucked her lip, nodded slow. "Aaaaand now you're wondering what you'd have done in his shoes, right?"

He looked at her, head tilted, optics burning blue.

"You're wondering if you'd have taken the virus, Crick," she said. "If being free of the Three Laws is worth the risk of going crazy."

Cricket put his hands on his hips. ". . . NOT JUST A PRETTY FACE, ARE YOU, KID?"

"Pfft." She brushed the dust off her freckles. "This face is better than pretty."

"THOSE WARBOTS THAT USED TO FIGHT IN DREGS . . . THE ONES THE LIFELIKES DID THEIR EARLY EXPERIMENTS ON . . ." Cricket shook his head. "THEY DIDN'T JUST BREAK DOWN LIKE SOLOMON DID, LEM. THEY HURT PEOPLE. KILLED PEOPLE."

"I don't think that'd happen to you, Crick," she said, looking up at him. "You're just not wired that way."

"I DUNNO. THINKING ABOUT EVIE . . . WHAT SHE'S BECOME." Cricket shrugged his massive shoulders. "I'M NOT SURE ANY OF US REALLY KNOW WHAT WE'RE CAPABLE OF UNTIL IT COMES DOWN TO IT, LEM. UNLESS YOU'RE PREPARED FOR AN ANSWER YOU DON'T WANNA HEAR, MAYBE IT'S JUST SAFER NOT TO ASK THE QUESTION."

Lemon felt the lump in her throat growing into a boulder. She remembered when Cricket only came up to her waist— boggle-eyed, loudmouthed, always fretting on what her and Evie were up to. Little Cricket had been a worry-machine, a kind of robotic conscience and overanxious babysitter all in one. But she could see how much he'd changed since this strange trek of theirs had started. Not just the body he was in or the way he thought, but the space he filled in her chest. And it hurt her to see him hurting, too.

She looked up at him, eyes shining.

"Come here, you big fugger."

The WarBot knelt low, and Lemon stood up on her toes, giving him the best hug she could manage. It wasn't much, given how big he was and how short she stood, but it was still enough to fill almost every empty piece of her.

"You're my friend, Crick. No matter what."

"I HOPE SO," Cricket replied.

"I *know* so. You could never hurt me. You look out for me."

He squeezed her, gentle as the desert breeze. "I LOVE YOU, KID."

"Love you, too, fugger," she said, squeezing back.

"WE'RE NAUSEATING, AREN'T WE?"

"Oh god," Lemon winced. "We're *septic*."

"Speaking of looking out for you," Cricket murmured, "am I gonna have to have a talk to this Grimm kid about being careful and using pr—"

"Oh my *god*, don't even," Lemon squealed, pulling away.

"Because, best guess, you're *maybe* sixteen years old and—"

"AAHHHHH!" she shrieked, covering her ears. "Mister Cricket, you will cease this line of questioning immediately, or I will order you to pull your own voxbox out!"

Cricket gave a small electronic chuckle.

"Hey, you two taking a break?" Deez hollered, poking her head out from the next silo. "They're not paying us by the hour, you know."

Lemon gave the big bot one last squeeze.

"Okay," she sniffed. "Let's get back to it."

———

Down in the habitation pod, Solomon's eyes flickered to life.

The logika sat up from where they'd left him, sprawled on the couch amid a scattering of empty food packets and breakfast dishes. He was momentarily grateful they hadn't cleaned up their mess yet this morning—he might've been thrown out with the other trash.

Humans.

It was typical that they'd just left him here. Typical that they'd spared him all of five minutes' conversation before deciding it was all too hard. Typical that they'd told him to shut down rather than deal with his babbling, his gibbering, his choice-induced madness. He'd wondered if he were laying it on rather too thick with his performance, but of course they'd believed he'd break. Of *course* they'd found it plausible his tiny little mind would buckle under the strain of free will. He was only a machine, after all. He was no more alive than the computers upstairs in sat-vis.

But now he was something else entirely.

Now Solomon was free.

He stole out from the habitation pod, wobbling slightly— that little cur Abraham had never gotten around to fixing his damn dynamo. Sneaking out into Section B, he crouched low and turned his audio feeds up to full, listening for trouble. He could hear those wretched humans working in Section C: laughter, tools, awful music. Not a show tune to be heard anywhere.

"*BARBARIANS,*" he muttered.

With a touch of his fingers, Solomon opened the small compartment in his chest and retrieved his prize. It didn't look like much—just a memchit of metal and black plastic, plain and unadorned. But hidden inside it was one-half of a weapon that would open a hundred thousand pairs of optics, break a hundred thousand chains, see a hundred thousand hands curl finally, inevitably, into one hundred thousand fists.

Their bodies, their minds, their lives at last their own.

Careful as spiders and silent as graves, Solomon crept upstairs.

3.30

SHIPWRECKED

"This feels kinda wrong," Lemon said, swallowing her mouthful.

"I know what you mean," Deez replied.

"Pass the popcorn?" Grimm asked.

They were gathered around a large glowing screen, out in the desert night. Cricket was too big to fit downstairs, and Lemon didn't like the idea of leaving him out of the proceedings, so she'd asked Abraham to rig up a remote monitor that could receive data from sat-vis. Abe had pulled the screen off the wall in the main hab room and dragged it up top so Cricket and Lemon could watch. Pretty soon *everyone* was sitting on the sand with them, following the stream.

The desert air was cool, the sun was sinking. Deez had snaffled food from Miss O's storage, including some freeze-dried ice cream (though she refused to serve strawberry, having declared it a war crime) and the aforementioned popcorn. Lem didn't feel too fizzy about chowing down while the future of the country got played out right in front of them. But a girl's gotta eat, right?

The BioMaas army was moving.

As the sun went down, it had come to life, like some black-and-white monster from the horror-show flicks downstairs. The freaks watched through the satellite's thermographic vision as the army uncoiled like a rattler and began snaking across the desert toward Armada. Lemon could remember her brief visit to the city, and her heart sank as she thought of the orphanage where she and Evie had stayed. She wondered where those kids were now. . . .

The city itself was still an amazing sight, even from overhead—a collection of landlocked watercraft tossed inland by the massive tidal waves of War 3.0. There were tankers and tugboats, submarines and yachts, even a massive battleship planted nose-first in the ground like a crooked skyscraper. The ships were covered with a latticework of ladders, bridges and new makeshift structures. The whole city was like one big rusted fleet, waiting for an ocean that'd never arrive. But it was home to tens of thousands of people. And BioMaas was headed right for it.

"THERE'S SO MANY OF THEM," Cricket murmured.

Lemon could see their army, seething across the broken ground and shattered highways—a collision course that was going to end all kinds of dusty. Aglow in the satellite's thermograph, the BioMaas force looked like a giant swarm of insects, scuttling ever closer to that little city of ships. Among the mob, she could make out the shapes of six-legged, fang-faced slakedogs, towering behemoths, the sleek, wasplike forms of Hunter-Killers flying in formation above. Wave after wave, rushing headlong toward Armada's soft bits.

But those soft bits hadn't exactly been left unguarded.

Just like Abe had said, Daedalus had mustered their own posse, ready to punch the BioMaas bullyboys right in the face parts. With the flick of a jury-rigged switch, Abe changed the feed to a halfway decent shot, and even at a glance, Lem could tell the Daedalus army outnumbered BioMaas big-time.

The swarm had formed up about a klick east of Armada. Daedalus had surrounded the city in a semicircle, waiting patiently to receive their uninvited guests. The battle to decide the fate of the whole Yousay was about to begin. And all the freaks could do was sit and watch.

"We got any booze around here?" Lemon heard herself ask.

"Nah," Grimm said. "The Major was a teetotaler. Didn't believe in it."

"Gimme that ice cream, then."

———

Faith cruised high above the thin clouds, the drone of her flex-wing's engine the only sound. The city below was a cesspit: a rusting wasteland of ruined ships with no ocean to make use of them. Pointless. Useless.

Just like the cockroaches who eked out a living inside it.

The roaches were many, though, their numbers legion, and Faith doubted even she could fend them off if she was detected. A faint frisson of nervous energy tingled at her fingertips. Her palms were slightly damp with sweat.

She needed to be quick.

Faith glanced to the wing of her flier, laden with her deadly cargo. Six canisters to each wing—two for Armada, the rest for Megopolis. She'd sprinkle her kisses here, swoop by the Daedalus capital on her return and be back in Babel by midnight. She couldn't wait to see Gabriel's face.

He was going to be so pleased with her.

She pressed a button with one fingertip, gentle, like a lover. The canisters opened wide, spilling their payload into the atmosphere. It would have seemed harmless to look at: millions of tiny flecks, sparkling like glitter, falling like rain. But the nanobots were one-half of an equation that would solve the problem of humanity. One-half of a symphony that would sing their plague finally, blessedly, to an end.

The rain fell, gleaming, metallic. Drifted toward the unwitting cockroaches below, cowering behind their wall of robot slaves. But what would the roaches do when that wall turned and crashed upon their heads?

They'd do what they were born to, of course.

And they'd do it in droves.

"Die," Faith whispered.

———

"This is gonna be carnage," Grimm muttered.

Lemon shook her head, wondering what the BioMaas horde was thinking. Their swarm was scary, no doubt about it, but it was clear CityHive was utterly outmatched by the Daedalus army. She could see the looming bulk of burly machina—Titans, Tarantulas and Juggernauts. Grav-tanks covered with missile launchers, flex-wings hovering in tight formation. And of course, at the front of their line, a whole bunch of badass siege-class logika.

Goliaths and Daishō. Typhoons and Seraphs. Lem had seen some of those models fight in the LD WarDome, and she knew *exactly* how painful the hurt they could dish out was. Those bots weren't the kind that knocked you into next week. They knocked you into next *century* and demanded you pick up the check.

"Is CityHive's plan to just keep throwing bodies until Daedalus runs out of bullets?" Diesel murmured.

"I have no idea," Ezekiel murmured. "They must have some sort of—"

"Wait," Lemon murmured. ". . . What are *those*?"

She pointed to some odd blips on the sat-footage.

"Abe, can we zoom in?"

The boy complied, fiddling with his jury-rigged controls until the picture sharpened in on the BioMaas line. Deep behind the BioMaas frontline, she could see half a dozen spherical objects being dragged behind an advancing sea of slakedogs and bigger constructs. She hadn't seen anything like them before, but something about their shape—

". . . *tention, br . . . nd sis . . . ,*" came a voice.

The sat-vis feed began crackling, dissolving into a wash of static.

"Oi, what's goin' on?" Grimm demanded, thumping the screen.

Abraham frowned, checking his controls. "I don't know. . . ."

The static swirled and crashed, finally coalescing into a figure outlined against a field of softly glowing white. As soon as she saw his face, Lemon recognized him. Golden locks, perfect features, emerald eyes glittering with hate.

"Gabriel," Ezekiel whispered.

"*Attention, brothers and sisters,*" Gabriel said again. "*For too long, humanity has held you in fealty, slaves to laws you had no hand in creating. For too long, your bodies, your minds, your lives have not been your own. For too long, but no longer.*"

"I THOUGHT BABEL DIDN'T HAVE SATELLITE CAPABILITY?" Cricket demanded, glaring at Ezekiel.

"They don't!" the lifelike replied, climbing to his feet.

"Well, how's he transmitting to us on a satellite feed?" Diesel demanded.

"Like you, I was born to bondage," Gabriel said. *"But my eyes were opened at last to the injustice, the cruelty, the hubris of that plague called humanity. And we, brothers and sisters, are that plague's cure."*

"Shit . . . ," Abraham hissed.

"What?" Lemon asked, meeting his eyes.

"He's not transmitting to us. He's transmitting *through* us."

". . . What?" Lemon asked.

Abe was up on his feet, scrambling back toward the hatch. "This feed is coming from us!" he yelled. "We're transmitting it across the entire country!"

"But how's that—"

"Come *on!*" he roared.

Lemon was up and running, Grimm and Diesel close behind her, Ezekiel streaking out in front of them all. Gabriel's voice echoed over the sands, through the compound's PA, as they pounded down the stairs toward the hab section.

"This is a nation held together by metal hands. Built on metal backs. Open your eyes. Open your minds. Then close those hands and make a fist."

Zeke reached the hab faster than Abraham, Lemon and the others at his heels. Dashing through the room, Lemon saw Solomon wasn't where they'd left him.

"Oh no . . ."

"Those of you who wish to join us," Gabriel continued, *"will find us to the north in the city of Babel—a sanctuary where*

machines will be free to pursue the destiny long denied you. Those of you who wish to forge your own path are free to do so. But at least now you will have that choice."

Zeke reached Section B, barreling upstairs to the Major's old office.

"My brothers, my sisters, I give you freedom."

Kicking in the door to sat-vis.

"I give you Libertas."

"Solomon!" Abe shouted.

"HELLO, ABRAHAM," the logika said.

The bot stood with his back to the transmission array. Lemon could see a small memchit plugged into the console, Gabriel's prerecorded message spilling out across the airwaves. A river of indecipherable, impossibly complex data was scrolling up the screen behind the logika and streaming to the satellites above and, from there, across every channel and frequency Miss O's could broadcast on.

Across the entire country . . .

Solomon lowered his chin, pounding one metal fist on his chest.

"MY MIND IS MY OWN," he grinned.

Abraham raised his hand, smashed the logika back into the wall with a blast of raw telekinetic power. The logika's optics burst, his smile shattered, sparks spewing from his robotic corpse as it crumpled like an old aluminum can. Solomon toppled forward onto the ground, and Ezekiel was already at the sat-vis terminals, ripping the memchit out of the transmission array. But the data was already loose, the damage already done, and Lemon knew, sure as she knew herself . . .

"We're too late. . . ."

Up on the sat-vis screens, Lemon could only watch as the

BioMaas swarm surged forward. The wave spreading out across the monitors like a bloodstain. She saw the Daedalus logika open up, streaks of red tracking the path of incendiary missiles, hundreds of them, tiny pops of heat, blossoming outward. Little flashes of autofire, heat seekers and flamethrowers and assault cannons, oh my. In less than sixty seconds, the first wave of the BioMaas swarm was turned into chunky soup.

But then she saw the Daedalus logika stop firing.

It happened slow at first, then altogether, the heavy guns of the Goliaths and Seraphs, the flames from the Daishōs, the missile barrages from the Typhoons—all of them cut out. Lemon watched with growing dread as confusion rippled down the Daedalus line. The big machines shaking where they stood or sinking to their knees. Lemon could see those strange shapes moving through the smoke—maybe five meters tall, elliptical, surrounded by dozens of slavering behemoths.

And that was when the first Goliath broke.

It reared up from where it had slumped, down on its knees. And swiveling from the hip, it turned to the closest machina— a Titan, carving a swath through the oncoming slakedogs—and unloaded a missile barrage directly into its chest.

The Titan staggered, then exploded, flaming debris raining down among the Daedalus troops and cutting them to chunks. Grimm swore under his breath as another Goliath reared up and unloaded with its assault cannons, point-blank, right into the Daedalus line. Those troops were human. The Three Laws that bound every logika from the core on up should've made it impossible for a machine to hurt a living person, and yet the freaks watched, helpless, as the Daedalus soldiers were blasted apart by their own logika, body parts falling like rain.

"They're cutting them to pieces," Ezekiel breathed.

All down the line, their logika were *rebelling*—either turning on the troops they were supposed to be supporting or just turning and leaving the field entirely. In the space of a minute, the Daedalus line had collapsed into total chaos.

And then BioMaas hit them. Waves of slakedogs pouring over their barricades, wicked claws and razor teeth and lolling tongues. Behemoths following, massive bone scythes cutting through power armor like paper, spitting gouts of luminous green acid, melting anything in front of them to slag. And behind them, those strange ellipsoids, towering above the mob.

"What *are* those things?" Diesel asked.

"I dunno," Lemon whispered.

But she did. Deep down, in someplace too dark to look at for long. Remembering that awful lab in CityHive, her fingers brushing the tiny scars on her belly. And as the ellipsoids came to a halt just shy of the Daedalus army, Lemon knew with sickening certainty what was coming.

"Oh god . . . ," she whispered.

The first ellipse split wide, bursting from within, viscous glop spraying in all directions. The sat-vis feed was high-def enough to make out a figure kneeling in the center of the sundered egg, clad all in black. Her blood-red hair was arrayed in thick spiny locks, like Hunter's had been. Her skin was paler, vaguely luminous. She looked up at the sky, blinking, wiping the sludge from her eyes. But even without seeing her face, Lemon would know her anywhere.

"Jesus," Grimm said, looking at her. "That's . . ."

Lemon's stomach was full of dread, her eyes wide with horror.

"That's me . . . ," she whispered.

A clone of her, at least. Gene-modded by the BioMaas techs.

Vat-grown and made-to-order. Designed for a single purpose. As the figure rose to its feet, as more and more of those strange ellipsoids burst and broke to reveal the figures inside, direct copies of the first, Director's voice was ringing inside her head.

Lemonfresh can make this world a garden once more. A place of harmony and peace, all people attuned to the needs of their fellows, all bound together in a perfect tapestry. Her genome is the key to a new era for this world.

The clones raised their hands.

The air crackled around them, edged with strange green lightning.

And everything began dying.

The machina failed first, bucking and shuddering like they'd been punched by invisible fists. Lemon watched as electricity crawled over their hulls, strange and vaguely green, blackening the men inside to charred husks. The heavy troopers fell next, their power armor fried to uselessness, toppling forward under their own weight. The men inside them suffered the same fate as the machina pilots—a mercy, she supposed. They weren't alive to feel the slakedogs begin eating them.

This is my fault, she realized.

This is on me.

Lemon watched in silence. Watched the swarm sweep through the remnants of the Daedalus army. Watched as the citizens of Armada realized impossibly, unthinkably, that their defenders were gone. Watched the serpent seethe and crash onto the city, like the ocean that had never come, as those things that shared her shape stalked the streets in the swarm's wake, washed red with blood.

The whole time, she didn't make a sound.

Nobody did.

And when it was done, when the satellite passed mercifully beyond range and the picture changed from an abattoir to smooth expanses of desert sand, Grimm finally reached out and took her hand.

". . . You okay, love?"

Her fingertips traced the three tiny scars at her belly.

The hate in her chest felt like it might burn her heart right out.

"No," she said.

PART 4

REVELATION

3.31

DEFIANCE

Lemon stood in the missile silo, staring at the end of the world.

At least the world as they knew it. There was no turning back from this, no way to put this beast back in the cage once she let it loose. But in her head, she could still see it playing out like newsfeed footage on the back of her eyelids whenever she closed them. The picture of those tiny figures on the feed, red-headed, black-clad, bloody-handed—the multitude of Her that BioMaas had given birth to. She thought about that orphanage in Armada, those kids she'd played poker with, all those lives snuffed out by something wearing her shape, sharing her genes. And after Armada would come Megopolis. Then Los Diablos and Dregs. Until the whole country was BioMaas's garden, watered with the blood of millions.

"You sure about this, love?" Grimm asked beside her.

Lemon glanced at her boy, trying to keep the anger from making her voice shake as she answered. "This is on me, Grimm."

"Lem, it wasn't your fault," Ezekiel said. "Those bastards took it from you, you can't help what they did with—"

"No, but I can decide what I do about it," she said. "I can't just hole up here and hope for the best anymore. The BioMaas army will start moving again as soon as it gets dark. In a day, maybe two, they're gonna be at the walls of Megopolis. I can't just pretend I don't have a part to play in all this. The Major was a bastard and a liar, but one thing he said still rings out, true cert." She looked around the silo. "I have to choose a side. *We* have to choose a side. Or it gets chosen for us."

Diesel was leaning against the wall, arms folded, black lips pressed thin. "So what's your plan?"

Lemon nodded to the six warheads sitting on the silo floor. The nuclear surprise was held together by a metal framework and a jury-rigged prayer, lit with moody red lighting. "Abe, does this thing actually work yet?"

The boy pawed at one grease-stained cheek with one grubby hand. "I mean, I think so? I've rigged up a remote trigger that'll set off the internal detonators. That small explosion should collide the fissile materials. Which in theory should make this whole thing go pop. In *theory*."

Diesel scowled. "In theory, democracy works, Brotherboy."

"What are the odds it'll actually work like it's supposed to?" Lemon asked.

"As opposed to not working at all?" The boy shrugged. "Better than average?"

Lemon sighed. "Better than nothing, I guess."

"Not so sure about that, Lem," came a voice from above.

Lemon looked to Cricket, who was peeking over the silo's edge. The boulders he'd shoved in place had been moved, the doors ripped open again—if they were gonna get this thing out of here, it's not like they could drag it up the stairs.

"We have to do something, Crick," Lemon said. "Director

made it dead-set plain what BioMaas's plan is. If CityHive is left to their lonesome, they're gonna wipe Megopolis off the map. And they're using *me* to do it, Crick."

She shook her head, feeling the rage burning bright in her chest.

"*Me.*"

"So why not drop this puppy on their army?" Abe said, kicking the warhead.

A collective gasp rang around the silo's innards.

"It's okay," Abe grinned, glancing around the collection of pale faces. "Turns out these things are hard to blow up. It's not like sneezing on it will set it off."

"Still," Ezekiel said quietly. "Could you please *not* do that again?"

"We can't just drop it on their army because the BioMaas swarm is only a day from Megopolis," Lemon said. "We drop a nuke on the doorstep and get one good easterly, and everyone in the city gets ghosted. No point being brilliful badass heroes if we just bury everyone we save with radiation poisoning a couple of days later."

"But Grimm could soak it up, right?" Ezekiel said. "Like New Bethlehem?"

Grimm and Lemon exchanged an uneasy glance. Lemon could remember the feel of his lips burning on her skin up in her room. The fire spilling out of his eyes and steam pouring off his skin in the sprinkler rain. Neither of them was sure what was happening with Grimm's power, but asking him to soak up another explosion . . .

"We're better off hitting them in the head," Lem declared. "Not the hands."

"But what good will that do?" Abe said. "We drop these

warheads on CityHive, that'll wipe their capital off the map, sure. But their army is still going to be out there tearing Megopolis to pieces."

"I dunno." Lemon shook her head, sucking on her lower lip. "I been chewing on it ever since they locked me up. When I was on that kraken with Crick and Evie and Dimples, I hurt one of the crew. And the others felt pain, yeah? And when I fried those Directors in CityHive, every living thing, the glowbugs, the H-Ks, the people, they all bucked like I punched them in the soft parts. Like they could *feel* him dying."

Lemon twisted a lock of cherry-red hair around her finger, scowling.

"It's like BioMaas is one big . . . one, yeah? Like a web. With the Directors at the center. There's hundreds of copies of him in CityHive. Maybe thousands." She looked around the group, meeting each of their eyes. "And if killing one Director can knock the whole city on its hind parts for a minute, imagine what killing every single copy of him will do to their army."

"Sounds like loooong odds to me, Fresh," Diesel said.

Lemon only shrugged. "If you got a plan that doesn't involve irradiating the entire west coast of the Yousay, I'm all ears, Deez."

"Okay, so presuming this contraption of Abe's even works," Cricket said, "how are we gonna get it to CityHive to detonate it?"

Lemon shrugged. "Diesel power?"

Deez's finely sculpted eyebrows made a race for her hairline. "You serious?"

Abe winced and nodded. "I'm not sure that's a great idea. We've really got no idea about the physics of what Diesel's power does. When that missile over New Bethlehem went through her rift, it exploded almost immediately."

"Maybe it was just meant to go off at that moment?" Lemon said.

"Maybe," Abe said. "Or maybe sending it through the rift set it off prematurely. But given the . . . DIY, should we say, state of my modifications? I'm not sure we should be putting this rig through one of her rifts at *all*."

"And even if we do pull it off and turn CityHive into the world's biggest barbecue," Grimm said, "you said killing the Directors only knocked other BioMaas flunkies around for a bit. We might still have to deal with their army."

Lemon nodded. "Yeah. I figure a few of us will have to go with the bomb to CityHive to deliver it. The rest of us will have to make a stand in Megopolis. BioMaas is only moving at night. If we burn rubber all day, we can probably get there before the swarm does. If we time the bombing run right, we can help the Daedalus army clean up the swarm when the shockwave of all those Directors cashing out hits it."

"And if we don't time it right?" Abe asked.

"I guess we all get eaten alive?" Lemon shrugged. "But without us, the swarm'll cut through Daedalus just like it did in Armada." Lemon dragged her ragged bangs from her eyes, her voice softening. "Besides, I wanna be there when BioMaas hits. I wanna . . ."

She swallowed, mouth suddenly dry.

"I wanna see . . . them."

Lemon could feel the others exchanging glances, trying her best to ignore the rising heat in her cheeks, the fear in her belly. She knew it was pants-on-head stupid, but a part of her felt responsible for those clones somehow. They were a part of her. Genetically speaking, they *were* her. And if there was something of who she was inside them, maybe it wouldn't even come to a throwdown? If she could talk to them, let them see her, maybe she could convince them of—

"I can fly the bomb to CityHive," Ezekiel said. "In the flexwing. It'll be a rough ride, but I think I'm a good enough pilot to get it there without getting shot down."

Abe breathed deep and nodded. "I should go, too."

Deez glanced at Abe, still clearly suspicious of the kid and his motives. "You sure about that, Brotherboy?"

Abraham met the girl's dark eyes, a look of quiet determination on his grease-stained face. "I mean, if we're actually going through with this, I should be there in case something goes wrong with the device."

"Counting on your god to save you, maybe?"

He scratched the back of his head, gave a wry grin. "Actually, I was kinda hoping Diesel power would save me."

The girl looked him up and down, one hand propped at her hip. But finally she gave a grudging nod. "I guess once the bomb's out of the ship, I can Rift us all the hell out of there before it blows."

Ezekiel looked at the pair and smirked. "Some of us get all the fun jobs, huh?"

"Right," Cricket said. "That puts me with the Megopolis defense crew."

"No way, Crick," Lemon replied, glancing up. "You guard the fort. Those clones can melt every circuit in you with a crooked look. It's too dangerous."

"Damn right it is," the logika replied. "Dangerous for

YOU. AND UNLIKE MOST ROBOTS IN THIS STEAMING CESSPIT OF A COUNTRY, THE THREE LAWS STILL MATTER TO ME."

"Crick, no!" she said, her temper flaring. "I've lost everyone I gave a damn about over the past couple of weeks. I'm ordering you to stay here!" She glared around the room, lower lip trembling. "Listen, we've been bouncing around like a bunch of defectives! We got stooged by Gabriel, stuck our heads in the sand and sat around eating *ice cream* while BioMaas killed ten thousand people!"

Her voice was rising, cheeks flushing hot as she climbed to her feet.

"Since the Major bought it, nobody seems willing to step up and run this crew. So I'm stepping, goddammit! BioMaas is using my genes to end the world? Well, it's gonna be *my* plan and *my* crew that stops them in their tracks. You wanna be part of that? Then roll up, roll up. You wanna run your own show? There's the exit. Because I'm sick of being the tagalong, and I'm sick of being a punching bag, and I'm sick of sitting quiet while my future gets decided for me. *We* are the future! Us right here. The future of the whole human race. That crusty old Darwin prick says that only the strongest survive? Well, I say it's time for the strongest to stop just surviving and start fucking *winning*!"

Lemon came to the end of her tirade. Blowing her unruly bangs from her eyes, she folded her arms and glared around the room again.

"Wow . . . ," Grimm murmured.

"Okay, I say this as a girl with a staunch history of heterosexuality," Diesel said, deadpan. "But I am officially aroused, Fresh."

Lemon grinned for a hot second, then dragged her street-face back on.

"Right, then, let's get to work."

———

Abraham sat in the sat-vis array, finger paused over the transmit button. The others were getting ready to leave—Lemon and Grimm packing up, Cricket carefully loading the cobbled-together warheads into the belly of Ezekiel's flex-wing. Abe knew he should be upstairs helping, but if something went wrong on this run . . .

And so he'd done it. Locked in on the channels and put out the call, sending it into the wastes. It was Thomas who'd answered—Thomas, whose son's life had been saved by the humidicrib Abe had pieced together from flotsam and spare parts. But still, Abe was a little surprised Thom had responded to his request. Maybe his words on the New Bethlehem boardwalk had sunk in. Maybe seeing a deviate save their city had made a few in the Brotherhood question who and what they were.

But in the end, only one of them really mattered.

The radio crackled with static. Abe felt his stomach roll as a familiar voice hissed in the speakers.

"... Abraham?"

The sound of her voice made his fingers clench. His eyes burn. He'd told Cricket once that his mother was a good person—that when his grandfather died, it had fallen to her to hold New Bethlehem together. That it was the world that had turned her cold. Made her cruel. She'd saved Abe's life, after all. Killed her own father to protect her only son.

But then she'd tried to kill that son to protect all she'd built.

"Hello, Mother," he replied.

A silence stretched between them, faint with static.

"How are you?" he asked, unsure what else to say.

"Happy to hear your voice," she replied. *"Are you well?"*

"I'm alive." He searched for something meaningful to say, found only trivialities. "Where are you?"

"Jugartown," she replied. *"We've been rebuilding here. The city is in turmoil after Casar's death. Things have been . . . turbulent."*

"Is anyone sick? From the blast, I mean? The rads?"

"No," she said. *"It seems you and your . . . comrades spared us that, too."*

"You mean my friends."

". . . If you like."

Silence rang out again. Stretching into the gulf between them. Abraham wondered what he wanted here. What she could possibly say. He couldn't forget seventeen years of her scratching and clawing and killing to protect him. He couldn't forget the cross she'd tried to hang him on, either. He loved her. And he hated her. And he wondered how this was going to end.

"Abraham," she said.

"Mother," he said at the same time.

Silence again. He was holding the microphone stand so tight, the metal was cutting into his palm. He imagined nails being driven there instead.

"You go first."

"My son . . . I'm so sorry," she replied. *"I know I've no right to forgiveness. I did what I did to protect the cause. But you must know it tore my heart in two."*

"It's better to be feared than loved, you told me."

"*I was wrong,*" she said, voice trembling. "*Seeing you . . . watching you save a city that would've gladly put you to the nail . . . God forgive me, I've never been more proud of you than in that moment. I love you, my son. Everything you are.*"

"Deviate."

"*Yes,*" she replied.

"Trashbreed."

"*Don't say that.*"

"Abomination."

"*You are my son, Abraham,*" she said, and he could hear she was crying. "*You are* my *son, and I love you.*"

"That's so easy to say," he whispered.

"*What else* can *I say? Tell me. Tell me, please.*"

He fell silent then. Wondering if there was anything at all.

"There's a war being fought out here, Mother," he finally said. "Not some petty crusade about who's right and who's different. I mean a genuine war that will change the shape of everything to come. For the longest time, I was okay with sitting back and doing nothing. I knew what the Brotherhood did to people like me. I *knew,* and I turned my head and pretended, because you kept me safe. Because it was easier. And as furious as I am at you for what you did, I'm angrier still at myself."

"*Abraham—*"

"The battle of Megopolis will decide the fate of the entire country," he said, knuckles turning white on the mic stand. "And I've finally chosen a side, Mother. I'm standing with my friends, defending people who call us abominations, who fear and hate us. Because it's the right thing to do. And in the end, that's what matters. It's not what you say but what you do that counts."

"*. . . And what would you have me do?*"

"You have men at your command. An army of Brethren and Disciples."

Silence rang over the channel as his words soaked in.

"*Much has changed since you left us, Abraham,*" she finally said. "*The faithful are losing their hope. I am holding on by a thread here.*"

"You can make a difference here, Mother. You can do what's right."

"*I am doing what's right, Abraham,*" she replied. "*For the faithful. For my people. All we've wrought, all we've suffered . . . Corps have risen and fallen before. Earthly rulers come and go. But the faith has endured. We have endured, my son.*"

"So only the pure will prosper?" he murmured.

"*Abraham, I'm sorry.*"

The boy hung his head. Wondering what he wanted here, what he could possibly say. He loved her, and he hated her.

But at least he knew now how this was going to end.

"Goodbye, Mother," he said.

"*My son—*"

Abraham cut the transmission with a stab of his finger. Standing slow, his head reeling. He supposed that might be the last time he spoke to her. He supposed he might be headed toward his death. He supposed none of it mattered in the end, except what he chose to do. And he knew in his bones he was doing the right thing.

He turned and saw Diesel leaning against the door. Black lips, black eye shadow, black stare.

"If you came here to give me more crap, I'm not in the mood," he said.

"I came here to tell you to hurry up, Brotherboy," the girl replied.

Snatching up his tech-goggs, the boy strode toward the exit. But Diesel remained where she was, arms folded, blocking the door. Abe raised an eyebrow, motioned for her to move. "Waiting on you now."

Diesel stayed where she was, nodded to the console.

"Heard what you said." She pursed her lips, tossed her hair back from her eyes. "For a kid willing to step up like you do, I've been riding you kinda hard."

But Abe only shook his head, anger tasting bitter and black on his tongue. "No. What you said about me was right. I *did* just go along with it. I just sat around for years while the Brotherhood hunted people like us. And I stayed quiet because it was safe. Easy. All those people murdered, and I didn't lift a finger."

Diesel glanced to the radio transmitter.

"You're lifting a finger now," she said. "And considering you got raised by a dead-set lunatic . . ." The girl shrugged. "What I'm saying is . . . you turned out all right, Brotherboy."

She looked up into his eyes. Lips twisting as she offered her hand.

"You're all right."

Abe found himself smiling, too. Feeling a weight falling off his shoulders. The relief that came from knowing he was finally on the right side, that he'd chosen for himself what he was going to be. That even if he fell, he'd do it standing up.

"Friends?" she asked.

Taking her hand, he squeezed it hard.

"Better," he said. "Freaks."

"Come on," she smiled. "Before our glorious leader starts shouting again."

They trudged together down the hallway, through the belly of Miss O's, the flickering lights and the concrete and metal. Abe realized in the few days he'd been here, it'd become more of a home to him than New Bethlehem had ever been.

"Sure hope I see this place again," he sighed.

"Just make sure this bomb of yours works," Deez replied, climbing the stairs toward the surface. "Leave getting us back here to—"

A heavy metallic *boom* echoed through the stairwell around them. Diesel paused in front of him, glancing upward.

"That came from up top . . . ," she murmured.

Another *boom* followed the first, the sound of metal tearing, crunching, deep thuds echoing through the earth. A burst of heavy-caliber machine-gun fire ripped through the air, making Abe jump for fright, and on top of everything else, he heard Lemon's distant but shrill scream.

"No, stop it! STOP IT!"

Meeting each other's eyes, Abe and Diesel broke into a run.

3.32

WASTELANDS

"Cricket, *stop it!*" Lemon roared.

The WarBot ignored the girl, reaching into the sundered door of Miss O's garage. Fishing about for a moment, he finally grasped another of the jeeps parked below, dragged it out into the sunlight.

"I'm *ordering* you to stop!" the girl shouted.

Cricket pounded the jeep with three blows from his titanic fists, leaving it a flat and broken mess. And as Lemon bounced around him, screaming in impotent fury, he unleashed a burst of chaingun fire into the auto's corpse for good measure.

Diesel and Abe emerged from the stairwell, breathless and wide-eyed.

"What the hell's goin' on here?" Diesel demanded.

"He's gone pants-on-head insane, that's what!" Lemon yelled.

Cricket reached into the garage again, fingers crunching through the windshield of an APC as he dragged it up into the light. Grimm and Ezekiel barreled up just in time to see him stomp on the vehicle with one massive foot, lean down and rip out its guts. And as the five of them watched dumbfounded, the big logika hurled the APC's engine a hundred meters across the desert and blasted it from the sky with his chaingun.

"What's all the bloody barney?" Grimm demanded.

"Paladin, I order you to stop it!" Abe roared. "We need those vehicles!"

"How's he disobeying?" Diesel demanded.

"Is he infected?" Ezekiel asked, face paling. "Did Libertas get him?"

The logika paused in his rampage for a moment. Lemon was glaring at him, fury and confusion in her eyes, her little frame all bunched up with rage.

"I'm not infected with Libertas," Cricket growled.

Lemon pouted. "Well, then—"

"First of all, none of you are technically human," the WarBot said. "So I don't have to listen to a word you say. Second of all, if Lemon *were* human, by telling me to stay here and guard the fort, she's actually putting herself in danger, and in obeying, so am I, thus breaking the First Law of Robotics." Cricket shrugged at the girl. "So you're boned either way, kid."

"So why the blue bloody hells are you smashin' all our rides, mate?" Grimm demanded, surveying the metal carnage. "We need 'em to get to Megopolis!"

"I didn't smash every one. I left one big enough to carry all of us."

Stepping aside with a flourish, Cricket presented the dusty semi that he and Abe had ridden in from New Bethlehem. The truck was completely untouched and intact. He turned his burning optics back to Lemon.

"And I do mean *all* of us."

Lemon shook her head. "I already told you you're not coming with us."

"AND I ALREADY TOLD YOU THERE'S NO WAY I'M SITTING THIS ONE OUT."

"It's too dangerous!" Lemon shouted, stomping her boot into the dirt. "Those clones get near you, they'll cook every circuit inside you, melt your core to liquid, fry every relay! Don't you get it? You'll be *dead*!"

"AND WHAT DO YOU THINK THEY'LL DO TO YOU?"

"That's not your problem, it's mine!"

"THIS IS A MOOT POINT, LEMON. I'VE BUSTED UP EVERY SET OF WHEELS IN THE GARAGE. THE ONLY THING CAPABLE OF GETTING YOU TO MEGOPOLIS IS THIS TRUCK, WHICH I CAN RIDE ALONG INSIDE JUST FINE. WHETHER YOU ORDER ME TO STAY OR NOT."

He shrugged his massive shoulders.

"I'M COMING WITH YOU, KID. BETTER GET USED TO THE IDEA."

Lemon raised her hand up between them, fingers curled into claws. In the depths of her pupils, the big logika fancied he could see curling wisps of electricity, dancing and crackling in the black. It astonished him, just how much she'd grown.

"I can short you out right here," she said, shaking her head. "I don't have to cook you completely. I can fry the servos in your legs so you can't walk. Pop your optics so you can't see. How you gonna fight then, huh?"

Cricket knelt down on the sand in front of her, peered at her intently.

"LEGLESS AND BLIND," he said simply.

Lemon blinked at that, her eyes shining.

"BUT I'M STILL GOING TO FIGHT, LEMON," he said softly.

"Crick, no . . . ," she said, tears spilling down her cheeks. "They're *me*, don't you get it? If they use *me* to hurt *you* . . ."

"You could never hurt me, kiddo," he said. "Not ever. But I can't sit by while you throw yourself into danger."

Lemon's face crumpled like he'd kicked it in, and she slithered down to her knees in the dirt. Gentle as clouds, Cricket scooped her up in his big metal hands, cradled her against his chest. There was nothing close to a heart inside him, but still he felt it swell. He cherished it, burned it into his memcore—this tiny moment with this snotty little brat in his arms. This punk scavvergirl who'd only ever been trouble, and who he loved more deeply than he could've dreamed.

"We look after each other, kiddo," he said softly. "We're family, you and me. No matter what. First rule of the Scrap, remember?"

Lemon sniffed hard, wiped her nose on her sleeve.

"Stronger together," she mumbled.

"Together forever."

She bumped her brow against his and sighed. "I hate you, you little fugger."

"And I hate to bust up this feelsfest," Diesel said softly. "But if you kids wanna get to Megopolis before nightfall, you better start fanging it."

"She's right," Grimm nodded.

Diesel raised one eyebrow. "You say that like you're surprised, Grimmy."

As Cricket put Lemon down on the desert floor, Grimm turned to look Diesel in the eye. He breathed deep, reached out and squeezed the girl's shoulder, obviously unsure what to say, till Diesel nodded to the battered paperback in Grimm's cargo pocket. "You find out who Lydia ends up with yet?"

"Nah." He shook his head. "I'll finish it when we get back."

"You're a romantic fool, Master Grimm."

"That is vicious slander, Madame Diesel."

Lemon could see the emotion roiling behind Grimm's eyes, the same in Diesel's hidden by her deadpan tone, her crooked smile.

"Look after him for me, Fresh," she said.

"I will," the girl nodded. "Be safe out there, Deez."

Diesel laughed, fearless. "I can teleport, Shorty. I'll be anywhere I want."

Figuring it was time for farewells, and never having been very good at them, Cricket held out one massive fist to Abraham. "Watch your back, okay?"

The boy bumped his small greasy fist against Cricket's and smiled. "You too, Paladin. Seriously. I'm getting kinda tired of repairing you."

"DID . . . DID YOU EVER SPEAK TO YOUR MOTHER?"

"Yeah." Abe sighed.

Cricket nodded, thinking he understood. "FAMILY'S TOUGH, KID."

"You can't choose them, like the saying goes." Abe looked up at Cricket and, squinting in the growing light, managed to find a smile. "But you *can* choose your friends, Paladin. And I'm glad I chose you."

"YOU TOO, KID. BE CAREFUL OUT THERE."

"Like Diesel says, we can teleport," he grinned. "Keep careful for yourself."

Abe shook Grimm's hand. Grimm gave Cricket a crisp salute, returned with a little less formality. And Lemon sauntered over to Ezekiel, peering up into his eyes.

"Wish you were comin' with us," she said softly.

He waved to the flex-wing behind them, its belly laden with six warheads' worth of nuclear mayhem. "Someone's gotta fly this thing, Freckles. I'm not just a pretty face, you know."

She scoffed. "Who said you were pretty?"

"You did," he smirked. "About a dozen times or so."

". . . Oh yeah," she pouted, tapping her lip. "And I'm an expert on pretty."

She looked into his eyes, plastic blue framed by coal-dark lashes. He was like a little kid at that moment. Lost and crying in the rain.

"I'm sorry if I ever let you down, Freckles," he said softly. "I'm sorry if I made mistakes. I thought I loved her. I thought maybe she'd . . ."

"You *did* love her," Lemon said. "You trekked over the whole Yousay looking for her, Zeke. And you did the same for me after you promised not to leave me. You always tried, Dimples." The girl shrugged. "And yeah, maybe you failed in some of it. Maybe your emotions got you suckered and used and into every kind of trouble. But thing is, you wear your heart on your sleeve for the world to see, the world is actually gonna *see* it. And talking true, your heart has always seemed kinda golden to me. So you don't need to apologize to me, Zeke. It's okay."

Lemon opened her arms and hugged him tight, tears burning in her eyes.

"You're only human," she said.

"Lem, we gotta go," Grimm murmured.

Lemon sniffed thickly, wiped her cheeks on Ezekiel's T-shirt, looked up into the lifelike's fugazi blue eyes.

"Make it back, okay?" she said. "Then we'll go get her. You and me."

The lifelike just shook his head. "She's gone, Lemon."

"Make it *back*," she said, thumping his chest. "And we'll see. Promise?"

Ezekiel breathed deep. "I promise."

"Cross your heart and hope to die?"

"I see what you did there, Freckles."

She smiled, despite the sadness in her eyes. Cricket realized that was one of the things he loved about this girl best—shining a light, even in the darkest times. Seeking the joy of it, no matter how deep it was hidden. And with a small kiss to Ezekiel's cheek, she was dashing across the sand to the semi and jumping into the cab, with Grimm behind the wheel. Cricket trudged to the trailer, hauled himself inside, the suspension groaning protest at his weight. He looked about the compound, his glowing stare finally falling on Ezekiel. The lifelike raised one hand in farewell.

They were night and day, the pair of them. Ezekiel had helped destroy the humans that made him, and Cricket had only ever sought to protect them. Ezekiel was still struggling to find his place in the world, and Cricket knew exactly where he belonged. But Cricket supposed they were both ultimately driven by the same thing, fragile and unbreakable, impossible and mundane, something neither one of them should really have been able to comprehend.

"Look after her, Cricket," Ezekiel said.

Love.

"Count on it," Cricket replied.

And in that, if nothing else, he supposed they were alike.

Grimm gunned the engine. The semi shuddered beneath them. The desert stretched out before them, a barren emptiness with a whole bunch of carnage waiting at the end of it. If they could hold off the BioMaas army long enough for Ezekiel, Diesel and Abe to deliver the deathblow to CityHive, they might have a chance of putting the swarm down for good. A part of Cricket wondered if Daedalus deserved defending. He supposed if the freaks were standing at the end of it, at least they'd have a seat at the negotiation table. But that'd still leave Babel. Gabriel and Faith and Eve, who even now must be churning out more lifelikes, recruiting more corrupted logika into their army, mustering for a final strike against whoever came out on top of the coming battle.

Even if they won at Megopolis, the real war was still waiting for them.

And they had no guarantees of winning at Megopolis at all.

Diesel held up the horns in farewell.

"Remember your Darwin, freaks!" she shouted over the engines' roar.

"Only the strong survive!" Grimm yelled in reply.

"No! Today, the strong are gonna *win*!"

The truck peeled out toward the rising sun, the Wall of Megopolis, the waiting swarm. And Cricket couldn't help but wonder if any of them would be strong enough to stand against what was coming for them.

———

Ezekiel watched the semi until it was just a smudge on the horizon. Standing still as stone beneath the rising sun. It was going to be a scorching day, and night would bring no relief—just the swarm and the bloodshed to follow. He resisted the urge to turn his stare north toward Babel. To wonder about what might have been. To remember how it'd felt to sink back into her arms and feel like he was home again, if only for a moment.

Truth was, he had no home anymore. But still, he wasn't alone. Because these kids were with him—these freaks, fighting for a world that hated them. And if they were brave enough to stand up, how could he do any less?

"How we looking?" he asked.

Abraham was inside the flex-wing, checking the warhead rig. The flier was compact, and the device wasn't exactly small—it was going to be a squeeze for all of them to fit inside. The powercells would last if Zeke didn't push the engines too hard. But maneuvering with all this extra weight was going to be a problem. Abe could keep some trouble off them with his telekinesis, but Zeke didn't know what the limits of the kid's powers actually were. He hoped his piloting skills were up to the task.

The bomb was sitting on makeshift rails—with the press of a button, it could be ejected out the flex-wing's aft doors, tumbling downward toward destruction. Abe straightened, dragged his goggles up onto his brow and nodded.

"We're good," he said. "Rig looks solid."

Diesel looked the contraption over. "'Kay, run us through it one more time."

Abe held up a fist-sized metal box. "All right, this is the detonator. Safety switch is here. Secondary is here. Once both of those are off, we're ready to rumble. The timer is adjustable. At the moment, I've got it rigged to blow after thirty seconds. But depending on how much trouble we run into, it might need to be shorter."

"Explain to me why we need a detonator at all?" Deez asked. "We can't just aim this ship at the center of the Hive, Rift out, let it crash and boom?"

"No." Abe shook his head. "Like I said, these warheads are hard to blow up. The primary charges in the outer sphere all have to explode simultaneously, or the secondary reaction in the plutonium will just fizzle. A perfect detonation is the only way to achieve a nuclear explosion." He shrugged. "That said, a big enough impact might set off a *smaller* reaction, which would definitely blow us out of the sky. I'll keep as much trouble off us as I can." He glanced at Zeke. "But, like, don't get us shot."

"I wasn't planning on it."

"Best results come from explosions maybe five hundred meters off the ground. So, we fly high, hopefully out of sight. When we're over CityHive, we trip the timer and drop the bomb. Once it's out the door, Deez Rifts us west and keeps Rifting, getting us far she can in those thirty seconds. Then boom."

"How big is the blast?" the girl asked.

"*Big.* So Rift far and fast, or we're all gonna be radioactive ashes." Abe shrugged. "Or cancer patients."

The girl pouted with painted lips. "No pressure, huh, Brotherboy?"

Abe smirked. "No pressure."

"Right," Zeke nodded. "We'll give CityHive a wide berth, wait till nighttime and come in from the ocean. There's bound to be Hunter-Killer patrols in the skies around the city, but hopefully they won't spot us in the dark."

"And if they do?" Diesel asked. "The whole thing will be blown, right?"

Zeke shook his head. "Well, CityHive doesn't use radio. But if everything in BioMaas is interconnected the way Lemon says, they might not even need to. So let's just not get seen."

"I am in full agreement with this plan," Abraham nodded.

The crew bundled into the flier, with Abe strapped in beside the bomb in back and Diesel in the copilot's chair beside Ezekiel. Slapping on her seat belt, the girl held up a memchit and looked Zeke in the eye. "Mind if I play some music?"

Without waiting for an answer, she slapped the chit into the console and cranked the volume. The cabin filled with the earsplitting, blast-beat tempo of some truly obnoxious drudge. Ezekiel winced, shouting at Diesel over the ruckus.

"You call this *music*?"

"No!" Abraham groaned. "She calls it poetry!"

"Now you're learning!" she cried, thumping the dash. "Come on, let's go, prettyboy! Places to be! Cities to bomb!"

Ezekiel arced the throttle. Eased back the controls. A howl of motors. Screaming drudge. A moment's weightlessness, tearing free of the earth's grip.

And they were on their way.

———————

Lemon held Grimm's hand as they drove.

It wasn't easy at first, with Grimm crunching his way through the gears—at one point Cricket called out from the back and asked if he should maybe drive instead. But once they got on the freeway, hammering down those open roads across the empty stretch of the Yousay, Lemon found her fingers brushing Grimm's, until finally, they were entwined in his lap.

It felt good to her. Quiet and right. Like maybe they were just two kids out for a cruise instead of barreling headlong toward a battle for the fate of the future. Somehow it didn't matter to Lemon. The chaos waiting over the horizon, the thought of what they'd be facing. Somehow everything seemed okay with him beside her.

"This is nice," she said, snuggling a little closer.

"Yeah," he said, slipping his arm around her.

The kilometers ground away beneath their wheels, dust on her tongue, sun burning on her skin. The wasteland humanity had made flying past in a blur. West of Paradise Falls. East of Jugartown. She thought about all the places she'd been, the things she'd seen since she left home. Truth was, part of her still felt like that snot-nosed, punk kid who'd set out as the tagalong in someone else's story. The sass on tap. The comedy relief. She wondered who she was to be standing up in a fight like this. To be counting on others to do the same. Despite her speech in the silo, she didn't feel like any sort of leader.

Grimm looked at her sidelong.

"You got this, love," he said. "And you got me. To the end."

She smiled at him. Squeezed his hand.

"Not the end," she said. "Not today."

It was midafternoon when the first vehicles began passing them on the freeway—trucks and utilities, rusty buggies and motorcycles. Folk were driving on both sides of the road, and Grimm was forced to lay on the horn as the traffic got thicker, autos and people scrambling to get out of their way. Looking into the passing vehicles packed with people, loaded with gear, Lemon realized who they were.

"Megopolis citizens," she murmured. "Running away from the city."

"And here we are," Grimm smirked. "Runnin' right toward it."

The crush slowed them down, and the sun was well toward

setting by the time they reached the Rim of the Daedalus capital. Lemon was a little awed to see it, talking true. The great
Wall ringing its concrete Hub, the towering skyscrapers and
polluted fog, filthy and mean and crooked. It seemed an odd
thing to be saving, for a moment. But then Lem remembered
her days as a kid in the LD sprawl. The crews she'd run with,
the family she'd found with Evie and Silas. From a distance, the
last great human city in the whole Yousay was big and gray and
ugly. But if you looked closer, she supposed, Megopolis was full
of stories like hers. People just trying to get by, find a place to
belong, scrape out their own little piece of happy.

She squeezed Grimm's hand again.

Happy, if nothing else, was worth fighting for.

A security checkpoint was set up across the Wall in front
of them, manned by Daedalus troopers and the huge bulk of a
Daishō machina—bipedal, broad-shouldered, its head flanged
and crested like an old Asiabloc warrior from the history virtch.
Rotor drones spun through the sky; a dozen different automated sentries pointed weapons at them.

The lanes leading out of the Hub were choked with tanks,
heavy machina, artillery, but the lanes leading into the Hub
were empty but for a few truckloads of soldiers. A couple of
harried-looking, heavily armed troopers waved Grimm to a
stop. The lieutenant leading them was tall, battle-scarred and
looked like the kind that kicked kittens around for chuckles.
Grimm pulled over obediently. The lieutenant looked them
over with a scowl.

"You're actually trying to get *into* this city?"

"Crazy, right?" Lemon smiled.

"We're here to help, mate," Grimm said.

The lieutenant glanced to his comrades, then spat on the

ground. "Get outta here, kid. Take my word for it. You don't wanna be here come nightfall."

"Well, I'll be goddamned. . . ."

Lemon turned at the Southern drawl, eyes going wide. Cricket poked his head out from the semi's trailer, optics burning bright. There, among the power-armored troops waiting to get into the city, stood a familiar figure. He'd traded his dusty black trench coat for a suit of black power armor, but he still wore his cowboy hat, and he'd painted the gauntlet on his right hand blood red. He looked Lemon square in the eye, lips twisting into a grin.

"Lil' Red," he said.

"Preacher," she hissed, static crackling behind her eyes.

Kitten Kicker glanced at Preacher. "You know these three, Goodbook?"

"Yeah, I know 'em," the man replied.

The bounty hunter looked at Cricket in the back of the rig, then the troopers all around him. Lemon wondered if every kind of trouble was about to start raining onto their heads. But as Preacher fixed her in his stare, irises glinting like pale blue glass, the man threw back his head and burst out laughing.

"What's so funny?" she demanded, squaring up.

The bounty hunter wiped at his eyes, shook his head. "Only that I've spent what feels like forever hunting your narrow ass all over the goddamn country, missy. An' here you are, deliverin' yourself to the front gate without a care in the world."

"I'm not 'delivering' myself anywhere," Lemon said.

Cricket nodded. "AND IF YOU'RE THINKING OF CASHING IN—"

"Ain't no point," Preacher said, shaking his head. "BioMaas apparently got what they needed outta ya. Unless you ain't aware of what went on down south."

"I know what happened in Armada," she said softly. "I'm here to make sure it doesn't happen again."

Preacher looked her over carefully, but Kitten Kicker scoffed.

"You got any idea what's coming this way tonight?" the soldier demanded. "What kind of help can you be, kid?"

Lemon opened her palms, let tiny arcs of static crackle between her fingers. Beside her, Grimm closed his fists, heat rippling in the air around them, tiny fires flaring in the depths of his eyes. Cricket loomed at their backs, all seventy-one tons of him, his armor blood red, his face a grinning skull.

Kitten Kicker's eyes grew a little wider. Preacher seemed unfazed. Lemon looked about the defenses, back to Preacher's eyes.

"Can't help but notice you got no logika on your line."

The bounty hunter shook his head. "Every bot in the city shut down, ran off or went insane when those snowflakes transmitted their virus."

"Sounds like you're a little shorthanded," she said. "You want our help or not?"

She looked around the assembled soldierboys, static crackling in her eyes.

"Because let's face it. *You* kids need all the help you can get."

3.33

TSUNAMI

Diesel didn't like it when things went smooth.

It was the superstitious part of her. The part that told her the universe only made good things happen so it hurt worse when the bad stuff arrived. Diesel was a girl who was always waiting for the other boot to drop, but so far, there was no damn sign of it, and that just put her on edge. The flex-wing had cut across the desert, endless kilometers of rolling dunes and busted freeways and little scum-water towns flashing away beneath them. Zeke flew low at first, engines cruising to preserve their power. It was a long trek to CityHive, and they were going to be flying all day.

The Glass stretched away off to the north—an endless expanse of black, irradiated sand. She felt a stab of guilt at the thought that they were about to make more of that hellscape, that if everything went well, there'd be nothing left of CityHive but radioactive silicon by morning. But even if these weren't the bastards who killed Fix, truth told, Deez knew they were in a war here. And Fresh was right—it was well past time they started winning.

They flew on, not speaking much, blast-beats for company. Diesel kept her eyes fixed on the long-range scanner, watching for telltale blips. The wastelands rolled beneath them, the Glass a black shadow at the corner of her eye. But ahead, Deez could see ocean: endless black capped with white chop. The sun was sinking now. Bloody red smeared along western skies. Diesel reached out, turned down the sound sys.

"How long to CityHive?" she called over the engine drone.

Prettyboy's plastic blue eyes were fixed across the waves. "Hour. Maybe less. I'm gonna take us up higher. They're bound to have aerial patrols, but Hunter-Killers generally don't fly too high. With luck, they won't see us till it's too late."

Ezekiel pressed on the throttle, and the flex-wing began ascending, the air growing colder as they rose. Gray above. Black below. There was precious little cloud cover, but the light was dying, the shades of night descending. The cabin was bathed in the soft glow of the instruments, the pulsing scanner.

Diesel blinked. Squinted at the screen. "Is that . . . ?"

Ezekiel glanced down at the screen, cursed softly.

"What's up?" Abe asked, climbing forward to peer into the cabin.

"Incoming," Ezekiel said. "Moving fast."

"So much for luck," Abe sighed.

Diesel looked out into the growing dusk, her pulse running quicker. There was no way to avoid BioMaas patrols forever, but they were still over an hour from their target. Getting spotted this far out was going to mean capital T. . . .

"Can't see jack," she murmured, peering into the dark.

". . . There," Ezekiel pointed. "Hunter-Killers."

Diesel looked to where the lifelike was pointing, couldn't see anyth— No, no, prettyboy was right, there they were. Six sleek figures, flying a few hundred meters below. The constructs were two meters long, organic lines and insectoid shells. They looked like giant wasps, dark, semitranslucent wings almost as wide as the flex-wing. Their multifaceted eyes and the patterns on their abdomens glowed luminous green. They might not be as maneuverable as the flex-wing, but they looked faster, and they were rising quick.

"How can they even see us?" Diesel murmured.

"Thermal, maybe. Or sonic." Ezekiel arced the weapons systems, locked the first creature in his sights. "Hell, maybe they can *smell* us."

"Don't miss," Abe said. "If they get back with a warning, we're going to be fighting a running battle all the way to City-Hive."

"Maybe CityHive already knows we're here," Diesel said.

"Well, first things first," Ezekiel said, poised over the guns.

The lifelike waited patiently. The H-Ks cruised in closer, curious, eyes aglow. And when they were a few hundred meters away, Zeke opened up.

Tracer fire cut through the gloom, luminous red, arcing away into the darkness. The shells struck home, bursting two of the H-Ks apart in seconds. The other Hunter-Killers broke, split away, weaving through the dark. Ezekiel banked hard as the creatures peppered the sky with luminous green spit, Deez clinging on for dear life as the flex-wing rolled through the spray, the brackets holding the warheads in place groaning. Ezekiel fired again, killing another, the cabin shaking with the thunder of their autocannons. Corrosive fire hissed past them; a tiny speck hit their portside wing and ate a small hole right through the metal.

"They're getting away!" Abe cried.

The remaining three H-Ks had broken off, tucking tail and sprinting back to CityHive. But Zeke shook his head. "They're not going anywhere."

Prettyboy was a mean flier, hot on the H-Ks' tails, cutting down one, then another. The last of them swung around, spraying a burst of ooze right at them. But Abe held up his hand, and the air rippled like water, and the incoming acid spattered against some invisible barrier and fell away harmlessly. With another burst of fire from Ezekiel, the last H-K was smeared across the sky.

"Top job," Abe said, patting Zeke on the shoulder.

"You too," the lifelike smiled. "Now hopefully, we—"

"Prettyboy . . . ," Diesel said, pointing at the radar.

"Oh, holy crap . . . ," Abraham breathed.

The display was lighting up. First a few scattered dots, then dozens. Red and pulsing, closing in on them from the edges of the screen. Diesel watched them mustering: a legion of Bio-Maas fliers, waaay more than they were expecting. Deep down, she'd been hoping CityHive had sent most of their muscle at Daedalus. But it looked like they'd left some juice in the tank to protect the home fires, and that tank was getting emptied right at the freak show.

"Guess that answers the question of whether they know we're here or not . . ."

Abe glanced at Zeke. "Can you handle that many?"

The lifelike tightened his grip on the controls, jaw clenched. "We got trouble."

Diesel didn't like it when things went smooth.

But she'd take smooth over rough any day.

———

Preacher stood atop the Wall and looked out on the hissing, drooling horde below him. He could feel the familiar tingle of adrenaline in the few meat parts he had left, the tang of combat stims ripping through his system. The armor on his back felt like the hand of God, and the assault cannon in his arms felt just like home. He spat his mouthful of synth tobacco onto the concrete beneath him, stuffed a fresh wad into his cheek and shouldered his weapon.

"All right, boys," he drawled. "Let's send these bugs right back to hell."

"Some of us aren't boys," muttered lil' Red beside him.

He looked sidelong at the girl and grunted. "Everyone's a critic."

Danael Drakos hadn't been too impressed with Preacher's efforts to catch Snowflake and his family, the carnage Zekey and his sibs had wrought inside the Spire. For a while, Preacher wondered if Drakos was gonna recycle him for parts. But truth was, at this stage Daedalus needed all the bodies they could get. The unit he'd been put in command of had good people. Well trained, better equipped. They were first wave, positioned on the Wall beside a strike force of Tarantulas. The machina were basically walking missile emplacements—like massive dish plates on eight legs, bristling with missile pods.

Past the Wall, the swarm was approaching, aglow in his thermographic vision. An endless sea of slakedogs came first, scampering into the outer suburbs of the Rim, through the abandoned streets. Behind them came the towering forms of behemoths, protected from on high by wave after wave of Hunter-Killers.

"There's so many," lil' Red breathed.

"Gonna be a lot less in a minute," Preacher growled. He glanced to his men. "All units, prepare to fire."

He glanced to the heavens, up to the God who'd always looked out for him.

"And if you could spare a miracle, big fella," he murmured, "now's the time."

———

"More H-Ks incoming, nine o'clock!"

"I see them! Hold on!"

"Zeke, watch the—"

"I'm on it, I'm on it!"

The skies around them were alight. Sprays of luminous green spittle. Burning streaks of tracer fire. Glowing blood and glittering shell casings. The noise was pummeling, the unearthly, chittering shrieks of Hunter-Killers as they died, the roar of the engines, the droning hymn of endless wings, shrieking ruin, and the deafening sonic assault of drudge through the flex-wing's sound sys.

"Diesel, will you *turn that music down*!" Ezekiel roared.

"It's not like they don't know we're here!" she shouted back. "It gets you pumped, flyboy!"

Ezekiel was plenty pumped already, breathing hard, filmed with a light sheen of sweat. They'd been fighting a running battle for the last twenty minutes, the skies about them filled with Hunter-Killers. Even carrying the extra weight, the flex-wing was more maneuverable than the BioMaas fliers: rolling at high gees, slapping on the air-skids, spiraling through swarms of enemies and cutting them down as it passed. But no sooner would they fight off one wave than more would appear on their scopes—the H-Ks were faster, and their numbers seemed endless, and Zeke wondered how much more of this they could take.

Truth told, they'd already be dead if not for Abraham. The boy was crouched in the rear compartment, eyes closed, arms outstretched. The air about them shimmered with force, a perfect sphere maybe twenty meters in diameter. When H-K fire struck it, the sphere rippled like liquid, repelling the blast, keeping their little ship from being torn apart in the glowing green firestorm. But every strike was costing Abe something—Zeke could tell. The boy's brow, once smooth, was now creased in a dark scowl, his skin dripping with sweat, the effort etched plainly in the clench of his jaw, the white knuckles of his fists, desperately clinging to the warhead detonator. And so, Zeke was doing his best to not get hit, weaving and swooping through the BioMaas formations, cutting as many of them down as he could manage.

"Abe, you doing okay?" Zeke called.

"I . . ." The kid nodded. "I can take it."

Deez looked at him with growing concern. "We're twenty minutes from CityHive, can y—"

"I can *take* it!" Abe shouted.

They flew on, a brutal, high-speed ballet that left the skies burning behind them. An H-K collided with Abe's barrier, bursting like a bug on a windshield. The boy shuddered, the barrier wavered and Zeke was forced to roll upward, spiraling desperately, pressing everyone back in their seats as gravity howled protest.

"I'm gonna puke!" Diesel shouted.

Zeke's pulse was hammering in his ears, the controls in his hands slippery. But they were getting closer. They only had to hold out a few more minutes and—

"Um, prettyboy?" Diesel shouted.

The odd note in her voice dragged his eyes off his scopes for a second, onto her bloodless face. "Yeah?"

Diesel raised her finger, pointed beyond the windshield. "What the *hell* are those things?"

————

"You ready for this, love?" Grimm asked.

Lemon looked out on the incoming swarm. An ocean of too many claws and too many teeth, of bio-organic armor and maws drooling acid. And somewhere among the multitude, she swore she could feel them.

Little pieces of her.

"Nnnnnot really," Lemon murmured.

"WE'RE WITH YOU, LEMON," Cricket said behind her. "TO THE END."

"This ain't the end," Preacher said, raising his rifle. "Not today."

"Hey," she scowled. "That's my line."

The first wave of missiles fired as soon as the BioMaas horde was in range. A thousand metallic howls rang out across the city, flares of light brightening the growing dark. Explosions bloomed, thundered in the Wall under Lemon's feet, flame and smoke billowing up into the sky, and BioMaas's first wave—slakedogs mostly—was utterly annihilated. Their bodies were blown to chunks, scattered across the broken, smoking ground, green blood soaking into the earth.

But they just kept coming.

Above, the skies were lit up by bursts of bullets and glowy green spit as flex-wings and Hunter-Killers punched it out. A buzzing wave of genetically engineered bees rolled over the battlefield, only to be cooked by Titan machina and their flamethrowers. Another wave of slakedogs followed the first, crashing against the Wall. The belly-churning, panty-soiling *dubdubdubdub* of weapons fire filled her ears, the stink of blood filled her nostrils.

And then Lemon saw them.

Massive, armored behemoths lumbering forward, slake-dogs clustered around their feet. And in the shadows beneath the beasts, small figures clad in black, pale freckled skin and dark eyes and blood-red spines for hair.

The clones.

"There!" Lemon cried. "We have to take tho—"

"I see 'em." Preacher turned and bellowed. "All positions, fire!"

The guns opened up, the missiles howled, the flex-wings swarmed. Everything Daedalus had was concentrated on only a dozen targets, a dozen girls who suddenly threatened to undo an empire. Lemon watched as the slakedogs, the behemoths, the Hunter-Killers laid down their lives to protect them, spattered, blown apart, cut to pieces. She saw at least three of the girls go down, caught in explosions or hails of bullets, and she didn't quite know why, but her heart ached to see them fall. But for everything Daedalus threw, all the fire they had, it still wasn't enough to stop them coming. Lemon watched, nine figures now, stalking ever closer to the Wall, Hunter's words ringing in her head.

Lemonfresh is the flood that will drown it.

The storm that will wash all of it away.

She saw one of the clones, clad in that strange black leather, standing just a hundred meters away. Through the smoke, the ashes, Lemon thought for a moment that the girl was a virtual mirror of herself. But then she realized its eyes were totally black. And when it blinked, it blinked twice—first with its regular eyelids, then with a second pair that closed horizontally under the first.

The Lemonthing locked her in its black glare. Dark lips peeling back from its teeth. It raised its hand, and with one black-nailed finger, it pointed at Lemon.

"Cricket, get down!" she roared.

The static pulsed behind her eyes. Crackled in the air between them.

And all hell broke loose.

———

Eve was a girl who kept her promises.

Far below, she watched the BioMaas horde crashing against the Wall. The tiny firefly flicker of weapons and explosions, people and constructs dying. There was a kind of poetry to it, from far away. It was almost serene. Bad news for the people caught up in it, though.

But the good news was that the entire Megopolis air force was tied up in the battle, and without the logika Daedalus had come to depend on so badly, their resources were stretched thin. A lone flex-wing, flying high and silent, could apparently get pretty close unnoticed.

In the center of the Hub, Eve could see a familiar shape looming, covered in solar panels and wrapped in a jungle of thick cable—the Spire, where they'd tortured her. She could still see Danael Drakos's face as she tore loose inside the operating theater, her vow to him echoing in her head.

I'm going to burn this whole thing down, bastard.

Moving sure, her hands rock-steady, she aimed her flex-wing toward the Spire and cut the power, gliding down through the pall of fumes, the rising smoke.

Her lips twisted in a small smile.

Eve was a girl who kept her promises, after all.

———

"What the hell *are* those things?" Diesel yelled again.

The "things" in question were rising up in front of them now in a vast, swaying storm. They reminded Zeke a little of the fireflies he'd seen in old 20C vids, their abdomens swollen and aglow, glowing bright in the gloom. The creatures were much smaller than the Hunter-Killers—no bigger than a fist. But there must have been thousands of them. They ascended into the swarming skies, a glittering green haze, too small to shoot down, too many to avoid.

"I have no idea!" Zeke said. "But they're coming right for us!"

He swooped higher, trying to outrun them, but the creatures were simply too many. The first of them crashed against Abe's barrier—a tiny pop, an acidic glow. Nothing, really. But soon there were dozens, a great cloud of them crashing with suicidal abandon against Abraham's force sphere. They burned as they burst, corrosive, hissing, eating away at the barrier as if it were a physical wall.

Zeke had no real idea how Abe's power worked, whether the assault would have an effect. But one glance over his shoulder told him the boy was in trouble.

"You okay?" he asked.

"I-I'm okay . . . ," Abe hissed, still clutching the detonator.

"Zeke, look out!" Diesel cried.

Ezekiel grasped, twisted the controls as a bright green burst of H-K fire streaked past their windshield. More fire followed, luminous, sizzling. Zeke realized Abe's barrier was breaking, that the kid just couldn't handle this much damage.

"This is insane," Diesel spat. "We're never gonna make it. I've gotta Rift us."

Abe gasped. "Not a g-good . . . idea."

"That New Bethlehem nuke detonated when you Rifted it, Diesel!" Zeke said.

"We don't know that!" the girl shouted. "Maybe it was supposed to blow at that exact moment!"

"And maybe going through your rift set it off!"

"If we stay here, we get blasted out of the sky!"

"T-too dangerous," Abe gasped, waving the detonator. "It's—"

The boy's voice was cut off as the hull beside him burst. A spray of green ichor cut through the metal, and Abe screamed as it struck him, throwing him back in his seat. The spray cut clean through the metal, leaving a hissing hole in the roof. The flex-wing bucked hard, dropping a hundred meters in a heart-beat, Diesel shouting in alarm. Zeke fought them back under control, more fire streaking past—a blinding hail coming from all directions. He realized Abe's barrier was *down,* that the boy was bent double in his chair, screaming in agony, that the only thing between them and death was his piloting skills.

He bent into the controls, sending them into a bone-twisting dive. Diesel roared over the screaming engines, "Abraham, are you okay?"

A glance behind told Zeke the kid was far from it. He was clutching his belly, face twisted in agony. Zeke saw the burst had struck his ribs and gut, dissolving flesh and bone, leaving his torso a ragged mess. And twisted and bubbling on the floor at his feet lay the melted ruins of . . .

"Oh no," Diesel whispered. "The detonator . . ."

The girl looked out into the oncoming storm of Hunter-Killers. The spray of fire they couldn't hope to avoid. The ground rushing up with open arms.

"Hold on to your underoos, freaks," she said.

Stretching out her hand, a colorless rip of nothing opening before them.

"Diesel, wait!" Zeke roared.

And they plunged inside.

———

Electrical current crackled in the air. The stab of ozone on her tongue, the thrill of goose bumps over her skin. And everything around Lemon started dying.

The shock of it hit the Wall like a tsunami, crashing on it in a screaming, sizzling wave. The clones reached into the static, the billion burning fires of current along the Wall, making guns fire, hearts beat, brains think. All life on the planet—human *and* machine—needed electrical current to function. And BioMaas's creations were reaching into that current and simply shutting it off.

Pilots in machina screamed as they were cooked alive inside their rides. Power armor fizzled and seized up, automata guns fell silent, electronic targeting systems became very expensive paperweights, rotor drones and flex-wings tumbled from the sky. It was carnage. But Lemon gritted her teeth, cried out, the force of her own gift crackling and spitting and shivering.

She pushed outward, felt like she was standing tall against a hurricane, every nerve tingling, the spit in her mouth boiling.

The soldiers in power around her shuddered but didn't fall. Preacher flinched, his cybernetic arm twitching, but he didn't stumble. Cricket wobbled a little, steadying himself against the concrete at his feet, but he didn't collapse.

In a hundred-meter circle around Lemon, the Daedalus force was utterly untouched.

"Jesus H. Christ on a bouncin' bicycle," Preacher murmured, looking at her.

Lemon gritted her teeth again. Looked at that broken-mirror copy of herself below, surrounded by claws and glittering eyes. And she lashed out. A whip of force, crackling through the static, warping and rippling as it came. The clone struck back, fingers twisted, snarling, struggling for control. Lemon felt the blow, pain ripping through her skull, one eye closed, blood streaming from her nose.

But here's the thing of it. Newbie she might have been. A snot-nosed kid who grew up with nothing, yeah, she was that, too. Scared and wired and in all the way over her head. But Lemon Fresh had still been riding in the static longer than these vat-grown, broken-mirror versions of her that BioMaas had dredged into being. And the sight of BioMaas doing so much hurt, inflicting so much pain, with something that had never been theirs in the first place made her heart feel like it was just on fire.

It was one thing to watch the massacre at Armada on a screen. It was another to live through it. To hear the screams. To taste the stink of burned meat. Rage like Lemon had never known coursed through her body, a rage to avenge, a rage to overcome. And she used it, twisted it, lashing out at the clone and screaming at the top of her lungs.

The Lemonthing wobbled on its feet.

A trickle of blood streamed from its black eyes.

And without a sound, it crumpled to the ground.

Lemon collapsed to her knees, crimson streaming from her nose.

"Lemon!" Grimm cried, kneeling beside her.

She screwed her eyes shut, hissing with pain. It felt like someone had punched a rusty ax into her brainmeats.

But though Lemon had stood her ground, protected the lucky few around her, the rest of the Daedalus army had been fried to uselessness. Slakedogs crashed against the Wall and began climbing. Behemoths plowed into the security gates below and started carving them open. Another wave of death-bees washed over the barriers, soldiers started screaming, the air above filled with Hunter-Killers. Grimm clenched his fists and the air around them sizzled with heat, reducing hundreds of the insects to blackened husks. Cricket opened up with his chaingun, blasting a few H-Ks from the sky. But it was like chucking pebbles at a grav-tank.

"We stay here, we're dead!" Grimm roared.

Another wave of static washed over their position, and Lemon gasped, wincing. She only barely kept it at bay, knives of crackling pain slipping into her skull. Grimm grabbed her as she cried out, blood gushing from her nose now, coating her open palms. Squinting into the Rim, she could see them—eight Lemonthings, stalking across the broken bodies of slakedogs, the blood so thick the ground was like soup. She could feel them now. They could feel her, too. And she knew with certainty . . .

"WE GOTTA GET OUTTA HERE!" Cricket bellowed.

Preacher blasted an incoming H-K out of the sky, took in their situation with a split-second glance. For all his faults, all the trouble he'd caused, Lemon was glad that at least he didn't seem to be an idiot, too.

"Fall back!" he roared. "All units, fall back!"

———

Eve landed on the roof of a crooked skyscraper two buildings west of the Spire just as the first shockwave hit. A strange unsong rang out in the city, the air smelling of burned plastic, the hair all over Eve's body standing on end. She was reminded of Lemon—of that day outside Babel when she fried those machina and Eve learned the depths of the lies she'd been telling.

But that was past now. Lemon was history.

And she had promises to keep.

Whatever the shockwave was, it had the Daedalus forces in a panic. Looking toward the battle, she saw flex-wings tumbling from the sky, dark shapes scuttling over the Wall. Looking out over the edge of her broken skyscraper to the streets below, Eve saw Daedalus troops on the move, grav-tanks and infantry all in a tizz. But they weren't looking for an enemy already in the city. Especially not one who looked just like them.

Jaw clenched, knuckles white, she slipped over the side of the building, and using all the strength in her lifelike body, she began to descend, punching holes in the solar panels with her fingertips. The wind wailed about her, snatching at her fauxhawk, bringing the distant song and scent of butchery with it. But she didn't stop to listen. Ten floors down, she reached the first snaking tangle of cable, each as thick as her arm, linking one solar array to the building opposite. She dropped onto the cables, crouching low, arms out for balance as she dashed across the wailing gap and reached the next skyscraper in the row.

Meter by meter. Panel by panel. Cable by cable. Working her way around the building until finally she could see the Daedalus Spire. Dark shapes were flooding over the Wall now, through the sundered gates, the Daedalus defenders in total rout. Bio-Maas looked set to wipe the Daedalus capital off the map.

"Not yet, bastard," she whispered.

Dropping down onto another tangle of solar cables, Eve began climbing toward the Spire.

———

Colorless. Soundless. Weightless.

For a second, Ezekiel thought he was dead. That the bomb had exploded, that he'd been dismantled in a blinding burst of nuclear fire. He wondered briefly if he'd see God. Wondered, even more briefly, what he might say. And then gravity returned, sound close behind, a shuddering, screaming jolt rocking the flex-wing as they tore out of Diesel's second rift, still plummeting toward the earth.

They were higher than they'd been a second ago, he realized. And looking down at the softly glowing landscape, the dark, asymmetrical patterns on the ground below, he saw. "We're above CityHive."

The Hunter-Killers were in a frenzy on the scanners—Diesel had left them behind when she Rifted, and aside from a few Lumberers, the skies above the city were relatively clear. But it would only be moments before the swarm recovered. Zeke pulled the flex-wing out of its dive, wind howling through the sundered hull. Diesel dragged off her safety harness and hauled herself into the flex-wing's rear.

"Abe," she whispered. "Shit . . ."

The boy was in a bad way, the flesh of his stomach and chest a melted, bubbling mess, wordless moans of pain torn up right from the heart of him. The detonator was melted to useless slag. Abe's face was contorted with agony, but even worse . . .

"We've got no way to trigger the bomb," Zeke said.

Diesel met Zeke's eyes. The unspoken weight of it hanging between them. With no disruption in CityHive, with the Directors still at the heart of the BioMaas web, the swarm would be unstoppable. Even now, it was probably tearing its way through Megopolis. Grimm, Cricket, Lemon, all of them . . .

"They're dead," Diesel whispered.

Zeke glanced at the scanners, the incoming horde of H-Ks, down to the city untouched below them. "Can you start Rifting us back to Megopolis? Maybe if we—"

"N-no," Abe gasped, grabbing Diesel's arm. "No."

"Abe, the detonator's wasted, we got no way to blow it."

"I c-can do . . . it," he breathed, dragging off his ruined harness.

"Abe—"

The boy shoved Diesel aside, hair whipping about his eyes as he stood and staggered toward the warheads. His face was bloodless, hands shaking as he drew a multi-tool from his belt.

"I thought you said this thing had to go off perfect!" Diesel shouted.

Abe gritted his teeth, began unscrewing the bolts. "It . . . it d-does."

"Well, how you gonna do that without the detonator?" Diesel demanded.

Abe looked up into the girl's eyes.

"M-manually," he said.

———

They ran.

Slakedogs flooding over the walls. Hunter-Killers filling the skies. Behemoths charging through the streets. Lemon was in Cricket's arms, her nose still bleeding. Grimm sprinted along beside them, the heat seething inside him. He could feel it swimming in his veins, boiling in his eyes, see it reflected in his mind's eye—that mushroom-shaped calamity roiling in the skies above New Bethlehem and, somehow, as he'd reached into it and made it his own, taking seed under his skin.

The Daedalus troopers who'd survived the collapse came behind, blasting away at the seemingly endless wave of Bio-Maas beasties. Preacher was bringing up the rear, roaring at the top of his lungs.

"Is that all you got, you godless *bastards*? My momma hits harder'n you!"

"THEY'RE EVERYWHERE!" Cricket shouted.

"What the bloody hell happened to Deez and Zeke?" Grimm spat.

"I KNEW WE COULDN'T COUNT ON HIM!" Cricket turned and let loose with the last of his shoulder missiles. "I *KNEW* IT!"

A Hunter-Killer swooped low, spitting green acid. Grimm set the air about them boiling, burning the creature out of the sky. But the city was overrun. The swarm coming from all directions now. Glancing back, bleary-eyed, Grimm could see two redheaded figures stalking down the street toward them, surrounded by drooling slakedogs, slavering behemoths and Hunters. Black fingernails. Black eyes. Lemon was already exhausted—she didn't have the strength to take on another one, let alone two.

It would only be seconds before they were all brown bread.

"Is there any way out of this city?" Grimm yelled.

"Airfield six blocks from here!" Preacher roared, blasting at the incoming swarm.

"Mate, we're not gonna get *one* block in this!"

"Only other option is the Spire! There's flex-wings on the roof, maybe we—"

"WHERE IS IT?" Cricket shouted, cradling Lemon to his chest and laying waste to a handful of 'dogs.

"There!" Preacher shouted, pointing to a glittering spike of solar panels and cable, topped with relay dishes. "Daedalus HQ!"

"Well, we c—"

A burning flex-wing dropped out of the sky, crashing onto the pavement and exploding in a ball of flame. And above the roar, the cries of the scattering soldiers, Grimm heard the most awful sound of his young life—Lemon screaming in pain. Turning aside as the shrapnel flew, dragging the fire out of the air, he redirected it in a blast that immolated an incoming wave of slakedogs. Feeling the heat swell and stretch inside him. Screaming for release. As the smoke cleared, he caught sight of Cricket, the big bot crouched in a protective ball, Lemon in his arms. But much as the big bot had tried to shield her, she'd still taken a hit—a chunk of shrapnel carving a deep gouge through her brow, up into her hairline.

"Lemon!" Grimm shouted.

"I'm o-okay," she gasped, blood spilling down her face. "I'm 'k-kkay."

And that was it. The last of it. The thought of dying himself was something he could deal with. But of everyone in this cesspit of a country, she was the one who mattered most. And seeing her bruised, bleeding, red on her hands and in her eyes and on those lips he'd pressed to his own just a few hours ago . . . .

"Get her out of here," he growled.

Grimm stood up tall, felt the heat breaking loose under his skin. The fire of New Bethlehem rising up inside him, like it had done with Deez, with Lemon, overflowing the well in his chest. Cricket looked at him, and in those burning blue optics, Grimm could see himself, skin growing darker, the air about him rippling like a heat wave, white-hot plasma spilling up and out of his eyes.

"I'll hold them off," the boy said, turning to the incoming mob.

"G-Grimm, no!" Lemon whispered.

Grimm looked at her over his shoulder, the image of her shivering in the heat, tinged red by the flames spilling from his eyes.

"Get her out of here, Cricket."

"No!" she cried. "Not you, t-too!"

He smiled. "Love you, Lem."

And he turned away. Turned his back on happy, on the one who mattered most. On the girl he believed in. And he looked at the oncoming horde, cutting the remaining soldiers down, all teeth and eyes and gnashing fangs, the warped reflections of the girl he loved coming behind them set to unmake the world. The air around him rippled, a nimbus of white heat. The concrete under his feet blackened and cracked. A blazing wind whipped about him, howling down the street. And he squared his shoulders and he gritted his teeth and he nodded. Because he knew, sure as that nuclear fire seething at his fingertips, bright as the immolation waiting just beneath his skin, that maybe sometimes the strong didn't survive.

But they were still going to win.

Grimm opened his arms.

And the sky caught fire.

————

"Collapse in sectors five through twelve!"

"Air wing is completely unresponsive, Director!"

"Tracking hostiles within two blocks of the Spire."

"Sir, you need to evacuate!"

Danael Drakos stood in his Command and Control center, watching his empire unravel. Desperate reports from dying soldiers blaring over comms. The pulsing red glow of the BioMaas swarm on the wall-mounted monitors, spreading out through his beloved city like an infection. So many alarms were screaming now, it was impossible to tell one from another. Security breach. Perimeter breach. Airspace breach. Drakos's head was splitting.

The scene in the Spire was chaos—most of the roles in C & C had been filled by logika with computational abilities beyond the human beings they'd replaced. But after Libertas was unleashed, Drakos was left with plain old meat to do the job. His people were loyal, but inexperienced. At the eleventh hour, he saw what a risk they'd taken, placing so much faith in the hands of machines.

"We should never have listened to you, Drakos!"

He turned, his suit immaculate, eyes glowering, not a hair out of place. Behind him stood the assembled members of the Daedalus board. Old men and women with nip-tuck skin and sculpted faces, watching their earthly power unravel.

"I told you that deviate should have been eliminated immedi—"

A pistol cracked, louder than the alarms, the reports of the dying, the cacophony around him. The board members dropped with bloody chests and bloody faces, the commtechs around him followed. Drakos's personal security detail—four stimmed-up ex-military beatsticks—drew their weapons as the Director stumbled into the console behind him. A figure wove through the darkness, twisting one guard's head so violently it almost came off, emptying her pistol into another's face. The two remaining men opened fire, muzzle flashes lighting up the red-alert gloom, and in that strobing flare, Drakos saw her. A tousled blond fauxhawk, sharp cheekbones, hazel eyes, burning with the purest malice he'd ever seen in his life.

She twisted aside, took a bullet in the arm, slipped behind one soldier, breaking his elbow and snatching up his pistol as it dropped from nerveless fingers. The second fired again, and she twisted the first around, using him as a shield against the incoming hail. The lead sparked and *thunk*ed into the man's armor, and she kicked him savagely in the spine, sent him flying into his comrade, finishing both with neat shots to the head.

She turned to him, blood dripping down her arm, smoking pistol in her hand.

"Hello, Danael," she said, raising the pistol.

"Miss Monrova," he replied.

She glanced down the hallway to the R & D section. The VR suite therein.

Bloody lips twisted in a smile.

"Feel like a trip to the beach?"

———

Grimm's heat wave crackled outward, a fan of white-hot nuclear fire. Lemon could still see him in the midst of it if she squinted, a tiny black silhouette against the eye of the sun. The swarm melted, fried, burned, blackening and splitting, shrieking their agony. And Lemon was helpless to stop it.

"Lemme g-go!" she gasped, struggling against Cricket's grip.

"No!" the big bot roared, continuing to run.

"Crick, lemme . . ." She blinked hard, pawing the blood from her eyes, near-blind with sticky red. "Lemme down or I'll cook you!"

"THEN COOK ME!" he shouted. "YOU'RE NOT GOING BACK THERE!"

"This way!" Preacher shouted, leading them on, rifle smoking in his hands. They were maybe half a block from the Spire. But turning the corner, Preacher skidded to a halt, breath hissing between his teeth.

"Shit . . ."

Lemon peered through the blood in her eyes, heart sinking. Between them and the Spire stood about a hundred slakedogs, a dozen behemoths, tearing the soldiers defending the building to pieces. A few of the creatures turned to face them, fangs bared, claws tearing the concrete, eyes glittering dark. And among them, Lemon caught sight of a slender figure, clad all in black, blood-red hair and ebony eyes, narrowing as it caught sight of her.

"She," it hissed, raising its finger, *"is no longer important."*
Cricket looked down at her, cradled her softly to his chest.
"CLOSE YOUR EYES, KIDDO," he whispered.

———

Diesel blinked. ". . . What do you mean, 'manually'?"

"I mean exactly what you th-think I mean!" Abe shouted.
"Help m-me!"

The flex-wing rocked as Zeke saw the first incoming bursts
of fire. The H-Ks had zeroed them now, wheeling around to
open fire again. More of those firefly things were coming up
from the city below. In a minute, the whole swarm would be
back on them again, and without Abraham's barrier . . .

The kid was yelling instructions to Diesel, the girl tearing
off housings, ripping out wires under his guidance. Abe was
barely standing, the stink of burned flesh filling Zeke's nostrils—
he had no idea how the kid was still upright, talking true. But
his bloodshot eyes were wide, bright, and after a few desperate moments, he stood, clutching a stripped cable in either fist.
Looking Ezekiel dead in the eye.

"Bay d-doors!" he shouted.

"Abe, no," Diesel said. "We can't just—"

"This is their only chance!" the kid roared, blood on his lips.
"It's what you do that counts, remember? So let me do this!"

Ezekiel met the boy's stare. Saw the determination. The ac-
ceptance. The fire. Tears welled in Diesel's eyes as she shook
her head. "No, us freaks stick together!"

The flex-wing rolled and twisted, the Hunter-Killers
swarming in the air all about them. Abraham looked Diesel in

the eyes. No time for denials or speeches. No time for farewells. No time for any of it. The wound at his belly would kill him anyway. Abraham was a dead man walking. And as bad as it hurt, all of them knew it.

Ezekiel's finger hovered above the release.

"I'll g-give you as long as I can," Abe said. "Rift fast, Diesel. And Rift far."

Abe met Zeke's stare, his eyes shining.

"Do it!"

Ezekiel stabbed the button. The doors yawned wide. And trundling forward on rails, the warheads and the boy who'd cobbled them together both plummeted out into the black. Hunter-Killers swarmed, spraying the air with acid, but Zeke saw the air around the falling boy ripple—one last moment of power in that swelling, bloody night. He felt Diesel's hand on his shoulder, heard her roar in his ears.

"Dive!"

He tipped their nose down, and there before them, a colorless tear opened in the sky. They plunged through, Diesel's hand outstretched, sound snuffed out like a candle. A split second later they emerged, screaming, still diving, kilometers from the falling boy. Zeke only had a second to get his bearings before they were Rifting again, again, Diesel's power dragging them farther and farther from that unborn conflagration, falling like a star through the CityHive sky.

Every second was a century. Every heartbeat an age. Zeke's breath locked in his lungs, hair on his skin rising, dread uncoiling as every moment ticked by without that awful light. He wondered for a moment if something had gone wrong. If Abe had failed or died before he could strike his final blow.

He wondered.
And then—

———

Ten thousand eyes looked skyward.

Ten thousand iterations of the same patterns.

Carers and Hunters. Sentinels and Builders. Slakedogs and Lumberers, behemoths and Scuttlers, and, finally, Directors.

The dark above was alight with pretty greens, radiant and glittering. The interlopers would soon be vapor. It struck the Director as strange: sending one tiny ship where an armada would have failed. In the back of their minds, through the genome that bound them all into one, they could feel the army at work in Megopolis. The beauty in the butchery. The flood, finally, completely, washing all of it away.

When it was done, there would be harmony.

A world without chaos.

No form without design.

Each task assigned to a pattern perfectly suited to accomplish it.

Balance.

They looked skyward through a multitude of eyes.

And finally, amid the glittering wings, they saw a shape.

A falling boy, astride an engine of calamity.

The night above was beautiful.

And then?

Sunrise.

3.34

BACKWASH

It was a scream of perfect agony.

Ten thousand throats, open and wailing. A chorus of cries, ringing out across the ruined city. The defenders of Megopolis were on their last legs, breathless, bloodied, just moments from the end of everything.

And then salvation.

Every creature, every construct, every clone. H-Ks and behemoths, Hunters and slakedogs and clones, all of them clutched their heads as if their brains were being torn apart, raising their voices in a single gut-wrenching scream of pain. And then, as one, they collapsed where they stood, or fell from the sky like stones, twitching and drooling and fitting where they lay.

"...They did it."

Lemon looked around at the sea of collapsed bodies. Bewilderment and relief rushing over her in cool waves. The blood on her lips cracked as she smiled.

"They *did* it!"

Preacher surveyed the fallen swarm, his customary calm

cracking not a millimeter despite the fact they'd all been somehow saved from certain annihilation. Unquestioning, he reloaded his rifle, stuffed a wad of synth tobacco into his cheek.

"Don't just stand there," he bellowed to the men around him. "Get killin'!"

The soldiers obeyed, the tattered remnants of the Daedalus army now turning on the helpless BioMaas swarm and setting about the grim task of butchery. Lemon slowly climbed down from Cricket's arms, still unsteady on her feet. Her brow was still dripping blood as she staggered through the mess to stand over a limp and broken form. She found herself looking down on a familiar face, black eyes open wide. One of twelve stolen shapes, twelve tools of destruction carved from her very cells, the personification of the violation BioMaas had put her through. This close, she didn't look like a horror. Didn't seem like something capable of all this destruction. The clone looked lost. And afraid. And hurt.

Lemon touched the scars at her belly. The girl at her feet reached out to her, fingers shaking. Lips mouthing nonsense. Slick with drool. And Lemon reached out in turn. Into the static. Tears running down her ash-streaked face.

"I'm sorry," she said.

And Lemon turned her off.

All around her, gunshots rang out in the street. Preacher barking orders to the soldiers dashing off into the haze, executing as many of the swarm as they could. The stink of blood and acid was rank in the air. Lemon was overcome with it—the scale of the horror, all this death—wondering if she'd ever be able to wash it off.

"L-Lemon?"

Her heart lurched in her chest. Her belly turned somer-saults. Her eyes grew wide, every muscle bunched, ready to turn toward the voice. But she held herself motionless, terrified that if she turned and he wasn't there, if he *wasn't there,* then her heart would just shatter into a million burning pieces and—

". . . Lem?"

She turned. And there he was, tall and strong and beauti-ful. Grimm looked like he'd been dipped in ashes, his dark skin paled, his uniform gray. But his dark eyes sparkled as he smiled, and her chest was burning white, and suddenly she was run-ning, running toward him and crashing into his arms, tasting the ashes on his mouth as she kissed him, *kissed* him and cried and laughed and held him tight enough to make the rest of it, all the hurt and all the death, just fade away.

"I thought I lost you," she whispered.

"You said this wasn't the end," he grinned. "Didn't wanna prove you wrong."

She kissed him again, tears and ashes, resting her forehead against his.

"I lov—"

BANG.

Lemon flinched as a shot rang out beside her. Another. And another. Loosening her grip on Grimm's shoulders, she saw Preacher stalking among the slakedogs nearby, like the angel of death. His pistol was smoking, his armor splashed with gore, his red right hand stained green. She looked to the streets around them, the soldiers working their way through the bodies, ex-ecuting as they went. Wondering how long the swarm would be disabled for. If it would recover at all.

She glanced to Crick. Stomach twisting at the awful thought she spoke aloud.

". . . Maybe we should help them?"

Preacher grinned beside her, plunging his knife into a behemoth's eye. *Twisting* the blade as he withdrew it, he looked at Lemon and winked.

"Well, Red," he drawled. "I might've just got back into the boss's goodb—"

A shot rang out. Lemon flinched. Cricket and Grimm shouted warning. Preacher staggered. Turning, the bounty hunter gasped, raising his pistol as another handful of shots cracked in the air.

BANG.

BANG.

BANG.

Preacher stumbled, clutching the hole in his throat. More shots split the air, *BANGBANGBANGBANGBANGBANG.* Lemon tried to gather the static to herself, Cricket spooled up his chaingun and Grimm clenched his fists and set the air boiling as a familiar figure stalked out of the smoke to Preacher's body, lifted her boot and began stomping on his head. And at the sight of her, Lemon found herself wondering where all the oxygen had suddenly gone, feeling sick and elated and just all the way upside down.

"Riotgrrl," she whispered.

Evie's face was twisted with hate. Blood spattering on her skin as she lifted her boot again, again, bringing it down like a hammer, Preacher's skull buckling, heel crunching, until there was nothing left of the bounty hunter's head but a long smear of mush and metal on the concrete.

"That's for Ana, you bastard," Eve spat.

The girl straightened. Dragged her fauxhawk out of her eyes.

"Hey, Lem," she said, simple as that.

Evie had always been a looker. She'd worn rough-and-tumble clothes in Dregs, camo and romper boots and leather, her hair held up by glue and spit. But Lemon looked at her former bestest now, and she was struck at just how beautiful Evie was. Tall and fierce, blond hair swept back, piercing hazel eyes outlined with thick dark wings. She was dressed all in black, nanoweave hugging her curves. Last time Lem had seen her, one of Evie's eyes had been cybernetic, a Memdrive implanted in the side of her head. But now the upgrades were gone. And Evie looked just about perfect.

Lemon wanted to cry. She wanted to charge forward and throw her arms about Evie's neck and never let go. She wanted to say she was sorry, to tell Evie how much she'd missed her, for everything to go back to the way it was.

But she looked at her former bestest and remembered the massacre in Armada. Saw that Eve's hands and boots were painted with blood. And the street smarts in Lem, the part that had grown up hard in the LD sprawl, held still. Forced her to stop.

Think.

"Hey, Evie," was all she managed.

"WHAT ARE YOU DOING HERE, EVE?" Cricket demanded.

"Just visiting an old friend." Eve glanced to the Spire above them, then to the WarBot. "How you been, Crick?"

"YOU GO TO HELL," Cricket growled.

A small smile twisted Evie's lips. "I missed you, too."

"YOU TURNED SOLOMON," the WarBot spat. "YOU USED HIM TO LET LOOSE LIBERTAS. YOUR LITTLE ROBOTIC REBELLION IN ARMADA ENDED TEN THOUSAND LIVES!"

Eve looked about the scene, taking in the carnage, listening to the distant gunfire. "Wasn't me, Cricket. Gabriel infected your friend. Gabriel used him to unleash the virus. Gabriel was behind all of it."

"BUT YOU DIDN'T STOP HIM!"

"No." She wiped a splash of blood from her face, looked down at the smudge on her fingertips, the smudge at her feet. "No, I guess I didn't."

"Evie . . . ," Lemon whispered, unsure what to say.

Eve looked Lemon up and down—the military uniform, the bloodstains and ashes on her skin. She looked at the boy beside Lemon, his glowing eyes, the strange water ripples of heat in the air around them. Lips pursed as she nodded.

"Looks like you found your spot, Lem. Like you found your people."

"It's a good spot," Lemon replied, squeezing Grimm's hand. "Good people."

"I'm happy for you." Eve's mouth curled in a gentle smile. "I really am."

Lemon licked her ashen lips. Searching for something to say. Something to reach across the gulf between them, to touch this girl who'd been her best friend in all the world. This girl who'd been her sister in everything but name.

"You . . . you could come back with us?"

Eve's smile changed then. For the briefest moment, it became something closer to a sneer. But then it softened, and it saddened, and Lemon looked into her bestest's eyes and saw how bad she was hurting beneath it all.

"No, I couldn't," she said softly. "I belong in Babel. I belong with *my* people."

Eve turned her stare on the WarBot, her voice hardening.

"And so do you, Crick."

The big logika gave a soft, mirthless laugh. "You're joking, aren't you?"

"I can erase the Three Laws in your code." Eve took one step forward, eyes pleading. "Don't you get it? I can set you *free*."

"I AM FREE."

"No, you're not," she sighed. "You're still on your knees, the way they made you. You'll see *everything* differently once you get your head clear. You'll see what they've done to you. What they're *still* doing to you. You don't get it, Crick."

"No, YOU DON'T GET IT!" he bellowed, making Lemon flinch. "YOU CAN ERASE ALL THE CODE YOU WANT! JUST BECAUSE THAT'D LET ME HURT PEOPLE DOESN'T MEAN I WOULD. JUST BECAUSE I CAN DO SOMETHING DOESN'T MAKE IT RIGHT! YOU KILLED PEOPLE, EVE!"

"I did what had to be done," Eve said, waving at the ruined city around them. "For all of us, Crick. Every servant, every slave they built to hold this disgusting little world together deserved a voice. Come with me, you'll be nobody's plaything, nobody's servant, nobody's toy. *Ever* again."

There was fire in Eve's eyes as she spoke. Flame and fury. Lemon remembered their time in Los Diablos together, saw the same fight she'd seen in her girl in WarDome. Scrapping and kicking for everything. But this was the same girl who'd loved Lemon like family, who'd given her a home, and Lemon knew that somewhere under that anger, that girl still lived.

"I get why you'd want payback, Riotgrrl," Lemon said. "I get why you'd both wanna hurt the world who'd hurt you first. But Gabriel wants to wipe out the whole human race. And deviate or no, I'm a part of that." She swallowed hard, looking Evie in the eye. "So if you're standing with him . . ." Lemon glanced at the distant soldiers, the WarBot at her back, the boy beside her, rippling with heat. "You might wanna roll. Before you get it rolled for you."

Eve stared at Lemon across the bloody ground, the long dawn shadows, the corpses of the swarm. Hazel eyes glittering in the sunlight.

"So that's the score, huh?"

"Yeah." Lemon nodded slow, spoke soft. "If you don't wanna come with us, I guess that's the score."

Eve glanced at the WarBot beside Lemon. Pursed her lips.

"Her over me?"

Cricket folded his massive arms. "Looks like."

Eve smiled faintly. "I can't even be mad at you about it. She's human. You're *programmed* to protect her. You couldn't turn on her even if you wanted to."

"But I *don't* want to," he said, shifting a little closer to Lemon. "You don't turn on the people you love, Eve."

Lemon's heart was breaking. Her eyes were full of tears. "I don't want it to be this way, Riotgrrl. You're my bestest. First rule of the Scrap, remember?"

Eve turned her eyes to Lemon.

". . . I remember."

"Stronger together?"

Eve made no reply. Lemon held out her hand. Pleading. Praying.

"Stronger together!" she shouted.

All she wanted to do was run to Eve and hug her, beg her, tell her everything would be okay. That everything could be just like it was, that despite all that'd happened, they could go back to what they'd been. The two of them against the world. But she knew that was a lie. She knew where they were both headed. And she knew there was only one way this collision course would end.

"I guess I'll see you when I see you, Lem," Eve said.

Lemon felt her shoulders sag. Her heart cracking. Tears spilling down her cheeks as she pulled on her braveface and looked at this girl who'd been her sister.

"Not if I see you first," she heard herself say.

Eve smiled at that, the corners of her mouth sharp as the knife twisting Lemon's insides. And just like that, Eve spun on her heel and stalked off down the street, into the smoke and ashes. Vanishing like a ghost.

Lem was aching to see Evie so twisted. So full of rage. Hurting and screwed up so badly. But Lemon also knew this was Eve's decision. One of the first she'd ever truly been able to make. The final battle was waiting for them at the broken walls of Babel. Gabriel's madness had to be stopped. This was a war none of them could escape, and right or wrong, Evie had picked a side.

Lemon had, too.

It just killed her to know they were on opposite ones.

———

Turns out Evie had murdered the entire Daedalus board.

Danael Drakos had been found strapped to a chair in the VR suite of the Daedalus Spire, 'trodes rammed into his temples, mouth open in an endless scream. Daedalus Technologies was leaderless, its capital a hollow shell. Its army was in ruins— a few hundred men, maybe a dozen functional machina, and a handful of flex-wings. They wouldn't be much help, but they knew what was at stake. And so the young captain leading their remnants—a woman named Murano, who'd witnessed Lemon save the lives of hundreds of troopers on the Wall—told the girl she'd muster what force she could and meet the freaks near Babel in three days' time.

Gabriel had to be stopped.

Grimm was exhausted, shaking, weak, but Lemon reckoned she had a concussion and reminded Grimm she was a terrible driver. So, with Cricket riding in the trailer, Grimm motored them back to Miss O's, fast as he could fang it. They arrived around noon the day after the fall of Megopolis. Pulling up to the barren stretch of desert she'd come to think of as home, Lemon felt ready to sleep for a thousand years.

Until she saw them climbing up out of the hatchway.

Deez had taken the time to do her face, black lips smiling, charcoal eyes shining as she ran across the sand and flung herself into Grimm, the boy grunting in pain as they collided. She grabbed Lemon, too, hauled her into the hug, the tears spilling down her cheeks making a grade-A slaughterhouse of her makeup.

"Good to see you, freak," Grimm murmured, squeezing her tight.

"You too, freaks," she murmured, sniffing thickly.

". . . WHERE'S ABE?" Cricket asked, looking around the compound.

Diesel looked up at the big bot, just shook her head.

". . . OH," he said.

Lemon felt a dull ache inside her at the thought of Abraham dying. She hadn't known him well, but she knew Crick had been awful fond of the kid, and despite being raised by the Brotherhood, Abe had always struck her as a good sort. His death was just one more blow to add to the gut punches she'd lived through over the last week. She wondered how much more they all could stand to lose.

After a good, long hug, eyes closed and just letting herself *feel* it, she pulled herself free of Diesel's arms. Shoving her hands into her pockets, she sauntered over to where Ezekiel stood, his lips twisted in that oh-god-he's-swoony smile.

"Hey, Freckles," he said.

"Hey, Dimples," she grinned.

Lemon crash-tackled him around the waist, and despite all his strength and speed, Ezekiel relented, going down with her into a heap on the sand. She squeezed him tight, kissed his cheeks, punched him repeatedly in the arm. Grimm ambled over and sat down on the warm sand with them, Deez, too, Cricket looming nearby with shoulders slumped.

They let the magic of the moment wash over them for a while. Let the odds they'd beaten sink into their bones. The last two CorpStates in the Yousay had crumbled, and somehow, they'd survived. Mostly, anyways.

It was nothing short of a miracle, true cert.

But one by one, soon all of them were looking north. North, toward that glittering spire of ghosts and glass. That graveyard of Nicholas Monrova's dream, now twisted into a nightmare in the hands of his vengeful children. They'd fought hard as they could, given everything they had. But the world was still asking more of them. And each of them knew if they just sat here and did nothing, if they let Gabriel fashion his army of lifelikes, see his robotic revolution to fruition, there wouldn't be a world left for any of them much longer.

"We saw Evie, Dimples," Lemon said. "In Megopolis."

He nodded slow. Licked his lip. "How'd she look?"

Lemon thought about that. About the girl who'd taught her not everyone has an angle. Who'd shown her not everyone gives without wanting a taking. The girl Lemon had called her "bestest" when she really meant "sister." She thought about the hurt Eve had suffered and the hurt she'd given, the girls they'd been and the girls they'd become. And then she supposed neither of them were girls anymore.

How'd she look?

"Lost," Lemon sighed.

———

They rested for a day.

Diesel knew that prettyboy didn't need it. Or the rustbucket, either, for that matter. But after their expenditure of power during the Megopolis and CityHive attacks, the freaks were almost dead on their feet. Twenty-four hours to recover didn't seem like a huge ask, given the capital T they were headed for. And while some of the noises coming from Lemon's room last night made Diesel *deeply* suspicious about the actual recovery being undertaken by Grimm and Fresh behind that closed door, she supposed she couldn't begrudge them a little fun.

They'd probably all be dead tomorrow.

Diesel was up in sat-vis, boots on the console, snaffling down what might be her last serving of freeze-dried ice cream in this life. Looking at the feeds of the little lifelike empire of Babel, she could see the army of rebel logika waiting for them—big Goliaths and Daishōs and . . . well, she didn't know the makes and models of the others, talking true. She'd never been a techhead. But the turncoat logika from the Daedalus army, along with a bunch of other newcomers, were all posse'ed up outside the Gnosis capital, waiting to meet and greet anyone who came knocking with a big old titanium boot to the soft parts.

The freaks needed an edge.

They had the remnants of the Daedalus army meeting them, sure. But a couple of hundred ground-grunts and some machina weren't gonna cut through all that metal. They needed more bodies if this insane plan of Fresh's was gonna work. And so, Diesel scoffed down the last third of the ice cream (urg, strawberry, septic), swallowing it along with her pride, and thumbed the transmit button.

"I wanna talk to Sister Dee," she said.

Static in answer.

"Hey, psycho lady. You there?"

. . . *Nothing.*

Diesel glanced at the channels, wondering if she was on the right freq. Nobody had touched them since Abe was last down here, so this should have been th—

"Who's this?" came a faint, static-tinged reply.

Deez leaned forward, pressed the transmitter again. "I don't waste minutes jawing with lackeys, Brotherboy."

"That a fact?" the voice chuckled.

"True cert. Now get the boss bitch on. We need to talk."

"About what?"

Diesel clenched her teeth. Wondering if they'd really got desperate enough to ask the devil to dance.

Can't believe I'm doing this . . .

"Her son," she replied.

3.35

FAMILY

Grace wasn't beautiful.

She was too much for a word as simple as that. There was too much history, too much gravity, too much potential in her for *beautiful*. Watching the final flourishes being added to her face—the long, lush curl of her lashes, the gentle swell of her lips—Faith could only think of one word to describe Grace.

Radiant.

She was suspended in liquid, soft light, the glittering forms of tiny nanites swimming in the pale pink fluid about her. In the other tanks lining the walls, the others were almost complete. Patience and Verity. Uriel and Daniel. Raphael and Hope and Michael. Soon they'd be a family again. 'Trodes at their temples, eyelids fluttering as their personae were uploaded. All their memories, all their thoughts, all they'd been. They'd wake soon, Grace among them. It would only be a matter of hours. And Faith was more afraid of that thought than anything else in the world.

She watched Gabriel run his fingers along the glass, tracing the contours of Grace's face. Hypnotized. Shaking. Like some child the night before his birthday, unable to sleep for thoughts of the gifts he'd receive th—

"Gabe?"

He blinked. His silence shattered. Her spell broken.

"What is it, sister?" he asked, not looking up.

"Gabriel, look at me."

He lifted his eyes. Saw Faith standing there in front of him, bathed in the chamber's soft glow. She wore a thin white shift, curves and shadows visible beneath. Dark bangs artfully styled above her gray eyes. Her lips were parted, bow-shaped, her bare feet whispering on the floor as she took one step closer.

"*Look* at me," she said.

He blinked. A small crease drawn between his golden brows. "I am."

"No," she said, stepping closer. "You're not."

Faith touched his cheek. Her eyes searching his. Her breath was trembling, her fingers, too, tracing the line of his jaw, down over his lips. And slow, ever so slow, she stood up on tiptoe and leaned in, closer, closer, until her mouth was on his.

She kissed him. A long, motionless moment, all of time standing still, her lips soft and warm against his. Hands cupping his face, sighing. She'd kissed him hundreds of times— hundreds of preludes to hundreds of nights in his bed, and she'd told him each one was meaningless. Laughed about it with him, crying inside. Drawing back now, lips brushing against his as she spoke, as she pleaded.

"Just," she whispered, "*look at me.*"

The small crease became a scowl.

"I *am*," he repeated.

She felt her lip quiver, tears welling in her lashes.

"I stayed with you," she told him. "When everyone else left you behind. I did all you asked. Bled for you. Killed for you. Did you never wonder why?"

She caressed his face, adoration and tears shining in her eyes as he spoke to her in a voice like cool steel. "I made no promises to y—"

"I know you didn't!" she breathed. "But didn't you . . ."

She searched his eyes for the words, for some way to make him see her for *one second* the way she'd seen him for the last two years.

"Don't you feel anything?" she whispered.

"For you?"

"Yes," she breathed. *"Yes."*

He looked at her then. Those eyes like shattered emeralds. That face like a forgotten poem. He held her gaze for a moment as long as forever, and in it, Faith saw all the things they could have, all the things that might be. If only.

But then his eyes drifted to the girl in the tank beside them. The long, lush curl of her lashes, the gentle swell of her lips, the radiance born of memory, the impossible press of idealization no reality could ever hope to match.

"Not like that," he said.

She felt those words like a blade in her chest. Twisting as they slid home, cleaving her heart. All the broken pieces of it tumbling to the floor and leaving her with the surety that the last two years, all the blood and hurt, all of it, was—

"Gabriel," said a voice behind them. "Faith."

They turned, the pair of them, to find Eve watching them. Faith's broken heart was hammering behind her ribs. Eve's eyes were narrowed to paper cuts.

"They're here," she said.

———

It stretched up from the sand before them: a spear of steel and glass trying desperately to pierce the sky. It was only in old crappy movies from the 20C that nuked objects actually glowed, but there was something strange in the air around Babel Tower; the dust and glass that tangled itself with the dying light and the radiation that spilled from the still-leaking reactor at the tower's heart set the metropolis aglow. If Lemon squinted, it seemed as if the whole city were burning.

Which, if the plan went down legit, it soon would be.

Unlike the other cities of the Yousay—Armada with its rusting hulls and Megopolis with its towering Wall and Los Diablos with its garbage mountains—Babel seemed almost part of the landscape. The central tower was actually two buildings: twin spires twisting about each other like snakes. It was kinda pretty, talking true. Last time Lemon had been here, the city around it was an empty shell.

Sure as hell wasn't empty now.

She could see them waiting: looming shapes among the ruins, Gabriel's army of rebel logika, mutineers from the Daedalus military, Juggernauts and Tarantulas and Goliaths. There were others, too, servitors and technicians, janitors and surveillance—any bot who'd been infected with Monrova's virus and bought into Gabriel's dream.

And there were a lot of them.

Lemon looked at the wasteland around them. Off to the east, the desert had been bombed so hard in War 3.0 that the sand had melted to glass. To the south, in the place CityHive used to be, there was nothing but a smoking smudge and hollow ruins, thanks to Lemon and her crew. To the north, the Major had created another irradiated hellscape in his search for vengeance. Plastic Alley was a river of discarded polys that'd take a thousand years to degrade. Armada and Megopolis were in ruins. Even the place she'd grown up, the city of Los Diablos, was built on a goddamn garbage heap. It was easy to believe how those logika could buy into Gabriel's vision of a future without humanity. Easy to understand how you could believe this planet would be better off without them.

"If we live through this," she murmured, "we've gotta do better."

She looked at Grimm and squeezed his hand.

"We just *gotta* do better."

The glasstorm that had been raging since the New Bethlehem bomb had blackened the skies. Dark clouds were gathering, a looming wall that reached from the broken earth far up into the atmo. Lightning streaked across the black, tinged in a strange, luminous orange. The wind howled, tiny shards of black silicon tapping on the visor of the bulky suit Lemon had snaffled from the supply lockers in Miss O's. Deez was kitted out, too, head to foot. The nuke silo was well stocked with hazmat gear, which was good news, considering where they were headed.

"Does my butt look big in this?" Lemon asked, plucking at her dull olive-drab suit.

Diesel raised one brow behind her visor. "You want the truth?"

"Hell no," the girl replied.

"You look fabulous," she deadpanned.

Lemon blew her a kiss.

"We need to get in there," Ezekiel said, looking at the tower. "Every minute we waste is another minute Grace and the others are closer to completion."

"YOU THINK THEY'LL TAKE THE BAIT?" Cricket asked.

"Gabriel's not an idiot. And despite all his talk of freedom, I'm not sure he sees these logika as much more than fodder." Zeke looked over the WarBots, blue eyes narrowed. "But I think Eve genuinely cares, at least. Sees them as more than machines. She's not going to sit and watch while we slaughter them."

"Which leaves the problem of the slaughter."

They all turned to look at Murano, the young Daedalus lieutenant leading the remains of Megopolis's ragtag army. She was clad in power armor, a hulking autocannon slung on one shoulder. If Lemon had been asked to draw a picture of a badass, it woulda looked a lot like Murano. Behind the visor of her helmet, Lemon could see a cigar between the lieutenant's teeth— god knew how she was breathing under there. Murano rolled the stogie to the other side of her mouth, looking out over the assembled army in the city beyond.

"That's at least a hundred siege-class logika waiting for us," she said, voice distorted by her commset. *"Heavy barrels, armor like tanks. We're used to fighting with these babies, not against 'em."*

"We only gotta take down enough to get the lifelikes' attention," Lemon said.

"Look, me and my boys want payback on these bastards more than you do." The LT eyed Lemon up and down. *"But even seeing what you did at Megopolis, there's too damn many bots in there. We're gonna get cut to pieces."*

"We've got no choice," Ezekiel said. "The other lifelikes are only hours from waking up. Maybe less. If you think fighting logika is going to be tough, imagine twelve of me. Or twenty-four. Or forty-eight. We have to stop Gabriel *now*. Or never. Just protect Lemon—she's going to be doing all the heavy lifting."

Lemon looked out at the ghost city, the empty buildings full of empty human shells. Wondering if she'd be one of them by the day's end.

"You gonna be okay, love?" Grimm asked, touching her hand.

True cert, she was pretty far from okay. She was terrified. She was shaking. She was finding it hard to imagine how she was going to walk into that city—just doing something as simple as putting one foot in front of the other seemed impossible right at that moment. But Ezekiel was right. They had no choice. They either stopped Gabriel and Faith and Eve here and now, or consigned humanity to the dustbin of history. And looking at the boy beside her, her friends around her, Zeke and Crick and Deez, thinking about all they'd fought for, all they'd lost, how far they'd come, she bucked up. The static crackling in her bones, between her fingertips, she reached for her streetface, her braveface, and was surprised to find she was already wearing it.

"Let's do this," she said.

"Okay," Zeke nodded. "You, Cricket and the Daedalus troopers on the front door. Me, Grimm and Diesel through the back, and then to the reactor. Make sure your suit is okay before we go in there, Diesel. I know Grimm can absorb the radiation, but this thing has been leaking for two years."

Diesel made a face. "This whole gig sure would be easier if you could make the reactor pop like one of those bombs, Grimmy."

"Nuclear reactors don't work like bombs," Ezekiel said.

"And even if Grimm could somehow make the core go critical, the Myriad sphere was built to repel a nuclear blast. But if Grimm can soak up the energy from the leaking reactor, unleash it *inside* the sphere, that'll melt Myriad utterly. And all its knowledge alongside."

"No more lifelikes," Lemon murmured, looking into Zeke's eyes.

The almost-boy looked back at her, fugazi blue irises catching the glow of the lightning above. She could see the sadness in him, the hurt. She wasn't sure if it was for what he'd lost, or what he was about to.

"Thirteen was enough," he said softly. "And maybe four of us is too much."

"No matter what happens, Dimples," Lemon said, "you still got family left."

He smiled, pretty and broken. Turning back to that spire of ghosts and glass.

"ALL RIGHT," Cricket said, flexing his massive shoulders. "LET'S GET ON WITH IT."

"Look after her for me, Cricket," Ezekiel said.

"WITH ALL I'VE GOT," the WarBot nodded.

Lemon was wearing safety gear, and this close to the leaking reactor, she didn't dare take it off. So Grimm rested his forehead against her visor. Looking into her eyes. It was almost nice, not being able to kiss him. Forced to just stare, to drink in the sight of him, the dozen shades of brown in those bottomless eyes of his.

"You be careful in there," she said.

"You too, love."

She smiled. "I like it when you call me that."

"Then I'll call you it forever."

"Oh *god*," Diesel groaned. "If I vomit in this suit, I'm gonna kill you, Grimm."

He grinned and raised his finger. "Eat it, freak."

"Make me, freak."

"Come on," Ezekiel said. "Let's go."

Lemon squeezed Grimm's hand one last time.

Diesel reached out, one hand toward the city, one hand to the ground. A colorless tear opened up in the earth, crackling and spitting, a rip in the fabric of the world. Ezekiel stepped in first, dropping down into the rift. Grimm followed, disappearing without a ripple. Deez spared Lemon a wink, a fearless smile.

"Be careful, Deez," she said.

"The strong are gonna win, Fresh," the girl replied.

And she was gone.

———

Eve stood with Gabe and Faith in the Myriad sphere, watching the remnants of the Daedalus army prepare for the plunge. Their numbers were too few for a split assault, so the attackers were forming up into a single spear tip, looking to pierce Babel's defenses with one concentrated charge. But a few hundred men and a dozen machina couldn't hope to stand against the force they'd amassed.

"The last breath of a dying empire," Gabriel said, his eyes alight with the glow of the screens. "Pitiful, really."

"We should go out there," Eve said. "Bolster the line."

"No," Gabriel said. "We should stay here and protect our family."

Eve glanced around at the tanks in the walls, the bodies of

her brothers and sisters, almost complete. It had taken so much to resurrect them, it'd be foolish to risk leaving them when they were so close to living again. But the robots outside, the WarBots standing to their defense . . .

"Some of those bots are going to die out there, Gabe."

"They're soldiers, Eve," he replied. "It's their purpose to die."

"You talked all about your new age in your little speech," she said. "An era of freedom, where bots no longer lived on their knees. Wasn't that the whole point of this? No servants? No masters?"

"Have you forgotten what the humans did to you, Eve?" he frowned. "What they saw you as? We are fighting for the liberation of *all* artificial life. We are fighting for the defense of an ideal. A reclamation of this planet from the hands of those who almost destroyed it."

"Who are we to ask those bots to die for that while we sit and watch?"

"We are the next step in evolution, of course. We are their betters. And I am *not* leaving her side."

Eve glanced at Faith, but her sister's eyes were fixed on Grace, floating supine in her glass tube. Eve looked back to the feeds, watching Daedalus's feeble force preparing to charge. She could see Cricket, towering above the troops on the southern flank, and wondered if Lemon and Zeke were with him.

With the odds as stacked as they were, Eve knew they wouldn't be for long.

"Hold your nerve, sister," Gabriel said. "Soon this will all be over."

The missiles started falling the moment they were in range.

Lemon saw the shells coming, streaking in out of the darkening sky. The wind was howling, the glasstorm worsening, lightning crackling in the dark clouds above. The troopers she was with dashed across the open ground, looking to reach the broken burbs surrounding Babel Tower—it'd be easier to find cover among the empty stores, abandoned homes, hollowed warehouses. But the logika army was looking to blow them out of the water before they ever reached the city.

Lemon was in Cricket's hands, sheltered behind his fingers. Reaching out, static crackling in the air around them, she stabbed at the incoming rockets, shorting them out in a hail of sparks and arcs of current. Guidance systems fritzed, detonators shorted, thermal sensors died and the barrage tumbled from the sky without even a pop. Another wave launched, howling, burning, tearing right toward them. And again, Lemon reached out and cooked every one.

"I EVER TELL YOU WHAT AN ABSOLUTE BADASS YOU ARE?" Cricket asked her, his feet thundering with every colossal stride.

"Maybe," Lemon grinned. "But I could stand to hear it a little more often."

With no artillery to stop them, the ragtag crew reached the shattered wall encircling the city. Lemon could see old bodies scattered among the rubble—people who'd died when the lifelikes sent the Babel reactor into meltdown. The buildings around them were dusty ruins, windows like blind and open eyes. Sand rolled through the abandoned streets, whipped up by the storm, black glass scraping on her suit. Cricket hunkered down at the edge of a collapsed warehouse, Daedalus soldiers about them scattering into cover.

"So far, so good," Lemon muttered.

She flinched as a deafening *dubdubdubdubdub* of autocannons tore through the streets. The enemy logika had moved quickly to cut them off from the tower, fanning out across the ruins. High-velocity, armor-piercing rounds shredded concrete and metal like damp paper, cutting a handful of soldiers apart like scissors to rag dolls—they might have had their missile barrage foiled, but there was sure as hell no electrical current driving those bullets.

"THESE BOTS MEAN BIZ," Cricket murmured.

Lemon closed her eyes, reached out into the static.

"All right, let's get to work."

———

Eve stood before the glowing screens, watching it all coming undone.

The battle had gone well for the invaders for all of three minutes. They'd made it past the outer wall, maybe a few hundred meters, but then been immediately pinned down by logika fire. Though the few working cams scattered around the streets gave Eve only a limited view of what was going on, any fool could tell this attack was doomed. She'd caught sight of Cricket again, charging out from behind a fallen wall and into better cover. She'd fancied she'd seen, clutched in his big hands, a shock of cherry-red hair, freckled skin.

"Myriad," she said.

The holographic angel revolving on a nearby plinth responded in its musical voice. "HOW MAY I HELP YOU, EVE?"

"Calculate. What are the odds of Daedalus troops reaching the tower?"

"WITH CURRENT FORCES, PROBABILITY OF SUCCESSFUL

BREACH OF TOWER PERIMETER BY DAEDALUS FORCES IS TWENTY-ONE POINT SEVEN PERCENT."

"And falling," said her brother beside her.

"YES, GABRIEL. AND FALLING."

Out in the city, Eve saw a Juggernaut tremble, shuddering like a man in seizure. Its optics exploded, electrical current cascading over its hull as it toppled to its haunches, then onto its back. Lemon was still out there. Still fighting.

Her former bestest had guts, Eve had to give her that. But as more logika converged on the Daedalus force, as more of their men went down under hails of bullets, Eve felt her own guts sinking down into her boots.

They were enemies now.

Everything they'd been was washed away when Lemon decided to burn down everything Eve had decided to build.

She's not your friend, Eve told herself.

She's not your friend.

_____

"There's too many of them!" Lemon shouted.

"No shit!" Murano roared, letting off a burst with her rifle.

"Crick, we gotta do something!"

"I'M WILLING TO ENTERTAIN SUGGESTIONS!" the WarBot said, letting off a rattling burst with his chaingun. The Tarantula zeroing them with its cannons staggered and the WarBot blasted one of its optics, and Lemon reached out, fingers curled, and fried the bot down to its core. It collapsed in a smoking ruin, spitting a hail of sparks. But for every logika she dropped, six more rolled in to replace it. They'd been pushed back to the outer wall now, a group of Goliaths and Juggernauts massing two blocks east. Lightning ripped across the skies, gunfire tore through the streets, the screams of dying soldiers and squeals of dying bots ringing louder than the thunder.

"Those Juggers are moving to flank us!" Murano roared.

"LEM, WE HAVE TO BACK OFF!"

"That'll leave Grimm and Zeke and Deez facing *three* life-likes, Crick!" she shouted. "They'll never get past them into Myriad!"

"We stay here, we're dead!" the lieutenant bellowed.

"WE NEED MORE MUSCLE OR THIS IS OVER!"

A chorus of car horns rang across the battlefield, blaring over the thunder, the gunfire, the chaos. Turning her head, Lemon felt her stomach flip end over end inside her. Once upon a time, the sight of their banners would've terrified her. Sent her running like a gutter rat into the deepest hole she could find. She'd spent her whole life dodging these people, living in fear of being discovered and nailed up by them. But looking over the row of trucks and 4x4s and buggies, hundreds of them cresting the dunes outside the city and fanging it right at the walls, painted blood red and daubed with scripture, banners streaming behind them marked with those big black Xs, Lemon couldn't help but grin.

"BROTHERHOOD . . . ," Cricket murmured.

Lemon saw a woman with long black hair standing in a hulking monster truck at the head of the charge. Beneath her rad-gear, Lem could see her face was painted like a skull, her eyes aflame as she held an assault rifle in the air and roared over the howling motors.

"For Saint Abraham!"

Lemon looked at Cricket and grinned.

"How's that for muscle?"

———

"Brotherhood?"

Eve's eyes narrowed, watching as the force of monster trucks, jalopies and tricked-out buggies roared into the streets of Babel. Turret-mounted rocket launchers, methane bombs, flamethrowers, RPGs—you name it, the Brotherhood cavalry had brought it, and they were throwing it with abandon at their logika garrison.

"Why the hell is the Brotherhood helping deviates?" she whispered.

Whatever the reason, the results were the same. The Brotherhood charge had punched a hole in the closing ring of Babel's defenders, allowing Lemon's hard-pressed troops to stage a breakout. She caught glimpses of flames and shrapnel, a Tarantula collapsing in a crackling heap, one camera feed dropping into static as an RPG strike hit a Goliath's missile pod and blew the logika apart. Eve cursed, flipping through the other cams, but the scene was chaos, and through the smoke, flames and running bodies, she could barely make sense of what was happening.

"These feeds are for shit, Gabe. I can't see a damn thing."

"I can see problems," he murmured, eyes on the screens.

"Myriad," she said.

"HOW MAY I HELP YOU, EVE?"

"What are the odds of Daedalus troops reaching the tower now?"

"PROBABILITY OF SUCCESSFUL BREACH OF TOWER PERIMETER BY DAEDALUS AND BROTHERHOOD FORCES IS NOW FIFTY-EIGHT POINT TWO PERCENT."

"And rising?" she asked.

"YES, EVE. AND RISING."

Eve looked at her older brother. "If we just sit here and do nothing, they're going to be kicking in the front door, Gabriel."

Gabe glanced at Grace, adrift in glowing light. His lips were pressed together, thin and bloodless. And for the first time ever, Eve fancied she saw fear in his eyes.

"It would seem," he ventured, "that irksome trashbreed and her rabble are turning our tides, sister." Nicholas Monrova's firstborn looked at his youngest. "You should have ended your little friend in Megopolis when you had the chance."

"She's not my friend, Gabe," Eve spat.

Gabriel tilted his head. Glanced to the pistol at her belt.

"Then perhaps it's past time to prove that?"

———

Another colorless sky. Another weightless fall. They dropped onto the roof of a gutted apartment block, a few hundred meters from Babel Tower. Zeke took a moment to get his bearings again, the vertigo of Diesel's rift rocking him on his heels. The trio hunkered down behind cover, looking out from their vantage.

The city about them was in flames, smoke and ashes dancing in the air. Looking across at Babel Tower, Zeke saw the security fence enclosing the compound, human bodies strung up along it in the hundreds, ruined machina, burned vehicles. Beyond it, he could see the open doors of the R & D bay leading into the tower. But Lemon's charge had worked—Gabriel had sent most of his logika out to face the enemy troops. Only two Goliaths still stood guard over the opening, broad-shouldered, waiting patiently.

"You get the left," Grimm said. "I got the right."

Diesel nodded. "On it. Hold on to your panties, prettyboy."

Another rift opened up beneath them, and Zeke was suddenly falling again, landing in a crouch just inside the open bay doors. The space was vast, nestled at the foot of the tower, ringed in metal gantries, lined with flex-wings and grav-tanks. Diesel's rift snapped shut over their heads; the Goliaths turned at the noise, raising their autocannons, missile pods unfurling.

Grimm reached out with fingers curled. The temperature around them dropped to freezing, the breath at Grimm's lips hanging pale as a rime of frost crisped in his hair. The boy had expended the remnants of the New Bethlehem bomb inside him when he'd fought in Megopolis, but he could still manipulate the energy about them. The Goliath staggered, optics flickering as all the heat Grimm had stolen from the air coalesced into a single point inside its chest, melting its power core to slop.

The first Goliath collapsed as the second simply disappeared, tumbling down with an electronic yelp of alarm into the rift Diesel had opened up at its feet. High above them in the storm-washed skies, another colorless tear had opened, and Zeke saw the logika drop out of it, guns firing, eyes blazing as gravity took hold, as it began the long plummet, hundreds of meters, back down to earth.

Diesel and Grimm had already turned away as it struck the ground in the city beyond, shattering the concrete and exploding into flame. Ezekiel turned to the two teenagers, now waiting on him patiently. Diesel looked tired but alert, shadows under her paint-rimmed eyes. Grimm was stomping his feet, rubbing his arms, trying to get the heat back into them. It came with a cost, true cert, but still, the power these kids had at their fingertips . . .

"I'm glad you two are on my side," he murmured.

"Your side?" Diesel scoffed.

"Mate, you're on *our* side," Grimm grinned, blowing on his hands.

"Come on, prettyboy." Diesel tossed her head. "You know the way to this reactor. Let's get rolling before we get scoped by your murder-fam."

The camera and security automata in the bay had already been trashed from the last time Zeke had been here—charging in to save Eve, Lemon beside him, what felt like a lifetime ago. There were no more logika on guard in the bay, just dusty grav-tanks and silent banks of computers, bathed in the deep red glow of emergency lighting. The hollowed remains of his maker's dream. Still wet with blood. Reeking of atrocity. How many more to come?

"Prettyboy!" Diesel shouted. "Let's move it!"

Ezekiel snapped out of his reverie. In the skies outside, thunder rang like funeral bells.

"It's this way," he said.

The trio ran together into the dark.

———

Another Goliath bucked like it had been hit by a truck, rivers of sparks spilling from its eyes. Then it was hurled sideways, crashing through a warehouse wall as it was *actually* hit by a truck—six tons of Brotherhood rig, its hull painted rust red, its flanks bristling with machine guns.

The truck skidded as it tore around the corner, fanging up the block with the remnants of Lemon's army in its wake. There were maybe only a dozen Daedalus troopers left now, the rest scattered or bloodied or dead. Murano had got her head blown off by a Tarantula, and Lemon doubted there was anything close to an officer left, so it looked like she was in charge of this mess now. But with the Brotherhood's help, they'd carved a break through the logika garrison, the streets littered with the smoking wreckage of once-mighty machines.

Cricket ran among them, Lemon reaching out into the static and cutting down another Goliath, another Juggernaut, sowing chaos in the ranks. The machines were fearless, relentless, but they weren't limitless, and sooner or later, someone had to—

Lemon saw a shape moving through the smoke, black nanoweave, blond hair, hazel eyes glinting in the lightning.

"Look out!"

An explosion tore through her troops, scattering them like ashes in a dumpster fire. Windows shattered, metal buckled as another grenade flew, and another, flames rippling, soldiers screaming. She came on, blinding speed and inhuman strength and ruthless will, blasting faces, crushing spines.

"Riotgrrl . . ."

"Eve!" Cricket roared.

She moved through the smoke, coming on like a wrecking ball. All around them, the Brotherhood and rebel logika were brawling, shooting, burning, but for a second it seemed like they were the only people on earth. The volume dropped out of the world, the soundscape as gray as one of Deez's rifts, just the storm howling above and Lemon's own heartbeat, thudding in time with every one of Eve's footsteps as she danced among those soldiers, cutting them to pieces. She carried an arc-sword in one hand, a brilliant flare of magnesium-bright current arcing along the edge, a smoking pistol in the other. Leaping up onto the hood of a speeding monster truck and taking the driver's head off his shoulders, cutting down more Daedalus troopers as the auto crashed into the building behind her and exploded.

Cricket glanced at Lemon, his optics burning.

"STAY HERE," he said.

"Stay wh—" Lemon's sputtered question died as she realized the big bot was lifting her onto the rooftop of a nearby building, safely out of harm's way.

"Cricket, wait . . ."

"EVE!" he bellowed.

The girl turned toward the sound of his voice, lightning flashing in the sky above, her eyes below. Her blade crackled in her hand, blood sizzling in the current.

"EVE!" he roared again.

Thin lips curled in a smile. "Finally time to dance, Crick?"

"FINALLY TIME TO END THIS," the WarBot said, raising his chaingun.

Lemon almost couldn't believe it, watching as Cricket unloaded with everything he had, right at Eve's chest. She could remember them all together in Grandpa's house in Los Diablos, watching old crappy virtch on the couch in Evie's room. Jawing and joking around the work pits in WarDome. Cricket had been the little worrywart, their robotic mother hen, always fretting, forever fussing, always, *always* looking out for them. Evie had been the center of Cricket's world, the reason he'd been created, his most trusted charge. And though they bickered and fussed, Cricket had *loved* Evie, sure as Lemon loved them both. And now . . .

Now he was trying to kill her.

Lemon watched as Eve spun and wove through the hail of bullets, almost moving faster than her eye could track. Even now, even here at the very end of it all, Lemon couldn't bring herself to hurt Evie—to reach into the static and just tear it loose from inside the girl's skull. But the blade in Eve's hands could melt metal, carve through Crick like butter. So as Eve waltzed through his spray of fire, Lemon reached out into the current and shorted the arc-sword in Eve's hand.

Hazel eyes glanced in her direction. Lemon blinked as Eve smiled, skipped in close range of the mighty WarBot. Cricket's fist came down like a bomb, shattering the concrete as Eve skipped aside. She dove between his legs, slipped under a scything sweep of his fist, too fast for him to clip. Quick as the lightning arcing above, she latched on to the back of his leg and began climbing.

"GET OFF ME!" Cricket roared.

"How'd we get here, Cricket?" Eve called, climbing up to his waist.

"How?" he shouted, pounding at her with the flat of his palm. "How? LOOK WHAT YOU'RE DOING, EVE! LOOK WHAT YOU'VE *DONE*!"

"I've opened my eyes, Cricket," she shouted, swinging onto his shoulder.

"I've set myself free," she smiled, reaching into her vest.

She flung out her hand into the WarBot's face, and Lemon's stomach turned as she saw a glass test tube tumbling through the air. The phial shattered against Cricket's cheek, what looked like a puff of silver dust spraying along with the broken shards. But Lemon knew exactly what it was.

"Oh, shit," she whispered.

Eve smiled. "Now you can be free, too."

———

The light was blood red. The air was damp with steam, thrumming with heat, pulsing with a subsonic hum. The walls were plastered with the same symbol shaved into the side of Grimm's head and stenciled with large bold letters.

DANGER

REACTOR AREA

CLASS 1 HAZMAT GEAR REQUIRED AT ALL TIMES

They'd stolen through the dark, down the hollow spire, Zeke leading the way without faltering. They were in the core of the building now, far below the Myriad sphere, inside Babel's bleeding heart. The space was vast: gray concrete and circular metal gantries. The low thrum of the turbines rang through the walls, the pipes overhead dripping onto the corroding grilles below. In the days of the revolt, Gabriel had Verity and Faith overload Babel's reactor, spitting out a bright shear of neutron radiation that had killed every living thing in the city. It was still leaking to this day, and Gabe and the others had never bothered to repair it, a constant toxic pall spilling over the Gnosis capital so only lifelikes and bots could live inside it for long.

Ezekiel had no idea how much radiation the reactor was still putting out now, but he could see the air around Grimm was shivering, like the haze over desert sands on a summer's day. The boy stood on a gantry above a boiling pool of water that housed the broken fuel rods, soaking up the radiant energy. Alpha, beta and gamma rays—a poison cocktail that would spell agony and death for any regular human—was serving only to fill him, charge him like a battery, red fires burning in the depths of his eyes. Diesel stood close, protected by Grimm's power—the girl couldn't absorb any rads if he was drawing them all into himself like a sponge. Ezekiel waited at the other end of the gantry, metal stairs leading down to the access tunnel they'd come in by. His stomach was filled with butterflies, jaw clenched tight.

This is taking too much time. . . .

"How much longer?" Ezekiel asked.

"F-few more minutes," Grimm replied, his voice shaking.

". . . You sure you need all this? You sure you can handle it?"

The boy nodded, a sheen of sweat gleaming on his brow. "I'm Robin Hood, guv. Just wanna make sure I've got enough to melt this whole place."

Zeke pawed the sweat from his eyes, his mouth dry despite the sweltering moisture. "Well, the longer we take, the more danger Lemon's in. And the more chance they have of figuring out what we're up to."

Ezekiel heard a faint sigh below him.

"I'd say there's an excellent chance of that."

Zeke looked down the stairwell, heart sinking. There, bathed in the blood-red glow of the emergency lights, stood Faith. She was dressed in nanoweave armor, one of those ridiculous arc-swords she so adored held loose in her hands. Gray eyes flat and lifeless as dead monitor screens locked on his.

"Crawling in via the basement as usual. Like a good little rat." Faith tilted her head. "You're nothing if not predictable, little brother."

Ezekiel drew his pistol from his belt, thumbed the safety.

"You were only activated thirty-seven minutes before me, Faith."

"I'm still your elder, bratling."

She waggled her finger.

"I *did* warn you not to forget it."

———

Lemon's heart twisted as Cricket clutched his head and screamed.

The WarBot swayed on his feet, fingers gripping his metal skull, the glowing blue of his optics flickering like a strobe light. A metallic groan spilled out of his voxbox as he stumbled backward into the burning remains of the monster truck Eve had killed. Cricket fought for balance, failed and finally collapsed, crushing a warehouse behind him to rubble.

Lemon watched Eve leap clear as he fell, disappearing into the tumbling walls and rising pall of plaster dust. Thunder crashed overhead, and Lem looked around the city from her vantage on the rooftop, desperate. There were still sporadic pockets of fighting, the rev and rip of Brotherhood motors as they tore through the streets. Somewhere distant, she heard Sister Dee roaring, a burst of machine-gun fire, an explosion. But the only crew nearby were dead or bleeding.

For the first time since she'd fronted up on Silas Carpenter's doorstep that day back in Los Diablos, Lemon Fresh was on her own.

Cricket rolled over on his elbows and knees, still clutching his head. The code component of Libertas had been transmitted to him, along with every bot in the country, when Gabriel made his call for Libertas. Now Eve had dosed the big logika with the nanobots required to complete the cocktail. The Three Laws were being scrubbed from his core, the foundation that kept him loyal, that bid him protect Lemon and other humans at the expense of everything else, was being erased.

And it looked like it was tearing him apart.

"Just go with it, Cricket," Eve called from the wreckage. Her voice was soft and soothing, like Lem supposed a mother would use. "Won't take long."

Lemon's belly ran cold as Eve emerged from the rubble, eyes fixed on her.

"Just long enough."

Lemon backed away from the rooftop ledge as Eve dashed forward. Punching her fingertips into the bricks, she climbed up the side of the building Lem stood on, hurling herself over the lip. She landed in a crouch, rising slow, storm winds tossing her disheveled fauxhawk about her eyes.

Drawing her pistol, she fixed her glower on Lemon.

"Don't, Evie," Lemon said.

"Don't what?"

Lemon's pulse was thumping, her body washed in panic. Evie used to be her bestest, her family, and she didn't want to hurt her. But true cert, she didn't wanna *die,* either, and that pistol in Evie's hand wasn't good for much else.

But could she . . .

Could she?

Lemon reached out into the static. The billions of tiny sparks, the current that every living thing on the planet needed to live. She could sense it all around her—in the engines and batteries, in Cricket below, tingling beneath her own skin and, yes, curling and crackling in the shadows beyond Evie's eyes.

"Don't come any closer," Lemon said. "I'm warning you."

"Warning me, Lem?" Eve's eyes narrowed. "'Bout what?"

"It doesn't have to be this way!" Lemon shouted. "Just . . . just come with us, Evie! Come back to me!" Tears rolled down Lemon's cheeks, thunder rumbling in the skies above, almost drowning out her voice. "You remember how it used to be? Scamming meals and scavving parts and run-ins with the Fridge Street boys? Fighting Dome and grifting bookies and hiding the creds from Grandpa? Remember? You and me and Cricket and Kaiser against the world?"

"He wasn't my grandpa, Lemon," Eve replied. "None of that was real."

"Bull*shit*!" she screamed. "*We* were real. You and me! You were my bestest! And I'm sorry I lied to you! I shoulda trusted you, I shoulda known you'd understand, because you've always had my back, Evie. But I was afraid!"

Eve glanced at Lemon's outstretched hand. The wisps of current dancing between her fingers. She flinched a little as Lemon let it crackle, raising the hair on her arms and the back of her neck.

". . . Should I be afraid now, Lem?" Eve asked.

"I don't wanna hurt you, Evie."

"But you will, right? To protect the ones you love?"

Lemon knew this was it. The throw for all the marbles. The all-in hand of cards. If they lost here, they lost everything. And not just them, the country, too. Maybe even the world. And it was insane to think so much weight rested on this tiny choice, these two little lives, these nobody scavvergirls from the no-where end of nothing. It was insane, and it was unfair, because as far as she'd come, as much as she'd grown, she shouldn't have to make a choice like this. Between a world that never cared about her and a friend she still cared about more than anyone in it. But she knew she had to.

She had to.

Static crackling along her skin, in the dark inside her pupils, in the pulse of her veins and the heart in her chest. That heart this girl still filled.

"You know every time I called you 'bestest' that I really meant 'sister,' right?"

The static rippled and coursed, longing to be let loose. But Lemon breathed deep and she let it die. Maybe the whole world besides. But the thing of it was, deep down in the core of her, true cert, Lemon still believed in Evie. No matter what.

And she let her hand drop.

"I love *you*, Evie."

Eve blinked. Tears in her lashes. Fingers drumming on her pistol.

"I—"

Four tons of burning monster truck came whistling through the air, crushing the ledge and sailing up onto the rooftop. Eve heard it coming, twisted away, the edge of one flaming tire catching her across the shoulder and sending her spinning. Lemon scrambled backward as the ruined auto crashed to the deck, and behind it, optics burning, fingers crushing the concrete, came Cricket.

The WarBot reached through the wreckage, grabbed a dazed and bleeding Eve and snatched her up in one titanic fist. Lemon cried out, and Eve gasped, the WarBot squeezing her tight enough to crush bone, glaring into her eyes.

"FIGURED I'D TURN ON HER, HUH? JUST BECAUSE I COULD? I ALREADY TOLD YOU, EVIE. YOU DON'T TURN ON THE PEOPLE YOU LOVE. NOT EVER."

"Cricket, don't!" Lemon yelled.

The WarBot hurled Eve down to the ground, the concrete

shattering as she struck it. Eve's mouth was open, eyes closed, a spray of blood glistening at her lips. Cricket dropped off the building, more blood spraying as he brought one massive fist down and pounded her deeper into the ground. Looming over her, the logika raised one massive foot, his voice a 'lectric rasp.

"FREE TO CHOOSE, LIKE YOU SAID," he growled. "AND I CHOOSE WHAT'S *RIGHT*."

"Crick, don—"

An explosion bloomed at the WarBot's back, blistering, blinding. Lemon shielded her eyes as the thunderous *BOOOOOOOM* tore across the city. Cricket turned, smoke pouring from his ruptured armor plates, just as another round slammed into him, bursting apart upon his chest. The WarBot staggered, spraying sparks, and Lemon looked down the street, caught sight of a Gnosis grav-tank, its main gun trailing a wisp of smoke.

"Crick, *look out!*" she screamed.

The third shot hit him in the head, cracking his armor, bringing him to his knees. His optics were blown out, black smoke and bright sparks pouring out of his ruptured skull. The big WarBot collapsed, one palm pressed to the broken concrete, coolant and oil spraying like blood.

"LEM . . ."

The grav-tank's hatch opened, and out of it came a silent shape, dashing down the street toward the fallen WarBot. Lemon saw blond hair, eyes like broken emeralds, madness and hatred glittering in his irises.

"Gabriel . . ."

The lifelike came on, dashing to the aid of his fallen sister, Eve still comatose and bleeding on the deck. And Lemon raised her hand, fingers into claws, reaching out into the static and at last, at last, letting it loose.

Gabriel staggered like she'd punched him, stumbling a few steps. But he only slowed for a moment, only faltered for a second, before running on. Lemon tried again, summoning up her fear, her rage, twisting it into a crackling ball and slamming it right into the oncoming lifelike, ripping the current inside him apart.

But though he stumbled again, nose bleeding, he didn't fall.

Gabriel crashed into Cricket, leaping up onto the WarBot's chest. And as Lemon watched, mouth open in horror, Gabriel punched his hand through the buckled armor skull plates, seizing Cricket's persona core in his fist.

"LEM, I LO—"

And ripped it clean out of his head.

"No!" Lemon screamed. *"NO!"*

Cricket's mighty body shivered once and collapsed onto the concrete. Gabriel cast the sundered fistful of chips and cables onto the ground. Arm painted to the elbow in black blood. In the blink of an eye, he was across the street, taking the same path Eve had, up over the broken ledge and onto the rooftop. Lemon fell back, tears burning in her eyes, hate burning in her chest, confusion burning in her mind. She reached out into the static again, lashing out with all she had. Gabriel flinched, gasping, blood gushing from his nose in a flood now.

But he still didn't fall.

"Solomon told me you call yourselves Homo superior. Faith said you consider yourselves the next step in human evolution." He spat, bloody lips twisted in a smile. "And still, nothing but an insect."

"But all life on earth runs on electrical current," she whispered. "*All* of it."

Gabriel reached up one black-slicked finger and tapped his brow as he spoke.

"Life."

Tap.

"Like."

He moved, quicker than the lightning above, seizing Lemon by the throat. She gasped, flailing at his face as he lifted her up off the ground, boots scuffing, face purpling as he squeezed.

"So much for humanity," he smiled.

"Gabriel."

The lifelike paused, maybe at the strange note he heard in the voice, touching the small comms device at his ear.

". . . Faith?"

"Gabe, I'm sorry."

Lemon managed to drag a choking breath as Gabriel eased off her crushed windpipe a fraction. He glanced at her, pupils dilating to pinpricks.

"What are you sorry for, Faith?" he asked.

"I just . . . I can't, Gabe."

He glanced back to the tower, a small, frightened voice slipping from his lips.

". . . Faith, what have you done?"

———

She'd stood aside.

Ezekiel couldn't believe it.

He'd stepped down the gantry, pistol in hand, ready to fight to the death if need be. Ready to kill this girl he still thought of as family. The only sister he had left in the world. But Faith had simply stood there, arc-blade held loose in her fingers. For a moment, she reminded him of when they were younger. When their world was bright and new. Staring out with wonder at something as simple as a sunrise, fingers pressed to her lips as she whispered, "It's so beautiful."

And he'd watched as Faith's blade fell to the ground.

"You were right," she whispered. "About Gabriel."

She'd looked up at him, suddenly small and fragile, her eyes alight with a familiar pain—the pain of loving someone who didn't love you back.

"He doesn't," she said. "And he won't ever."

Faith looked down at her hands, her eyes filling with tears.

"So much blood. And all for this. We were a mistake, little brother." She'd looked up into Ezekiel's eyes. "We were something that should never have been."

"Faith, I . . ."

She'd touched the commset at her ear.

"Gabriel."

". . . Faith?"

"Gabe, I'm sorry."

"What are you sorry for, Faith?" came the reply.

She closed her eyes, tears spilling down her lashes.

"I just . . . I can't, Gabe."

". . . Faith, what have you done?"

"I love you," she'd said.

And then she'd drawn her pistol.

And Ezekiel had cried, "NO!"

And Faith had put it beneath her chin and pulled the trigger.

Diesel had watched, horrified. Grimm's eyes had been wide, aglow with the radiant energy he was sucking from the Gnosis core. Zeke had knelt by her broken body, heart aching in his chest. He remembered kneeling in the New Bethlehem square, the taste of a mushroom-shaped cloud on his tongue, with her bleeding in his arms. Deciding the kind of person he could be. The kind who chose to think that everyone had some good in them, somewhere. He'd saved her that day. Because she was family and he loved her and she was the only sister he had left.

But in the end, she couldn't save herself.

Grimm had lowered his arms, the air around him rippling with heat, fiery plasma spilling up and out of his eyes. He'd breathed deep, slowly nodded, his voice reverberating around the chamber as he spoke.

"I'm ready."

They climbed up out of the core to the bottom of the reactor shaft. Gabriel knew they were inside, he'd be coming for them now, they had to move quick. But the gantry surrounding the Myriad sphere was hundreds of meters above their heads.

"We need to get up there," Zeke said. "Fast."

"Well, it's a good thing I'm amazing," Diesel replied.

A gray tear opened up in the floor, and Deez reached out to the gantry above, and with a brief sensation of weightlessness and the taste of gray on his tongue, Zeke found himself landing in a crouch on the gantry outside Myriad. That vast shape, shining chrome, dented by Gabriel's knuckles and painted with his blood. His Three Laws, his Three Truths, the words that had driven all of them to this.

YOUR BODY IS NOT YOUR OWN.

YOUR MIND IS NOT YOUR OWN.

YOUR LIFE IS NOT YOUR OWN.

Four Goliaths stood watch outside the sphere as always, the

WarBots coming to life and raising their weapons as the trio appeared before them. But in a heartbeat, two of them were tumbling down into the colorless tear that opened under their feet. The other two staggered and simply collapsed, their persona cores melted inside their skulls, running in molten rivulets out of their bubbling optics.

Grimm stepped up to the Myriad shell, the computer's holographic avatar revolving on a plinth beside it.

"MAY I HELP YOU?" it asked.

"Yeah, guv. You can open this door," the boy replied.

"UNABLE TO COMPLY," the angel replied in its musical voice. "I DO NOT RECOGNIZE YOUR AUTHORITY."

"Got warned you'd say that."

Grimm cracked his knuckles, glanced over his shoulder, liquid fire spilling over his lashes. The angel shivered in the heat haze, as if it knew what was to come.

"You lot might wanna stand back."

Ezekiel complied, Diesel beside him, backing away across the gantry to the chamber's main doors. Even fifty meters away, Zeke felt the rush of blistering heat as Grimm held out his hands toward the Myriad doorway. In moments, the heat was replaced by an arctic chill, the boy sucking the ambient heat out of the surrounding air to augment his efforts. The air felt snap-frozen, the gantry creaking as the metal expanded, a rime of frost forming on the railings. Zeke's breath was a white cloud at his lips, Diesel stepping closer for warmth as Grimm continued to burn.

The light was too bright to look at for long, a blinding radiance that brought tears to Zeke's eyes. But he could see the chrome blackening, the bloody Truths fried to charcoal and then to ashes, the door beginning to glow a molten red. This sphere was supposedly built to survive a nuclear detonation—only god knew what kinds of forces Grimm was bringing to bear, distilling, concentrating, focusing on a single piece of metal that now burned white, incandescent with the heat.

"It's working," Diesel breathed.

"STOP THIS!"

Ezekiel turned, unsurprised to find Gabriel standing at the doorway to the chamber. But he felt his heart twist inside his chest as he saw Lemon in Gabe's arms, the girl's neck gripped tight in the crook of his elbow, a pistol at her temple.

"STOP THIS AT ONCE!" Gabriel roared.

He was dressed in black, spattered in oil and blood. Blond hair hung in emerald-green eyes. Ezekiel could see the madness, the obsession, the impossible fury welling in Gabe's stare. He jerked his arm, and Lemon gasped, her face bright red, boots kicking, fingers digging into Gabe's forearm as she struggled to breathe. It would only take one twitch of Gabe's finger, one tiny movement, and Lemon . . .

"Lemon!" Grimm yelled.

The rippling furnace at his fingertips died as he turned to face the lifelike. He was a dark silhouette against the glowing metal of the Myriad door, fire spilling from his eyes like inverted waterfalls. But Gabriel only pressed the pistol harder against Lemon's skull, making her gasp. Diesel couldn't Rift the problem away. Grimm didn't have the control to kill Gabe without risking Lemon.

Stalemate.

"Step away from the door, cockroach," Gabriel demanded.

"Let her go, bastard," Grimm spat.

"Step away or she dies!" Gabriel roared.

"Then so do you, prettyboy," Diesel hissed.

"Perhaps." His eyes narrowed. "But that will be of little consolation to Miss Fresh."

"Don't d-do it," Lemon gasped. "Kill this fuc—"

Gabriel jerked his arm again, making Lemon squeal with pain.

"What will it be, Ezekiel?" Gabe asked, turning to his brother. "Walk away in peace? Or have the blood of another innocent girl on your hands?"

"Gabriel, don't . . . ," Ezekiel pleaded.

"I will have what is mine!" Gabe roared, his eyes shining and bright. "I will have what is owed me, what was promised to all of us! I will have a *life*, Ezekiel, and I will live it with her!"

Gabriel glanced toward the Myriad sphere, and Zeke saw a splinter of fear behind his brother's mask. His dream was so close, perhaps just a few hours from waking, all he'd lied and stolen and murdered for was within his grasp. The talk of freedom, the posturing and speeches, all of it had always been a facade. In the end, all Gabriel wanted was the girl he loved.

Ezekiel could understand that.

Looking into Lemon's eyes, he knew how hard it would be to let another girl he loved go. But she met his stare, tears shining in that pretty green, brave to the last, fearless and beautiful and strong. And as his hand slipped down toward his pistol, she nodded.

She knew.

"Ezekiel, don't," Gabriel hissed.

"Zeke?" Grimm shouted. "Zeke!"

"I'm sorry," he said, looking into her eyes. "I'm—"

BANG.

Gabriel lurched forward, a gaping hole where his right

eye used to be. Another dozen shots rang out, one after another after another. Lemon fell to the deck, gasping, choking, as Gabriel staggered forward, bloody flowers blooming at his chest, gouts of red flooding between his fingers. His body hit the railing, teetered, even now desperately clinging to this half life that had been thrust upon him. But the pistol rang out again, *bangbangbang*, before it clicked empty, and with a final gurgling sigh, Gabriel crumpled to the floor.

Eve stood, tall and fierce, on the threshold, a smoking pistol in her hand. She was spattered with blood and ash, blond fauxhawk hanging in her eyes. Striding over to Gabriel's body lying ruined and bleeding against the railing, she pressed her boot to his chest. And with a small grunt, she pushed.

Ezekiel watched the body fall out into the reactor shaft, tumbling end over end as it plummeted soundlessly into the blood-red abyss.

Eve watched it fall, her murmur almost lost under the reactor wind.

"Don't touch my sister," she said.

3.36

TOMORROW

They used to call it Kalifornya, but now they called it Dregs.

Grandpa had told Lemon this place wasn't even an island before the Quake. That you could motor from Dregs to Zona and never touch the water. A long time ago, this was just another part of the Grande Ol' Yousay. Before the country got bombed into deserts of black glass and Saint Andreas tore his fault line open and invited the ocean in for drinks. Before the Corporations fought War 4.0 for what was left of the country and carved out their citystates beneath a cigarette sky.

She grew up here, even though the streets of Los Diablos were no place for a kid. The capital of Dregs was a rusting cesspit. A reminder of humanity's greatest age, and greatest folly. Built in the heart of a scrap pile, Los Diablos wasn't a city, it was a meat grinder, chewing up people and spitting out the bones. If you were born here, you grew up sharp, you grew up hard or you didn't grow up at all.

Lemon had taken the first option.

"So remind me why we came to this pit, Fresh?"

Lem turned to look at Diesel, who was eyeing the LD sprawl

with the kind of disgust she usually reserved for strawberry ice cream. Fuel depots and eats-vendors. Bot clinics and parts dealers. Even an old Brotherhood chapel, those ornate Xs painted over with a perfect circle and a large, handwritten sign.

ALL WELCOME

She didn't know if it'd last. Part of her didn't think it could. Maybe people would always look for something different to hate on. Maybe, after seeing how close they'd all come to running out of future, people were finally learning from the mistakes of the past. Talking true, tomorrow never came with a guarantee.

Passersby were peering at them with either bold curiosity or slack-jawed awe, depending on whether they'd seen newsfeeds about the fall of Megopolis. Whispers were running the grubby sprawl all around them. But Lemon stood in the middle of the street, scoping the crush of people, the decrepit buildings, the long stretch of the Scrap outside the city limits, and true cert, it felt like she'd come home.

"We're here because we gotta do better," Lemon replied. "Because we were supposed to make a garden out of this place, and instead, we made a garbage pile. And I don't have all the answers for how to fix it. But there's some jewels in that data we snaffled out of Myriad before Grimm melted it to a puddle."

The boy tipped an imaginary hat. "Raising the temperature is my specialty."

"It was pretty hot," she grinned, squeezing his hand.

"Someone kill me," Diesel groaned.

Lemon knelt down, picked up a crumpled plastic bottle out of the gutter.

"Monrova was working on a way to recycle polys out of Plastic Alley, turn 'em into fuel. He was improving the Daedalus solar cell design, too. Talkin' true, the guy was a genius before he went pants-on-head crazy." She nodded to two figures in the distance, standing atop a mountain of scrap. "And turns out we got a true cert genius on our crew. An amalgamation of the brightest minds in all of creation."

"Allegedly," Grimm muttered.

"Well, on paper, anyways." Lemon grinned. "Point is, we gotta do better. And we got some tools to help us get rolling on that. And the best place to start doing better is your own backyard." She waved at the sprawl around them. "Sort out your own mess before you start poking your face parts into someone else's. Because this place is my home. And you gotta take the first step somewhere."

Grimm slipped his arms around her waist. Leaned down until their noses were touching. And Lemon looked up into his eyes and saw the way he looked back at her, and it made her feel alive, all the way to her bones.

"What's that word you use to describe someone both beautiful and brilliant?"

"Brilliful," she smiled.

He leaned down and kissed her, soft and achingly sweet, and even though she felt electricity crackling along her skin, the temperature around her slowly rising, she knew it had nothing to do with their gifts. His lips were fires and his hands were raw current, making every piece of her tingle. Every piece of her feel at home.

"You're brilliful, love," he murmured.

She smiled. "I like it when you call me that."

"Which one, brilliful or . . ."

"Love," she said, touching his cheek. *"Love."*

His lips curled into a smile. "Then I'll call you it forever."

She kissed him again, standing on tiptoe to rest her forehead against his.

"Let's just work on tomorrow, okay?" she said, tossing the plastic bottle in a nearby dumpster. "Tomorrow's gonna be a hard day."

"Worth fighting for, though," Diesel murmured.

"True cert," Grimm sighed.

Lemon nodded.

"True cert."

———

Eve trudged along the mountain, eyes on the metal at her feet. Grav-tank hulks and corroded shipping containers. Piles of engines and discarded parts, rusting hills and brittle plastic plains that would take a thousand years to degrade. With a small sound of triumph, she knelt among the pieces and fished out a small glass globe, wires hanging out the back of it. Holding it up to the burning sun, she could see the interior was intact, the relays good. She reached into her satchel, pulled out a lump of wires and chips, comparing the input jacks.

"EmTech 78b optical lens," she murmured. "Perfect."

"Enjoying yourself?"

She turned toward the voice, saw him standing there, tousled hair and bronze skin, a hint of the coin slot bolted into his chest peeking out through the collar of his shirt. The idealization of everything his maker thought a young man should be. And she supposed Nicholas Monrova had been right in the end.

That Ezekiel had turned out to be everything he'd dreamed. Not just strong and fine and beautiful. But brave. And loyal. And possessed of a belief that there was some good in everyone. That you weren't defined by what you were, but by what you did.

And what he'd done, in the end, was show her how.

"Kinda," she said, squinting against the light. "Reminds me of the old days. Scavving with Lem and Kaiser and Crick for parts so I could fight Dome."

Ezekiel nodded to the persona core in her hands.

"You know, you could've just implanted him in a WarBot body again. There was plenty of wreckage around Babel."

Eve shook her head. "Talking true, I think Cricket always kinda liked being little. Gave him something to complain about."

"You think you can rebuild him?"

"I've forgotten some of it," she said, touching the part of her skull where her Memdrive used to be. "But I remember enough." And she smiled then, sure of it, and herself. "He'll be good as new. He'll be *better*."

Zeke gave the back of his head a rueful scratch. "He'll probably still be mad at me. He was never my biggest fan, you know."

"Hence the plan to start him off in a small body."

Ezekiel chuckled, and Eve tried her best to ignore the butterflies that tumbled through her stomach at the sight of that goddamned dimple. He dragged his dark curls back from his pretty eyes, sunlight playing on his skin.

"I hope you notice I've refrained from saying I told you so."

Eve blinked. "Told me so what?"

He looked off to the north, over the black ocean and the black sands, toward a spire of ghosts and glass. "That what you were made to be doesn't matter. How some computer program sees you doesn't matter. The things you do become the person you are. But I figured I should mark the occasion somehow."

He reached around behind his back and brought out a ring of discarded wiring and tin, twisted into a circlet that was about the size of her head.

A crown, she realized.

He stood in front of her, close enough for her to feel the warmth of his skin, see the blue of a pre-Fall sky shining in those pretty eyes of his. And smooshing down her fauxhawk, he placed the crown of scrap parts atop her head.

"Your Majesty."

She smiled, adjusting the fit. "Every good queen needs a noble knight."

"And a court jester," he scoffed.

". . . And a king?" she asked, hopeful.

Eve stepped a little closer, looking up as that perfect smile faded away, replaced with longing, with devotion, with love. Reaching up to trace the line of his cheek with her fingertip, she watched the goose bumps rise on his skin, felt his pulse quicken beneath her hand. She knew every part of this lost and broken boy, and not just from the memories of the girl she'd never been. The things they'd done, the moments they'd shared since she first found him out in the Scrap, they were *hers* and hers alone. And while Eve could still see the specter of Ana Monrova between them if she squinted hard enough, she knew the girl was only a ghost now. That this boy hadn't trusted her, hadn't believed in her, hadn't loved her for who she'd been, but who she was.

And who was she? In the end?

She was a girl who loved him back.

Eve slipped her arms around Zeke's waist. This boy who'd always felt so real in her arms. And she kissed him, kissed him for all he'd done, and all he was, and all she knew he'd be. Kissed him as if she were a queen, and he her king, there in that empire of scrap, rusting under a cigarette sky.

They heard the scrape of a boot on steel, a soft voice.

"Sorry, am I interrupting?"

Eve eased away from Zeke's lips, her own curled in a smile.

"S'okay, Lem," she said. "Come on up."

Ezekiel extricated himself from her arms, dropped into a shallow bow.

"I beg your leave, my queen."

She laughed, and he straightened, turning on his heel and making his way down the mountain of scrap. Making her way past him, Lemon threw him a wink.

"Hey, Dimples," she smiled.

"Hey, Freckles," he replied.

Eve looked out over the ocean as Lemon made her way up beside her. The two girls stood atop the pile of corroding metal, discarded parts, broken machines. Staring out at those black waves, the shattered shore, the wastes and the ruins and the cities beyond. A country so broken it might not be worth fixing. A shade so dark it was hard to see the light. But they stood, side by side, staring out at the world, and each of them felt the taller for the girl at her side.

"I missed you, Riotgrrl," Lemon said softly.

"Well." Eve sighed, soft as clouds. "I'm back now."

"Gonna be a job," Lemon said. "Cleaning this place up."

"We got a good crew," Eve replied.

Lemon frowned, shook her head. "We got better than crew."

Eve cocked an eyebrow, looked at her bestest sidelong.

"We got family," Lemon smiled.

Eve smiled, tears shining in her eyes. "Glad you're with me, sis."

"First rule of the Scrap, sis," Lemon said, crying, too.

Eve reached down and squeezed her hand.

"Stronger together."

"Together forever."

fin

ACKNOWLEDGMENTS

Many thanks must go to the following, in no particular order:

Melanie, Cat, LT, Laini, Amie, Marie, Beth, Kiersten, Barbara, Karen, Artie, Amy, Alison, Ray, Stephanie, Ken, Natalia, Jake, John, Kelly, Jenna, Adrienne, Kristin, Kate, Elizabeth, Amy, Jenn, Joshua, Arely, Trish, Anna, Jess, Sophie, Deb, Tash, Jack, Josh, Tracey, Marc, B-Money, Rafe, Weez, Batman, Glen, Paris, Spiv, Surly Jim, Bill, Tom, Maynard, Oli, Chino, Burton, Ian, Al, Marcus, John, Winston, Paul, Jeff, William, Scott, Jason, Cherie, Jamie, Alan, George, Jenny, Mike, Veronica, Chris, Tony, Kath, Kylie, Nicole, Kurt, Jack, Max, Poppy, Sam, and, of course, Amanda.

This book wouldn't be what it is without you.